THE CALLER

Also by Alex Barclay

Darkhouse

ALEX BARCLAY

The Caller

HarperCollins*Publishers*

HarperCollins*Publishers*
77–85 Fulham Palace Road,
Hammersmith, London W6 8JB

www.harpercollins.co.uk

Published by HarperCollins*Publishers* 2007

1

Copyright © Alex Barclay
asserts the moral right to be identified as the author of this work

Daphne Du Maurier quote reproduced with permission of Curtis Brown Group Ltd on
behalf of the Estate of Daphne Du Maurier copyright © Daphne Du Maurier 1938

A catalogue record for this book
is available from the British Library

ISBN-13: 978 0 00 719533 6
ISBN-10: 0 00 719533 8

This novel is entirely a work of fiction.
The names, characters and incidents portrayed in it are
the work of the author's imagination. Any resemblance to
actual persons, living or dead, events or localities is
entirely coincidental.

Set in Meridien by Palimpsest Book Production Limited,
Grangemouth, Stirlingshire

Printed and bound in Great Britain by
Clays Ltd, St Ives plc

Mixed Sources
Product group from well-managed
forests and other controlled sources
www.fsc.org Cert no. TT-COC-2139
FSC © 1996 Forest Stewardship Council

To Ciaran, Ronan, Lorraine and Damien

With screaming eyes
And weakened breath
'Twas not for life
He begged,
'Twas death.

Anonymous

PROLOGUE

The room was eight by ten and windowless. Weak shafts of light stretched through the bars that ran from floor to ceiling across one wall. The small television, mounted on a black shelf outside, was full-volume white noise. On a tray by the door lay the shrivelled remains of an overcooked dinner.

The bed, pushed against the right-hand wall, was perfectly made, each corner tight under the thin mattress, the coarse green cover smooth except for where he sat, hunched and focused. Sweat darkened the folds and underarms of his blue shirt, the odor mixing with the rising stench from the discarded food.

He opened his eyes and turned to the desk lamp beside him, flicking the switch. Under the brilliant white light, he held a model; a plaster replica of the thirty-two human teeth he could recall so easily as he traced his thumb over the contours; the imperfection of a prominent incisor, a pointed canine tip, the uneven surface of a chipped premolar. Only once had he seen the teeth in a smile: at the beginning, a quick flash before the terror struck. For hours afterwards, they had been clamped shut in agony or visible only as the lips curled back from them in a silent scream.

He bent forward and slid a box from under the bed, pulling it up to rest on his knees. Twisting his body, he removed a key from his pocket, then unlocked the box. He looked at the model one last time, then set it down inside with the others. One, two, three. Four.

The day after you watch your first victim die is not very different to the day before. You still wake up. Maybe you skip breakfast, even lunch, but you will eat . . . eventually. And you'll sleep. And you'll slip into a rhythm. Not identical to the one before; there might be an erratic beat, but at least it's a silent beat. Yours.

He pushed the box under the bed, where other reminders lay – of lives taken and lives spared. He closed his eyes and breathed in the warm, captive air.

My prison is a tool, a training ground, a stopover. I look at the bars behind me, the space around me, the confinement. I think of where you are and how tragic for you

*it is that here I am, there you are, but oh so quickly,
there I am. Right with you.*
   Entrance. Exit.

He switched off the desk lamp. He returned the
key to his pocket, stood up and walked to the door.
He slid back the bolt and stepped outside. He
reached up and turned off the television, watching
as the light was sucked into a tiny circle at the
center and turned to black. Then he walked across
the floor and up the steps, pausing as he crossed
the threshold into his bright, air-conditioned home.

She was twenty-nine years old, small and slender,
dressed in a white tank, pale pink cardigan and
jeans, her dark hair twisted and secured with a
dragonfly clip at the nape of her neck. Her skin
was sallow, her eyes winter blue. Beside her was
a doll, made from instructions that lost her interest
before the mouth was sewn and the brown wool
hair could be bunched and tied with bows. Beside
that lay a clay ashtray, half-painted and dented
by pressured thumbs.
   She couldn't remember why she had sat down.
She opened the desk drawer and took out a lami-
nated prayer card and red St Pio rosary beads.
Wrapping them around her fingers, she bowed
her head and began to pray. She told St Joseph
that she dare not approach him while Jesus
reposed near his heart.

From nowhere, it rose, a familiar unsettling pressure in her stomach. Her only relief was that somewhere mixed in with the fear came a euphoria she had never found anywhere else. But only the fear washed over her now. Her left hand shot out and slammed down onto a notepad. She slid it across the desk towards her, her head feeling free from her body as she tried to make use of what was happening to her. A dark reel unwound behind her eyes; edited razor-sharp, black and grey shapes, a frenzied acceleration of badly lit scenes. Her right hand groped the air, her fingers searching for two short vertical lines that would make it all pause, then backwards arrows to make it rewind. But this was nothing she could control. Coursing through her was the impulse to stay in the moment, not to go back, not to cast any light onto dark half-memories. But before she got a chance to write, she was gone, sliding to the floor, dragging paper and pens and pencils on top of her. The last thing she saw was her friend, standing in the doorway, shrunken to the size of a child.

Detective Joe Lucchesi sat with his head between his knees, tears streaming down his face and dripping onto the carpet below him. His face was grey, his forehead dotted with sweat and newsprint from the fingers he had pressed against it before the real pain had kicked in. Half an hour earlier he had arrived at his dentist's office for emergency treatment – with pain he had gauged level eight. Now it was off the scale and rising. Nausea ripped through him, but he stayed doubled over, letting out a growl that choked in his throat.

'Joe? Joe?' A receptionist rushed in from the hallway. 'Stay with me, sweetheart.'

She glanced around the waiting room. 'Did anyone see what happened?'

'He was sitting right there reading the news-paper, he took a call on his cell. He sat back down and then he started not to look too good.' Joe knew it was the voice of a kind-faced older man who was sitting opposite him when he arrived.

The receptionist laid a hand on Joe's shoulder. 'Dr Makkar will be along right away. Is there anything I can get you in the meantime?'

'Would he maybe take a glass of water?' It was the man again. He had stood up – Joe could see his brown suede loafers on the carpet in front of him. Joe managed to raise a shaky hand that said no to both offers.

'I don't think he was even able to talk to whoever called him,' said the old man.

But Joe knew it wasn't the pain that had stopped him from talking. He just had no answer for the voice that came twisting its way back into his life, drawling and heavy and laden with unfinished business.

'Detective Lucchesi? Every time you look at the scars on your wife's pretty little body, right down . . . low down

on that tight little belly. Or when you flip her over onto her front. She's light, you can flip her easy, can't you? There's some scars there too – makes me feel like I'm the gift that keeps on giving. Well, what I want to know is this: when you see them scars? Do you still want her?' He paused. *'Or do you want me more?'* He laughed long and loud. *'Tell me. Who's gonna get it in the ass? Little Anna Lucchesi or Big Bad Duke Rawlins?'* His breath was gone, lost in a dead silence. Then his voice struck up, one last time. *'And Detective? You'll never bury me. I. Will. Bury. You.'*

ONE

Detectives Joe Lucchesi and Danny Markey stepped into the elevator that would take them to the sixth floor office of Manhattan North Homicide. They were three hours into an eight to four tour. A short skinny man shot in after them, jumpy and light on his feet.

'You know, I can read futures by your hands.' He had weathered skin and a droopy left eye. He stood an inch from Joe's chest and looked up at him with a gentle smile. Joe looked at Danny and held his palm out.

The man stepped back, banging his head on the elevator doors.

'Not your palm!' he shouted. 'Not your palm! The back of your hand! I will know you from the back of your hand.' Joe turned it over.

'The other one too. You too,' he said, looking at Danny. 'Both hands. Both hands. Many hands make Jack dull.'

Joe and Danny smiled and did what he said.

'You're laughing too early,' said the guy. 'This could be bad news, what I see here. This could be too many ducks spoiling the bush.'

'We don't want to hear no bad news,' said Danny. 'Right?'

'Right,' said Joe.

'Right,' said the man. 'But I'm not just the messenger here. You gotta appreciate that. I'm how it all begins. I'm what sets it all in motion. I'm, like, bang. And the future I see will start from right here in these nine stitches.'

Joe nodded slowly.

The man reached up and adjusted the purple crocheted hat on his head, pulling the ear flaps around so one of them hung in front of his face. He rotated it again, then looked back at their hands.

'Yeah,' he said. 'I'm seeing things. I definitely am,' said the man. 'My name is One Line, by incident. One Line. King of Madison Avenue. Your product in one line. Your brand in one line—'

'You were a copywriter?' said Joe.

'Your future in one line,' said the man, staring at the hands in front of him.

'OK,' said Danny. 'So what is it?'

The bell chimed and the elevator doors opened on the sixth floor. Joe and Danny got out. As the doors slid together, One Line pushed his face close to the gap.

'One line: you're fucked, both of you. Is that two lines? Could that be two?' The doors closed.

They laughed.

'Another EDP for the HPD,' said Danny. An EDP was an Emotionally Disturbed Person. The HPD was the Department of Housing Preservation and Development – one of their jobs was to give out Section 8 housing subsidies.

'Let's send him into Internal Affairs, let him tell *them* they're fucked,' said Danny.

'I'd like him to come up with a whole jingle for that,' said Joe.

Sixteen detectives worked in three teams out of Manhattan North Homicide, a modern open plan space with a small glass-walled office in the corner, shared by the sergeant and the lieutenant. The NYPD was one of the only law enforcement agencies in the country whose officers weren't put through regular fitness checks, leaving Sergeant John Rufo free to work his way up to 230 pounds and into his current predicament of trying to work his way back down.

'Your mental agility is being impaired,' he said, pointing at Joe and Danny with something beige speared on a fork.

'Is that tofu?' said Danny.

'No it is not tofu. It is marinated steamed chicken. Tofu. Gimme a break.'

Joe and Danny exchanged glances.

'It's eleven o'clock in the morning,' said Danny.

'Eat little and often,' said Rufo. 'Them's the rules.' He pointed to his plate. 'Vegetables, protein . . .'

'Yeah, boss,' said Danny. 'Tomato sauce, meat-balls: I got it covered already.'

'How do you stay so trim?' said Rufo.

'You mean, "Have I been working out?"' said Danny.

Rufo rolled his eyes. Then poked his fork through his salad. 'Who's up today?'

'Me,' said Joe. 'And I eat well, by the way.'

'You gotta watch that French food,' said Rufo, looking up at him. 'It's tasty . . .' he raised a finger in warning, '. . . because it's rich. Your wife is genetically wired for it. You might not be. You're in shape now, but who knows down the line . . .'

Joe laughed. 'Yeah, Sarge, thanks for looking out for me.'

'A varied diet,' said Rufo, 'that's what—'

The phone interrupted him. 'Ruthie, yeah – put him through.' He nodded. 'How you doing? OK. Yeah. OK.' He listened, then scribbled on a notebook in front of him. 'Right away. Detectives Joe Lucchesi and Danny Markey. Yeah. Uh-huh. Take care.' He put down the phone. 'Gentlemen, we have a homicide on West 84th Street. Here's the address. Guy found in his apartment.' He ripped out the page and handed it to Joe. 'The Two-Oh is at the scene already.'

*   *   *

Joe and Danny crossed Broadway to the parking lot under the railway bridge.

'Who says "trim"?' said Danny.

'People who aren't,' said Joe.

'It's unbelievable,' said Danny, 'we get sucked into food talk every time we go in his office. I wind up starving.' Danny was short, wiry and had no extra weight. He'd been wearing the same suit size since he was eighteen. He had pale skin and fading freckles, light brown hair and blue eyes. Joe was six-three, dark and broad.

Joe stopped. 'Aw, shit . . .'

'What?' said Danny.

'Would you look at that?' Joe walked over to a silver Lexus. 'That fucking shit.' He pulled his keys out of his pocket and opened the door of his car, popping the glove box. He took out a cloth and started rubbing at a lump of tar on his windshield.

'I've a pain in my fucking ass with that crap,' he said. He looked up at the bridge from where the tar dripped in the heat.

'Least it was a fresh one,' said Danny. 'How come you don't have the ghetto sled?' The ghetto sled was a detective's B-team car, the one he could park two blocks from the projects and not have to worry about.

'We got a meeting at Shaun's school today, I'm going straight there. Or at least I would have been. Anna's going to have to go it alone.' Shaun was Joe's eighteen-year-old son.

'She won't like that,' said Danny. 'What's he been doing now?'

Joe shook his head. 'You name it.'

'He's been through a lot.'

'Yeah, but it's fucking wearing me down. And Anna doesn't need this kind of shit, going up to the school every month to answer to this asshole teacher fifteen years younger than us.'

'Shaun's a good kid,' said Danny. 'He'll be in college next year, you won't have to worry. Try having four under ten. I love them, but, man . . .' He breathed out. 'Now, come on. Say goodbye to the nice car and get into the shit one.' There was a pool of five cars at Manhattan North. Any damage during a tour and the driver was left to face a bawling out by Rufo. The newer the car, the more likely Joe would take the wheel. Today, they had the oldest car – a grey Gran Fury; 'You get a scratch on it, who gives a shit?' said Danny. They pulled out and joined the traffic heading south on Broadway.

'Can I ask what happened with Dr Mak?' said Danny.

Joe grunted. 'I staggered in, I got more Vicodin, I walked out.'

'That's it?'

'That's it,' said Joe.

'You mean that's all you let it be, right?'

'Who are you? Psych services?'

Danny ignored him. 'I'm guessing you went

in, told him you were real busy, just needed a
prescription, gotta go.'

'What else am I going to do?' said Joe.

'Let him treat you,' said Danny.

Joe had TMD – Temporo Mandibular Joint
Dysfunction. The least it would do was make his
jaw crackle when he opened his mouth, the worst
– spark excruciating pain all over his head. For
years, Danny had watched him pop over-the-
counter painkillers and decongestants. He'd
recently moved on to Vicodin.

'It's getting worse,' said Danny.

'Yeah, so are you.' Joe turned away. Yesterday's
phone call had jerked him back too far – to events
he had spent wasted months trying to forget: the
botched rescue of an eight-year-old kidnap victim
and the near-destruction of his family. The little
girl had been returned to her heartbroken mother
and the two clung to each other, happily, desperately. Seconds later, the scene turned to graphic,
bloody images he still couldn't shake – the
kidnapper had blown them up in retaliation for
calling the cops. Joe confronted him moments
later and pumped six bullets into his chest. His
name was Donald Riggs.

After the case, Anna wanted Joe to take time
out. She was offered a job in Ireland and they
went with Shaun. After eight great months, everything went wrong. Donald Riggs had an associate
– Duke Rawlins – a killer he had spent years on

a murderous spree with, someone who wouldn't let Riggs' death go unavenged. Fresh from a maximum security prison, he had caught up with Joe and tried to destroy his family. During their time in Ireland, Shaun's girlfriend, Katie, had been murdered. Shortly after, Rawlins had abducted Anna and left her so physically and mentally scarred, she struggled every day to get past it.

They pulled up by the patrol car outside the apartment block on West 84th Street. A well-dressed couple stood under the green and gold awning, aware something was going on, but more concerned about where they were going for brunch. The doorman inside was a neatly groomed older man with a moustache and a badge that read 'Milton'.

'Terrible,' was all he said, shaking his head, gesturing with a white gloved hand to the elevators.

'Has someone spoken with you yet?' said Danny.

Milton nodded.

'All right,' said Danny. 'We'll be back down to you in a little while.'

'Why were you shouting at him?' said Joe when they got into the elevator.

'Didn't he look a little deaf to you?'

Joe raised his eyes to the ceiling. They got out at the third floor and walked down a grey tiled hallway to apartment 3E. A detective in a navy blue suit walked out, his eyes on the notebook in his left hand. His right hand was pressed to his stomach. He turned slowly their way. Danny and Joe made their introductions.

'Tom Blazkow from the Two-Oh,' he said. The twentieth precinct covered everywhere from 59th Street to 86th Street, west of Central Park. Blazkow was in his mid-forties and bulked-up, with a grey buzzcut, a massive jaw and bloodshot blue eyes. He turned to the detective walking out of the apartment behind him.

'This is my partner, Denis Cullen.'

They all nodded. Cullen was in his early fifties and dressed in a limp brown suit and a tie from a bowling league with a stars-and-stripes pin. He had pale red hair thinning on top and broken veins across his nose and cheeks. He looked eager, but worn out.

'So what have we got?' said Joe.

Blazkow spoke. 'Ethan Lowry, graphic designer, DOB 04/12/71, married with a young daughter. 911 got a call from his diet delivery people. Every morning, they bring his meals for the day. He didn't open the door. First time in eleven months he didn't. Delivery guy saw a drop of blood in the hallway, got a bad smell.' He pointed to a pale, wheezing teenager. 'The two uniforms tried the bell, banged on the door, no answer, went around the back, climbed up the fire escape, couldn't see nothing through the

window, so they called ESU. Body was right inside
the front door. No sign of forced entry. Balcony
door was locked. No response from the wife's cell
phone. We got a uniform down by the elevators.
He knows who to look out for. You're going to
have to knock.' He pointed to the apartment.
'Careful going in. You might slip on a chunk of
face.'

Joe reached into his jacket pocket for a handkerchief and a small bottle of aftershave. He shook
some drops onto the white cotton and held it to
his nose, taking in a few deep breaths. He knocked
on the door and they walked carefully into the
apartment. Ethan Lowry lay on his back, naked,
his body pressed up against the baseboard behind
the door. His arms were stretched out above him.
His head was turned to the right, but there wasn't
much of a face to face that way. Ethan Lowry had
been savagely beaten, more blows than were needed
to kill someone who had clearly been finished off
with a bullet. The damage was entirely to his face.
Where the skin wasn't plumped up and tight, it
was pulped. His nostrils were plugged with dried
blood.

'What's in his mouth?' said Danny.

'His mouth,' said Joe.

'Aw, Jesus,' said Danny, leaning in closer.
Lowry's mouth looked like it had been turned
inside out. It covered his whole chin and left side
of his face like raw meat. Only one tooth was

visible. The rest were hidden under the swollen mess, broken or lying alone on the floor beside numbered evidence cards. Joe sucked in a breath. The skin was split at Lowry's left eye socket where a gun had been fired point-blank.

'Hey,' said Danny to Kendra, a smiley, bulky crime scene technician, who was squatting on the floor beside him.

'Hey, Joe, Danny. I'm having an *MTV Cribs* moment. Here is the hallway. And this is where the magic happened. See all this?' She gestured around the body and in an arc above it. 'We've got expirated mist on the floor, on the wall. We've got cast-off blood on the ceiling. We've got it all basically. Over there we've got high-velocity spatter from the gunshot wound. Small caliber.' She shook her head.

'And—'

'God bless you, but God slow you down too,' said Joe. 'Just give us a moment.'

'Sorry,' she said. 'I get so—'

'Cheery,' said Danny.

Kendra turned to him. 'I love my job,' she said. 'And if that's an emotion that for some reason confuses you . . .' She shrugged.

'How could you not love this?' said Danny, pointing to the body. Beside Lowry's head was a black, blood-streaked cordless phone. Joe put on a glove, picked it up and hit the dialled calls button.

'Someone was alive in here last night at 10.58 p.m.,' said Joe. He took down all the incoming and outgoing calls.

'Let me call Martinez,' said Joe. 'Unless you'd like to.' He smiled. The year before, on his year out, Aldos Martinez filled in as Danny's partner. Now, with Martinez's partner, Fred Rencher, they made up the D team at Manhattan North, the only four-man team.

'Hey, Martinez, it's Joe. Do me a favour – could you do a victimology on an Ethan Lowry, 1640 West 84th Street, DOB 04/12/71. Thanks. Great. See you in a little while.' Joe paused and looked over at Danny. 'Yeah, he's here. You need to talk to him?'

Danny shook his head violently.

'Oh, OK,' said Joe. 'See you later.'

'What did he want?'

'Just to say he misses you.'

'Look at this,' said Danny. He was crouched down beside Lowry's wrists, pointing with his pen to a series of holes in the floorboards. 'His arms must have been restrained by something hammered in here. There are two holes on each side of each wrist.'

'Did you find anything he could have used to do this?' said Joe to Kendra.

'Unh-unh,' she said. 'Perp's not going to leave them behind – my guess is they're his special toys.'

TWO

There were six doors off the hallway in Lowry's apartment: into two bedrooms and a bathroom on the left; into the kitchen, living room and office on the right. The kitchen was painted citrus lemon with green glossy cabinets and cream worktops – all tidy and undisturbed. The living room had a deep red sofa, wide-screen TV and a pile of children's toys in one corner. In the other was a yoga mat and two pink dumbbells.

'I'm not sure any good graphic designer would have been involved in this interior,' said Joe.

'Maybe he was a bad graphic designer,' said Danny. 'Why do you always make victims nicer or more talented than you actually have any proof they are?'

'No, I don't.'

'When they're in a nice house, you do.'

'Yeah, well they're hardly ever in a nice house, so that's bullshit,' said Joe. 'They're decomposing on the bare springs of a bed in some skanky crack den or some place that hasn't seen a bottle of bleach . . .'

They walked into Ethan Lowry's office.

'This is more like it,' said Joe. 'See what I mean? Clean lines.'

'People love crime shows. People love interior shows. You mix the two, Joe, you got a job for life. Extreme Make-over: Home Invasion Edition. CSI: Brownstone.'

Joe smiled. It encouraged Danny. 'Detective Joe Lucchesi: investigating your death *and* your taste. What were your last movements? And why did you choose *those* drapes with *that* carpet? Find out after the break. This season, green kitchens are all the rage. Speaking of rage, savage beatings are—'

'All right, already,' said Joe. 'Let me think.'

Ethan Lowry's office was tidy and minimalist. Across one white wall was a long grey desktop, mounted on steel legs. A twenty-inch flat-screen monitor sat at the centre, running the screensaver – a slideshow of Lowry's family photos. Joe hadn't set his up on his laptop yet, because he couldn't think of anything he wanted to be reminded of. He paused in front of this happy montage of a dead man's life. From the photos and the food deliveries, it was clear that Ethan Lowry had worked hard to slim down. The new, lighter body he had fought for was sad and pointless, lying in a pool of blood by his front door. The camera, a professional digital SLR, was on a low table to the right, beside two tall stacks of clear plastic drawers. Joe pulled a few of them open: receipts, paper clips, rubber bands, stamps.

'Look,' he said to Danny, 'he *was* a good designer.' The bottom drawer was filled with design awards that were gathering dust. 'And,' said Joe, 'he was obviously modest enough not to display them. Which would lead me to believe he might have been quite a nice guy.'

Danny rolled his eyes.

Underneath the desk, the cables that ran from the computer, the printer, the disk drive and the lamp were grouped together neatly with cable ties and ended in plugs with icons. On the floor beside a well-made single bed in the corner was a pair of navy track pants, with a white T-shirt and a pair of white jersey boxer shorts thrown on top. A bunch of letters addressed to Ethan Lowry in girlie script and tied with rubber bands lay beside them. A seventeen-inch PowerBook was on top of the bed, its tiny white light pulsing. Beside it was a remote control vibrator and a short, stiff leather whip. Joe lifted up the screen of the laptop, which quickly flashed up a series of images from soft-porn DVD covers; oiled, topless men in jeans bearing down on tiny, lost blondes. Huge-breasted lesbian liplocks, cheerleaders, repairmen, soldier girls, soldier boys, police officers.

'We're a few shy of the Village People,' said Danny, moving up beside him.

'Tame,' said Joe.

'He's no Marv.' Marvin was one of the first dead bodies they had to guard as rookies, a morbidly obese victim of his own eating habits. All he had in his apartment when they found him was a tower of Krispy Kreme boxes, a mountain of crispy Kleenex and the sickest collection of amateur porn that Joe or Danny had ever admitted to seeing.

They moved into the master bedroom. Another tidy space, with a queen-sized bed and a pale green satin throw folded over the bottom half.

'I wish Gina would let me have a bed this easy to climb into,' said Danny. 'Instead of taking a hundred fucking pillows out of the way first. Does that make sense to you ever, why women do that?'

'No.'

There were books and bottles of water on each nightstand, some headache pills and a bracelet on the wife's side, a wallet and a watch on the husband's side. There was a chair in the corner with a pair of jeans and a grey sweatshirt on it. Up a step on the left-hand side of the room was a raised dressing area that appeared to be Mrs Lowry's domain and the most disturbed by the attack. There was makeup, shoes, belts and bags everywhere. In a corner, two linen baskets were stuffed and spilling over with clothes, a suitcase lay half unpacked, the dressing table was covered with hair products and more makeup. A small stool was upturned on the floor. Joe studied the room for several minutes before deciding the perp hadn't made it in here. It looked more like a case of opposites attract.

Joe took notes of where he needed photographs to be taken and checked with Kendra when he got back to the hallway. He drew a sketch of the apartment, marking in the smallest of details.

After three hours, everyone was winding down and heading back to the twentieth precinct.

'What do you think?' said Danny as they got into the car.

'Well, it's not a burglary,' said Joe.

'Yeah, with the wallet just lying around—'

'Two wallets,' said Joe.

'What?'

'Yeah. In the hallway, the little table was knocked over. There's a kind of bashed-up wallet there. And a new one.'

'Both the vic's?' said Danny.

'Both have his cards in it. And money.'

'Yeah and then the expensive watch on the nightstand and shit . . .' said Danny.

'With the computer and the sex toys and the naked body, it could be something sexual.'

Danny nodded. 'Do you think maybe he had something going on on the side? Blazkow said the wife was in Jersey with her ma for the night.'

Joe nodded. 'I'd say yeah.'

He took out his cell phone. He had eight missed calls. Six were from Anna: one voicemail, four hang-ups and a final voicemail:

'Asshole.'

With her accent, Joe liked when Anna said asshole. He didn't like the volume, though, and the crash of the phone as she slammed it down. He looked at his watch. He hadn't made Shaun's meeting. And he hadn't called.

'Shit,' he said. 'Shit. I forgot to call Anna.'

'You're a dead man,' said Danny, reversing out of the space. 'Speaking of dead men, did you hear why Rufo lost all that weight?'

'No.'

'His brother died, forty-nine years old, heart attack. Bam. No warning.'

'Yeah, I remember that.'

'No, but there's more. Apparently, at the funeral, Rufo had a few too many and one of the guys heard him tell some old aunt that he didn't want to go down the same road as his brother because – wait for it – he'd never been in love. Specifically, he'd never found true love.'

'Rufo?'

'Yes.'

'I'm seeing him in a whole new way now.'

'Yeah,' said Danny, 'in soft focus, running through a cornfield.'

'How long ago was that?'

'Three years ago.'

'And we haven't seen him with a woman yet.'

'It's sad. For all of us. He could have kept his fuller figure and we could have been spared the salad, quinoa, couscous talk.'

'You go ahead in,' said Joe when they got to the twentieth precinct. He walked past the entrance and called Anna. 'Hey, honey, I'm sorry. I'm not gonna make—'

'I know,' said Anna. 'Because I've already been to the school and now I'm back home.'

'I caught a homicide. I've been tied up, honey. How did it go?'

'Oh, well the principal was there and she started off by—'

Joe saw Cullen and Blazkow walk from their car into the building. 'Honey? I'm sorry. I can't get into the details right now. But did it go OK?'

'That depends,' she said stiffly.

'I gotta go, look, I'm sorry. I'll call you when I get back to the office, OK? It'll probably be late. I love you.'

'I love you too,' she said, her voice tired.

Joe made his way up to the second-floor office. Everyone was standing around drinking coffee.

'So what have we got?' he said.

'Closed homicide, no witnesses? A bag of shit,' said Blazkow.

'Any video?' said Joe.

'Not so far,' said Martinez.

'Not even from across the street?' said Joe.

'Nope.'

'Not everyone was home in the building,' said Blazkow. 'So we'll see what comes up, but neighbors on either side heard nothing and the doorman didn't see shit.'

'What about the wife?'

'She's at her ma's with their kid,' said Martinez. 'She was a mess, tried to hold it together for the daughter, but . . . fuck. I got what I could from her, which was not a lot. She has no idea why this happened. They don't socialize a lot, they hang out together most of the time.'

'OK – Rencher, can you pull Lowry's phone records?' said Joe. 'Cullen, could you run the plates of all the cars on the street? Tomorrow, we've got the autopsy. When we've got an idea of the time of death, we can work out about canvassing the building again.' He turned to Blazkow. 'You get anything from BCI or Triple I?'

Anyone who was arrested in New York got a NYSID number – New York State Identification. The Bureau of Criminal Investigations had the records. If Lowry had a criminal record, a phone call to the BCI would have details and a photo. A Triple I check would show if Lowry had an out-of-state record.

'Nada,' said Blazkow.

'OK,' said Joe.

'Grab a desk,' said Blazkow. 'You want coffee?'

'Thanks, yeah,' said Joe. He took off his jacket and sat down. When he looked up, Denis Cullen was standing over him.

'Uh – Joe? Can I put myself forward for going through the financial records, maybe the phone records?'

Joe laughed. 'That's the first time in my life I've ever been asked that.'

'Yeah, well . . . I guess I've kind of got an eye for it.'

By 1 a.m., Joe was slumped in his chair, his fingers stiff from typing. He had crossed the coffee threshold. It was now sending him to sleep. He never realized he was ODing until it was too late.

'I'm outta here,' he said, standing up, suddenly.

'You OK?' said Danny.

'I'm tired. I'm going back to the office. You coming?'

'Sure. You not going home?'

'Not tonight. Not with the autopsy first thing.'

The dorm in Manhattan North was off the locker room and had four metal beds with thin mattresses and covers that nobody risked sleeping under. Working the 'four and two chart' meant four days on, two days off. The first two tours were 4 p.m. to 1 a.m., the last two were 8 a.m. to 4 p.m. The turnaround tour ended at 1 a.m. and was followed by an 8 a.m. start. Most detectives stayed in the dorm on those nights or at least told their wives they did. Anna didn't like being alone at night any more, so Joe had been coming home; because they lived in Bay Ridge, he didn't have far to go. But the first few nights on a major case, she wouldn't expect to see him. He called her anyway.

'Sweetheart, it's me again. I'm staying at the office tonight.'

'I know,' said Anna.

'Well, it's just I hadn't said, so I thought—'

'It's fine. Don't worry.'

'Will you be OK? Is Shaun home?'

'No. But he'll be back.'

'What happened at the school?'

'Well, the principal was very nice. I think she likes Shaun, but understands he's . . . changed. She said he's been rude and uncooperative.'

'That's the French blood.'

Anna laughed. 'Yes. His falling grades they've put down to the American.'

Joe laughed. 'They said the same thing about his charm and his looks.'

'And low self-esteem . . .'

'What was the bottom line?' said Joe.

'Just that they will give him a chance to improve. They think he's tired in class, staying out too late and—'

'Did they give us a hard time?'

'They didn't have to say a word.'

'Look, are you sure you're going to be OK tonight? Would you like me to get Pam to come over and stay?'

Pam was his father Giulio's second wife.

'Pam?' said Anna. She laughed. 'Yeah, baby-sitting by a woman the same age as me . . . who is my mother-in-law.'

'Step.'

'Whatever.'

'It wouldn't be babysitting. You could ask her over for a glass of wine and a movie. I'm just trying to help.'

'Just to remind you – it's after one in the morning. And I'm OK. Sleep well whenever you get there.'

'Thanks. I'll see you—'

'In a few days. I know.'

'I love you.'

'Me too.'

'Honey?'

'Yeah?'

'I love laughing with you.'

'Me too,' she said. 'And Joe?'

'Yeah?'

'At least I know you sleep in the dorm.'

'I wouldn't want it any other way.'

Anna was right. He did sleep in the dorm. But Gina Markey thought the same thing about Danny.

THREE

Stanley Frayte had an hour to kill before he showed up for work. He drove down Holt Avenue in his white Ford Econoline van stamped with the chunky blue lettering of Frayte Electrical Services. He pulled into the parking lot at the south end of Astoria Park. At 8.30 a.m., it was quieter than it would have been an hour before when the dawn walkers, runners and swimmers were making their way back home to take a shower before work.

He got out of the van and let the cool breeze from the East River raise goosebumps on his bare arms. Where he stood – by the park, under the Triborough Bridge – was Astoria as it had always been to him. On the Shore Boulevard side, the luxury condos that looked over the tennis courts on one side and Manhattan on the other repre-sented change. Like Brooklyn, Astoria had lured people out of the city and was going through the makeover to prove it. Stan liked it all. He was just happy to be anywhere he could feel the sun, look out over beautiful water, walk through the trees, sit on a bench. When it hit 8.50 a.m., he went back to his van.

He drove down 19th Street and pulled into the small parking lot of the apartment building he had been working on for the previous two weeks. He unloaded his equipment and walked up the flag-stone path. He stopped halfway and bent down, laying his gear beside him and pulling a penknife from his utility belt. He flipped it open and sliced at a weed that was pushing up through a gap in the cement. June, the receptionist, waved to him from behind the front desk as he walked towards her. He pushed through the front door into the lobby. The smell was lemon disinfectant, rising from the shiny floor tiles. June's desk was on the left-hand side, a crescent moon that curved towards the door. The walls were pale gold with a cream dado rail that traced around the corner to the elevator bank. Behind the desk, free-standing plastic barriers closed off the corridor to everyone except the construction workers who were renovating that section of the building all the way up to the fourth floor.

'Hey, Flat Stanley,' said June, smiling up from her desk. Flat Stanley was a character from a chil-dren's book who in a tragic accident got flattened to 2-D. The Stanley standing in front of June was not flat; he was Stanley with a belly inflated to bursting point. Stan grunted, shifting the utility belt that only ever came to rest under his gut, no matter how high he tried to move it.

'Anything I need to know?' he said.

'Just that Mary Burig on the second floor is going to plant that little strip of flower-bed you've been kind enough to lend her.'

'Mary?' His face lit up. 'Today?'

June nodded. 'Yup.' She smiled. 'I think someone has you wrapped around her little finger.'

He frowned. 'She likes flowers.'

Mary Burig checked her smartphone. It held everything she needed to remember: phone numbers, addresses, bank account details, appointments, shopping lists, birthdays, anniversaries, maps and guides. She spent fifteen minutes tidying her living room, starting by the front door and working clockwise through each corner. She moved into the kitchen and wiped down the surfaces. She was about to unload the dishwasher when the doorbell rang. She jogged back to the front door and opened it.

'Hi, Magda,' she said. 'Come in. I'm working hard here. Tea?'

'Coffee,' said Magda, hugging her. 'Thank you. I can make it.'

Magda Oleszak was in her early fifties, with a healthy glow from eating good food and walking everywhere. She came to New York from Poland with her two teenage children ten years earlier, learned perfect English, but never lost her accent.

'The place looks great,' said Magda, walking around as she took off her light vinyl jacket. Upside down and open beside Mary's bed was *Rebecca* by Daphne du Maurier.

'Are you reading *Rebecca* again?' said Magda.

'I know,' said Mary. 'It's cheating because I know it inside out.'

'It's not cheating,' said Magda, turning to her, holding her hands passionately. 'Don't ever let me hear you say that again, Mary. It's beautiful what you and Rebecca have. You are friends for life. She'll always be with you, won't she? Or whatever that girl's name is. Does she have a name? I don't think she does, does she? I get confused myself, see? *I* get confused. You don't. It's wonderful, Mary. You hang on to that feeling. You remember what *Rebecca* brought you when you were lying on your bed as a young girl.'

Mary smiled.

'Now, because we are talking about books,' said Magda, 'I have some good news for you. Stan Frayte, you know Stan, is going to do your makeover on the library.

Mary clapped. 'Cool.' Then she frowned. 'So do you think it'll wind up looking more like a library than a store window?'

'Nothing is happening with the glass if that's what you mean. We want to make sure no-one's making trouble in there.'

'No-one makes trouble in libraries.'

'They do, going right to the dirty bits in all those romance novels. Hot throbbing whatever.'

'Magda!'

Magda laughed.

'I wish they'd do something about the other windows,' said Mary. 'They're too high up. You can't see out if you sit down. You're just staring at a blank wall.'

'You know what?' said Magda. 'I like to think that the reader uses it as a blank screen and they project onto it the world of whatever book they're reading at that time.'

Mary thought about it. 'I'll go with that,' she said. 'I like it.'

'Oh, you want to know how they got the money to do the library? Stan himself. He said he got a discount on some light fixtures for the hallway. I'm not so sure.'

'That's so kind,' said Mary. She paused. 'There's something sad about Stan.'

Magda went into the kitchen. 'You're out of coffee, Mary.'

'Oh. I'm sorry.' She hit Tasks on her phone menu and added coffee to her grocery list.

'So,' said Mary, 'what's going on?'

'David's coming this morning, isn't he?'

'Yes,' said Mary. 'There's cake in there. I'm not hungry, but you can help yourself.'

Magda opened the bread bin and pulled out a cake wrapped in aluminium foil. It was covered in mould. She flipped the lid of the bin and threw it inside.

'Thanks,' she said, 'but I've eaten.' She came back into the living room and sat down on the sofa. 'Will I stay until David comes?'

'That would be great,' said Mary. 'Today is ironing day, so I'm going to start now, if you don't mind.'

'Go ahead,' said Magda.

David Burig was thirty-four years old, looked younger, and spent most of his time dressed in a suit so his staff would take him seriously. He ran a successful catering business he bought after offloading an overvalued software firm nine years earlier.

'Hello there,' he said, hugging Mary and kissing her on the cheek.

'David,' she said. 'Yaaay!'

'If only everyone had that response when they saw me.'

'Yaaay!' said Magda.

He laughed. 'Why thank you, both. I feel very special. So,' he said to Mary. 'I believe it's time for bed.'

Mary frowned. She looked at the clock. 'But it's only 10 a.m.!'

He smiled. '*Flower*-beds.'

She shook her head. 'Is that supposed to be funny?'

'Yes.'

'Just because you say so, I'm still not sure that means it is.'

He held his hands up. 'It actually wasn't funny at all.'

'It was dumb,' said Magda.

'Worth a try, though,' said David. 'Let me go change. And can I ask? *What* are you wearing?'

'Do I look nuts?' said Mary.

'You look . . . creative.'

Mary smiled because David did. 'I thought it was kind of cool.' She was wearing a pair of orange baggy cotton pants that tapered at the ankle, a green vest and white sneakers.

David laughed and disappeared into the bedroom with his sports bag.

'OK,' said Magda. 'Have you got what you need for gardening?'

Mary pointed to the tools lined up on the table: 'Two trowels, mat to kneel on, watering can, fork thing . . . is that everything?'

'Yes,' said Magda. 'There's a faucet at the back of the building.'

David appeared in a battered pair of jeans, a blue long-sleeved T-shirt and green retro Pumas. 'Right,' he said. 'I am ready to garden. I am proud – no, I'm shocked – to be assisting in such a noble endeavour. Come on, lady in scary pants, let's go down and bring that dirty brown soil to life.'

'I'll take the elevator with you,' said Magda.

*　　*　　*

Mary laid down the mat in front of the flower-bed that ran along the edge of the property, fifty feet away from the back of the apartment block. A row of pots filled with chrysanthemums in bright shades of yellow, orange and magenta was lined up against the wall.

'They're so beautiful,' said Mary.

'They are,' said David. 'Stan always sticks with the same colour theme, doesn't he? Just changes the flowers in fall.'

She nodded.

David turned to the bare flower-bed and laughed. 'Look – he's marked out where we can plant: the shadiest, quietest corner—'

Mary smiled. 'In case we do it wrong?'

'I'd say so.'

'But I've helped him before, he knows I'm good.'

'You. But not me.'

'OK,' said Mary. 'We need to take the flowers out of the pots, break up the roots gently and plant them here in a pattern.' She handed him a piece of paper with a rough diagram.

'That should be easy,' said David.

Mary knelt down on the mat and started to dig a hole. David tended to the pots, pushing a small trowel into the first one, working it around the roots, pulling the plant free and shaking off the excess soil.

'Everyone I know is at the office right now,' he said. 'Do you know how good that makes me feel?'

Mary smiled. 'Thanks for helping me.'

'Helping you? I'm helping myself, here,' he said. 'This is therapy. This is what life's all about. Outdoors, fresh air, office avoidance.'

He spotted a weed, growing by the grass at the edge of the flower-bed. He pulled it out and held it up. 'Isn't it funny?' he said. 'How easy it is for beauty to attract such ugly, clinging things.'

'Like the garden in Manderley,' said Mary.

'Yes!' said David. 'Exactly.'

They worked on, talking and laughing for over an hour. David stopped and watched his little sister, her concentration unwavering, stooped over the bright petals, holding them gently in her tiny hand, pouring her heart into the job.

'How are you doing?' he said.

She looked up at him. 'I guess I'm OK.'

He squeezed her hand. 'That's good. That's good, Mare.'

She smiled. They continued in silence until David stopped again. He looked at her and started a quote from *Rebecca*: '*We all of us have our particular devil who rides us and torments us.*'

Mary smiled sadly and continued. '*And we must give battle in the end. We have conquered ours . . .*'

David let out a breath. '*Or so we believe.*'

FOUR

The body of Ethan Lowry was laid out on the perforated surface of a stainless steel table in the basement of the Office of the Chief Medical Examiner. A body block lay under his back, forcing out his trunk that had been emptied of its organs. A handwritten, bloodstained list with their weights lay by the scales.

Joe and Danny were dressed in scrubs, gowns and gloves, with face masks hanging around their necks. Joe's digital camera and notebook were on the counter beside him. He had taken photos and notes and asked questions through every step of the three-hour autopsy.

Dr Malcolm Hyland was young for an ME. Cops liked him because he didn't expect them to be doctors, but he didn't expect them to be stupid either. He was soft-spoken until he had to use the microphone – then he turned stilted and loud.

'OK, doc,' said Joe. He grabbed the notebook and flipped it open again.

'OK,' said Hyland. 'Estimated time of death somewhere between 11 p.m. and 3 a.m. Cause of death was a point-blank GSW to the head – you saw the small entry hole by his eye socket and the bruised and battered twenty-two caliber bullet taken from the skull cavity. The bullet's trajectory was left to right, lodged in the temporal lobe. You remember the grazing around the wound margins as the bullet was spinning in. Because it was directly over bone, you got the radiating splits in the skin and the stellate effect – that star shape. Mechanism of death was an intracerebral bleed.

'But before we even get to the gunshot, we had evidence of compressive asphyxia which is what I was saying about the diaphragm not being able to expand. I'd say the killer sat on the guy's chest or pressed a knee down on it and the vic got the full force of his body bearing down on him. Subdued like that, the killer was able to assault him with what was probably a medium-sized hammer. With regard the facial injuries – you already saw that – extensive bruising and swelling, several irregular lacerations. The upper and lower lips showed external and internal lacerations . . . this is very common in homosexual killings.'

'He was alive for all the facial injuries,' said Danny.

Hyland nodded. 'He'd inhaled blood and teeth fragments.'

'And what you're saying is this guy was already dying when he was shot, he wasn't able to breathe properly,' said Danny.

'Yeah,' said Hyland. 'I guess I could understand if the killer bashed his head in, then asphyxiated him. But on top of that, he shoots him? It's cruel stuff. You can imagine, the man's fighting for his every breath, putting all his strength into that, then he's slammed in the face with the hammer. He's focused on that agonizing pain, then back to fighting for breath, then pain again, everything mounting right 'til the end. Then a gunshot wound. And that's it. He's gone.'

'These wackos always got their own screwed-up reasons,' said Danny. 'Some of it is looking familiar to me, I gotta say. You remember William Aneto?'

Joe shook his head.

'Oh yeah. You weren't here. It was me and Martinez. This gay guy on the Upper West Side. It just . . . there's something about it rings a bell.'

'If we're done here . . .' said Hyland. He pointed to Joe's notebook. 'I'm sure you got it all there.'

'Yeah, until I get back and I find one word I can't make out and nothing else makes sense without it.'

'Well, if you need anything else, call me.'

Joe nodded. 'Thanks.'

'Good luck,' said Hyland. 'You know, I wish

when I dissected a brain I could find a little reel, like a victim's-eye movie, so we could just sit back and watch a replay of what happened. It'd be fool-proof in court for you guys, wouldn't it? Slam dunk. Wouldn't that be great? Or if I could find, like, a mental black box that would log the minute-to-minute psychological impact of what the victim's been through. Although I'd say with this guy, it was all so horrific, a circuit somewhere would have blown.'

Anna Lucchesi lay on the sofa in her pyjamas with a light fleece blanket over her. She was watching the fourth episode in a row of *Grand Designs*. A couple had renovated a country estate somewhere in England and she was now watching the car wreck that was their 80s taste in interiors. When she first started watching the show in Ireland, it was from a different vantage point in a house that fit. She was a rising star at *Vogue Living* and had overseen the renovation of a lighthouse and the keeper's home beside it outside a small village in Waterford. She was doing the job she loved in a beautiful loca-tion with her husband and son cheering her on. Watching *Grand Designs* now, she felt like a discon-nected outsider, sitting in a grim two-storey brick frame house in Bay Ridge, Brooklyn – not Brooklyn Heights, not Williamsburg, not even DUMBO. It was older, it felt safe, the neighbors were nice, but it held no spark for Anna.

She stared towards the window, missing the sea view and waves that could get so loud, you had to close the window to hear people talk. The house had been peaceful and comfortable, with simple furniture and neutral tones. Then everything it represented was gone, shattered by Duke Rawlins. He wanted to destroy Joe. But he had underestimated his resilience. And when Anna thought of it now, she didn't admire Joe for it, she resented him. Joe killed Donald Riggs and she paid the price. He was uninjured, back on the job. She was in her pyjamas in the afternoon.

For two months after Ireland, she stayed with her parents in Paris. Joe and Shaun came for the first three weeks, but the tiny house started to close in on them. She felt like Joe was trying to rush her recovery and make things go back to a kind of normal she knew they never would. She eventually persuaded him to take Shaun back to New York.

When she followed them over, she spent time adjusting to the new house in the new area she had been too depressed to take an interest in choosing. She would wake in the morning, wondering why she was there, but never able to figure out where she would really like to be. But she knew she wanted to avoid the outside world. And that meant embracing the four walls.

Her boss, Chloe da Silva, had allowed her to work from home, but had made it clear that it was only a temporary arrangement – Anna was too good an interior designer to lose on the big jobs. That was fine at the start, but as the months went by, Anna felt a rising insecurity that any day she would be fired and the only thing keeping her sane would be taken away. She liked styling shoots from home, choosing products from catalogues or jpegs or from the packages that were sent nearly every day to the house. It was unorthodox, but it worked. She hoped.

She dragged herself up off the sofa and was about to go into her makeshift office when the phone rang. She heard the harsh clatter of being punched off speaker phone in Chloe's office.

'It's me again.'

Anna held her breath.

'I'm sorry to land this on you, but, Anna, I really am under serious pressure here. There's a major shoot at W Union Square tomorrow morning and Leah has let me down big time. Anyway, the shoot is bedrooms – models in hotels slash extravagant homes, sleeping off all that hard work they do – walking and um, staring. A lot of our major advertisers are involved and, here's what I'm hoping you'll go for: the photographer is Marc Lunel. You can work with someone who doesn't pronounce Moët wrong. Come on. Please. Please. Please.'

Anna paused, watching the couple on television directing two men into the house with a red leather sofa. 'Only if I get the main credit,' she said finally.

'You'll do it?' said Chloe.

Anna's heart was beating rapidly, but not out of excitement. 'Yes.'

'God, if I'd known it was going to be that easy, I would have called Marc months ago.' Her laugh was shrill. Anna was silent.

Chloe jumped in. 'Oh, listen to me being so insensitive. Of course you needed all that time—'

'Please,' said Anna. 'Email me the details.'

'Of course. Done. Darling, thank you. Thank you so much.'

Joe leaned into the mirror in the men's room, snipping away the nasal hair that had spent three hours soaking up the smell of death. He never figured out if it was a practical or a psychological routine or both. He didn't like seeing his face up close, seeing the new lines around his eyes, the extra grey hairs at the side of his head; more things that were out of his control. He went to his locker and grabbed a bottle of tea-tree shower gel that Anna had given him. He got undressed and threw his suit into a plastic bag.

'The smell of that crap,' said Danny walking in. 'I think I'll go back to the autopsy.'

'Screw you,' said Joe. 'I'd rather smell—'

'Like weird-ass tea—'

'Like – clean, than how you go out with your

cheap foaming shit that doesn't cover up
nothing.'

'If a woman can't handle the smell of death
from a man—'

'She can't go out with a deadbeat.'

'Shit,' said Danny, closing his locker door. 'I'm
all out of shower gel. Give me some of that crap.'

Joe went back to his desk and checked his email.
Danny walked over a few minutes later, smelling
the back of his hand and frowning.

'Get over the fucking shower gel,' said Joe.

'Let me pull that file,' said Danny. 'The one I
told you about – Aneto.'

Joe made space on his desk, laying a stack of
files on the floor beside him. Danny came back
and opened William Aneto's file in front of him.
Aneto was thirty-one, slightly built, handsome,
with collar-length black hair. Joe looked at his
head shot and saw a TV actor's face; the four-line
max guy, two or three steps back from the main
action. His role in a Spanish language soap opera
was the friend of the brother of the leading man.
He was killed almost a year earlier, his body discovered in his Upper West Side apartment by a female
friend. The case had quickly gone cold. As a victim,
William fell into the high-risk category, promis-
cuous on the gay scene, known for disappearing
at the end of a night with a stranger. Danny and
Martinez had interviewed hundreds of Aneto's

friends, acquaintances and lovers and had gotten nowhere. His murder was down as a hook-up gone bad.

Joe pulled out the next photos and laid them in rows on the table in front of him. Danny stood beside him. Like Ethan Lowry, the body was found in the hallway. But behind William Aneto, hair smears of blood curved across the grey tiled floor like tracks through red paint from a dried brush.

'Yeah. It's all coming back to me,' said Danny. 'Most of the action happened in the kitchen. He was killed there and then dragged to the front door to be finished off. Wait 'til you see the kitchen. Hand prints, foot prints, all over the floor, up the wall – kindergarten art class. You know – if all the paint was red. And the children were Damian.'

Joe studied the photos of the kitchen. He pointed to the bloodied corner of a granite counter top. 'So I'm the perp, standing here behind the vic, bashing his face off this.' Blood was spattered onto the wall, the counter, the floor, misted across the granite.

Danny nodded. 'Yup.'

They looked at a wide shot of the hallway – the crumpled corpse, the spatter of a gunshot wound, the pooled blood under his head.

William Aneto's face was more damaged than Ethan Lowry's, destroyed by injuries that left the entire surface pulped and bloodied. His right eye socket was completely impacted from one of the blows, obliterating the entry wound from the bullet that, based on the autopsy results, followed a similar trajectory to Lowry's.

'Yeah. It's a no-brainer,' said Danny.

'The caliber was too low,' said Joe.

'Funny guy. Shit, the phone – look,' said Danny, pointing to the tiny silver cell phone beside Aneto's body. 'I forgot about that.'

Like Ethan Lowry, it looked like William Aneto could have made a call just before he died. Joe flipped through the file to a statement from a Mrs Aneto.

'Yeah,' said Danny. 'His mother said the call was just to say goodnight.'

'Maybe you should talk to Mrs Aneto again.'

'She no likey me,' said Danny, making a face. 'Maybe Martinez could warm her up again.'

'Yeah, that's one I won't be tagging along for.'

'Why's that?'

'Maybe you should ask Martinez,' said Joe.

'What the hell's that supposed to mean?'

'See how he looks at me? I'm a homewrecker. He had eleven good months with you, I show up, you take me back, the guy's life is over.'

Danny shook his head.

'He gets that glint in his eye when you're around,' said Joe.

'Screw you. What you are seeing is professional admiration.'

'Come on. Let's go talk to Rufo.'

'Gentlemen,' said Rufo when they walked in.

'We got a link,' said Joe. 'Between Ethan Lowry and William Aneto.'

Rufo frowned. 'The guy I've been getting all these calls about this week?'

Danny nodded. 'Yeah. The year-anniversary-still-no-answers thing.'

'Interesting timing,' said Rufo. 'Tell me more.'

'Both happened at home, no sign of forced entry, similar facial injuries, similar twenty-two caliber gunshot wound, phone found beside both of them, bodies left in the hallway behind the door.'

Rufo nodded. 'That's good enough for me.'

Shaun Lucchesi lay on his bed staring at the ceiling. The stereo blasted the same lyrics over and over: *left behind/left behind/left behind*. It had been almost a year since his girlfriend, Katie Lawson, was murdered. They had met on the first day in school when he arrived in Ireland and they had been inseparable until she died. What made things worse was that Shaun had started out as the prime suspect, convicted by most of the small village until they learned the truth.

For months after Katie's death, Shaun had woken up with a void inside him that had ached like nothing else he had ever known. On the good days, he was lifted by memories. On the bad ones, he was trapped in a loop of images that started from the time he picked her up that night and ended at the last moment he saw her. Everything now seemed unimportant. He came back to New York and met his old friends and went to the old hangouts, but it was such a different life to the one he had with Katie, it was surreal. His life with her was stripped down to how they felt about each other, how they made each other laugh, how they lay on his bed wrapped around each other for hours, just talking or watching movies. It wasn't about who your friends were, where you went, what you owned, who you were sleeping with, who had the latest cell phone, who had the fastest car. Sometimes he was so overwhelmed at the thought of never being that happy again, he almost couldn't breathe. He turned off the stereo and went to his closet. From the top shelf, he pulled out a small, chunky round tin. A thin layer of wax coated the bottom of it and a short black wick twisted from the centre. It was Katie's favourite candle – Fresh Linen. He took a lighter from his drawer and lit it. He could only burn it for a few minutes at a time, it was so low. He couldn't bear the thought it would ever burn out completely.

Everyone else would remember the anniversary of Katie's funeral three weeks from now. But this night, one year ago, was the night he nearly had sex with her for the first time. But then they had fought. And then she had run away from him. And then she was killed. He lay down on his bed, closed his eyes and, for half an hour, let the tears run down his face onto the pillow. Then he sat up and grabbed his cell phone and scrolled through his photos. Katie at school. Katie on the beach. Katie in his room. Delete. Delete. Delete.

FIVE

Joe sat at his desk, pressing his fingers against his forehead, pretending to read a report that had started to blur a few minutes earlier. His phone rang. It was Reuben Maller from the FBI, Eastern District – the office that covered the whole east coast. They got on well since their first case together. The last one they worked was Donald Riggs.

'Can you talk?' said Maller.

'Go ahead,' said Joe.

'How are you all doing?'

'Who?' said Joe. 'You mean here? Manhattan North?'

'You, Anna . . . Shaun. How are you holding up?'

Joe paused. 'We're good . . . why? What's going on?'

Maller let out a breath. 'OK,' he said, lowering his voice. 'Off the record, I got some news from the Bureau in Texas. On Duke Rawlins.'

Joe stopped breathing.

'Before you say anything, Joe, it's sketchy, I don't have a lot of details. And you do not know this.'

Joe fought the nausea rising in his stomach. 'Tell me,' he managed.

'Duke Rawlins' home town, Stinger's Creek? Geoff Riggs – Donald Riggs' father – said he had a visit last week from Rawlins. Geoff Riggs is in really bad shape, Joe. No-one knows the last time he was sober. He walks through town, railing about things, not making a lot of sense. Last week, he said to some young kid in the liquor store that Rawlins was out at his cabin the week before. The kid was freaked out and called the cops. They went to speak with Riggs. I have it written here verbatim. Geoff Riggs said, real calm: "Sure, I had a visit from Dukey. He was wanting to say Hi, catch up. Been years. Wanted to take a look around Donnie's bedroom. I said, 'Knock yourself out, buddy'. Not a lot in there since y'all turned it upsideways last year. So Dukey comes out, then he go on out to the shed out back where I keep my tools and I say, 'Sure you can, Dukey. You're a good boy.' He seemed kinda aggritated. Had some sort of bug in his bonnet. Anyways, last I saw of little Dukey."'

'That's it?' said Joe.

'Yep.'

'Geoff Riggs didn't call the cops, nothing?'

'No – this guy's brain is so fried. That statement I just read to you took two hours to extract from him. My guess is Rawlins is taking advantage of the relaxed surveillance.'

'The no surveillance,' said Joe.

'Yeah,' said Maller. 'It's been a year – he hadn't shown anywhere anyone expected him to. And his visit to Geoff Riggs is only part one of the story. The second part is that a few days later, the custodian of the Stinger's Creek cemetery was doing his rounds and when he got to Donald Riggs' grave . . . well, there was another one opened up right beside it.'

Joe paused. 'Someone was dug up?'

'No. Someone had just dug a grave. It was empty. It was thoroughly searched and there was nothing or no-one in it.'

'Jesus Christ,' said Joe.

'What we have got to remember is everyone out there knows what Rawlins and Riggs did. And on the one hand, you've got people baying for blood. On the other, some of the officers from the sheriff's department who went to investigate this, spoke to a group of stoners who were all, "Man, Duke Rawlins is, like, sick." In a good way. So it could have been an angry relative of a victim, it could have been a teenage prank.'

'Maller, why don't we cut the crap, here? You know what this is. Alcoholic witness or not. It's not a coincidence – we hear Rawlins shows up, pays a visit to a tool shed and within days a grave is opened up next to his old buddy. Come on.'

'Yeah,' said Maller. 'It's just I know what this

man has done to you. I mean, that's why I called you on this . . . yeah, I don't think this one's a false alarm.'

'Jesus Christ.'

'I have to ask,' said Maller, 'has he tried to get in touch with you?'

Joe did not hesitate. 'No.'

Anna Lucchesi sat at her dressing table in her bathrobe, her hair pulled back with a black jersey headband, her face pale, her eyes shadowed. She opened a packet of cleansing wipes and started wiping down her makeup products, getting rid of dust and dried-in foundation and caked powder. She grouped them together and lined them up, ready for the following morning. A photo beside the bed showed her as she used to be, her hair dark and glossy, her cheeks healthy, her eyes alive.

The notice board at Manhattan North was covered with badges from police departments all over the country and around the world. Joe stood in front of it, thinking about Duke Rawlins. Every evil thing Rawlins had done had settled close to the surface and deep down inside. He didn't know what would end it, but every day a new scenario took him away from where he was supposed to be.

'Joe? That's your freakin' phone,' yelled Martinez.

Joe grabbed the receiver.

'Joe? It's Bobby Nicotero. From the 1st.' Bobby's

father was Victor Nicotero – Old Nic – a retired
cop and close friend of Joe's.

'Jesus, Bobby. What's up?'

'Not a lot.'

'How's Old Nic?'

'You tell me.'

Joe paused.

Bobby's laugh was off. 'I was going to ask you
the same thing. How *is* my father?'

'Well . . . last time I saw him was at that
barbecue, couple weeks back. You had to be somewhere with the kids, I think. He was good, taking
it easy, enjoying writing.'

'Writing what?'

'Oh,' said Joe. 'He's working on a book.'

'Yeah, well, I've been busy . . .'

'Yeah – your old man's writing his memoirs.'

Bobby shot out a laugh. 'I got a few chapters
of my own I might like to add to that.'

'Really?' said Joe. 'What can I—'

'Actually I'm calling because I think I've got some-
thing you might be interested in. The Upper West
Side homicide you got? Your vic – Ethan Lowry.
Was there a phone by him when they found him?'

'Yeah. There was. Why?'

Bobby sucked in a breath. 'Sounds a lot like
this case I caught in SoHo back in December. Guy's
name was Gary Ortis, badly beaten about the face,
gunshot to the head, phone in the hallway beside
him. We never got the guy.'

'Jesus. And it looks like we're already linking this one to a case a year back. Was your guy gay?'

'He was single and he dated women,' said Bobby, 'but who knows? Yours?'

'Ethan Lowry was married with a kid,' said Joe. 'William Aneto was gay.'

'Hmm.'

'I know where you're coming from,' said Joe, 'it has that feel about it. That was some hardcore facial damage and I don't know about you, but last few times I saw shit like that, it was two guys, lovers' spat. No-one died, but . . .'

'Yeah, I know,' said Bobby.

'Look, why don't you call in to the Two-Oh, bring what you got.'

Joe put down the phone and reached into the inside pocket of his jacket hanging on the back of his chair. He pulled out two pills and took them with a can of Red Bull.

'Guys,' he said. 'That was Bobby Nicotero from the 1st. Looks like he got a third vic, happened back in December. He's on his way over.'

'Holy shit,' said Danny.

'On Lowry's records? said Blazkow. 'The last call at 10.58? Was to a woman – Clare Oberly. Lives on 48th Street between 8th and Broadway.'

'OK,' said Joe. 'Danny and I'll go check her out this evening.'

*   *   *

Half an hour later Bobby Nicotero walked into the twentieth precinct with his partner. Bobby was thirty-nine years old with a thick neck, broad shoulders, short legs and suits too cheap to flatter any of them. He had close-cut black hair, a heavy brow and a range of facial expressions that stretched to pissed off.

'Hey,' said Joe. 'Good to see you.'

'You too,' said Bobby, shaking his hand. 'This is my partner, Roger Pace.'

Pace was shockingly gaunt with eyes set deep into dark sockets.

'Nice to meet you,' said Joe, shaking his hand. 'Thanks for coming in.'

'No problem,' said Pace, slipping back behind Bobby.

'OK,' said Joe, walking over to the others. 'Bobby, you know Danny Markey. And this is Aldos Martinez and Fred Rencher from Manhattan North. Tom Blazkow and Denis Cullen from here at the Two-Oh. Everyone, Bobby Nicotero and Roger Pace from the 1st.'

Everyone nodded.

'Do you want to tell us what you got?' said Joe.

'Sure,' said Bobby. 'I read the paper and I just saw our friend, the "source close to the investigation" saying that the vic was found naked and his face was severely beaten. I figured there could be something to it, could be nothing.' He opened the file.

'Our vic's name was Gary Ortis, DOB 07/10/69, cause of death – GSW to the head from a twenty-two. There were signs of oxygen deprivation, you know, petechial hemorrhages. He was found naked in his apartment on Prince Street in SoHo.'

'Body behind the door,' said Joe.

'Yup.'

Everyone nodded. 'That sounds like our guy,' said Joe. 'Any leads?'

Bobby shook his head. 'Nothing. We thought it was a gay thing, but the guy had lots of girl-friends—' He shrugged. 'Not that that means anything.'

'Yeah,' said Martinez looking at Danny.

Danny rolled his eyes.

'Looks sexual to me,' said Blazkow. 'They're all found naked like that, beaten so bad.'

'We got the ME talking about a homosexual motive,' said Joe.

'Makes sense when you look at the physical damage,' said Rencher. 'When I was in the 17th, I caught this case – a high school junior, one of those small, pretty boy types, hooked up with this forty-year-old guy, they had a thing going on for a while. Then we're called out, the boyfriend has beaten the crap out of the poor kid, totally smashed up his face and, I mean, like our vics, he was unrecognizable. The boyfriend was out of his mind with grief, crying and saying he just wished the kid hadn't spent so much time talking to that cute barman, that he would have been still alive if he had. Unbelievable.'

'And remember that guy in Jersey who shot his boss?' said Cullen. 'He'd been arrested for beating the crap out of his boyfriend with a hammer a few years before that.'

'But then, there's no damage to the genitals with our vics,' said Joe. He shrugged. 'That usually goes along with it.'

'Also – on the sex thing,' said Rencher. 'According to Lowry's wife, the DVDs and whip and shit were just theirs, they liked to watch porn together, no big deal. She figures he was just going to watch some that night while she was gone.'

'OK. But what else was left lying around the other scenes? What was in the bedrooms?'

'There was a sexual element at the Aneto and Lowry scenes,' said Blazkow.

'Yeah, same for Ortis,' said Bobby. 'Toys, DVDs. Some of them were a little dusty, I remember, but they were out there on his bed. But there was also work papers, diaries, photos.'

'Yeah, we got photos at Aneto's too,' said Danny.

'There were love letters from Lowry's ex-girl-friend by his bed.'

'Oh, there were boxes of wax strips at Aneto's,' said Martinez.

'And Preparation H at Ortis's place,' said Bobby.

'It's kind of like they were all looking for

something,' said Blazkow. 'Pulling out drawers, looking through closets. Do you think maybe the perp was after something?'

'Maybe,' said Bobby. 'Maybe they could have all ripped him off.'

'Let's take a look at what they've got in common,' said Danny. 'We got a Wall Street guy, an actor, a graphic designer . . .'

'Faggoty jobs?' said Martinez.

'Yeah, I see that sensitivity training worked out well for you,' said Danny.

'It's cool, I'm dating the guy who gave the talk,' said Martinez.

'You're such a dickhead,' said Danny.

'What about success?' said Blazkow, ignoring the interruption. They all nodded. He continued, 'Perp could have a chip on his shoulder. All these guys were successful . . . at least, on the surface, like if you saw them on the street.'

'The Wall Street guys are all about surface,' said Danny. 'Why else do they freak out so much when they're caught with their pants around their ankles burying it in some ten-dollar whore? My neighbors, my clients, my wife . . .'

'Yeah,' said Bobby. 'And then the pricks tell us they're paying our salary, like that's going to help their situation. How to win cops and influence whatever.'

'OK – phone calls,' said Joe. 'All the vics made calls the night they died. Looks like while the perp was in their home. William Aneto calls his mother – she says it was just to say goodnight.'

'Gary Ortis calls his former business partner just to say hi, he says, see how he was doing,' said Bobby.

'Hmm,' said Joe. 'Maybe not. We need to go talk to these people again. And how is he choosing the vics? Is he following them home? If so, from where? If not, how is he meeting them – on line, at work, in a bar, at the gym . . .'

'Why, though? Why is he killing them?' said Blazkow.

'It's going to be a long night,' said Danny.

'What's Denis Cullen's story?' said Joe later, when he was alone with Danny.

'That's Denis Cullen who the 10-13 benefit's for next month. Well – it's for his daughter. She's got cancer, she's only thirteen years old.'

'Shit,' said Joe. 'I didn't know that. I thought he'd just been through a divorce or something.'

'Nah, they're a real close family. He's a good guy. When he's not here, he's at the hospital with his wife and daughter the whole time.'

'When's the benefit?'

'A couple weeks at the Bay Ridge Manor. There's a poster up on the board. It's black tie.'

'Black tie? What's up with that?'

Danny shrugged. 'It's terrible – it's because they're not sure, you know, if she's going to pull through and you know, make her prom, her wedding . . . so it's kind of a fancy affair for that.'

'Jesus Christ, you think you have problems . . .'

'I know.'

Anna Lucchesi lay in bed as wide awake as she had been when she got in. She wanted so badly to sleep, but one part of her was listening out for Joe to come home, the other for Shaun. Over the past few months, she had been kept awake by a strange humming sound somewhere off in the distance, maybe out across the water. Tonight, at least it was quieter, just the sound of cars going by below on the Belt Parkway, a soothing sound that usually lulled her to sleep. She pulled the sheet tightly around her, up over her shoulder and high under her chin. Just as she settled, she heard the screech of a car pulling up outside the house. A door opened, then closed, then silence. No footsteps. Nothing. She leaned up on her elbow and listened. She looked at the clock. It was 4 a.m. After a minute, she heard faint electronic beeps from outside. Then a short five-note melody. Then more beeps. Shaun's cell phone. She got up and walked over to the window when she pulled back the blinds, she saw a body lying on the street outside the gate. Her heart leaped. She looked closer and recognized Shaun's sneakers. Her legs went weak. She grabbed her cell phone off the nightstand and dialled Joe's number as she ran down the stairs.

'Joe, Joe, get home now,' she screamed. 'Something's happened to Shaun. He's lying outside the house on the street.' She hung up. Shaun was on his back with his eyes closed, his arms stretched out by his side.

'Shaun,' said Anna. 'Shaun.'

She crouched down beside him and put an ear to his chest. He was taking in deep guttural breaths and breathing out a rancid mix of garlic, cigarettes and alcohol.

'Shaun,' she hissed. 'Wake up.'

He frowned and rolled his head from side to side. Anna looked around to see if anyone was watching her in her pyjama bottoms and cami kneeling beside her drunk teenage son. Shaun's eyes flickered open and he slowly turned to her, his head loose on his neck, his eyes wildly trying to focus, first on her, then randomly on either side of her.

'Mom?' he said finally.

'Yes,' she snapped.

'Dad?' he said.

She reached down and grabbed his arm. 'Get up. Into this house.'

He wrenched his arm away. 'Get off of me.'

'Just get inside,' said Anna. 'It's four o'clock in the morning.'

He laughed.

'It's not funny.'

'It is,' he said. 'C'mon, it is funny getting the

time whenever you come home. Every kid gets the time when they come home. Like we care. Like it matters.' He lifted his head off the concrete. 'Am I on the sidewalk? Jesus Christ.' He laughed again. 'How the hell did I get here?'

'Oh my God – how did you get here? You don't know how you got here?'

'Jesus Christ,' he said, rolling onto his side, then dragging himself up onto his elbow. 'I have no idea.'

'OK. I'm going inside and you can follow me in. Now.'

'Ugh.'

'And your father is on his way.'

'What? I thought he had a—'

'Yes he does,' said Anna. She reached the front door. 'So God help you.'

Shaun stayed where he was, then dragged himself to the top step of the house. Eventually Anna opened the door and came out.

'Get up now, Shaun.' She walked back into the hall. 'I'm closing the door.'

'I never asked you to open it.'

She slammed the door and turned on the porch light.

'Aw man,' he said. 'Come. On.' He leaned a hand back on the step and pushed himself up, knocking against a plant pot. 'Turn off the goddamn searchlight. I'm right here.' He banged on the door. Anna opened it. He walked in and sat on the first chair he found.

'Don't get comfortable there,' said Anna.

She heard the beeps again, outside the house. She pulled open the door and grabbed his cell phone.

'Give me that,' he said.

She held it up. 'When you go up and get into bed. Where were you tonight?'

'Out.'

'Tell me where you were. Or I will not give this back.'

Shaun laughed. 'What? Give me my phone.' He glared at her.

'Don't try anything with me,' said Anna. 'No more. I'm tired of this.'

'I'm the one who's tired of all this,' said Shaun, standing up, 'this fucking house. It's so depressing. I hate being here. I can't bear it. You go to anyone else's house and you have fun. You come here and it's all, like, ugh.'

Anna reached into his jacket pocket and pulled out a bottle of beer. She shook her head slowly. 'What are you?' she said. 'A wino now? Walking around the streets with bottles of alcohol?'

'I didn't want it to go to waste,' said Shaun.

'It's disgusting,' said Anna. 'When did you turn into this . . . this person?'

'What person?' said Shaun.

'Stop it,' she shouted. 'Stop being so aggressive with me.' Tears came out of nowhere. Shaun swayed in front of her, blinking slowly. She turned quickly and walked into the kitchen, wiping her eyes. She sat down at the table and took some deep breaths. She remembered the advice she once heard that it was never too late to start your day over. She looked at the hands of the clock at 4.20 a.m. and wondered which day she would be re-starting. In the hallway, Shaun's cell phone beeped again. Anna boiled the kettle and made a mug of Sleepytime tea. Within minutes, she could feel its effects and wanted to stay exactly that way – alone, warm and calm in the soothing steam.

Beep. Beep-beep. Beep-beep. Beep. Beep.

She put down her mug gently. And made an angry burst for the hallway.

'Turn that phone off,' she roared.

Shaun jumped. They both turned towards the door when they heard the keys.

'Oh no,' muttered Shaun.

'Hey, what's going on here?' said Joe.

'What do you think?' said Anna. 'He arrived home drunk – again. This time, he was lying on the pavement. Someone had pushed him out of a car and left him there.'

'What?' said Joe and Shaun.

'Yes,' she said, turning to Shaun. 'You don't even remember that part. What nice friends you have.'

Joe knew by looking at Anna that she hadn't slept yet.

'Go to bed, honey,' he said. 'You need sleep. I'll take care of this.'

'What do you mean you'll take care of this?' she said. 'You haven't done anything—'

Joe turned to Shaun. 'You, stay where you are. Anna, can I talk to you upstairs?'

Anna shrugged. They walked up the stairs and stood on the landing, leaving Shaun muttering after them.

'If he sees us fighting, we're going to get nowhere.' Joe struggled to keep his voice low.

Anna stared at him, her eyes wide. 'Really?' she said. 'But if he doesn't see you at all, that's better?'

'What the hell is that supposed to mean?'

'You know what that means,' said Anna. 'I'm trying to discipline him alone. And I'm not able to.'

'Yes you are.'

Anna laughed. 'Obviously.'

Joe stared at the ceiling.

'Do you know he hasn't done anything about his college applications?' said Anna.

'Yeah, well, he's doing that to piss us off. Because we didn't go see them with him.'

'What? He knows we couldn't. I was just back from Paris, you were—'

'Yeah, yeah, working, I get it.'

'But you were!'

'Of course I was! Where else is the money going to come from?'

Anna stepped back. Joe stared at her. 'It's true,' he said.

Her eyes were black with anger. 'I can not believe you. After what you put me through—'

'What *I* put you through?' His voice cracked. They looked at each other. 'Jesus Christ, Anna. Is that how you feel?'

'I don't know,' she said. 'I'm tired. I'm going to bed. You blame me for him, I blame you for me, you blame yourself for nothing. Goodnight.'

'Wait – you have to answer me. You've never said that—'

'I *said* I don't know what I feel. Now let me go to bed.'

'What has happened to us?' said Joe. But she was gone.

Joe leaned against the banister, his breath shaky. He slowly made his way down the stairs.

'Shaun,' he said, crouching down in front of him. Over the past year, the brightness had gone from Shaun's eyes and his skin was starting to look pale and waxy.

'What?' said Shaun, drowsy and irritated.

'Where were you tonight?'

'Not again,' said Shaun. 'I was out, OK? Just let me go to bed.'

'What's going on with you?' said Joe.

'Nothing,' Shaun snapped. 'Nothing, OK? Nothing.'

'Your Mom and me are worried.'

'Yeah, well, get over it.'

'This isn't you talking,' said Joe. 'You're my boy, you're a good kid. I don't know where this nasty piece of—'

'Leave me alone,' said Shaun. 'I want to go to bed.'

'Your mother was up at the school today, I know you haven't done anything about college—'

'Why are you talking to me about this shit now?' said Shaun. 'What is wrong with you? It's, like, late. Or early, whatever.'

Joe moved back and let Shaun struggle up from the chair.

'Shaun – this is the last time you're going to do this, come home like this, OK?'

Shaun snorted. 'Whatever.'

'Don't,' said Joe. 'EVER say that word to me like that, OK?'

'Whatcha gonna do?' said Shaun, taking a step towards him, staring him down.

'Don't make this any worse for yourself,' said Joe.

'Worse than living in this house? With Mom moping around all day?'

Joe grabbed his arm. 'Listen carefully, Shaun. I married your mother. That was a *choice* I made. I love your mother. And I never have and never will listen to anyone disrespect her, least of all her own son. Now, get the hell out of my sight.'

SIX

Danny and Joe pulled up across the street from Clare Oberly's apartment building and parked outside a dry cleaners. The elderly owner stood against the plate glass window, smoking a cigarette and staring at them.

'That Pace guy looks kinda funny, doesn't he?' said Danny.

Joe smiled.

'Kind of like parts of his face are trying to make a run for it,' said Danny. 'His eyes are busting out, his Adam's apple . . . it's like he's so thin, there's no nourishment there for them. They're out of there. Know what I'm saying?'

Joe shook his head. 'You're a cruel son of a bitch.'

'Just saying what everyone else is thinking.'

'You are so full of shit.'

They walked over to the building, past a huge moving van and into a brightly lit foyer with floors

streaked with black marks. A couple walked by
them in shorts and T-shirts, carrying a chest of
drawers, the man sweating heavily and trailing
foul air behind him.

'Jesus Christ,' said Danny to Joe. 'Deodorant.'

One of the elevators was held open by the
couple moving. Joe and Danny took the free one
to the tenth floor, found apartment 10B and rang
the bell.

'Hello,' said Joe. 'Clare Oberly?'

'Yeah. Hi.' She was an attractive blonde in her
mid-thirties, dressed in a lime green chiffon top,
white jeans and red and green platform shoes.
Strings of expensive multi-coloured beads hung
around her neck.

'My name is Detective Joe Lucchesi. My partner
and I are investigating a homicide. You received
a phone call round about 11 p.m. last night?'

She paused. 'Yeah. Why?'

'Who was the call from?' said Joe.

'Ethan Lowry.' She looked at both of them.
'Why?'

'What's your relationship with Mr Lowry?' said
Joe.

'Oh, we dated in college. Is he OK?' she said.

'Can we come in?' said Joe.

'I'm sorry. Yes. I'm so rude. Come in.' She
brought them into a neat, open plan apartment
with a huge Miró on one wall. She sat down and
gestured to the sofa opposite.

'I'm afraid Mr Lowry's been the victim of a homicide,' said Joe.

'Oh my God,' she said. 'Ethan?' She shook her head. 'Oh my God. He's so . . . what happened? He's just so not the type . . . if that makes any sense.'

'He was murdered in his apartment. We think he may have called you right before it happened. And we need to find out why.'

'God. I don't know. I mean, I don't think it would be anything to do with why he was murdered. We don't even know each other that well any more. Like, I'm not a person he would call if he was in trouble. We're just not close.'

'When was the last time you spoke with him?'

'A year and a half ago. At my brother's funeral. It was really sweet of him to come. Ethan was very kind like that.' She bowed her head. 'I can't believe this.'

'What did he say to you when he called?'

'Not a lot. He just called to say hi.' She shrugged.

'How long were you two dating?'

'Six years.'

'What happened?'

'Nothing major, the usual, we were too young, I was too ambitious, he wanted quiet nights in, I wanted to party. We drifted. It got boring, I guess.'

'And you both moved on.'

'I did more than he did, I guess. But then he met his wife and he got married shortly after.'

'So why do you think he called you the night he died?'

'I have no idea.'

'You have no idea,' said Joe. 'Really?'

She smiled sadly. 'I'm such a bad liar. The worst. I guess I'm worried . . . his wife's just lost her husband . . .' She sighed. 'OK. What I tell you? Does his wife get to hear it?'

'Not necessarily, no,' said Joe.

'I don't want to make things worse for her. Even though I haven't done anything . . . just, the only weird thing that night was Ethan told me . . . that he loved me.'

Joe frowned. 'What? And you hadn't seen him in how long? A year and a half?'

'Yeah. He said he was just calling to say he loved me.'

'What did you say to him?'

'I was shocked. I mean, he sounded pretty normal except for what he was actually saying to me. That was it. I didn't know what to say back. I mean, he's married, I heard he has a lovely wife and daughter and . . . I don't know. I mean, I don't love him. Didn't. I said that to him. I said about his wife and that I'd moved on.' She shrugged. 'Now I feel terrible. For him. For his wife. I'm guessing she has no idea. Do you think . . . I mean, he didn't kill himself or anything?'

'No,' said Joe. 'Had he hinted about his feelings when you met at your brother's funeral?'

'No,' said Clare. 'He was really sweet to me. But that's Ethan, he just is. There was no major interaction between us, no plans to meet up, I didn't encourage him, nothing.'

'Is there anyone you could think of that had a problem with Ethan? Was he ever in trouble?'

'It was eight years ago when we broke up. But before then, Ethan was, like, normal, just a nice guy. I never saw him even have an argument with anyone. He was low-profile, you know what I mean? He'd be the last person I would think would end up murdered.'

Rufo was sitting at his desk pressing keys on his cell phone when Danny and Joe walked in. He held up his left hand to silence them. They looked at each other. Joe shrugged. Rufo spent another few minutes focused on the tiny handset. He was smiling to himself. He hit one last key and put the phone down.

'Texting,' he said. 'What a great way to communicate. You should check it out.'

'I lived in Ireland, remember?' said Joe. 'It's nearly taken over from drinking.'

'Who were you texting?' said Danny.

Rufo looked up at him. 'None of your business, Markey. Now, to what do I owe the pleasure?'

Joe spoke. 'I'm thinking of setting up a meeting with Reuben Maller in the Eastern District, get some sort of profile worked out on this perp . . .'

'Sure. Go ahead,' said Rufo. 'As long as we're all clear it's his friendly assistance you're after.'

Joe nodded. 'I'll see what comes out of the profile. If there's anything we think he should stick around for, anyone he'd like to interview, we'll see, but you know Maller, he's a good guy, he does his thing, then disappears back—'

'Under his rock,' said Danny.

Joe rolled his eyes. 'Do you ever think it might be you?'

'What the hell's that supposed to mean?' said Danny.

'You know? The whole world's an asshole or a dickhead. Did you ever think it might be you?'

'Ladies, take it outside,' said Rufo.

Anna stood outside Bay Ridge subway station, searching through her huge navy bag. She found her white headphones, but as she pulled them out, she realized there was no iPod attached.

'*Merde.*' She remembered seeing it in the speaker dock in the kitchen. '*Merde.*'

She checked her watch and thought about running back home for it, but instead, she forced herself to walk into the heat of the station and down the steps. Raised voices echoed up and when she reached them, she saw a tall well-dressed woman push a scruffy teenage boy by the shoulders, slamming him against the ticket machine. He spat in her face. She threw money at him and walked away. Anna had no interest in working out what had happened, she kept her head down and moved as far away from him as she could. It annoyed her that her heart rate shot up. It happened too easily, any confrontation, any sudden movements, any loud noises. When she had her iPod on, Mozart made her feel that she could drift everywhere untouched by her surroundings, a gentle soundtrack for a different place, a different set of scenes.

She swiped her Metrocard and waited on the platform, glancing over at the woman in the suit, keeping her where she could see her. The woman was tweaking – coming down off crystal meth, radiating crazy. Anna could hear the young guy behind her shouting – 'Crazy bitch! She took my money, the crazy bitch!' Then, 'No! I got it here! Crazy bitch threw it back at me!'

Nervous energy ran through the crowd. The woman walked away swinging her briefcase, her head held high, her own special tune playing in her head. The R train pulled in and everyone moved on. It was rush-hour cramped and Anna, small and slight, got pushed into a tight spot against a huge student who smiled an apology down at her. She smiled back.

For the first part of the journey, everyone was focused on their books and newspapers or talking to their friends. Anna stared through the window at nothing. Then the subway doors slid open at

Cortlandt Street and stayed open. Panic struck up in her again. Announcements boomed from the speakers on the platform. No-one could hear them. People started to look up, then around at everyone else.

Anna felt a sickening urge to push her way through and burst onto the platform, but was held back by the attention that would attract, everyone staring at this women who was alarmed because a train stopped for two minutes longer than it was supposed to. She could feel the sweat soaking into the fabric at her back, the heat of the platform, of the people around her, of their breath. The doors slid closed and the train started up again. She breathed out and talked to herself all the way to her stop, telling herself she was stupid, then brave, then irrational, then strong, then stupid. She almost ran up the steps into Union Square, relieved to hit air that wasn't suffocating her. She peeled her top away from her skin and let the light breeze cool her. '*I can't do this,*' she said to herself. '*There is no way I can do this.*'

She straightened up and looked across at Barnes & Noble and felt the pull of a morning spent drinking coffee and flicking through design books of faraway houses on stilts in the ocean or on beaches or cliffsides. A shiver ran up her spine. She took a deep breath and walked towards the W Hotel. She stood at the window and saw everyone gathered in the early morning darkness of the bar. She recognized the back of Marc Lunel's head, his long, black shiny hair, the red tab on his Prada shoes. She saw four models, two makeup artists, two hair stylists, the intern from *Vogue Living* . . . everyone waiting for her guidance. She saw her reflection in the glass, her tired eyes, her downturned mouth, the sheen of sweat on her forehead. She turned away. She started walking. And she hailed the first cab that passed by.

When Joe got back to his desk, a white envelope lay there, stamped and addressed to him. Most of the mail he got was yellow-envelope inter-departmental. He picked it up. It was light but bulky; cheap paper with no return address. He grabbed a ruler from his drawer and sliced through it. The thin white pages were folded in half and sprang open, both sides covered in scrawled writing and short sentences: *Dear Detective Lucchesi, The noise this morning was almost unbearable. I could try to create it in letters and words. I got out of bed. I wouldn't know how. Two directions. And it's agony. I get anxious sometimes if I do. And actually what I need is peace to find my way through everything. There was no point in just laying there. One forward, one back. I made coffee and fixed myself scrambled eggs. I still know how to do that. I'm not sure which is harder. But it was loud. Not everyone else does. I don't think I can figure it all out without quiet. Bass and drums. There are times when I'm nearly there . . .*

Joe paused, rubbing his temples. He flipped the page over and kept reading. On it went, a random series of thoughts and the vague sense that there was a story inside, one that only the writer knew. It was a complexity of simple facts, observations, theories and descriptions. What Joe read on the sixth page made it relevant to him. Vertically, in the right-hand margin was written: *Lying, badly beaten. Lowry is the result. I don't know if I could have done anything differently.*

Something cold shot up the back of Joe's neck. He scanned quickly through the pages that followed, through writings about rooms and stories and calculators and theatres. It ended after sixteen pages, signed off namelessly: *More will come. Captured at the right time.*

'Jesus,' said Joe. 'What the fuck was that?' He called the others over.

'Guys, I just got a letter about Ethan Lowry.'

'A letter?' said Danny. 'From who?'

'A randomer,' said Joe.

'Who's Arrandoma?' said Rencher.

'Randomer. A random person. Person unknown. It's something I picked up from one of Shaun's friends in Ireland.'

'OK, what's this randomer saying?' said Rencher.

'A little and a lot,' said Joe.

'Don't be fooled by the rocks that I got,' said Danny.

Joe ignored him and looked down at the letter.

'OK, so we got a lot of information on exactly where the salt is in the kitchen for when the guy is microwaving his eggs in the morning, a bunch of other stuff about what he likes to do – major detail there . . .

'Did he sign it?' said Rencher.

'Yeah, sure he did,' said Danny, 'with his address too, that's why we're all sitting around here, trying to figure out who could have sent it.'

'Yeah, I meant with anything—'

'What? Like, *From the killer* . . . ?' said Danny.

'Shut the fuck up,' said Rencher.

'Shut the fuck up all of you,' said Joe. 'Let me read this out to you.' He read through the letter and waited in the silence that followed.

'Are we taking this seriously?' said Rencher.

'I think we should be,' said Joe.

'But *"lying badly beaten"* – you could get that from a media report, that's no insider information there,' said Rencher.

Joe looked down again at the letter and shrugged. 'I think there's something in this. Let's just take it that there is.'

'*"More will come, captured at the right time"*,' said Danny. 'More victims?'

Joe shrugged. 'Or more letters?'

'Maybe,' said Danny.

'I mean, what is the point of this letter?' said Martinez.

'Someone is reaching out,' said Rencher.

'But are they trying to help?' said Cullen. 'Are they giving us any information?'

Joe glanced down at the pages. 'I think somewhere in here there's information. I think they're trying.'

'Seriously, could it be from the perp?' said Rencher.

'Doesn't sound like a psycho, but then, *"Lowry is the result. I don't know if I could have done anything differently"*.'

'Yeah,' said Joe. 'That could be talking about anything. I don't know. Look, I'll go ahead, copy this a few times, if anyone has any ideas, get back to me.'

'Will Question Documents be able to tell us more?' said Rencher.

'Probably not a whole lot,' said Joe, 'Looking at this, the paper, the envelope, the pen don't look like anything special. If we get another letter in, they can tell us if it's from the same guy. And if there's any problem when we track him down, they can use samples of his writing to match it up. That's about it. First thing is to get it to Forensics, see if we can get some prints.' He pointed to his notebook. 'I mean doesn't whoever wrote it get that it's pretty fucking easy to trace? I've got the time and place where it was mailed right here from the stamp. I'm going to get in touch with the post office, see if we can get any video. Bobby, can you pass me the Ortis file?'

'Sure,' said Bobby, handing it to him.

The others were talking among themselves as Joe slowly started to flip through the pages.

'You got the VICAP form?' said Joe. He looked up at Bobby.

'For Ortis?'

'Yeah,' said Joe.

Bobby shrugged. 'I guess I didn't fill one out.'

'You didn't fill out the VICAP form, Bobby?' Joe's voice rang loud in the room.

'Yeah, like, you fill them out every time?' Bobby glanced around at everyone. 'Come on, a hundred bullshit questions that are no use when, like, the whole fucking country isn't filling them out too? Everyone knows that. Spending hours answering questions when I could be out on the street getting somewhere?'

'So you don't see how making a link here might have helped Ethan Lowry?'

Bobby snorted.

'And to answer your question, yeah, I did always fill out the form,' said Joe. 'And I still do . . .'

'What's that supposed to mean?' said Bobby.

'Nothing,' said Joe. 'If I'm working with a squad detective and they haven't filled one out, I have to do it for them.' Joe was looking down, his tone neutral.

Danny got up. 'Right,' he said. 'On that VICAP bombshell—'

Nervous laughter broke out, but died away just as quickly.

William Aneto's mother Carmen lived above the grocery store she owned on 116th Street in East Harlem. Martinez had rung the bell, but there was no answer. The door was freshly painted bright green with a gold knocker he slammed against the wood.

'Nice smell,' said Danny, glancing into the store. He reached out to ring the doorbell again.

Martinez slapped his hand away and did it himself. 'This is my show.'

Mrs Aneto opened the door and gave them a weary look. She was a small woman in her early fifties, dressed in a navy blue suit and low heels. Her hair was held neatly in a bun at the base of her neck. She wore no makeup. Martinez greeted her in Spanish, introducing himself and Danny.

She stared at Martinez. 'You must be the token guy,' she said.

He frowned.

'Match the skin of the detective to the skin of the victim,' she said.

Martinez turned back to her and spoke again in Spanish. She gave a defeated smile and led them in, up a narrow flight of stairs into a small apartment.

The living room was well worn and looked like the centre of entertainment for Mrs Aneto. There were women's magazines on the sofa, two books balanced on the arm, a tray with a teapot and one cup on it. A bowl at the centre of the coffee table was filled with candy. The TV was widescreen and behind it, there were tall shelves of DVD cases and at the bottom, rows and rows of cassettes with white stickers and handwritten titles.

Mrs Aneto sat down in a high-backed armchair and put the footstool in front of it to one side. Danny and Martinez sat side by side on the sofa. Martinez leaned forward, resting his forearm on his left knee. He spoke in Spanish. 'The night your son died, you said when he called you it was to say goodnight. Did he say anything else?'

'Let's not be rude to our white guest,' she said and switched to English. 'Why are you asking me this now?'

'Because there have been some new developments in the investigation and—'

'What kind of new developments?'

'We believe there may be another victim.'

Her eyes were wide. 'Was the victim white?'

'Yes,' said Martinez. 'In fact, there may be two of them.'

'Both white.'

'Yes,' said Martinez. 'We've spoken with another victim's family member who got a phone call the night their loved one died – well, a different kind of call than the one you got. We're wondering if there's a connection . . .'

Mrs Aneto closed her eyes. Her lips moved in silent prayer. Then she took a deep breath. 'My son begins his introduction to detectives as a Latino victim. Strike one. William is gay. Strike two. Strike three would have been what I told you about the phone call. You people did nothing to find William's killer. Nothing. You did not give a damn. And you're only back around now because some white boys have gone the same way. I'm telling you now what I didn't tell you before, because it might be connected. And you will work harder now for three victims than you ever would for William, a lone victim with the wrong-coloured skin—'

'Mrs Aneto—' said Danny.

She held up a finger. 'There is nothing you can say to me that will change my truth.'

'Your truth, Mrs Aneto,' said Danny.

She stared him down. 'I have spent a year having my anger and bitterness grow inside me. And this is my break. I won't cry for those white boys, because maybe they'll help me lay my William to rest. This is a tragic spotlight to have shined on my son, but I'll take the light where I can get it.

'I have two dead sons,' she said. 'Pepe, my youngest, was killed three years ago in drive-by crossfire, some gangs in Alphabet City. I was told he was scoring drugs. I never believed that. Something never seemed right about that to me. His killers have never been found.

'On the night William died, as you know, he called me. But no, it wasn't just to say goodnight.' She paused. 'I could barely hear him. He sounded drunk, he was sobbing, breathing so badly. He said to me, "Mama? I killed Pepe." I said, "William. Is everything OK? What is the matter?" He said everything was fine. Then he told me what happened. He told me that he had sent Pepe to pick up drugs for him. And that was why Pepe was there. And that's why he was shot. William apologized. Over and over. I was so angry with him, but I was so scared for him, he sounded so hopeless. When the police came the next morning to tell me he had been found, I thought it was suicide.'

'So William was a drug user.'

'I didn't know he was. But he must have been at one stage. I knew William was clean when he died – his toxicology proved that – but if I told you what he said in this phone call he made, you wouldn't get by the fact he had been involved with drugs.'

'Mrs Aneto, every victim is important to us,' said Danny. 'Every single one. No-one gets treated any differently because of the colour of their skin, the lifestyle they have, the choices they make, nothing. We want to find your son's killer. And we just want all the information we can to do that. We're not judging that information, running it through any filter. They're just facts to us – black and white – things that may or may not lead us to a killer.'

Mrs Aneto reached for a photo of William from the sideboard, framed in shiny black wood. She stared down at it. 'I'm only talking to you today, detectives, because I have hope. I am still bitter, I am still angry, but I have hope. I'm not sorry I didn't tell you this a year ago. I stand by that decision. Because I hate to think how bad your efforts would have been if you had known he had been into drugs.'

Joe grabbed his suit jacket from the back of his chair. He looked around the office.

'I haven't eaten yet. I'm going to get breakfast. Anyone need anything?'

He took three food and drink orders and as he was getting out of the elevator, his cell phone rang. It was a number he hadn't seen in over two years and had never deleted from his contacts: Anna (W).

He frowned. 'Anna?'

'Do you know where she is?' It was Chloe. Her tone had none of its usual confidence.

Joe could not speak. Anna cannot be anywhere other than the W Hotel in Union Square. The number he had programmed into his phone that morning. Just in case.

'What?' he said. His hunger had gone, the void in his stomach now filled with something else.

'I'm sorry. It's Chloe here. Anna didn't show up at the shoot this morning. I've been trying her cell, the home phone – nothing. I dragged your number out of some next-of-kin thing we had for her. I'm sorry to bother you—'

'Whoa,' said Joe. 'What's going on? I left her this morning and she was taking the subway to Union Square and everything was fine—'

'She never showed. It's not like her. Have you been speaking with her?'

'Obviously not.' He had no time to deal with Chloe. He needed to go.

'And she seemed fine to you this morning?'

'Yes. Yes she did,' said Joe, wondering what fine was and if he'd know it if it slapped him in the face.

They both paused. 'Well?' said Chloe. 'What will we do?'

'Leave it with me,' said Joe.

'Thanks,' said Chloe. 'I'm . . . worried about her.'

Sure you are, thought Joe. He stood in the street, his shaky fingers punching buttons on his phone, searching for a text message he'd missed, a phone call he hadn't heard, anything. Then he dialled Anna's cell, then the house. Voicemail both times. He looked across the street at his car. And ran for it.

Anna lay on the bed, back in her pyjamas, asleep, curled into the tiniest ball she could, gripping a pillow tightly to her chest. Her body jerked from side to side, then she was on her back, rigid, the pillow thrown to one side. Images washed over her, pinning her down, taking a psychological grip on her that felt physical. Her mouth was clamped shut. She wanted to scream, but she couldn't. Choppy and ghost-like, strange eyes and mouths hovered over her, sweeping up her chest, pausing before her face, threatening, then sweeping away again to be replaced by another and another, each one making her feel that the next one was going to be the one to take her away. Her hands were in fists, her eyes pressed shut, a scream desperate to explode from her closed mouth.

She could hear her name being called. Over and over . . . but the voice was warm. She could associate it with someone kind. Someone who would look after her. Something inside her relaxed. And the scream came out, mixed with a dreadful, plangent moan.

Tears streamed from her eyes. They shot open and Joe was beside her, pulling her onto his lap, stroking her hair, kissing the top of her head.

'It's OK, sweetheart,' he said. 'It's OK. I'm here.' He paused. 'You're safe. It was just a nightmare. Everything is good. Everyone's OK.'

The relief in her eyes nearly broke his heart. 'It was sleep paralysis again,' she said. 'I hate it. I thought it was gone. All these terrible—'

'Shhh,' said Joe. His voice was gentle. 'It's over

now. And you're going to come with me to the
kitchen. And I'm going to make you some herbal
tea. And I'm going to make myself a liter of coffee,
find myself an IV line . . .'

'How come you're home?' she said. 'What time
is it?'

'I am home,' he said, 'because I missed my wife.'

SEVEN

'Did you fly back to Ireland to milk some fucking cows?' said Rencher.

'Lattes,' said Joe, 'are for pussies.'

'That's it?' said Rencher. 'That's all you got for me?'

'That and your latte,' said Joe. 'With two extra muffins.' He put them down on Rencher's desk.

'What?' said Rencher. 'I look like I need fattening up to you?'

'You look like you need to smile,' said Joe. 'Where are the other guys? I've got more coffees to hand out.'

'Well, in the two hours since you've been gone, they did the weirdest thing – they went out on police business.'

'And I did not?' said Joe.

Rencher tilted his head.

'Back to your work,' said Joe, smiling. He sat down at his desk and sighed. He pulled up the address book on his computer and searched through his contacts for Reuben Maller's phone number.

He picked up before Joe even heard a ring tone.

'Reuben, it's Joe Lucchesi.'

'Hello, Joe.' His voice was cautious.

'Don't worry,' said Joe. 'It's about a case I caught.'

'Oh, OK. Good. I don't have any update for—'

'I know,' said Joe. 'I know. Look – do you remember William Aneto?'

'Yes, that got a lot of coverage.'

'Yeah. Well, we think we've linked him to two other recent homicides – another on the Upper West Side and one in SoHo a while back. Would you maybe take a look at the file, see if there's a profile you could come up with? It's always good to have an extra pair of eyes.'

'Sure, not a problem. Let me swing by the office later.'

'No, I'll drop it in to you.'

'Great. Joe? Do you really need my help or . . .'

Joe laughed. 'I'd like your help, OK?'

Maller laughed. 'All right. I had to ask.'

Joe put down the phone. He turned to his PowerBook and clicked his favourite icon, the pen and inkpot that opened up Pages, a programme for creating newsletters, journals, flyers, brochures. It was filled with templates in bright, shiny colours with photos of happy, smiling people. He opened

his own template, VICS, and created a new file.
He wondered what the software designers would
think. He opened iPhoto and dragged photos onto
the document, one of each of the victims taken
while they were alive, their faces smiling, bored,
relaxed – not battered beyond recognition. Joe
wanted to look them in the eye. He wanted to do
something for these three guys he could have
walked past on the street or had a drink with at
a bar or stood behind in line at the grocery store.
Not three guys who he knew only by standing
over their dead bodies.

His phone rang. He picked up. 'Yeah?'

'Joe, hi. It's Mark Branham, Gay Alliance.'

'Hey, thanks for getting back to me, Mark. How
you been?'

'Great. Busy. It's the first anniversary of William
Aneto's death, as you know, so we're trying to
help the family rustle up some publicity. Is that
why you're calling?'

'Kind of. We're just talking here, OK?'

'Sure, Joe.'

'We think the case may be connected to a
couple of other murders over the last few
months.'

Mark sucked in a breath. 'Really?'

'It's early days.'

'Were all the victims gay?'

'No. But we're wondering if any of them hadn't
come out or maybe if they, you know . . .'

'What? Gave off gay vibes? Tried it for a night? Bi now, gay later?'

Joe laughed. 'Whatever. Maybe had two things on the go, you know?'

'OK. So what do you think the killer was after?'

'We've got a few options: maybe he likes to play rough, took it too far, got to liking it; guy is a homophobe and wants to teach the victims a lesson; or he's just a guy whose pool of victims may be gay because that's his circle.'

'He could be your classic homophobe with repression issues who gets drunk and tries it out some night and blames the guy he picked up, takes out decades of anger on him. I've seen assaults – never murders – for that reason. Very badly beaten men. Is that what you have?'

'Yes. Their faces were really messed up. The ME has seen it before in these kinds of cases.'

'Not good. What can I do?'

'Keep this quiet for now, first of all. But also, are you familiar with 3B?'

'The club? Bed, Bad and Beyond? Yeah. William Aneto was there his last night.'

'Yeah. I'd like to talk to whoever runs it, but don't want a big deal made of it.'

'OK. Well you need Buck Torrance. Promoter by night, pet accessory guy by day. Dawg On It in Chelsea. Eighth Avenue between 21st and 22nd. He's a good guy. No drama. You can tell him you're a friend of mine and that it's about the first anniversary thing. If you're asking about those other guys, you can say they were friends of the victim's, whatever. Anyway, he's discreet.'

'Thanks, Mark. We'll get to him tomorrow. How's Kevin?'

'He's great. How's Anna?'

'Not doing too bad. You take care.'

'You too.'

Joe left the office at seven to drop the file in to Reuben Maller. He decided to visit Old Nic on his way home; the only reason he had left for going back to Bensonhurst. He was unlikely to see a familiar face there now – almost everyone he knew had made the move to Staten Island in the Nineties. It was like all trace of his childhood had been swept away with the old storefronts. To Joe, Bensonhurst was the opening sequence to *Welcome Back, Kotter*; if they shot it now, nothing would be the same.

Joe took a left off 86th Street and drove a special route, past the house he grew up in, past Danny's old house, Gina's parents' house. He avoided the apartment he spent three years living in with his mother and sister after his parents' divorce. To him, that was three years of knowing his mother had cancer and a year of knowing she wasn't going to make it. Bringing her to hospital appointments weak and unsteady, taking her home weaker.

He remembered their first visit to Kings County Hospital when he was fourteen. She told him it was a routine health check. He was embarrassed to hold her hand, but she was gripping him so tight, it would have been wrong to let her go. He waited outside the room, not knowing that inside, his thirty-six-year-old mother was being diagnosed with breast cancer. Joe was too busy worrying about being recognized; Kings County was the same place he would go to when he got into a bad fight. He used to hang outside waiting for a young intern to come on break. The same guy would always show up and shake his head when he saw Joe with a split lip or a slash through his eyebrow. Then he'd sneak him into an empty room to patch him up with his big, careful hands.

Joe knew that even to drive by the old apartment building would break his heart. He did it once and he thought he saw her walking down the front steps. Maria Lucchesi was a small, round woman. She always wore a red coat. The woman he saw was so similar, Joe had slowed the car. Then he pulled over. He remembered sitting with his head against the steering wheel, older than his mother was when she died, weeping like a child for the woman that always kept it together. One hug from his ma was bigger than anything else that was happening in his life.

Joe pulled up outside the Nicoteros' small framehouse and walked to the front door. He rang the doorbell and heard the familiar shuffle of Old Nic's slippers.

'Hey, buddy,' he said, hugging Joe. 'What a nice surprise.'

'I came over all nostalgic,' said Joe.

'Good – you're not coming to tell me Bobby's been misbehaving in class.'

Joe laughed.

'Come in, come in,' said Nic. 'Patti's not here. I'm out on the deck.'

Joe took a seat beside Old Nic at a small ornate metal table.

'So how's things working out with Bobby?' said Nic, smiling. He opened a bottle of beer and handed it to Joe.

Joe took a mouthful. 'Good. We're good.'

'Yeah?' said Nic. 'Well I think you're different.'

Joe looked at him and smiled. 'What?'

'Don't bullshit a bullshitter,' said Nic. 'You guys are too different to ever get along.'

'Maybe,' said Joe.

'And you've been tainted by your association with me,' said Nic. His eyes were down. 'Isn't that sad?'

'His loss,' said Joe. He shrugged.

'What's on your mind?' said Nic. 'Business or pleasure?'

'Well something that should be pleasure,' said Joe. 'But I'm sorry to say, I've screwed that all up.' He stared out over the tidy garden. 'Anna's on my mind.'

Nic nodded. 'How's she doing?'

Joe let out a breath. 'She . . . kind of lost it yesterday. You know she's been hanging around the house a lot. Well she got herself together yesterday and went out on a shoot for work. She got as far as the hotel where it was being done and she just freaked out.'

'What happened?'

'I don't think she's even telling me the full story. All I know is she felt everything close in on her and she ran. She got in a cab and came home. She even turned off her phone and didn't tell her boss. She hasn't even turned her phone on today she's so scared. I mean, she could lose her job. I'm worried she was that scared that that didn't matter to her.'

'OK,' said Nic. 'What I want to hear about is you.'

'Pardon me?'

'You've told me about Anna. You always tell me about Anna. That's easy. She's got all the problems, right? You don't have any?'

Joe frowned. And said nothing.

'Me and Patti went through some pretty hard times,' said Nic. 'Do you want to know the biggest mistake I made? Thinking she was the only one who had to change.'

Joe stared down at the cracks running across the deck.

'And Anna . . .' said Nic, 'well, she had a hard time.'

Joe nodded. He squeezed the bridge of his nose.

Nic took a deep breath. 'You don't think you're her hero any more.'

'What?' said Joe, staring at him.

'I'll let you in on a little secret,' said Old Nic. 'What you think is a knight in shining armour to a woman and what they think are two entirely different things. I spent too long trying to be this hard-ass protector guy who solved all the problems of the universe. But I'm not that. No-one is, Joe. You're going to have to get past what happened because it wasn't your fault. Shit happens. Very, very bad shit sometimes. So – you can let this Rawlins guy sink your relationship, put the final nail in the coffin or you can say "Screw you, you motherfucker, you came close to my family once, you had your chance, you blew it, you don't get a second chance and I'm not spending my whole fucking life acting like you will." Give that psycho the power to alter the course of your life? Fuck that, Joe. You owe it to Anna and Shaun not to let that happen.'

'It's not as simple as that,' said Joe.

'It is. Let me tell you something. Patti thought the sun shone out of me when we got married. I was the big, tough cop. No-one around here messed with Victor Nicotero. We walked down the street together and I knew she felt proud and she felt protected. And I fucking loved it. It made me feel great. Then one day I was at work and she wasn't feeling great and I didn't get home in time. She was two months' pregnant – it was before Bobby – and she lost the baby. And there was nothing I could do, Joe. And something changed. For a year after that, I thought she saw me as a weaker man, that I'd let her down in some way.' He shrugged. 'And do you know what she said to me? "Thank God," she said. "Thank God you know you are not invincible. And I'm sorry if I ever gave you that impression." And she was right. I believed what she told me. Then she said to me, I'll never forget it: "A hero means a lot of things. It's about strength of character, it's sacrifices, it's sometimes just laughter or quietness. It's not wasting energy thinking you can control all the bad things in the world and then getting angry and frustrated when you can't. I don't want that angry, frustrated man. And I'm glad he's gone." That's what she said to me. And then she just walked out of the room and finished whatever she was in the middle of doing.'

'Patti's something else,' said Joe.

'No woman wants to be with a weak man,' said Nic. 'And that you are not.' He paused. 'Talk to Anna. Really talk to her, not in an angry way. Just tell her how you feel.'

Joe laughed. 'You're getting soft in your old age.'

'Don't give me that bullshit,' said Nic. 'Everyone looks for advice from the person they know is going to tell them what they want to hear. You come to me because you know I'm going to say how good you and Anna are together and you have to stick at it. You don't want to go to the guy who's going to tell you it's gone too far to ever go back to the way it was.'

'But what if it has?' said Joe.

'It hasn't,' said Nic. 'All right? It hasn't. Drink your beer. I'm worn out with all that wisdom.'

Hours later, Joe pulled into the driveway and turned off the engine. Even after six months in the house, he couldn't shake the disappointment he felt when he arrived home. He had been forced to make a decision on it while Anna was in Paris. It came down to money – the rent was low because the owner was another cop who wanted to help a colleague out and trusted Joe enough not to bother him while he travelled around the world.

When Joe went to look at the place, it was on two hours' sleep and lots of painkillers. Sonny, the owner, had managed to get a lady friend to clean it up and put some vases and air freshener around. The kitchen appliances were just six months old and the bathroom had been renovated, but Joe's usual attention to the tiny details left him as soon as he walked through the door. A strange sense of relief took over. He could imagine the three of them leading a wonderful life there and he floated through the rest of the viewing on a positivity warped by desperation. Three things tricked his eyes – the sections of stainless steel countertops in the kitchen, the cream L-shaped sofa in the living room and the old-fashioned wrought-iron bed in the master bedroom. It was Anna's style.

He worked hard to get the house ready for her. Danny put in long hours with him, but opened with, 'Rather you than me, buddy, when Anna shows up,' and, 'Man, you're screwed.' He became more useful when he started writing a list of things that needed to be done. It was a long list that they decided they could bypass Sonny to tackle. This came after they found a canine tooth in one of the kitchen cabinets and when they realized one of the main storage areas in the house hadn't been emptied of Sonny's stuff.

The day they moved in, Joe saw that the nice cream sofa had been swapped for a stained orange one and instead of the wrought-iron bed, there was a beige base and mattress from a discount furniture store. The only blessing was that Anna had arrived at the house after an eight-hour flight from Paris. She glanced around, got the vague sense of somewhere clean and tidy, then went upstairs, exhausted enough to sleep on the cheap bed. Shaun had been coached by Joe to create enthusiasm and distraction and it had worked – at least until Anna got up the next day. The problem was that short of rewiring, replumbing and calling in a carpenter, the place was doomed to appear unfinished, however freshly painted the walls were. Everything wooden was a series of misjudged measurements: baseboards that were too long or too short, doors that were too narrow, cabinets that wouldn't close. Some of the doors had been hung with just two screws in each hinge. The bedroom doorframe had come off in Joe's hand. Upstairs, by the bathroom door, light shone through from the recessed lighting in the kitchen.

Anna had taken it well. She was so touched by the effort Joe had made, she hadn't made a fuss. But over the months that followed, Joe would hear random shouts from around the house when things broke or handles came off or heads were banged against surprise corners.

'It's only me,' said Joe, always reassuring her every time he came home. 'Hey,' he said, kissing her on the lips. 'How you doing? You look cute.' Anna was small, with sallow skin and pale green eyes. She was barefoot and dressed in jeans and a black tank. She shrugged. 'I'm OK.' She ran her hand over the back of her hair, trying to flatten the tangles.

'Did you call Chloe in the end?' he said.

'You are not going to believe my luck,' she said.

'Luck?'

'Yes. The photographer from yesterday has a new girlfriend, who is, maybe, twenty-two. Anyway, she styled the whole thing. He offered her as a solution to Chloe, which she had to accept, because she had inconvenienced him. And I'm not fired.'

'You are kidding me.'

'You thought I'd be fired?' She smiled.

'No. But Chloe is . . .'

'I know. But she's schizophrenic. We've agreed she pushed me into the shoot, so for now I can just stay working from home.'

'That's . . . wonderful.'

'I know.'

'Honey,' said Joe. 'I just want you to know . . . I love you.'

'Thank you,' she said. 'I love you too.'

'And I feel . . .'

'You feel?'

'Just . . .' He shrugged. 'I guess I feel . . .'

They could hear keys in the front door and voices in the hallway.

'He's back early,' said Anna, leaning out towards the sound.

Shaun walked into the kitchen, throwing his book bag on the floor.

'Mom, Dad, this is Tara.'

It almost killed Joe not to flash a look at Anna. Tara was about seventeen, blonde, five foot nine, painfully thin and in very low cut jeans and a skinny yellow T-shirt. An oversized pink bag hung on her forearm.

'Hey,' said Tara. 'Nice to meet you.'

'You too,' said Joe.

'Yes,' Anna managed.

'I'd shake hands but I, like, just got these,' said Tara, wiggling her fingers and a new set of sparkling acrylic nails.

'They're very pretty,' said Anna.

'*I* thought so,' said Tara. 'My dad is, like, having a pool party tonight. I live with my dad. So I *so* had to do something outrageous. There's some, like, TV guy friend of his coming. And that's what I want to do – TV. So we were, like, in the city earlier.' Every statement sounded like a question. She smiled at Shaun. 'We were bikini shopping.'

Shaun tried to smile back. 'I got some CDs.'

'Did you find anything, Tara?' said Anna.

'I did,' she said, swinging a miniature paper bag from its white rope handles. She started by pulling out a red string that turned into a bikini top, then dug in again and pulled out a small pair of red hipster shorts.

'Wow,' said Anna.

'Yeah,' said Joe, turning quickly towards the fridge.

'Oh and check this out,' said Tara, rubbing a hand up her tanned arm. 'This is this new fake stuff? Instant but waterproof. SplashBronze. You should try it.'

'Thanks for the tip,' said Anna.

'We're going to my room,' said Shaun.

'OK, bye,' said Tara, with a little wave.

'Would you like to stay for supper?' said Anna.

Tara glanced at the cubed beef. 'Ew, no thank you!' she said. 'I mean, you know, I don't do red meat. Just white. Or fish. Some fish. Red Snapper and stuff that doesn't taste very fishy.' She shrugged and followed Shaun into the hallway, about to slip her hand into his jeans' pocket until she remembered her new nails.

Joe walked back to Anna, drinking from a carton of juice.

'What do you, like, think and stuff?' said Joe.

Anna shook her head, smiling. 'Hooker.'

'How do you really feel?'

She shrugged. 'What can I say?'

'Yeah, I know. It's weird. He looks so unhappy and it's like she doesn't even notice.'

'Or care.'

'Hey, she could be a hooker with a heart.'

Anna laughed. 'I want him to be happy again. His poor sad eyes.' She shook her head. 'To her, he's just this handsome—'

'Poor kid.'

Anna laughed. 'She's going to try that bikini on for him up there.'

'Want me to go break it up?'

Anna laughed as he grabbed her from behind and kissed her cheek.

'Don't worry,' he said, 'she's not my type.'

'She's not Shaun's type either.'

'Teenage boys don't have types. That's their mothers' job.'

'I would never expect him to go for anyone I'd like.'

They both went quiet, thinking of Shaun's girl-friend Katie. She was a girl the whole family had fallen in love with.

EIGHT

Joe and Danny sat in the hot, cramped back room of the post office where the letter had been mailed. A small television screen ran black and white video footage of the mailboxes inside the building. An over-excited manager hovered around behind them.

After a quarter of an hour, Joe turned around to him.

'Hey . . . Simon, if you want to leave us here doing our thing, we'll call you if we see anything we need your help with.'

'Sure,' said Simon. 'Absolutely. No problem. I'll be right outside.'

'Yeah, thanks,' said Danny.

'God bless him,' said Joe.

'I fucking hate this shit,' said Danny pointing to the screen. 'I have nightmares about video tapes. Watching the same thing over and over and over until I lose my mind, I'm in a fucking straitjacket.'

They watched in silence for ten minutes.

'We're looking for someone mailing a single small envelope between 9 a.m. and 11 a.m. OK – here's one guy,' said Joe. 'Let's still that. Go bring Simon back.'

Simon rushed in ahead of Danny. 'You got something?'

'Do you know this guy?' said Joe.

Simon put his face within three inches of the screen, then shook his head sadly. 'I'm sorry. No. Do you want me to bring any of the others in?'

'Yeah, that would be great,' said Joe.

No-one recognized the man. Or the nine other men and five women who mailed letters around the same time. Danny wrote down all the relevant frames on the footage and they took the tape with them. TARU – the Technical Assistance Response Unit – had sent equipment to Manhattan North, so they could transfer the tape to DVD and print stills when they got back to the office.

'OK,' said Danny. 'We still doing Chelsea?'

'Yup.'

Dawg On It Pet Accessories was a long, skinny building between a closed tapas bar and a men's T-shirt store on Eighth Avenue.

'We're too early,' said Danny, pointing at the poodle-shaped hours of business sign and wandering into the T-shirt store instead. Joe followed him in. It was small and crammed with free-standing circular rails, wall-mounted rails and shelves of T-shirts. A hanging metal rack behind the counter was stuffed full of greetings cards. A three-foot long CD rack filled with hundreds of CDs behind glass was mounted like a shelf behind the counter with a sticker that said, In Emergency Break Glass. Resting on top, was an iPod hi-fi.

Danny pushed hard through the rails on the wall and pulled out a navy T-shirt.

'Kind of cool,' he said to Joe. 'I need something for the weekend.'

He went to the counter and took out his wallet.

'I'm going out on a limb here,' said the guy behind the counter. 'But would I be right in saying you two are not, like, together?'

'That would be right,' said Joe.

'And you never would be.'

'He's not my type,' said Danny.

'Well, you need to look a little closer at the graphic on that T-shirt,' he said to Danny. 'Because you might not be sending out the message you want to.'

'Oh,' said Danny. 'That's not what I thought it was. You're right. Thanks for that.'

'Don't worry about it. Happens all the time. If you seemed like assholes, I would have let you go. And get hit on, like, ten times, when you're out with your wife.'

Danny headed quickly for the door. Joe followed, laughing.

'You should have bought it. I wish he'd let you.'

'I'm not an asshole, remember?'

'Here we go,' said Joe. 'Open.'

They walked in to Dawg On It and the backwards motion of Buck Torrance in a purple cowboy shirt and tight white jeans with purple diamanté paw prints on the pockets. He didn't hear them over the vacuum cleaner, but turned it off when he caught their reflection in the mirror.

'Hi. Buck?' said Joe.

'Yes.'

'Detectives Lucchesi and Markey, NYPD. You're the promoter at Bed, Bad and Beyond?'

'Yes, sir. I am. Can I help you?' said Buck.

'I was speaking with Mark Branham from Gay Alliance. He said you were the man to talk to. We're looking into some pretty violent attacks on men that have happened over the last year,' said Joe.

'Gay men,' said Buck.

'One of them was gay. We were wondering if we showed you a few photos . . .'

'Sure. Go ahead.' Buck took the photos. 'No to this guy, doesn't look familiar. No again. And yeah. I know this guy's face. That's William Aneto.'

'Did you know him?'

'I'd seen him around – in bars, in the club, whatever, so I knew his face. And then there were the posters all around the place last year. People lit candles on the street by the club, that's it. I'm sorry.'

'Did you notice him with any particular crowd, any one guy?'

'I just didn't know him that well. Do you want to leave those photos here with me? I could ask around for you?' said Buck.

'No. We'll hold onto them. Thanks for your help.'

'My pleasure. If you need anything else, let me know.'

'Sure,' said Danny.

'Should guys be worried around here?'

'Don't be,' said Joe. 'And you don't want people staying away from the store because you're freaking them out.'

'Yeah. Who's going to dress all the dogs in the neighborhood if you go out of business?' said Danny.

'Sweetheart? Those dogs you see out there? A lot of them? Don't even have names.'

Danny frowned.

'Those little doggies are sniffing butts so their owners can. The ohmygod-let-me-stop-talk-to-you-bout-your-dog/enough-about-the-dog-what-about-me approach. I mean, this store is, like, a major pick-up joint. You want to check out the dog run at Waterside Park. Sit on a bench there and you'll have a date in no time.'

Danny was standing at one of the shelves trying to put something back where he found it.

'That little red dog collar isn't you,' said Buck.

'You haven't met his wife,' said Joe.

'Wife?'

'Funny,' said Danny.

'I know,' said Buck. 'Look, seriously? I know it's hard for you to work a case like this. I've seen it before. I mean, gay men spread themselves far and wide. But they get to know the ones who like it rough and the ones who like it *way too*. So if I hear anything, I'll let you know.'

'This guy is really wrong,' said Joe. 'He's not someone you want to be alone in a room with.'

'Oh don't worry about me.' He laughed. 'I'm straight, sweetheart.'

Danny and Joe paused, then walked out onto the street and took a left towards the car.

'He is fucking serious,' muttered Danny, waving back to Buck.

'He is,' said Joe.

Back at the office, Reuben Maller called again.

'Joe? I've come up with a loose profile for you. Want me to fax it through?'

'Machine's bust,' said Joe. 'Can you run it by me now?'

'I would say – surprise, surprise – white male in his thirties, most likely lives alone. He will come across as quite a regular guy. He won't give off any weird vibes. He lives in the city – we've got one victim in SoHo, two on the Upper West Side. He's mobile, drives to and from the scene. Reasonably stable work history, but probably with gaps in between jobs or maybe with a job that means he works alone, but has intermittent interaction with people. He must spend a lot of time alone to finely tune this fantasy of his. There's hardcore evidence of overkill at the scenes, which suggests all this is personal, so maybe you should be looking at linking the victims or maybe they're people who slighted him along his path.

'The guy is a mixed offender. He plans well: he gets in to the apartments easily, no forced entry, so he must be doing something right. He brings tools with him: his hammer, his twenty-two caliber handgun. He doesn't leave behind any evidence. Yet his attack is frenzied, which implies he also lets his control slip.

'Think carefully about the locations. Killers usually ease themselves into it by operating in an area that's very familiar to them, so we could be looking at someone who lives on the Upper West Side or grew up there, same goes maybe for SoHo.'

'Great,' said Joe. 'Thanks for that. Did you come up with anything sexual? You know, the whole nudity thing?'

'I'm just not getting that. It seems more like a humiliation thing. Or a control thing. I'd be surprised if there was a sexual motivation. But as they say, guarantee: no guarantees.'

'Sure.'

'Listen, if you need anything else—'

'Yeah, I'll be in touch.'

*   *   *

When Joe got home, Anna was sitting at the kitchen counter with a stack of pages she had cut out of magazines. Joe kissed her on the cheek, then reached out to pull open the tall narrow cabinet that was wedged between the fridge and the wall. It rocked wildly from side to side.

'This thing feels like it is going to fall apart every time I touch it.'

'Pull it quick,' said Anna, 'and lift it at the same time.'

He closed it and tried it again.

'I have a lot of practice here all the time,' she said.

'Well maybe I can tempt you out on Friday. It's Gina's birthday. Danny has booked a table for the four of us in Pastis. Are you OK with that?'

She paused, but then nodded. 'I think so.'

'You can always cancel at the last minute. No pressure.'

'Thanks.'

'But I'd love you to be there.'

'I know'.

'Let me go change,' he said. He went upstairs, took a shower, then came down in jeans and a blue T-shirt with the logo of a bar he never remembered being in. He sat down on the sofa and turned on the television. He barely noticed the channels he was changing until he hit a press conference. The Police Commissioner was standing at a podium reading from a statement.

'. . . established a link with two previous murders, the first of which happened in September last, that of William Aneto, and the second in December of Gary Ortis.' The room erupted. The Commissioner continued. 'All three victims were male, aged between thirty and forty years old and were brutally attacked in their place of residence and shot dead. A twenty-two caliber handgun was used in each of the crimes. There was no sign of forced entry, so we're investigating the possibility that these men knew their killer. A task force working out of Manhattan North Homicide has been put together to handle the investigation.'

Questions were shouted from all over the room:

'Are you saying there is a serial killer loose in New York?'

'What I'm saying is that we have established a pattern between three homicides that have taken place in the city in the past year.'

'Why did you not establish a pattern sooner? The first murder happened almost a year ago.'

'These three crimes were committed in different parts of the city over a period of a year and did not initially appear to be connected. For reasons I can not go into at this time, when we went back and got together with detectives handling each case, a pattern emerged.'

'How did he gain access to the apartments?'

'Like I said, there was no sign of forced entry. We have to presume for now . . . the . . . uh . . . caller . . . was let in by the victims or someone familiar with the residences.'

'Were these doormen buildings?'

'One was.'

'Have you spoken to the families? How did they respond?'

'Yes. We have already spoken to each of the victim's families and have impressed upon them our commitment to finding their sons' killer.'

'William Aneto's mother has been extremely outspoken in her dissatisfaction with your handling of her son's case—'

'We have spoken with Mrs Aneto who continues to assist us with our investigation. That's all I have to say on that matter at this point.'

'Have you established a connection between the victims?'

'That is something we are looking into.'

'Gay Alliance has recently been raising awareness of the first anniversary of the murder of William Aneto. Do you think there is a homosexual motive to the killings?'

'It is important not to jump to any conclusions in the early stages of an investigation.'

'What advice can you give the public?'

'No-one is to panic, here. I would say what we always say: be alert, don't open your door to strangers, ask to see ID from anyone purporting to be from the gas company, etc. And obviously, if anyone out there has information on any of these crimes, could they please contact Crimestoppers confidentially at 1800 577 TIPS. That's 1800 577 TIPS.'

'Do you have any suspects?'

'We are working through a list of names that are linked in some way to our three victims. Ladies and gentlemen, that's all we have time for here, today. Thank you for your cooperation.'

'Yeah, thanks for letting me know, you fucking douche-bags,' said Joe. 'And what about – hey, we didn't make a connection because people don't know how to fill out a form or fucking communicate with people?'

He changed channels again and every news broadcast he saw had the story.

'This perpetrator comes to the homes of his victims. We have no information right now as to how he gains access . . .'

'This dates back to last year's murder of thirty-one-year-old actor, William Aneto. His body was discovered in his Upper West Side apartment . . .'

'The last person to see Gary Ortis alive is with us right now . . .'

'We'll be back after the break with information on how you can secure your home.'

'. . . being dubbed The Caller . . .'

'A detective who chose not to be named described the scene as . . .'

'Fear, fear, fear,' said Joe, turning the television off. Every day, articles in newspapers ran stories with headlines that screamed Deadly. Anger. Fear. Killer. Disease. Alert. Threat. These murders were not typical for New York. You were more likely to be killed by someone you knew than by the stranger who had now been given the title The Caller.

'I'm going to take a shower.' Anna walked back into the room. She leaned over and kissed him.

'OK.'

He grabbed a magazine from beside the sofa and started flicking through it. He could hear the water running upstairs. He wanted to walk up, open the door, slide in behind her and do something they hadn't done for months. His patience was low. He felt bad. But really, he was angry. He threw down the magazine and turned the television back on.

Anna came down half an hour later. Joe didn't bother to look up. When he did, she was leaning over the counter with her back to him, opening a bottle of red wine. She was wearing the tiniest black shorts, no top. Her shoes were high and black with skinny heels and red soles. She turned around. He couldn't decide where to look. When he made it to her face, she held his gaze and walked slowly towards him.

NINE

Mary Burig stood in the doorway of the library with her smartphone in her hand, open on a drawing programme. With the stylus, she drew a rough sketch of the room, L-shaped because a small storage area had been built in the back right-hand corner. Bookshelves ran around all the walls of the library and in the left-hand corner, the top of the L, was a circle of six low-backed chairs in worn orange fabric. Mary used the eraser tool to take the chairs away. She drew them into the space right inside the door. Then she put them back where they were, saving the drawing and putting the phone in her pocket. She walked over to the poetry section, pulled out a book and went straight to the page she had kept marked with a pink Post-It.

Stan Frayte opened the door and stuck his head in. 'Hey, cut out the noise in there,' he said, winking. 'I got work to do.'

Mary looked up and smiled. 'Come here for a second,' she said. 'Listen to this. "No night is endless, dark and bleak / When in the rising dawn, a weakened light / Erupts to blaze and fire / And guide me past a spirit tired / By heavy hopes and wingless dreams / To find another future's gleam / And when I search the brightness' source / I find your heart, a blinding force."'

'I don't think the source of light was a heart, Mary. It was, like, a bulb, a lamp, something an electrician worked real hard at.'

'Maybe it was,' said Mary, smiling.

'No maybe about it.' Stan walked into the room, pulling a measuring tape from his utility belt. 'It's so great that you've got a library in the building.'

'I know,' said Mary. 'But not a lot of people use it.'

'That's a real shame,' he said.

'I mean, I don't want you to think all your work will be for no-one.'

'If it'll make one person happy,' said Stan. 'That's good enough for me.'

'Thanks so much,' she said.

'So what would you like?'

'Well, this corner,' she said, 'where all the chairs are, there are no outlets. I think it would be nice to have some desk lamps here instead for night time, because,' she pointed to a fluorescent strip-light on the ceiling, 'that is really glarey. It hurts my eyes.'

'OK,' said Stan.

'And I think that's everything for the electrical department.'

He laughed. 'Well, what about some lighting in the shelves? At the top? That could be neat.'

'That would be great,' said Mary. 'I'd love that. If it's not too expensive.'

'Don't worry about that,' said Stan. 'Also, the walls could use some paint.' He nodded. 'I can do that at the weekend. Anything else?'

'Thank you so much. Magda's going to get some magazine racks. Most people who come in here read magazines. I prefer poetry.'

'I don't know a lot about poetry,' said Stan, 'but I like the idea of it. I like that you have to say everything in as few words as possible.'

David Burig parked outside the apartment block in his black Mercedes. He grabbed a gift bag from the passenger seat and got out. June was on the reception desk and waved him through. He took the elevator to Mary's floor and knocked on the door.

'Hello, there,' he said. He handed her the bag.

'What is this for?' she said, smiling.

'For the hell of it,' he said.

'OK. Can I open it?'

'No. Save it for Christmas.'

Her face fell. David rolled his eyes. 'Of course you can open it.'

'Yay!' She ran to the sofa and opened the bag.

He closed the door behind them and waited for a reaction.

'Ohmygod! This is so cool,' said Mary. 'So cool.'

'Do you like it?'

'No.'

'Very funny.'

Mary was holding a huge grey scrapbook with 'There's Something About Mary' written across the top. On the first page was a photo of her – age two – almost in silhouette with a random streak of light covering her head. The caption read: Why Mom Should Never Have Taken Photos. Mary laughed out loud. The next photo was of Mary holding up the winning end of a giant Christmas cracker with David beside her, his face frozen in the shock of defeat. The caption read: Traumas of David's Young Life: Part I.

'Is there a Part II?' said Mary.

'See page twenty-five,' he said.

'Oh God,' said Mary when she found it. Sellotaped to the page was a Motley Crue/Whitesnake ticket stub from Madison Square Garden 1987. And beside it, a photo of a tanned and sweaty David in tight jeans and vest top with long shaggy hair and bandana, giving the peace sign.

'It needs no caption,' said David, shaking his head.

Mary laughed until she cried. 'Oh my God! Do you remember meeting that girl afterwards and she said, "What's your name?" and you said, "David" and she said, "David who?" and you said, "David. Lee. Roth, baby."'

'I did not!'

'You did, you loser.'

'Hmm. Yeah, I may have filed that memory under "Destroy. Destroy."'

'What is it about teenage years that no matter who you are, you look back and are like, "What the hell was I thinking?"'

'It's so that no matter who we end up being, we can never take ourselves too seriously. Because at one point, we were all proud to wear snow-wash.'

Mary glanced down at her jeans.

David laughed. 'Like, I'd ever let you do that again. Anyway, look, I'd love to stay and talk, but I've got to get back to the office. I just wanted to drop that in.'

'It's the best present ever. Thank you.'

'Wait 'til you see the secret compartment at the back.'

He hugged her and left before she had a chance to open it. He jogged down the hallway, nodding at Stan Frayte as he passed.

Mary turned to the back of the album and to a flap in the cover with a loop of red ribbon. She pulled it and it opened a little door. Inside was a disk: *Rebecca* on DVD with a note saying, 'Can't believe you've never seen this. Awesome! XX'.

Magda Oleszak rode the elevator to the second floor. She stepped out and was hit with the grinding stop/start sound of drilling from down the corridor. She took a right then a left, away from the noise and towards Mary's apartment at the end. As she got closer, she sensed something wasn't quite right. She walked a little faster, holding tight to the shoulder bag that banged off her hip. When she reached the door, it was open. Stan turned to her, his face stricken. Mary was lying on the floor at his feet.

Magda rushed to Mary's side. 'What the—'

'I don't know! I have no idea.' Stan's voice was pitched high. He wiped the sweat from his face with a stained yellow cloth from his belt, his eyes moving everywhere around the room.

'Did you hurt her?' said Magda.

'What? No!'

Magda shook Mary's shoulders gently, looking up at Stan. 'What were you doing in Mary's apartment?'

'Coming to show her paint samples. That's all.'

'Did you call the doctor?'

'I just got here! Right before you walked in.'

'What's all this?' she said, looking at the floor around the body. 'Did she do this while you were here?'

Stanley shook his head. 'I don't know anything about this.'

'Call the doctor,' she snapped. 'And get security up here.'

Mary's eyes flickered open.

TEN

Anna sat at the kitchen table in a long black silk robe. Her eyes sparkled, she was smiling, she was eating pancakes. It reminded Joe about how everything used to be.

'This is great,' he said. 'Seeing you sitting there, eating pancakes.' He walked over to her, took her two small hands in his and pulled her towards him. He hugged her tight.

'You're a midget,' he said, stroking her hair, kissing the top of her head. They stayed there for minutes, quietly, holding on.

'How does he kill them?' said Anna.

Joe pulled away slowly. 'What?'

She stayed with her head against his chest. 'The Caller guy,' she said. 'I saw the news.'

Joe tilted her chin up, but still couldn't get eye contact. 'Are you for real?'

She nodded.

'I'm not going to go there with you,' he said.

Anna finally looked up. 'Please.'

Joe put a hand on her chest and felt her heart beat rocketing underneath it.

'This is not good, you thinking this way.'

'What way?'

Joe's expression was patient. 'Come on,' he said.

'But what if it's . . .'

'Sweetheart, I've been to the crime scenes. This is not Rawlins. This is no-one that has anything to do with Rawlins. This is a different guy. Trust me enough that you don't need to know the details.'

'But if I knew the—'

Joe shook his head. 'You're so beautiful. I look at you and it breaks my heart that inside that head . . . there is so much pain and fear.'

Tears welled in her eyes.

'I know what that feels like,' said Joe. 'But I'm used to it. So you're going to have to trust me. I'm not about to come home with all the details and add more to what you've already got going on.'

'Is it worse than what the papers—'

He smiled with sad eyes. 'You know the answer to that.'

'You can't filter the world for me forever, you know.'

'Yeah?' said Joe. 'Well, I'll die trying.'

Anna went to the worktop and took a tissue to wipe her eyes.

'Do you want to go on a date tonight?' she said.

'What?' said Joe. 'Are you serious?'

She laughed. 'That's so depressing.'

'I didn't mean it like that,' he said. 'I'm just—'

'Yes or no: do you want to go out?'

'Yes,' said Joe. 'I'd love to.'

'Then we will.'

'Where would you like to go?'

'Cardino's.'

He smiled. 'Cardino's? I don't know. I think I got some lightweight French girl drunk there once and she ended up having to marry me. *"I am a French woman! We do not drink beer like this!"'*

'That is the worst accent.' She smiled, about to walk away, but her robe slid wide open and off her shoulders. She slowly shook her head. Joe dangled the black silk belt high in his hand.

'You gotta be quick,' he said.

Artie Blackwell was the shortest journalist in the five boroughs. He had short, spiky grey hair and a perfect, tight grey beard, yet always managed to look unwashed. When he walked, he leaned left, weighed down by one of a number of free, branded shoulder bags. He was hovering outside the Manhattan North building, sweating in the early morning sun.

'Woo, Case Detective Lucchesi. Someone's being good to you.'

'Artie,' said Joe, glancing down. 'Pleasure.'

Artie snorted. 'You got to admit – it's an odd choice, all things considered, what with the shooting and the whole Rawlins fiasco.'

'You know the deal,' said Joe, smiling and calm. 'I caught the Lowry case. My partner caught the Aneto case. Oh, and I was cleared of any wrongdoing in the Riggs shooting, so here I am. And here we are, Artie.'

'Good to see you again,' said Artie, tipping his dark blue fisherman's hat.

A breeze rose from nowhere and Joe was forced to turn away; Artie always smelled of his last meal. Sadly for Joe, none of them ever had been.

'Creepy name too: The Caller . . .' said Artie. 'Does the perp make a phone call to his victims before he shows up?'

Joe rolled his eyes. 'No. Under the bright lights of the cameras, the Chief got flustered and said "caller". And some . . . journalist thought it sounded creepy enough to freak the public out. I could think of a lot of other names for the guy . . .'

'Like what?' said Artie.

Joe stopped. 'What can I do for you?'

'You got anything for me?' said Artie.

'Unless you want to do a nice three-way with the DCPI, no.'

'I could do that.'

'Come on, Artie. You know I'm not in a position to say shit. OK? Now, I'm coming into work a very contented man this morning, so please . . .'

'Just something that no-one else's got. Throw me something.'

Joe looked at him like he had lost his mind. 'Why are you even here?'

Artie shrugged. 'I was in the neighborhood.'

Joe laughed.

Artie had to jog to keep up with him. 'Have you made any further progress on the Duke Rawlins investigation?'

Joe spun around. 'That's not an investigation I'm directly involved in,' he said. 'And you know that, you—' He paused. 'Go talk to the FBI. Just go, find out who the hell you're supposed to talk to. Goodbye, Artie.'

Joe sat at his desk with Aneto's file in front of him. He spread out the photos of the hallway and the close-ups of the blood stains, looking for anything about him that made him the reason why the killer started here. There were no guarantees he was the first victim, but it was unlikely he wasn't. All the squads knew to look through their files for anything similar – nothing had come up – and the chances of a body lying undiscovered in a New York apartment for over a year were non-existent. He went slowly through the images. He had seen them before, but he was looking for another angle and he had a fresh cup of coffee to back him up. Six photographs in, he stopped.

It was taken in the hallway – a close-up of Aneto's torso, nothing remarkable, except for a dark spot at the edge of the photo. He looked closer. If it was what he thought it was, it was totally out of place. He pulled a magnifying glass out of his drawer, looking around quickly before he held it over the photo. He was right. It was a dermestid beetle. Joe had spent two years studying entomology before he dropped out to become a cop. His father was a professor in Forensic Entomology.

Joe turned back to the photo. Dermestid beetles weren't there for William Aneto – nothing on his body would interest them yet. They came to corpses at the end. After the flies had arrived to lay their eggs and the maggots had crawled off into the dark to pupate, dermestids showed up to feed on the dried tissue. William Aneto didn't have any dried tissue. The body was found within twenty-four hours of his murder with eight hours of night time in between when insects would not have been active.

Joe laid out all the photos of William Aneto's apartment looking for anything else that could have attracted a dermestid beetle – they also fed on hide and hair. A bad taxidermy job could have brought them out, even the horse hair from a violin bow. Joe studied the apartment, but it was modern and minimalist, lots of plastic and chrome and smooth shiny new surfaces. There was no mounted stag's head on the wall near the body, nothing that Joe could find that would account for the dermestid beetle. The only thing he could think of was another dead creature in the house, a mouse or a rat. But then there would have been more beetles and there were none in any of the other photos.

'You've got mail,' said Rencher, holding up a white envelope with Joe's name on it.

Joe looked at the envelope. 'He strikes again.' He pulled a pair of gloves out of the drawer and put them on. He sliced the letter open: more pages, squashed into an envelope made to take only two or three. Rencher hovered by the desk.

'I'll let you know,' said Joe, tilting his head towards Rencher's desk.

Rencher shrugged and walked away. Joe walked over to the copier, made a copy of the letter for everyone, then put the original in an envelope. They hadn't got prints from the first one, so he was hoping for better luck this time. He sat down with his copy and read through it, marking parts as he went along. When he had read it three times, he called everyone over.

'Reminds me of school,' said Rencher. 'Getting a letter was the highlight of your day.'

'You went to boarding school?' said Martinez.

'Yes I did,' said Rencher. 'Got a problem with that?'

'Relax,' said Martinez.

'OK,' said Joe. 'Letter two, same kind of envelope, same writing, mailed around the same time from the same post office. Similar kind of shit: talking about going to some gallery, going to the park, being spiritual, baking cookies in someone else's kitchen – whatever the hell that's about.' He flicked through more pages. 'There's a lot of stuff about forgiveness here and redemption. And good and evil. And then we come to the case: "*It strikes a chord with me. I'm not sure why. I follow The Caller investigation with interest when I get the chance.*" Then: "*But I know that somewhere inside me I, personally, wish you luck.*" And it's signed off – "*God be with you. May angels rest on your shoulders and lighten your load.*"' Joe shrugged.

'And can you feel God with you right now?' said Martinez.

'I look at you guys and I think "Jesus Christ". Does that count?' said Joe.

Rencher shrugged. '"*I wish you luck*" because I want to stop, maybe? Is this the perp wanting to get caught?'

'I don't think I could bear the cliché if it was,' said Danny.

Joe laughed. 'Nah. He's been so careful all along.'

Rencher shrugged. 'Well could it be the perp and he *doesn't* want to get caught?'

'Then why engage us at all?' said Joe.

'For a mind fuck,' said Rencher.

'To me,' said Danny, 'the letter reads like your

neighbor trying to give you some friendly advice
– the kind of advice that's useless because really,
you know he's an EDP.'

'Your neighbor's the one should be worried
about living next door to an EDP,' said Rencher.

'I see where you're coming from, Danny,' said
Joe.

'". . . somewhere inside me I, *personally*, wish
you luck". This could be someone who knows The
Caller,' said Rencher.

'Or has witnessed the crime,' said Bobby.

'Or has been the victim of a crime,' said Rencher.

'Or has been a victim of The Caller,' said Joe.

They looked at him. 'Woo,' said Danny.

'It doesn't sound like some sick twisted psycho,'
said Joe. 'But I can't make up my mind if it's one
of those harmless loser psychos who lives with
Mom.'

'Maybe the guy doesn't know who or what he
knows,' said Bobby.

'And maybe, just maybe . . .' said Danny. 'This
is all just a load of bullshit.'

They stood in silence, their eyes moving
between the letter and the photos still laid out on
Joe's desk.

Bobby spoke first. 'We worked this case, don't
know if any you guys saw it – the mugger who
was targeting those Columbia University girls? We
got in touch with the papers, fed them some stuff
and within, like, a week, we had our guy.'

'No,' said Joe. 'I'm not going to do that. We don't know enough about—'

'Do you know the case I'm talking about?'

'Yeah,' said Joe, 'but it doesn't matter.'

'What do you mean it doesn't matter?'

'Look, Bobby,' said Joe. 'How far into your investigation were you? Come on. What you were doing with the papers was after – what? – nine, ten attacks? You knew a lot about the perp. What are we? At the start of a *homicide* investigation, no witnesses, no nice descriptions, no suspect, nothing predictab—'

'I still think he could—'

'No,' said Joe, too loud. 'I'm not doing it.'

Cardino's on Broome Street was small, loud and pumping out angry music. Anna was sitting in the corner in jeans, a black off-the-shoulder top and scuffed black ankle boots. Her hair was in a ponytail and she had dangly silver earrings on.

Joe was laughing as he walked over to her. She laughed too and kissed him on the lips. He guessed by her eyes she was about two glasses of wine down.

'Is that what you were actually wearing?' he said.

'Nearly. The jeans and boots are. But I don't think I can do these for much longer.' She let the ponytail down and pulled off the clip-on earrings.

Joe looked around the bar. 'All the girls here are going for the same look.'

'Yeah – they're about twenty years old. You get to do every look once,' said Anna. 'That's the rule. Second time round, you're always going to be too old.'

'I never knew that,' said Joe.

She nodded. 'It's true.'

'Does that mean I never get to wear skinny jeans ever again?' said Joe.

'Who said you could the first time?'

'My physique.'

'Oh my God. Are we back in time? Can I change my mind?'

They laughed. But Joe got a flash of something that made him wonder how Anna's life would have turned out if she had walked away from their first date.

'Let me go to the bar,' he said. 'You want some Coors for old times' sake?'

'You know what happened that night—'

'Exactly.'

'Sauvignon Blanc, please.'

She watched him walk away. The man beside her got up and left his newspaper behind. Anna waited a few minutes for Joe, then dragged the paper across the seat towards her and started reading. She jumped as Joe put the drinks down on the table.

'Am I boring you?'

'Never,' she said, folding the newspaper and pushing it back where she got it. 'Thanks.'

'Cheers, sweetheart. Thank you for going on a date with me.'

'My pleasure,' she said.

'And thanks for putting out on the first night.'

Shaun Lucchesi sat at his desk, scrolling through his cell phone. His myspace profile was open on the laptop in front of him. Behind the Explorer window was iTunes, behind that was Skype and hidden at the very back was a blank Word doc he had opened an hour earlier to write an English paper. His phone rang and Tara's face filled the screen. He turned the sound off on the computer.

'Hey, Tara.'

He clicked onto iTunes as he listened to her. 'Nah,' he said. 'Just English. And I have not written one word. I can't even remember the title.'

As she kept talking, he lost interest in the screens in front of him. 'Hmm. I'd like that a lot,' he said, spinning around in the chair and standing up.

'Wow,' he said. 'I . . . don't know what to say back to that.' He paced the room, listening to every word she breathed down the phone.

He sat on the bed, then lay back. 'OK,' he said, 'I'm not good at this. I'm too sober to have this conversation.' He glanced at his watch. 'Why don't you come over?'

Joe and Anna arrived back from the bar hungry. Joe went to the fridge and pulled out a dish of leftover meatballs. He slammed the door and slammed the dish onto the counter.

'Shhh,' said Anna, pointing upstairs.

Joe ignored her and put the meatballs into the microwave.

'What is wrong with you?' said Anna.

'Nothing.'

'There is something wrong. Just tell me.'

'I didn't want to stay that late, that's all. I've a lot on.'

'It was fun.'

'After lots of drinks, maybe.'

'What's that supposed to mean?'

'Nothing,' said Joe. 'Do we have bread?'

'Yes,' she said, pointing to a baguette right in front of him.

'Oh.' He grabbed a knife and started cutting it.

'Come on,' she said. 'You enjoyed yourself.'

He was somewhere else, staring ahead, his face set.

'Do you know who I liked?' said Anna. 'I liked Ireland Joe. I mean, before everything . . . the guy whose face was relaxed, who didn't have a frown all the time, who made jokes, actually laughed.'

'I still know how to laugh.' He glared at her.

'Maybe you just don't put it into practice, then.'

'Come on, Anna, there's always something.'

'No there isn't.'

'We were having a nice night,' said Joe.

'And then we weren't. Because you had to—'

'No, no, because *you* had to,' said Joe. 'You can't face what's inside you, so you look outwards, you've got your little roaming red crosshairs. Who can they land on? Who can they land on? Oh yeah, nearest person: me.'

'It's not that at all. You can't bear anyone criticising you.'

'Ditto.'

She shook her head. 'You can't. You come home from work complaining every time your judgment is called into question. Maybe it's you who can't face who you are or what you've done.'

'What is that supposed to mean?'

'I think you feel guilty.'

'About what?'

She stared at him. 'I think that's obvious.'

'If you're talking about you, damn right I feel guilty. What guy – not to mention detective – is not going to feel guilty that he nearly got his wife killed?'

'I'm not saying there's anything wrong with you feeling guilty—'

'Since when did I need your blessing on what I can or cannot feel?'

'Joe, stop.'

He took a breath. Anna reached out and held his hand.

'I'm just saying, I think you feel guilty, but you're not dealing with your guilt and . . . you're like a time bomb.'

He tilted his head. 'OK. Well, I think you feel scared, but you're not dealing with your fear and you're like a time bomb.'

'You are impossible to talk to.'

'So are you.'

She dropped his hand. 'How old are you? Grow up.'

'Oh,' said Joe, 'just to let you know, I knocked over one of your boxes last night. I think something broke.'

Anna turned to him. 'Which box?'

'I don't know. A navy blue one?'

'No,' said Anna, raising her hand to her mouth, running down the hallway into the front room. She grabbed a pair of scissors from the floor and cut through the tape on the box. She pulled it open.

'Oh, no, no,' she said, gently lifting out one half of a broken glass lampshade. Joe stood behind her.

'Sorry,' he said. 'Was it expensive?'

'You don't want to know . . . because you'll have to replace it.'

'What?'

'It's only on loan for a shoot. I'm responsible for it. You broke it.'

'Well, how much is it?'

'Eight hundred dollars.'

'Eight hundred dollars. You are shitting me. For a lamp?'

'Oh, come on,' she said. 'I'm not working for the *Bay Ridge Gazette*.'

'I don't really have to replace it, right?'

'You do,' she said. 'It's in my care.'

'Tell them it broke in transit.'

'They know it arrived here OK.'

'I don't have that kind of money to hand over to some fucking . . . and who the hell spends eight hundred dollars on a lamp?'

'You'd be surprised.'

'I am surprised. I'm also surprised that more things don't get broken in this house. It's out of control, Anna. It's crazy. It's like a bomb site in here. I can't live this way. Meanwhile, you're happy as can be, getting a ton of new stuff in every day. Every day's your birthday. Every time, you open the door to the mailman, UPS guy, whoever, sign, take the package, walk five steps into the front room, throw it in there, maybe open it, see what's inside or hey, just leave it lying there—'

'You don't need to reconstruct everything in your life, Joe. I'm here, I'm not a dead body. You can just *ask* me what I do when my doorbell rings.'

Joe rolled his eyes.

'Go ahead,' said Anna. 'Ask me what I do when my doorbell rings. How much fun it is for me.'

'Spare me,' said Joe. 'It's pretty clear what happens and how all this crap piles up in the front room.'

'You're leaving some things out. Here's what happens: the doorbell rings and wherever I am in the house, I freeze. Then my heart jumps and starts to beat faster. I wonder will I go and open it or will I wait until they go away. If I'm near a window, I can check. I look at the uniform, see if it's correct, I look at the person's face, see if I am looking at an honest one, I see if I can see their truck, I check if anyone else is out there on the street. In the middle of this, guess what else I'm thinking about?'

Joe stared at her and it was clear that anger was winning the fight over sympathy.

'Maybe,' said Anna, 'if you paid attention at home, you would have a better understanding of things that are not black and white or follow some sequence that you imagine in your head because you're not around to see it.' She walked across the room and yanked open the top drawer of an old mahogany bureau, grabbing with both hands the piles of cards inside it. 'Sometimes,' she said, throwing the contents at him, 'things don't always work out the way you think.'

Joe stood still as all around him FedEx and UPS failed delivery slips floated to the floor.

ELEVEN

'Shaun?' Anna knocked on the bedroom door lightly and pushed it open. The quilt was gathered in a huge mound, hiding his face . . . *and the face of the girl lying beside him* she realized when she saw two abandoned strappy sandals on the floor. Anna's stomach gave a jolt. She walked backwards out of the bedroom and closed the door quietly behind her. The she stormed back in to Joe.

'That little . . . *salope* is in there with Shaun,' she hissed.

'Oh,' said Joe. 'No.'

'Yes. In bed with him!'

Joe stared at her. 'I didn't think she'd be on the floor.'

'She will be in a minute. And the smell of beer in there!'

'OK, OK, don't do anything crazy that will scar him for life,' said Joe. 'Let's see how he handles this first.'

She glanced towards the door.

'No,' said Joe. 'Come back to bed for a few minutes. I promise I'll de-stress you.'

'So, we're friends now?' she said.

'Of course we're friends. We're united against the teenage enemy.'

Anna choked back a laugh, then put her finger to her lips. 'Shhh,' she said. 'I'm going down for breakfast.'

'I'll make it,' said Joe. He jumped up and ran after her to make sure she wasn't going to do anything. He ran back at the last minute and grabbed a pair of jeans in case Tara was going to arrive down for breakfast and be scarred too. Anna was sitting at the table with a glass of grapefruit juice. Joe took charge of making pancakes and distracting her. With every break in the conversation, she was leaning an ear towards the door.

'Stop that,' said Joe, looking around at her.

She shrugged. 'I'm just—'

'I know,' he said. 'But . . .'

'Have you got a dentist's appointment this morning?' she said, glancing at a calendar pinned to the wall.

He paused. 'Maybe.'

'Do you need a hug?' she said, smiling.

'What are you talking about? Do I look like the kind of guy who needs a hug before going to the dentist?'

'Yes.' She walked over to him, grabbing him

from behind, leaning her head against his back. He pretended to shake with fear. They were laughing when Shaun strolled in, dressed in board shorts and a T-shirt, his eyes puffy, his hair on end.

'Get a room.'

Anna's smile faded quickly.

Shaun pulled a carton of orange juice out of the fridge, drank straight from it, then put it back in.

'Is that empty?' snapped Anna.

'Yes,' said Shaun.

'Stop doing that,' said Anna. 'I've told you over and over.'

'Big deal,' said Shaun. 'It's just a carton.'

'If I'm going to the store, I don't know what I need to buy if you keep . . .'

Shaun flung the fridge wide open, knocking bottles against each other, pulled out the carton and threw it in a pile for recycling.

'There,' he said. He waited a beat. 'Hey, Mom? If you're going to the store? We need juice.'

'Don't be a jerk,' said Joe.

Shaun made a face as he put a bagel into the toaster.

'What time did you get home last night?' said Anna.

'About three o'clock,' said Shaun. 'I had to drop Tara home.'

'Really?' said Anna, raising an eyebrow to Joe.

'Yeah,' said Shaun. 'Why?'

Anna stood up and walked upstairs, opening the door to Shaun's room, then the bathroom. No Tara. She walked back into the kitchen and sat down. She shook her head at Joe. Anger simmered behind her eyes. Shaun grabbed his bagel, smeared cream cheese on it and left the knife on the counter top by the open tub.

'Your knife,' said Anna. 'The cheese.'

Shaun kept walking.

Joe slid into the seat beside her. 'There it is,' he said. 'The Mom's approach to a problem. You start by identifying the issue – girl in Shaun's bed – you can't say it right out, so you survey the child going about his business and pick apart all the other things he's doing. That's good.'

'Ugh,' she said. 'Tara. Ugh.'

'Hey, even I feel dirty.'

Shaun stuck his head around the door, his cell phone in his hand. 'Guys, I'm going out to meet Tara.'

Dr James Makkar had accepted two important things about Joe Lucchesi: a. he didn't do alternative therapies to alleviate stress, therefore, his symptoms and b. he was surgery-phobic. Joe and Dr Mak had an understanding.

'Hello, Joe. Nice to see you for a scheduled visit.' Dr Makkar was dressed in white scrubs with a white mask hanging around his neck. He was in his late thirties, but his silent-movie grooming added years. 'Need me to wipe that sweat off your brow?'

'You're not supposed to make fun of me,' said Joe.

'You are looking for a nurturing environment?' said Makkar.

'I don't know why I come here,' said Joe.

'You need me.'

'Right. But thanks again for helping me out last time.'

'Temporarily,' said Makkar. 'With all the limitations you put on me, my hands are tied. Which is obviously how you like them.'

Joe smiled.

'Follow me.'

Joe walked behind him down the short corridor.

'Take a seat. Let's have a look at that jaw.'

Joe sat down and opened his mouth when he was told.

'How's work?' said Makkar.

'Crap. How about you?'

'Fantastic, of course. It's all about smiling.'

'Or crying out in pain.'

'You wouldn't come to me if I caused you pain. The amount of times I've numbed your mouth before you even knew I was in the room. Your *condition* causes you pain; *I* make it go away. I'm good cop.'

Joe raised his eyes, one of the few responses open to a patient in a dentist's chair.

'You get very close to people's eyes in my business,' Makkar had told him before. 'We see right
in, all those little reactions. I think I'd make a
great jury consultant if I wasn't doing this. Or a
cop, of course.' Joe wanted to smile at the thought
of this slight, dapper Indian cop, patrolling the
75th precinct, but he couldn't.

'OK,' said Makkar. 'First of all, how are your
symptoms?'

'Not as bad as the last time. Pain in my jaw,
cracking when I open my mouth.'

'And,' said Makkar tapping Joe's chin and
looking inside his mouth, 'grinding your teeth.'

Joe nodded.

'Your options are . . . well, keep taking
painkillers. But that's getting a little tired in my
opinion. It's not getting you anywhere. I'm
thinking you really should consider surgery.'

'What?' said Joe, struggling to sit up. 'We've
been here. I don't do surgery.'

'Joe,' said Makkar, laying a hand gently on his
shoulder, 'if you shattered your leg in an accident, you'd do surgery. You'd have no choice. Of
course, you do have a choice in this case, but
you can't keep going on as you are, suffering
with this unnecessarily. The pain does go away,
but it's been years now and I think your lifestyle
and what you've been through – and are probably still going through – are taking their toll.
Those problems are not quick-fix ones. It's likely

you'll be signing up to a lot more pain for a lot longer.'

'That's positive thinking.'

'I'm being realistic. Hear me out. I know you fear surgery—'

'It's not fear, it's—'

Makkar tilted his head patiently. 'I know you *fear* surgery, but this is different. I mean, I don't even need to call it surgery.'

'Doc, I'm forty. I'm a big boy. Call it what it is.'

'OK, then: arthroscopy. Here's the deal – you go under general anaesthetic. The surgeon makes a little incision right here in front of your ear.'

Joe touched the side of his face. 'I don't like the sound—'

'Oh, shut up. He inserts this tiny instrument with a little lens and a light and he has a look around. If he sees inflamed tissue or whatever, he'll remove it. Or he might need to realign the disc. Or he might inject liquid steroids if you need it. You'll have a couple of little stitches, some swelling afterwards, that's it. No overnight stay in hospital. It's way less hardcore than open-joint surgery. Recovery time is quick, there's no major scarring. And a few weeks of physical therapy, just twice a week.'

Silence.

'OK,' said Makkar. 'Why don't I tell you about an alternative: joint replacement procedure. You go under general anaesthetic. You're out. And

then you wake up with a new jaw. Recovery
period – six weeks, jaw wired shut.'

Joe laughed. 'Let me tell you about the clippers guy. When I was a rookie, my partner and
I were called out to an apartment after we got a
load of reports of a bad odor in the building. We
break down the door and let's just say I'm glad
I can't mentally store smells the same way I've
stored the pictures from that night. Our victim
is face down in the hallway in a pool of puke
etcetera, with a cut finger and a pair of clippers
across the floor from him. His jaw had been
broken a couple weeks beforehand when he was
mugged and then it was wired shut by doctors
in the ER. And as you know, he was given the
clippers so he could clip the wires in case he
needed to puke or whatever. The poor guy, who
was only eating liquids through a straw himself,
was making dinner for his girlfriend and cut his
finger real deeply while he was slicing through
some peppers. It turned his stomach and he knew
he was going to throw up. So he went to grab
his clippers, but his hands seemed to be covered
in this olive oil marinade, the clippers shot out
of his hand across the floor, he couldn't hold on
much longer, he puked and choked on it. And
he wasn't found for two days, because the girlfriend had stood him up.'

'Women can be such bitches.'

'Yeah, that's not exactly the message I got from

that little story. Jaw, wiring and shut: no thank
you.'

'You're married, your wife's not gonna stand
you up.'

Joe shook his head.

'So, arthroscopy sounds good, right?' said Makkar.

'Better.'

'Here's what I'm gonna do. I'm sending you for
a consultation at the Facial Pain Clinic at Columbia.
They will do a better job of encouraging you.
Please. Humor me.'

Joe swung his legs off the chair and stood up.
'I can't promise anything.'

Desk space was tight at Manhattan North, with
twelve extra detectives drafted into the task force
to add to the original eight. Martinez walked over
to Joe's desk with Rencher, holding a sheet of
paper above his head.

'We have a match,' said Martinez. 'Between 11
and 11.30 a.m. both Mondays, we have this guy.'
He put two photos down in front of Joe. Danny
came over to join them.

Joe nodded. 'Good work. Anyone at the post
office know who he was?'

'No,' said Rencher. 'The guy there made a big
effort to help us, though.'

'Do you think he's our guy?' said Martinez,
pointing to the photo.

'He looks like he ticks a few of those profile

boxes,' said Joe. 'But who knows? Next Monday, Danny and I'll be waiting for him, see if he's trying to send us anything else. While you're here, I was going to fill you in on something I noticed in the Aneto crime scene photos. There was a dermestid beetle there that didn't really have a place.'

'Oh no – not a domesta beetle,' said Martinez. 'Shock. Horror.'

'Dermestid,' said Joe.

'Whatever.'

'This could mean something,' said Joe. 'Dermestid beetles only feed on the dried tissue of a body. Like when it's practically skeletonized, which Aneto's body wasn't even close to being. Put it this way – dermestid beetles are used by museums to clean animal bones so they're all nice and white for the display. They put the bones in a box with a colony of dermestids and any skin, tissue, muscle, whatever, is eaten away.'

'Yawn,' said Martinez.

'So,' said Joe. 'I'm thinking this is a hitch-hiker bug. It could have come in on the killer.'

'Hey!' said Martinez. 'Someone put a call in to the Natural History Museum. See if they've got an escaped dinosaur skeleton with maybe a hammer he robbed from the cave man exhibit.'

'Callersaurus Rex,' said Rencher. 'The Calleraptor, The—'

'You know, you're a bunch of fucking retards,' said Danny.

Joe shook his head. 'Look, all I'm saying is this one little bug is out of place. It's something to think about. I mean, maybe the guy owns one of the businesses that breeds dermestids for museums, that kind of thing.'

'Suuure,' said Martinez.

Anna flashed a glance at the bed and her pyjamas lying there and thought how comfortable her night could be if she tucked herself back in. Joe arrived home earlier than she expected.

'Hi,' she said, forcing herself to get up, slipping out of the bathrobe and putting on the jeans and top she had thrown on the chair earlier.

'You look beautiful,' said Joe, grabbing her and kissing the top of her head.

'Thanks.'

'You ready?'

'Nearly. By the time you're finished in the shower, I will be.'

She went downstairs and put on Shaun's Kanye West CD and started tidying anything that wasn't going to mess up her clothes.

Joe came into the kitchen, grabbed a glass of water and knocked back two Vicodin.

'If there was no dole you would have a serious problem,' said Anna. She tried to sound light, but failed.

Dole testing was the NYPD's random drug test. Every day a list of officers were called at random, without notice, to the Medical Division in Queens to give a urine sample. If they fail, they're fired. If they test positive for prescription drugs and don't have an up-to-date prescription, they're fired.

'What are you talking about?' said Joe. 'I have a prescription for these.'

'What about the times you go to your friend in the Village?'

'It's no big deal,' said Joe. 'You really think I'm a better person or a better detective when I'm going around in fucking agony? Or when my brain has other things to focus on other than pain?'

'I worry about you.'

'Let's go.'

The night was warm and still and the traffic into the city was light.

'So,' said Anna. 'Would you like to bet with me? Whether Gina will be wearing red and black with gold jewellery, red and black with red jewellery or gold and black with gold jewellery? Boobs squished together and out or separated, up and out?'

'Well, that's bitchy,' said Joe.

'Come on,' said Anna. 'It's true. Red lipstick or red lipgloss? Black eyeliner or black*er* eyeliner?'

'Gina likes to make an effort. That's all. She's home with the kids all day, she likes to dress up when she goes out, make a statement.'

Anna's smile faded. She stared out the window.

'What?' said Joe. 'What did I say?'

'Nothing,' said Anna. 'Nothing.'

He stared ahead.

'Don't let her take me over,' said Anna. 'I don't want to get into a big conversation with her asking me lots of questions. It can be too claustrophobe.'

'Claustrophob-ic.'

'She's just question, question, question . . .'

'Oh for Christ's sake, why the hell did you come out? Have you got anything good to say? About anything?'

'This is hard for me,' said Anna, her voice rising. 'OK? I'm doing my best.'

'OK, sweetheart. I apologize. I'm sorry. I appreciate what you're trying to do here. I'll keep an eye on Gina.' He took a deep breath. The rest of the journey passed in silence.

Gina stood up and waved as they walked in to Pastis. She was wearing a tight black skirt, a black blouse with a lace cami underneath and a wide red patent belt. Anna squeezed Joe's hand. He squeezed back. Gina moved around the side of the table and hugged Anna tight.

'Honey, you look gorgeous. It's great to see you out. My God, have you lost weight? Like this girl needs to lose weight. I mean, really. But you look amazing.'

'Thanks,' said Anna. 'So do you. Happy birthday.'

'Hey, beautiful,' said Danny, kissing Anna on

both cheeks. Joe hugged Gina. 'Happy birthday, sweetheart.'

'So Anna, what's been going on with you?' said Gina.

'Not much. A little bit of work.'

'Danny tells me you're working from home.'

'Yes.'

'Good for you. And what's it like? Is it hard to discipline yourself? I know I couldn't do it. I'd be thinking of the laundry or tidying the bathroom or I'd be in the fridge all the day . . .'

'It's good. I'm enjoying it,' said Anna.

'How does it all work?'

'All these companies who want their products to appear in the magazine send me them – or photos of them – and pray I'll put them in.' She laughed.

'They actually send stuff to your house?'

Anna nodded.

'That's gotta be so much fun,' said Gina, 'opening gifts all day. Do you get to keep any of it?'

Joe leaned in. 'Unfortunately, she does. She keeps lots of it, don't you?' He was smiling.

'Ooh, Anna's not taken too kindly to that,' said Gina. She patted Anna's hand. 'Don't listen to him, sweetheart. All these guys get on the job is dead bodies and—'

'Dead ends,' said Anna, smiling.

'Ouch,' said Gina. Joe was already turning back to Danny.

The waiter arrived and took their order – four Steak Béarnaise, well done for Gina and Danny; extra fries for Danny, extra sauce for Anna, side salad for Gina that she never ate.

'I went to see Old Nic the other day,' said Joe.

'Aw. Mr Nicotero,' said Gina.

'Mr Nicotero, that's cute,' said Danny.

'I can't get past it,' said Gina, laughing. 'When I was dating Bobby, you know – his father was always going to be Mr Nicotero to me.'

'You dated Bobby Nicotero?' said Anna.

'He was the handsome quarterback, I was the head cheerleader.' She laughed.

'He's a big guy,' said Anna, 'but he doesn't look like an athlete.'

'He was really good,' said Danny.

'He's a jerk-off,' said Joe.

'Come on,' said Danny. 'He's not that bad.'

'He treats his old man like crap,' said Joe.

'Old Nic says that?' said Danny.

'I say that,' said Joe. 'Old Nic's too nice a guy.'

'Maybe he wasn't always,' said Anna.

'No,' said the others at the same time.

'Old Nic's adorable,' said Gina.

'I'm surprised Bobby ended up a cop,' said Danny.

'Why?' said Anna.

'Bensonhurst, honey,' said Gina. 'In those days, you were either a wise guy or you went into the service. Bobby was in gangs, that was his thing.'

'You know,' said Danny, 'Gina tried out a few of the bad boys before she gave in to me – didn't make my life too easy, that's for sure.'

Gina leaned away from him and slapped her hand on the table. 'Well, about time. That's the first time ever he's admitted that I gave in to him. Read the small print: he hounded me. He pursued me relentlessly, 24/7.'

Danny looked away. 'Whatever you say, sweetheart.'

Joe and Anna laughed.

'Now that I recall,' said Joe, 'you arrived on my doorstep a few times to hide from some wiseguy with a baseball bat.'

'I'm proud of you, honey,' said Gina. 'As far as I'm concerned? You gotta prove you want to die for someone before you—'

'Here's our food,' said Joe.

Dinner was over and two empty wine bottles had been taken away from the table. Gina got louder. Anna got quieter. After three barbed comments in a row she directed at Joe, Danny put up his hand.

'OK, who here ordered a side of marital discord with their steak? Anyone?'

Gina shook her head. Joe locked eyes with Danny, warning him off the humour route. Anna didn't look up from her plate.

'C'mon, I'm kidding,' said Danny. 'But I'm

sending it back, it doesn't taste right. It's kind of . . .
sour.' He turned to Gina, 'Hey. Where's my
laughter track tonight, baby?'

'I'll laugh when you say something funny. That's
how it works. Joe, how's your tiramisu?'

'It's totally sick,' said Joe. 'As I heard Tara say
to Shaun yesterday.'

Anna smiled. 'It's so funny to listen to her. For
me, sometimes, it's like a whole new language.'

'The other day,' said Joe, 'I heard her bitching
to Shaun about some guy who had "storked" one
of her friends.'

'Stalked?' said Gina.

'Storked. Like "porked", but with the end result
being that the girl winds up pregnant.'

They all laughed.

'That makes Danny a serial storker,' said Gina.

'And I am a lone storker,' said Joe.

'Shooting blanks for years,' said Danny.

'Amen to that,' said Joe. 'Sad and all as it will
be, Anna and I will be packing off our beloved
son to college next year and then we'll have the
freedom to—'

'Argue at full volume,' snapped Anna.

'Jesus, Anna,' said Joe. 'What's your—'

He watched as she bunched up her napkin, slid
her chair back from the table and stood up.

'I'm sorry,' she said. 'I have to go. I forgot to . . .
I have a conference call with . . . Paris.' She looked
at her watch.

Joe stared at her. 'No, you—'

'Enjoy the rest of the evening,' she said to all of them.

'Wait. I'll come with you,' said Joe, standing up, hitting the table hard with his knee.

'Stay,' said Anna. 'Please.' Her voice was cracking.

Joe looked from Danny to Gina.

'Stay,' said Anna. 'Have a night out.' She walked quickly through the restaurant, her head bowed.

'Guys, I really apologize,' said Joe. 'I have no idea . . .' He shrugged.

Gina squeezed his arm. 'She's had a rough time,' she said. 'You go. You look after her. She needs you.'

Joe followed Anna through the restaurant but he couldn't avoid stopping at one table.

'Oh. Hey, boss,' said Joe. 'How you doing?'

'Joe,' said Rufo, sliding his hand away from his date's. 'Good. I'm doing good.'

Joe nodded and looked towards the door where he could see Anna standing on the corner about to step out onto the cobbled street to hail a cab.

'This is my . . . this is Barbara Stenson,' said Rufo. He wiped his mouth with a napkin. 'Barbara, Detective Joe Lucchesi.'

Joe turned back to them, hovering.

'Hi,' said Barbara. 'Nice to meet you.'

'Likewise. Great place for dinner.'

'One of the best,' said Rufo.

'We like it.' Barbara nodded.

'You on your own?' said Rufo.

'Uh, no,' said Joe. 'I've had to rush off. I just left Danny Markey and Gina on their dessert.' He stared at Barbara as he spoke. She held his gaze.

'Well,' she said. 'After this, we were going to take a walk, have dessert somewhere else.'

Rufo frowned. 'We were?'

'Oh, yeah,' she said. 'My little surprise.'

Rufo looked like the happiest man alive.

'Catch you later,' said Joe, nodding.

'Take care,' said Rufo.

Joe didn't tell him he had sauce on his tie. And he definitely didn't tell him Danny had slept with his girlfriend.

TWELVE

Joe shared the elevator to the sixth floor with Irene, who he knew only from her name badge; black backing, gold print. They had never spoken. She had thin lips, flossy grey hair and sharp metal glasses. Joe pitied anyone who had to go through Irene to get what they wanted. They had taken the elevator with babies, bouquets of flowers, beautiful people, singing people, even a clown, and none of them had cracked her. She represented a day he hoped he wouldn't have.

The smell of Colombian coffee filled the office, but when he went to get some, both pots were empty. The detectives in the task force corner all had fresh cups.

Denis Cullen sat alone at his desk.

'Yes,' he said suddenly, slamming his hands onto the desk. He stood up. 'Everyone? I've got the perp's way in.'

'Go ahead,' said Joe.

'He's got something the vics want,' said Cullen. He cleared his throat. 'All the vics cancelled their credit cards a week or two before they died.'

Some of the men nodded. Others waited for more.

'Right, OK,' said Joe. 'So they all had their wallets stolen. That would explain Lowry's two wallets. He got the cards re-issued. Then he gets his original one back. The night he died.'

Cullen nodded. 'Perp's got their wallet means he has their address, phone number, place of work. Calls them up, they're so grateful. And hey, everyone's going to trust the guy who's honest enough to return a wallet.'

'He can spend as long as he likes with it before-hand,' said Joe, 'thinking about the victim's poten-tial, looking through their things, checking where they shop. He can call the house at different times, see whether there's always someone home. He might rule someone out if they've kids, someone with kids is going to have photos in the wallet—'

'Lowry had a kid,' said Rencher.

'Yeah,' said Joe, 'but every Sunday they went to her ma's. The perp could have noticed that, Lowry could have mentioned it on the phone, we don't know.'

'Also,' said Cullen. 'He can take a wallet and never choose that person as a victim. He could have wallets of people he's never called.'

'Bobby, Pace – you were on the phone records,

right?' said Joe. 'No-one noticed they all must have got an incoming call the night they died?'

'That's not for sure,' said Bobby.

'Well, did you notice anything unusual in the incoming phone records?' said Joe.

'We would have said,' said Pace.

'Do you mind if I take a look at them?' said Cullen.

'Sure. Go ahead,' said Bobby. 'Knock yourself out.'

Joe was walking away when the phone on his desk rang.

'Detective Lucchesi? Joe Lucchesi?'

'Yeah.'

'My name is Preston Blake.'

'Yeah?'

'I . . . uh . . . is this confidential?'

'If that's what you want, sure,' said Joe.

There was silence at the other end. Then faint breathing, deep, but quiet.

'Sir? What can I do for you?' said Joe.

'You're working on The Caller case. I saw your name in the paper.'

'Yeah.'

'I think . . . The Caller . . .' He inhaled, long and slow.

Joe waited.

'He tried to kill me.'

Joe sat down. 'Kill you?'

'Yes.'

'When did this happen?'

'Six months ago.'

'Mr Blake, have you been following all the media reports on the investigation?'

'Yes . . . but that's not why I'm calling. This is real. This really happened.'

'Is this your first time getting in touch with us, Mr Blake?'

'Yes. Why do you ask?'

'No reason,' said Joe. 'Please, tell me what makes you think it was The Caller.'

'I let him into my home, he stripped me naked and beat my face and pulled a gun on me.'

'How did you get away?'

'I overpowered him and he ran.'

'Are you sure it was the same guy?'

'Did any of the victims have . . . was there a phone near them . . . ?'

This time Joe went silent.

'Mr Blake, can I take some of your details? My partner and I would like to pay a visit to your house, talk to you a bit more, if that's all right with you.'

'I . . . don't know if it is.'

'Let me start with getting a few details, OK? Your name again.'

'Preston. P-R-E-S-T-O-N Blake.'

'Date of birth?'

'04/16/72.'

'And where do you live?' said Joe.

'1890 Willow Street in Brooklyn Heights.'

'Me and my partner would like to drop by. You home this afternoon?'

'I don't know if I can do this. I . . . no-one has been here since . . . no-one.'

'You've made this call, Mr Blake. That means you want to help. We're not going to do anything to make things worse for you. I can promise you that. We'll stop by, ask you some questions and then we'll be outta there. If this is the killer, you'd like to see him caught, right?'

Blake sucked in a deep breath. 'You must have seen what he did to his victims. You must have seen their corpses . . . the living proof might be harder to take.'

Brooklyn Heights was a quiet upper middle class neighborhood, one subway stop – but a world away – from Wall Street. At three o'clock on a Wednesday afternoon, the main action on the residential streets was nannies with strollers taking kids to the tiny playground by the promenade.

'These are some very nice houses,' said Joe.

He took a left onto Willow Street, lined with trees and perfectly kept terraced brownstones. Preston Blake's house was on the right-hand side, close to the corner, a narrow, three-storey over-basement Anglo-Italianate design with an antique black door.

Joe rang the bell and spoke into the intercom.

'Mr Blake? It's Detectives Joe Lucchesi, Danny Markey.' They held their badges up to a small security camera mounted in the right-hand corner above the door. After several seconds, they heard a series of muted beeps from inside. They waited, then counted the halting slide of bolts that ran from the top of the door to its base. The door opened inwards, but was hinged on the same side as the keyhole. Joe and Danny exchanged glances. No-one appeared. Joe pushed the door gently and walked inside. His chest was hit with a constricting spasm as he took in the vast white expanse around him. Suspended from the ceiling by thick steel cables were evenly spaced rows of six-foot tall, two-foot wide white perspex bookshelves. White, high-gloss floor tiles shone with the reflected overkill of hundreds of shelf-mounted spotlights. Joe stepped forward and felt a surge of regret. Every book title was a desperate search for relief, a net cast wide across disciplines; acupuncture, angels, auras, Buddhism, meditation, reflexology, reiki, yoga. Joe and Danny hovered, emotional intruders. They turned to the man who didn't look like he'd found an answer in any of these pages.

Blake raised his hands. 'Don't worry. I have *The DaVinci Code* too.' He flashed a lopsided smile from the right-hand side of his mouth. A small pool of saliva leaked onto his lower lip. He dabbed at it with a handkerchief. 'But codes . . .' He gestured

to the security panel by the door. 'I'm sure
someone could . . . well, maybe that's not a great
leap.'

Joe smiled.

'Anyway, hello.' Blake stretched out his hand
from behind the door.

'Thanks for letting us come over,' said Joe,
shaking it firmly.

Blake was lean and stooped. Whatever he had
been through had left his face older and shadowed, his most striking feature, loose flesh hanging
under dark, weary eyes. The skin on the right side
of his chin was lumpy and uneven. He was dressed
in baggy chinos and a lightweight black turtle-
neck. A red baseball cap was pulled low on his
head. Panic flickered in his eyes. Danny followed
his gaze to the open door and quickly closed it.
Blake walked past him and ground the bolts back
into place.

'Follow me,' he said when he was finished.

He led them through the complex of shelves
and through heavy white double doors into a
sparse and spacious living room. The floors were
polished oak, the walls soft yellow. There was no
dining table, no sideboard. Heavy green drapes
hung down by the windows.

Blake sat on a white sofa facing the door and
gestured to the matching one opposite. Danny and
Joe sat down.

'You've got a nice home here,' said Joe.

'Thank you,' said Blake. 'Can I offer you something to drink, coffee . . .'

'Coffee would be great,' said Joe.

'Yeah,' said Danny. 'Thanks. Black for both of
us.'

Blake paused, but got up and walked across
the room to a discreet door that led into a dim
hallway. Joe stood up and wandered over to a
vase of dried white flowers that stood by the huge,
empty fireplace. Just behind it, Joe noticed the
corner of a picture frame. He bent down and
picked it up. In it was a faded colour photograph
that looked like it was taken in the eighties – an
older couple, the man thin and stern, the woman
chubby, heavily made up and with a sparkle in
her eye.

'My parents,' said Blake, coming back in, smiling
at the photo. 'They adored each other.' He set a
tray on an ottoman between them with three
mugs of black coffee.

'How long have you been living here?' said Joe.

'All my life. My parents both passed away. I
have no siblings.'

'What do you do for a living?'

'I make jewelry.'

'Did you make that?' said Joe, pointing to a
black leather cuff Blake was wearing.

Blake nodded.

'My son wears things like that.'

'I have more up in my—'

'I'm sorry,' said Joe. 'I didn't mean—'

'It's not a problem. It'd be a pleasure.'

Joe smiled. 'Thanks, but he needs to get a handle on his schoolwork before I come back with any gifts for him.'

'Well, let me know if he does.'

'Thanks,' said Joe. 'So, where do you work?'

'Here.' He gestured upstairs.

'So does that mean customers come to your home or suppliers or whoever? I'm just trying to get a feel for people who would know you, know the house.'

'I have a small client base. I design high-end pieces, made to order. I will meet with a client at their home, discuss designs, go away and create. None of them come here.'

'OK. Suppliers?'

'I get the leather sent here. Metals and diamonds I go to 47th Street.'

'You have cleaning staff? Delivery people coming through?'

'No. I'm the cleaning staff.'

'For the whole house?'

'I got a lot of time on my hands,' said Blake.

'Have you ever been the victim of another crime?' said Joe.

'Like what?'

'A burglary, a robbery?'

Blake shook his head. 'No – why?'

'Or even had your wallet stolen?' said Joe.

Blake frowned. 'No. Never. Why?'

'Just wondering. OK. Do you think you could talk us through what happened that night?'

'I don't know,' said Blake.

'You take your time,' said Danny. 'We think you'll be able to do it. We really do. That's why we're here.'

Blake took off his baseball cap, smoothed down the black, wiry hair that bounced up, then put it back on. He took a deep breath. 'It was Monday night. March 13th, I think. I was home watching a movie . . . two movies. Back to back.'

'What about that morning?' said Joe. 'I'm going to need as much detail as I can about what you were doing that day, where you went, who you spoke with . . . I'm sorry, but it's important. If the perp chose you, it could be that by some twist of fate, a change in your routine meant you crossed paths with him. Monday, you stop for coffee at the deli outside your apartment building, Tuesday you hold off 'til you get to the subway, right next to the killer's hotdog stand. You get the picture.'

'OK,' said Blake. 'I got up. And I started work immediately. I didn't go out that day. And no-one called. I get so absorbed in work sometimes, I lose track of time. Which, I guess wouldn't make me the most reliable witness.' He smiled. 'I can't even tell you what time he called to my door.'

'Don't worry,' said Danny. 'Neither of us know,

here, what details might help. That's why we'll go back and forth with some questions and answers and see what comes up. How about that?'

Blake nodded. 'I'm sorry. This is so hard.'

'I understand that,' said Danny. 'But I'm betting you'll feel a hell of a lot better once you've got it all out.'

'It was late,' said Blake. 'He . . . he called to my door, saying he was a realtor. He was admiring the building and asked to talk to me about selling or wanted to tell me about house prices in the area . . .'

'And you let him in.'

'Yes. I let him in. He had material from Acheson & Grant, the realtors on Montague Street . . . and yes, I know, it sounds kind of dumb.' He took in what looked like it would be a deep breath, but ended up halting and shallow.

'It's the way we are,' said Danny, 'most of us want to trust people. Even I want that.'

'Thanks,' said Blake. 'So I invited him in to the foyer and next thing I remember, I was under the kitchen counter—'

'Sorry – before that,' said Joe. 'When you opened the door, did you get a good look at the guy? Could you describe him?'

Blake shook his head. 'I wish I could. What I can tell you is he was slightly shorter than me, maybe five nine? He was normal build, that's the best I can do. And his clothes were black – you

know, as opposed to the usual bright pink crimi-
nals wear.' He smiled. So did Danny and Joe.

'He must have looked like a realtor to you –
so, was he in a suit?' said Joe.

Blake shrugged. 'From what I remember. I
think. But I couldn't swear to it.'

'What about hair color?'

'I don't know. Blond? Grey? I think it was light.'

'Or any facial features that stood out?' said Joe.

'Not that I can think of. Believe me,' said Blake.
'I've spent so much time going through that night,
replaying everything . . . if I haven't remembered
already, I don't think I ever will.'

'It's OK,' said Danny. 'Don't get yourself worked
up about it. Something might come back to you
again. Let's go back to after you woke up on the
kitchen floor.'

'Everything felt wrong. I remember peeling one
eye open, literally, with my fingers, because it was
stuck shut with blood. I was lying in a foetal position under the island at the centre and I could
make out, above me, the corner of the work
surface.'

'Can we go take a look at the kitchen?' said
Joe.

'Sure.'

Blake led them down the hallway. A bike leaned
against the wall with a black helmet hanging from
the handlebars. The kitchen was a modern chunky
design, granite, walnut and stainless steel. Blake

stood by the island and rested a hand on the corner.

'My own blood was dripping down onto me from here. I remember raising my hand up towards it to prove it. I thought I was in the middle of a nightmare; you know the part where you start to realize what you're experiencing isn't real and something physical you do will wake you up; like, you wake up when you're just about to walk out in front of a speeding car?

'I can't describe how I felt knowing that this was real, just the combination of sensations in my head – these throbbing, aching, piercing, stabbing pains. And I can not describe the terror of hearing his footsteps come back towards me.' He looked away. A tear ran down his face.

'He came back?' said Danny.

Blake nodded. 'And somewhere inside me, I got this overwhelming urge to get away, like an actual physical sensation. I . . . I basically dragged myself off the floor and was on my hands and knees by the time he walked back in. I made it look like I was about to collapse back on the floor, but instead when he came closer, I kind of jumped up and I punched him, really hard. He staggered backwards into the foyer. That's when I saw he had a gun in his waistband. And when I looked past him, I could see he had laid something out on the floor, I don't know what it was. But I knew he was going to do something to me

there. So I punched him again, back towards the
door. He had my phone – the cordless phone.
That went flying out of his hand. He didn't go
pick it up. And then, he . . . I mean, I guess he
wasn't expecting I would fight back. He grabbed
what he had left by the door and . . . he was
gone.'

'Did he tell you why he was there, why he was
doing this to you?' said Joe.

'No.'

'Did he speak at all?'

'No.'

'What do you think he had left in the foyer?'

'I couldn't see.'

'What did you do after the attack?' said Joe.

'I cleaned myself up, I took some sleeping pills
and I went to bed.'

'Didn't you need stitches?' said Danny.

'Probably. I managed. Well,' he said pointing to
his chin. 'Maybe not. But I didn't want to see
anyone, didn't want to go to a doctor. I just wanted
to get into bed and sleep through it all.'

'Why did you not come forward earlier?' said
Joe.

Blake sighed. 'There are several reasons, I guess.
The first is, like anyone, I didn't ask for this, it
was forced on me. If you're a private person to
start with, you're definitely not going to want to
be public at the most personal, damaging time of
your life. Do you know what I mean? When I see

people on TV with a microphone thrust into their face as they're walking away from an explosion or a shooting, I can't bear it. I turn it off. Everyone wants to be inside everyone else's pain these days. I don't think it's right. Do you remember when you could watch the news or read the papers and you would barely see blood or dead bodies and it was all just too sanitised? Then they gradually began showing us more of the reality of war and violence and it worked to an extent, it woke people up to what happens in the world. But that point has been made. Now it's all about satisfying this imagined prurient curiosity we all have. We want to see how violent death looks on someone's face. We want to see how losing your wife two minutes ago looks on someone's face. It's not right. I would never want to be looked at that way. I think it's the worst kind of invasion. Worse for me than this Caller entering my home.'

'This will be kept within the task force,' said Joe. 'You don't have anything to worry about.'

'Thank you. I'm also thinking of my neighbors. Another reason I didn't come forward – this is going to sound nuts – was the residents' association around here. They work so hard for everyone, making sure the neighborhood is not compromised in any way. It would devastate them if they knew about this. Also, if in any way . . . you know . . . I invited this on myself—'

'This is not your fault,' said Danny.

'Other people might feel differently.'

'And why did you come forward now?' said Joe.

'When I saw that press conference, I felt I would have support. I would have the backing of the Police Commissioner and the detectives investigating this. And I guess I felt I could speak out for the guys who didn't make it.'

'We appreciate you talking to us,' said Joe. 'We don't always have a victim who gets away.'

'Why do you think he's targeting us?' said Blake. 'Me and the other victims.'

'He mightn't like what you represent to him,' said Danny.

'But—' said Blake.

'We're not sure why,' said Joe. 'We're looking at different things. Talking to you helps us get closer to what that might be.'

'Do you think he's crazy?'

'Did he seem crazy to you?' said Joe.

'Uh, I guess not. I don't know. Isn't he crazy to do what he's doing?'

'Maybe not,' said Joe. 'We'll know when we find him.'

'Do you think you're getting close?'

'We have lots of information we're working on, some very reliable directions to go in.'

'Do you think . . . look, I guess what I want to know is . . . do you think he'll come back for me?'

'I see no reason why he would do that, Mr

Blake. He left when he had the chance. I don't think he's going to come back around. Why would he?'

'The house appears to be very safe,' said Danny. 'Look, if you're ever worried about anything, take our cards, call us.'

'Thank you.' He stood up. They shook hands and walked to the front door.

'Did you have that security system all along or just . . . after?' said Joe, pointing to the keypad by the door.

Blake nodded. 'After.' He shrugged. 'But even if I had it before, it wouldn't have mattered if I was going to go inviting the guy into my house anyway. I mean, a security system is only as good as the guy with the codes.'

'We had a guy once who wrote the combination to his safe on the ceiling above it,' said Danny. 'We have people who never change the factory settings, which are the same in a lot of places. That's one thing you got to do.'

'Oh, I do everything that has to be done,' said Blake. 'I keep closing the gate and the horse has bolted so long ago . . .'

'You do whatever you need to feel safe,' said Danny.

'Thanks for coming. I guess I'm lucky I can hole myself up here and not have to face the world if I don't want to.'

Joe thought of Anna and felt a stab of guilt for

making a link. 'Thank you for your time, Mr Blake.'

'Yeah,' said Danny.

'No problem,' said Blake. 'Take care.'

THIRTEEN

Rufo sat in his office chewing cherry Gas X, thinking it was time to give up on raw broccoli. Just because something was good for you, didn't mean it tasted good. Or that your body reacted well to it.

'So,' he said when Joe and Danny walked in. 'How did Brooklyn Heights work out for you?'

'The guy's name is Blake,' said Danny. 'Rencher did a work-up on him and he's clean. Lives in a nice house – he's got a foyer. He has never been in trouble, pays his taxes. He looked expensive—'

'Yeah, but did you see those Target bags in the hallway by the bike?' said Joe. 'Maybe he doesn't like to spend his money too much.'

'Either way,' said Danny, 'he's another rich guy who finally realizes it doesn't protect you from shit. I feel sorry for him, don't get me wrong. There's something just so fucking tragic about him.'

'Gay, straight?' said Rufo.

'Straight.'

'What makes him think he was a victim of our perp?' said Rufo.

'He talked about letting the guy into the house,' said Joe, 'no struggle, he was bashed off the corner of a work surface, guy had a gun—'

'But,' said Danny, 'the wallet ruse wasn't used on him – the guy said he was a realtor.'

'Yeah,' said Joe. 'But it's just not like on TV. No-one is going to work the same way every time. It's not natural. Like no-one does anything exactly the same way every time . . .'

Danny nodded.

'I think what's important to the perp is bashing in the vics' faces and finishing them off with a twenty-two,' said Joe. 'They're the two things that have not changed in each homicide. He doesn't care how he gets there. So he chooses one mode of entry, restrains them one way, one time, another way the next.'

'Maybe the only thing he cares about is bashing in their faces,' said Rufo. 'And shooting them is just to make sure they'll never identify him.' He shrugged.

'Jesus, Blake's face was something else . . .' said Danny. 'I mean, I was firefighting.'

Rufo looked at him. 'You were what?'

Joe answered. 'Firefighting. It's when there's a bunch of reactions Danny wants to have, but can't because they're not appropriate. He imagines them as fires inside his mind that he has to put out—'

Danny nodded. 'First I wanted to shout out "Holy shit!" Then I wanted to puke. Then I wanted to reach over and just feel that weird skin. Then I wanted to take a picture with my phone. So,' he said reasonably, 'I had to put my energies into controlling these impulses. Firefighting.'

Rufo shook his head. 'Do you have one of those firefighter's poles inside too so's we can get the happy pills into you quicker? You're a fucking nut job, Markey. Really, I'd like to know what one of New York's finest looks like to another human being when all this firefighting shit is happening.'

'Don't worry about it, boss,' said Joe. 'He's worked it into some sort of sane-looking stare.'

'Sometimes I tilt an eyebrow,' said Danny, 'touch a few fingers to the chin area.'

Rufo shook his head. 'I spend my whole time shaking my head around you, Markey. It's an impulse I just can't control.'

'Hey, I think I can work with you on that,' said Danny.

'Get out, get out of my office,' said Rufo, smiling.

Victor Nicotero was sitting at his kitchen table with a beer, a notebook and a silver pen. Joe walked right in.

'Nice security system,' he said.

'Patti,' said Old Nic shaking his head. 'The

woman is like a force of nature. Closing doors, turning off lights, they're just not things she thinks about.'

Joe laughed. 'It was wide open.'

'Your serial guy could have butchered me to death.'

'I think he likes the city too much.'

'Let's go out on the deck. I'm done here.'

'You're writing it all longhand?'

'Longhand,' said Nic. 'I'm writing it. That's what it's called – writing. Whether my hands are long or short doesn't come into it.'

Joe took a beer from the fridge and sat out beside him.

'Would you like to move in?' said Nic.

Joe smiled. 'And live with your grumpy ass? No. I'll take my chances with an out-of-control teenager.'

'Easy when there's a beautiful French woman tied into the deal. How are things there? You take my advice?'

'Course I did. And things were better,' said Joe. 'And then she storms out of dinner last night.'

'Hormones,' said Nic. 'They go nuts. Every frickin—'

The kitchen door banged open behind them and heavy footsteps tracked through to the sliding door. Joe and Nic looked up. Bobby leaned out, a cheap bouquet of flowers in his hand. He frowned, then glanced around the garden.

'Is ma here?' he said. He barely nodded at Joe.

'She's at the store,' said Nic. 'Do you want a beer?'

'Uh – no, thank you. Ma wanted me to fix some door in the bedroom, there's some problem—'

'I took care of it,' said Nic. 'Sit down, it's a nice evening.'

'You took care of it?' said Bobby. 'When did you do that?'

'This afternoon. She's been bothering me about it for weeks.'

'Yeah, which is why I came over,' said Bobby.

'You were here with her at the weekend – why didn't you do it then?'

'What are you talking about? You were the one who was supposed to—' Bobby glanced towards Joe who had picked up a magazine from the table.

'Have you eaten?' said Nic.

'No,' said Bobby and Joe àt the same time.

'Sorry,' said Joe. 'I thought you meant me.'

'I meant both of you,' said Nic.

'I can't hang around,' said Joe.

'No, you stay where you are,' said Bobby. 'I'm going to go see the kids, now that I'm out here. These are for ma,' he said, raising the flowers. 'I'll leave them by the sink.'

'OK,' said Nic. 'You take care.' He let out a breath and turned to Joe. But Joe sat in silence, staring into the distance, thinking about Shaun.

*   *   *

The next morning, Joe made it in to the office
early to get his suits ready for the dry cleaning
service that picked up three times a week. He liked
to keep two full sets of clothes in his locker, but
he was down to one. He was walking back to his
desk when his phone rang.

'Joe, it's Giulio.'

'Hi. Everything all right?'

'Yes. I saw your name in the paper the other
day.'

'Yeah?'

'Yes. It's a shame.'

'What's a shame?'

'All that attention.'

'What attention?'

'Can't they leave you out of it?'

'Who?'

'The media.'

'Dad, I haven't even spoken to one journalist.
They do their thing. I'm someone who was
involved in some prominent cases. They make
something of it, that's not my fault.'

'What I mean is you're in the spotlight again,
people are dredging up what happened to you and
Anna and Shaun. You've got to think what this
is doing to the family every time you put yourself out there.'

'Here we go,' said Joe. 'I am not "putting myself
out there" for the hell of it. I am heading up an
investigation. It's not like I heard there was a few

homicides and some media attention and I said, "Great, yeah, sign me up for that, please make me the case detective."'

'I'm just saying—'

'I know what you're saying. Your facts are wrong. You can't control the whole world, OK?'

'I'm . . . concerned.'

'Yeah, great. Look, I gotta go.'

Joe put down the phone and walked over to the coffee machine. It stank of sour milk and burned coffee. There were rings on the surfaces and coffee grounds scattered on the floor.

'Everyone, clean up, already,' he shouted. 'Stop leaving this for Ruthie to do. She cracks because she can't stand the mess. It's not her job. She is too busy doing every other fucking job for you lazy sons of bitches!'

'Thank you, Joe!' shouted Ruthie from the reception desk.

'Sorry, Mom,' shouted Martinez.

Joe grabbed a paper towel and started wiping the surfaces. He bent down to pick up a ball of paper that had missed the bin. It was a stray print-out from the Pages program he used. He opened it out. Someone had written 'Season's Greetings' across the top in red felt-tip pen and drawn Santa hats on all the victims. Handwritten under the photo of Gary Ortis was: 'Greetings from the Ortis family. This year Gary was murdered! His battered body was found in his hallway! He spent hours

being tortured! And his killer's still on the loose!
Haaappy Holidays!'

Joe looked around the room at the people who
first came together on this case: Denis Cullen – a
man who would rather stare at figures all day so
he could save his energy for visiting his sick little
girl. Tom Blazkow – tough and thorough, Aldos
Martinez – dedicated, but narrow-minded, Roger
Pace – nothing more than Bobby Nicotero's long
skinny shadow, Fred Rencher – good guy, but not
too sharp. And then Bobby Nicotero – Joe glanced
down at the page – and his girlie handwriting.

'For Christ's sake, Lucchesi, that's your freakin'
phone,' shouted Martinez from across the room.

Joe threw the paper back into the bin and went
to his desk.

'Detective Lucchesi? Preston Blake.'

Joe couldn't tell whether it was the line that
had a hiss in it or Preston Blake's voice.

'Oh, hi—

'You fucking asshole.'

'Mr Blake?' said Joe, sitting down.

'You clueless son of a bitch.' He was sobbing.

Joe looked around the room, but couldn't find
anyone to get eye contact with. His cell phone
vibrated on the desk in front of him. It was
Danny.

'Mr Blake, could you hold a moment?' said Joe,
punching the button anyway.

'Joe? It's Danny. I'm on my way in. Have you

seen the front page of the *Post*? Do not take a call from Preston Blake until you do.'

'What the hell is going on? And you're too late – I've got him on hold.'

'Uh-oh. Go to Martinez's desk. He'll have a copy. Blake has been named by the press as "the one who got away". How the hell did that happen?'

'How do I know?' said Joe, walking over to Martinez's desk and picking up the newspaper. 'Shit,' he said. 'We were the only ones who knew. I mean, very few people knew I was there. Rencher, Martinez, me, you, Rufo.'

'Think you can hang up on him? Think the line might be faulty?'

'I'd love to.'

'Or tell him you think you hear someone at his front door.'

Joe laughed. 'I'll do the honorable thing . . .'

'What? Put him through to Rufo?'

'Something like that. Gotta go.'

'Call me after.'

Joe took the handset back up. 'My apologies, Mr Blake. Could you give me the opportunity to read through the article before we have this conversation?'

'Let me save you the trouble. *"Preston Blake, seen here in happier times"* – insert smiling photo – *"before he became the alleged victim of The Caller, the only one lucky enough to survive his horrendous attack."* And *"Preston Blake has been living the life of a recluse in his luxury Brooklyn Heights brownstone, rumoured to be the location of his vicious assault six months ago. Mr Blake refused to comment on The Caller's latest victim, following the discovery of the mutilated body of Ethan Lowry on September 7th."* And let's skip down here: *"While unclear how prolonged his ordeal was at the hands of The Caller or how extensive his injuries, Mr Blake has been visited by Manhattan North Homicide Detective Joe Lucchesi for assistance in his inquiries. Detective Lucchesi came to prominence –"* and then there's a bit about your tale of suffering and woe. You have my sympathies for that, as do your wife and son, but I am furious here. I am betrayed and exposed.'

'I feel for you, Mr Blake. I really do. But I can promise you I had nothing to do with this disclosure. I have respected your wishes throughout this whole process. Would you like us to have someone watch the house? Would you feel safer?'

'No. I invited you into my home, Detective. Do you know how many people have been inside my home since the attack?' He paused. 'I don't have visitors. I spend months, sequestered, happily, if that makes sense, you show up and the game is up. Did you see? I've made the news. "How ironic" people will think in the way that stupid people do not understand the meaning of the word ironic—'

'I don't know what happened here, but I can

assure you this did not come from me or anyone involved in the investigation.'

'I just don't buy that. Because it sure as hell did not come from me. This should not have gotten out. Can you imagine how violated I feel? Violation after violation. Is that what I can expect from life now, Detective? Do I sit back and accept that fate?'

'You don't. This will pass. The press are more interested in the perp. Because they didn't have a bright, shiny new victim this week, yours is the story they went for. How they got it, we don't know, but they'll move on.'

'Just like me, Detective. I've nothing more to say. What you need to do now is read and re-read every word of what I told you the day I was foolish enough to let you into my home. And here's hoping you'll find enlightenment in those pages. Because my cooperation ends there.'

'It can't.'

'Oh yes it can.'

'But you're the only one who has seen—'

'I've told you everything. And honestly? I can't imagine a time where I'm sitting on the stand pointing at The Caller across a courtroom. Because I can't imagine a time where you will gain the insight to apprehend him. If you ain't got him now, Detective, you ain't never will.'

'I disagree, Mr Blake. My colleagues and I won't let that happen.'

'Your colleagues and you are leaking, Detective.

And a leaky vessel won't hold water. And a leaky vessel sinks.'

Joe hung up on the dial tone and went to Rufo's office.

'Come in,' said Rufo. 'Close the door.'

'You see the—'

'*Post*? Yeah I did. What's going on?'

Joe shook his head. 'Blake is really pissed. He just called saying all kinds of shit, me and Danny ratted him out, left him exposed . . .'

'What did you say?'

'I set him straight, obviously, but he didn't want to listen.'

'Do you know the guy who wrote this? Artie Blackwell? Why don't you make a few calls, see if we can find out who did tip him off.'

'Artie fucking Blackwell. I didn't notice.'

Rufo scanned the page again. 'Whole thing seems kinda weird to me. You think Blake likes the attention?'

'Not if you heard him on the phone just now. The guy's like a recluse, far as I can tell.'

'Was he screaming for the Chief, the mayor, Larry King Live?'

'Nah.'

'Was he looking for anything else? Did you tell him we can have a few guys watch the house?'

'Yeah. He wasn't interested.'

'OK,' said Rufo. 'Let me put a call in to him, see if I can't talk him off the ledge.'

'Danny and me are heading out,' said Joe. 'Surveillance on the post office.'

'Good luck,' said Rufo, reaching for the phone.

There was never a weekday quiet time on 21st Street. Danny and Joe were parked opposite the post office where the letters were mailed. The air conditioning was on high and the sun was beating down on the shiny black hood. Danny and Joe were quietly focused on everyone entering and leaving the building.

Suddenly, something slammed against the driver's window. Joe turned to see the white hairy crack of someone's ass pressed up against the glass. Outside someone else was roaring, 'You mother-fucker! You fucking motherfucker!'

A huge paper cup landed on the car, splashing strawberry milkshake up onto the windshield of Manhattan North's new Chevy Impala.

'Son of a bitch,' said Danny.

Joe hammered his forearm against the glass and shouted. 'Get away from the car.'

Danny got out the passenger side. 'What's going on here?' he said to the two men.

'None of your business,' said the guy forcing the other one against Joe's window. He was massively overweight and the skinny guy under-neath him was feeling the pressure.

'You're going to suffocate him if you don't get up off of him,' said Danny. 'And either way, my friend in there is going to climb out the passenger door and kill you both. Now, back away from the car.'

The overweight guy pulled his friend off the door and Joe got out.

'What's going on?' said Joe. 'That I need to get so intimately acquainted with your spotty ass?'

The skinny guy checked behind him and pulled up his jeans.

'I . . . I . . .' said the fat guy, gradually realizing he was dealing with two cops.

'We don't care,' said Danny. 'Long as you're not going to hurt your friend here, we just want you to get away from our car.'

'Sure,' said the fat guy.

The skinny guy had a plastic Gristedes shopping bag beside him on the ground. He bent down and pulled out a liter bottle of Poland Springs and handed it to Joe.

'For the car,' he said, pointing at the milkshake.

'Thank you,' said Joe, turning to Danny.

'This is a caring neighborhood,' said Danny.

Joe poured the water over the hood and got rid of as much of the milkshake as he could. They got back in the car. Joe ignored the greasy smear on the driver's window. He flicked on the wipers and a watery mix of milkshake and soap washed across the glass. As it was clearing, Danny sat forward. 'Check this guy out,' he said.

The man walking towards the post office was

about five foot eight, in his mid-forties, dressed in pristine blue Carhartt workpants, heavy black boots and a denim shirt with two buttons open and the sleeves rolled up. He had light brown hair, thinning on top and an unremarkable face. They looked at the photos they had printed from the tape.

'That's our guy,' said Joe. 'Let's go.'

They jumped from the car and ran. 'Police,' shouted Joe, flashing his badge. The man didn't move. He stood, frozen, with his letter. Joe grabbed his wrists, yanking them hard behind his back and snapping cuffs on him.

'Tell us your name, sir. What is your name?'

'Stanley Frayte! My name is Stanley Frayte! What are you doing? What have I done?'

FOURTEEN

Danny pushed Stanley Frayte into the back of the car and Joe drove them silently the half mile from the post office to the 114th precinct on Astoria Boulevard. They left Stan in the interview room alone and waited outside. Joe got some gloves and opened the envelope. This time, the writing was on a cheap napkin stained with ketchup and mustard. He photocopied it and put it in a plastic bag.

'Jesus, this one is different,' said Joe. 'He sounds very anxious. Listen to this: *"Oh, God. But he can find me now. If it's a game, I don't understand. My life is here. I'm terrified. Please, please. It can't change. Look closer. I thought you would find him. It can't change. I don't know if you're playing a game. It's so wrong. I don't want it to change. Ask more questions. I can't have it taken away. Something is not right. Just not too many. You can't find me too"*.' He put it down. 'Well I think we found you now, you son of a bitch.'

'Short and sweet,' said Danny.

'And really scrawled,' said Joe. 'I mean, even more than the other one. This looks really rushed.'

'Well I guess it's easier to rush a napkin,' said Danny.

'It's weird shit,' said Joe.

'Let's see what Mr Frayte has to say,' said Danny.

When they went back in, Stan was asleep. Danny and Joe exchanged glances; the ones who slept when they were taken in were usually the guilty ones. An innocent man would spend the time desperately trying to work out why he was there. There was often a relief in the guilty that the lie was over, the game was up and they could relax enough to snooze.

'Mr Frayte,' said Danny, shaking his shoulder. 'Mr Frayte.' He shook harder.

Stan woke up, irritated, then tried to calm himself when he saw where he was.

'I'm sorry,' he said, rubbing his face.

'Do you know why you're here?' said Joe.

Stan shrugged. 'No.'

'Well why don't you have a think about what you were doing when we picked you up,' said Danny.

Stan paused. 'Mailing a letter,' he said.

'Glad you seem so happy about that,' said Danny.

'Yes. I was mailing Mary's letter,' said Stan.

'Who's Mary?' said Danny.

'Mary Burig.'

'Yeah?' said Danny. 'Who's this Mary Burig?'

'Please,' said Stan. 'Can we tone this all down? You're making me anxious.'

Danny looked at Joe.

'I've done nothing wrong,' said Stan, shifting in his seat, sitting up straighter.

'Tell us about Mary,' said Joe.

'Mary is a patient,' said Stan, 'well, not a patient, a *client* at the Colt-Embry Homes, a couple of blocks away. Part of the Rehab Clinic.'

'Meaning?' said Danny.

'Meaning what?' said Stan.

'Patient/client – what's that all about?' said Danny.

'I guess Mary – like all the other clients in the building – is there because she got a brain injury.'

'Everyone staying in these apartments has a brain injury?' said Joe.

'Yes. You go there after rehab, but before you go home. To help, you know, initiate yourself into society.'

Danny locked eyes with Joe and slowly shook his head.

'So what you're saying is this Mary is brain damaged,' said Danny.

Stan's jaw clenched. 'No. I am not saying that.' He paused. 'In fact, I would hate to say that.' He shrugged. 'I guess you guys can say what you like.'

'What's your relationship with Mary, exactly?' said Joe.

'None. I mean, I kind of know her, she's a nice girl. I'm an electrician/handyman working in the apartment building she lives in. That's it.'

'Why were you mailing letters for her?' said Danny.

'Because she asked me to. Jeez. There's no mystery to this. She's a nice girl. She asked me a favour. I go out on my morning break. I mail her letters.' He shrugged.

'Did you know why she was mailing them?'

'No idea. To be honest, I didn't even read the envelopes. None of my business.'

'You never read the envelopes,' said Joe.

'Sure,' said Danny.

'I did not,' said Stan. 'Privacy is a big thing there. Clients have got to feel respected. I would never want to upset anyone. Look, I've told you everything. Can I go now?'

'No you can not,' said Joe.

'You're an electrician, right?' said Danny.

'Yes.' Stan nodded.

'So you got the keys to a lot of houses, a lot of apartments,' said Danny.

'What do you mean?' said Stan.

'Do you or don't you?'

'Sure I do. But so do lots of people. A lot of people have a lot of keys.'

'You gotta understand,' said Joe. 'That not a lot of them are mailing letters to the case detective of a serial homicide.'

'Homicide? Oh, no. You're not investigating that Caller guy, are you? You think . . . Oh my God. No way. No way. What's Mary mailing you guys for?'

'Well that's what we'd like to know,' said Joe. 'If Mary really is the person who wrote them, why? And why you are the person mailing them to me, without allegedly looking at the address or the name of the person.'

'I didn't know what I was mailing!' said Stan. 'If I thought it was something weird, I wouldn't be walking right up there to the Astoria Post Office in broad daylight with no gloves on or nothing, mailing it. I'm truly sorry that this has caused you problems, I really am, but I did not know. Please talk to Mary. She'll clear this up.'

'That seems fair,' said Joe to Danny.

Stan got up to leave.

Danny laughed. 'Buddy, I'm afraid you're going to have to sit it out while myself and my partner here take a visit to this Colt-Emory.'

'Embry,' said Stan. 'Embry. You'll need to speak to Julia Embry. She's the boss.' He shook his head sadly. 'They're good people there.'

In 1992, Madeline Colt and Julia Embry came together at The Mount Sinai Hospital of Queens to watch their teenage sons paint. Separately, they had turned away and walked crying into the hallway outside.

'My son used to hike,' said Madeline.

'Robin made us laugh so much,' said Julia. They had both looked back at their sons, one with the easel lowered to the level of his wheelchair, the other having his brush guided around the page by a nurse. The women looked at each other and smiled.

'But they're here,' said Julia.

'They are,' said Madeline. 'We're blessed.'

Ten years of campaigning and fundraising later, the Colt-Embry Rehabilitation Clinic was founded to support patients with traumatic brain injuries. It sat on a one-acre site between 19th and 21st Street in Astoria. Tucked into the north-east corner were the Colt-Embry Homes, a small block of twenty apartments to ease the transition for patients from rehab to home.

Julia Embry sat at her desk, pressing a Kleenex carefully under her eyes to catch the tears before her mascara did. She held a photo of Robin in her hands. It was taken at his eighth birthday party. He was wearing a huge black pirate's hat and a white shirt with a red kerchief tied around his neck. An eye patch was beside his plate, a glass of orange beside that. His chin was so far forward and he was grinning so wide, that he almost didn't look like himself. But what Julia loved about it was just how happy he looked, how bright those eyes were, how gentle the little blond boy looked as a fearsome pirate.

The last time she had a visit from two detectives, it was to tell her about Robin's car accident.

He was seventeen years old when the car he was driving was involved in a crash and the other driver left the scene. Robin was rushed to the hospital where his bones were repaired and his wounds eventually healed. But his brain injury was too severe and after hanging on for a year in rehab, he died. The police never caught the driver.

There was a knock on the door.

'Come in,' said Julia, putting the photo back on the desk facing her. She stood up.

'I'm so sorry about all this, detectives,' she said. 'Please, sit down.'

Joe and Danny introduced themselves and took a seat.

'Firstly,' said Julia. 'I really would like to reassure you about Stanley Frayte, for what it's worth. He's worked with me for so long now. He's the best. He really is. He was trying to do the right thing by Mary. But, you know, he doesn't know everything about everyone. He's been with the clinic and me for ten years, but he's only been working here in the apartment building several weeks, so . . .' She smiled. 'Poor Stan.'

'We'd like to talk to you about Mary Burig,' said Joe.

'OK,' said Julia. 'What would you like to know?'

'Let's start with how she came to be here,' said Joe.

'Mary was found last year, wandering the street three blocks from her apartment. When they got

her to hospital, doctors discovered the TBI. She
had no recollection of what happened to her.'

'So Mary has never spoken about her accident.'

Julia shook her head. 'No. She can't remember
it. It's not uncommon. It's kind of like the brain's
defence mechanism.'

'Can you talk us through her, uh, situation,
condition . . .' said Joe.

'First of all, Mary is a person . . . who suffered
a traumatic brain injury.'

'I understand,' said Joe.

'Not a brain injury sufferer.'

Joe nodded.

'So Mary as she was before – what we call pre-
morbidly – is still there, but she's got a new set
of behaviours. Every program is individual here.
This is Mary's.' She handed a copy to each of them.
Joe flicked through twelve pages on Mary's treatment and details of how each one would help her.
He paused at psychiatric. Impairment: brain injury.
Function: emotional regularity. Participation:
inability to regulate emotions/thoughts.

Joe looked up. 'Let's say Mary can make sense
of these letters—'

'She might not,' said Julia. 'She might not
remember writing them at all.'

'OK, but let's say she does. Can we believe what
she is saying to us?'

'I would say so. Yes. If you can decipher it.'

Danny looked up from his notebook. 'How do

you think her injury might have happened?'

'Her medical records are confidential, as you can appreciate. Unless Mary gives you permission to access them. Or her guardian does.'

'Who's her guardian?'

'Her older brother, David Burig.'

'We'll get his details from you, if that's OK,' said Joe.

'Sure,' said Julia. 'Mary's lucky to have David. There's not a lot of support out there for people with a TBI. Places like Colt-Embry are not common. Most of the time, people are released from hospital into rehab and after that, they're on their own, back home expected to function as they did before. It's crazy. And a lot of people are not covered to stay in a place like this. If they don't have the right insurance, they better have a wealthy family. Can you imagine? Just to be able to live normally? It's crazy. And because a lot of people physically look the same as they did before the injury, people expect them to act "normally" and when they don't, they can't handle it. It's a very hard thing for everyone to have to adjust to.'

'How does Mary's injury affect her, like day to day?' said Joe.

'Mary suffered right temporal lobe damage. The temporal lobe is all about memory, emotional stability, reading social cues – crucial parts of everyday life,' said Julia. 'Someone who's had the right side damaged, like Mary, would have problems interpreting facial expressions, so would find it hard to know if you're angry, sad, etc. Also there would be tone-of-voice issues – their own speech patterns are quite flat and also, they won't recognize, for example, sarcasm in your tone. They're not great with humor. Anything non-verbal: faces, music, shapes – she'll have a problem with. A lot of Mary's long-term memory is intact. Her short-term memory is where she has difficulties. For example, she may remember someone visiting her apartment this morning, but she may not remember why.'

'What about all her writing?' said Joe.

'That's because she has temporal lobe epilepsy and what can go along with that is hypergraphia. Basically, she is compelled to write. She can't help herself. The length of what she writes can vary, so can the quality. Dostoevsky was hypergraphic. Poe was. And Lewis Carroll – you know *Alice in Wonderland*? Apparently the inspiration came from what happens in the aura part of a seizure when objects will seem to be getting bigger or smaller. You can go into Mary's room and find her writings everywhere. She likes fancy notepaper, so she's got stacks of that. She's written on toilet paper, the back of receipts, cereal boxes, even the wall once.' She smiled.

'Do you read what she writes?'

'No. Just because Mary has a brain injury doesn't mean we can all waltz right in there and invade her privacy. She has an apartment, it's her space, what she does there is her business. I mean, within reason. Obviously, we need to keep an eye on things.'

'Why do you think she's writing to us?'

'I don't know. You can ask Mary. I told her you were coming in. It really distressed her, just so you know. She's been a little at sea, because her TSS was away.'

'TSS?' said Joe.

'Sorry – that's Therapeutic Support Staff. Her name is Magda Oleszak, but she's been on vacation. Someone else was filling in, which always unsettles Mary.'

'OK,' said Joe. 'We'll bear that in mind. Back to why Mary got in contact with us . . .'

'Right. It may be she saw you on the news, in the newspaper. It's common that someone like Mary might feel responsible for every ill in the world. You and I could watch a news report on a murder or a natural disaster and feel terrible for the victims and their family, while Mary might feel genuine guilt and wish she could do something about it. The religious element to her condition taps into this too. She wants to reach out, help people. People with brain injuries can be very me-centric. Mary is no different. But she is also concerned with other people's welfare in her own way. She's very kind to the other clients here.'

'Is Mary on any medication?' said Joe.

'As usual, I'm torn here, with what I can reveal to you.' She sighed. 'But I want to help. Let me check the file.' She looked through it. 'When she got here, Mary was taking 300mg of Dilantin – an anti-seizure medication – but that didn't agree with her. So the doctors moved her over to 500 mg of Sodium Valproate three times a day, but her hair started to thin out. When she started losing patches of it, she was very upset, so she stopped all medication. And she was fine. Up until three months ago, when she had the first seizure.'

'We received the first letter a month ago.'

'Yes. And she's had more seizures since then.'

There was a knock on the door.

'Yes,' said Julia. 'This will be Mary,' she said to them. 'Come in, Mary.'

Mary Burig squeezed through the tiny gap she made for herself in the door and closed it behind her. She was dressed in a pale pink oversized cardigan, a blue silk tank, jeans and flip-flops. With her head bowed, her hair – black and shiny, parted in the center – hung down in front of her face.

'Hi Mary,' said Julia. 'Come on in. Sit down.'

Mary raised her head slowly and looked first at Danny. Something caught in his chest.

'Hi Mary,' said Joe. 'I'm Detective Joe Lucchesi.'

'Oh, hi,' she said, reaching out to shake his hand.

'Detective Danny Markey,' said Danny, half standing.

'Hi.'

'Take a seat, Mary,' said Julia.

'We met Stanley Frayte earlier,' said Joe. 'He was mailing a letter for you. We have your letters here. Did you write these?'

'Yes.' She frowned. 'How many do you have there?'

'Three,' said Joe.

'But I sent you fifteen.'

'Fifteen,' said Danny. 'You've been busy.'

She smiled. 'Can I see the one you have there?'

Mary took the plastic bag with the napkin and stared down at it, slowly reading through it, her head bent, her hair falling down to cover her cheeks. She shifted in the chair, pushing her feet back underneath it, crossing her legs at the ankles. Several minutes passed. Joe looked towards Julia Embry who gave a tiny shrug. He gave her a small smile and waited. Lights flashed across the bottom of Julia's phone. Her focus stayed on Mary, whose hair was now covering most of her face, until she tucked one side of it back behind her ear and they could all see the tears streaming down her face. When she looked at Julia and then Joe, the pale eyes that had seemed so shining and clear were now dark with fear and confusion.

'Mary, does this letter mean anything to you?' said Joe.

'No,' she said. 'I'm sorry.'

FIFTEEN

Someone had brought Stanley Frayte a Coke and some chocolate. The can was crushed as small as it could go and the chocolate wrapper was twisted tightly and rammed into the hole. He jumped when Danny and Joe walked back in.

'OK, Stanley, we spoke with Mary' said Joe. 'She's confirmed what you told us. So we're done here for now. You can go home.'

'Thank you,' said Stan.

'Hey, why don't we give you a ride?' said Joe.

'You sure?' said Stan.

'Not a problem,' said Joe. 'Back to Tuckahoe?'

'No. My van's at the clinic.'

'Sure, OK.'

Joe had asked a lot of people if they wanted a ride home after spending hours grilling them in a small interview room. They often said yes because they felt it was a test. Maybe if they said no, it would be like they had something to hide. Sometimes they said no because, innocent or guilty, they just wanted to get the hell out of the station house. It looked like Stan thought he was passing a test. When they got to the car, he glanced at the milkshake stain on the hood.

'Don't ask,' said Joe, throwing Danny the keys.

They got in and drove the short journey to 21st Street. Joe turned in his seat to talk to Stan.

'So how long you been an electrician?'

'Eight years,' said Stan.

'Really? You like it?'

'Yeah,' said Stan, 'yeah I do.'

'What did you do before that?'

'I drove a truck.'

'My father was a truck driver. What was your route?'

'I delivered a lot to Riker's Island.'

'No shit. With who?'

'Barbizan Trucking.'

'Did you give it up because of all the Frayte jokes?'

Stanley smiled. 'Something like that.'

They pulled up outside the clinic.

'Here,' said Joe. 'Here's my card. If you think of anything else or if you need anything, let me know.'

'Sure,' said Stan. 'Thanks for the ride.'

'Thanks for your help today.'

Stan walked over to the van. In the rearview mirror, Joe could see Julia Embry standing at the front door, waving to Stan to come in.

'Your father's a truck driver,' said Danny, taking a right out of the clinic. 'How many jobs have you given Giulio over the years?'

'Hey, it's the only time I get to see him as a regular guy,' said Joe.

'Jesus, you're cruel.'

'So what do we make of Miss Mary?' said Joe.

'Those eyes,' said Danny.

'Mary's?'

'Yeah. They're like those dogs. What are they called? Those wolfy dogs.'

'Huskies.'

'Yes. That's it.'

'Down, boy.'

'It's just her eyes I'm talking about. You gotta admit, they were really something.'

'Yeah.'

'I mean, not that the rest of her . . .'

'You're not right, Danny. The girl looks like she needs to be wrapped up in cotton wool and, I don't know . . . let nowhere near you, that's for sure.'

David Burig sat on a short wooden bench in the grounds of Colt-Embry. Mary was beside him, facing him, her legs curled under her body. Her eyes were red and tired.

'Mary, Mary, Mary,' said David. 'What am I going to do with you?'

'Go to a movie?' she said.

David smiled and hugged her. 'Sending letters to the cops. You really thought you could help them.'

He could feel her nod against his chest.

'You have a good heart,' he said, rubbing her hair. 'Remember the little kid around the corner who cried all the time and I used to say to him, "would an ice-cream make it better?" and he'd say, "yes" and I'd say, "well, when you're at the store, will you get me one too?" Your little face – you'd laugh, but you felt so bad for him at the same time.'

She smiled. 'I remember him. You were so mean.'

David pulled her away gently and looked at her. 'Do you want to talk about these things? I don't know if you do. I don't know if I'm upsetting you.'

'I do,' said Mary. 'Because I remember them. They mean that I had a good life. And people loved me. And I did things myself.' She stared down at the ground. 'I know I'm not intelligent any more.'

'God, that's heartbreaking,' said David.

'But it's the truth,' said Mary.

'Look at you,' he said, 'you're just so pretty and you look . . .' He trailed off. 'You made me laugh so much, Mare.'

'And I don't any more.'

'Don't say that. You do make me laugh. You

cheer me up. You remind me that the world is good and pure . . .' He stopped, because sometimes she reminded him that the world was a terrible place.

'Look at your shirt,' she said.

He looked down. 'What?'

'It's shaking. Is your heart beating really fast?' She frowned and reached out her hand.

'No,' he said, quickly taking hold of it. 'That's just the breeze.' He smiled.

Mary looked at him. 'Do you get tired of visiting me?'

'No, no, no,' said David. 'Please don't tell me you think that. It's you and me, Mary. It always was. And always will be, OK?'

She nodded. 'Thanks.' She paused. 'I'm sorry about the letters.'

Joe and Danny were pulling up at the car wash on Columbus Avenue when Joe's phone rang. He pulled it out and flipped it open.

'Joe? It's Rencher. This Mary Burig broad? She was admitted to Downtown Hospital nine months ago, GSW to the head from . . .' he paused, '. . . a twenty-two caliber automatic.'

Julia Embry had been paged to reception in the main clinic by the time Joe and Danny arrived back. She leaned over the desk to the receptionist. 'Send Magda to the coffee shop when she comes in. Thank you.'

They took a quiet table in the corner and got coffee.

'I'm sure you know every shooting is reported to the police in the ER,' said Joe 'so when we ran Mary's name, it came up.'

Julia nodded. 'I didn't know if it was relevant.'

'I don't know if you've been watching the news or reading the papers, but The Caller is killing his victims with a similar weapon . . .'

'Oh my God,' said Julia.

Joe nodded. 'It's looking like Mary could possibly have been a victim.'

'But weren't the victims all male?'

'So far, yes,' said Joe. 'But it's too much of a coincidence that Mary has been sending in these letters, she seems to have some information about the crimes and now she has an injury just like the other victims.'

'I suppose you need to speak with her again.'

'Yes,' said Joe. 'How was she when we left?'

'She was down, frustrated that she couldn't help. And scared. She's back at her apartment now. I can take you over there.'

'We don't want to do anything to upset Mary,' said Danny. 'We just think there might be more information there that could be useful. If we can jog her memory in any way . . .'

'OK. First, you can speak with Magda. Here she is. I called her when all this happened with Stanley earlier. She said she needed to come in.'

Magda walked towards them with a blue canvas tote bag clutched to her stomach.

'Hello, detectives. My name is Magda Oleszak, Mary Burig's support worker.'

She took a seat in front of them and pulled the bag onto her lap.

'Hi,' said Joe. 'How you doing?'

'Here,' she said, reaching in, taking out a large brown envelope. 'These are from Mary.'

'She asked you to give this to us?' said Joe, taking the envelope.

Magda shook her head. 'No. I mail letters for her sometimes. But she writes so many I can't mail all of them. Like the one she wrote to welcome the new Pope. Or the ones to you. She saw the news conference. Lots of people saw it, but they don't send you letters. When I came back from Poland, I heard she told you she mailed you fifteen letters. She didn't. She has problems with her memory. But she did write these other things that I can give you now. She writes sometimes before she has a seizure. Stan will tell you that. He arrived one day after she had a seizure and her papers were on the floor all around her.'

As Joe sliced through the envelope, the contents spilled out: receipts, Post-Its, strips of newspaper margins, toilet paper, magazines, floral notelets, Rolodex pages, greeting cards, the pale cream interiors of cereal boxes. Every surface Mary could have found to write on, was covered with text and stuffed into envelopes.

'It was distressing for her,' said Magda. 'Mary tries to make sense of what she has written and she can't. Not all of it. I see her crying, I see how I can make that go away and I do it. I take these writings away. For her. Stan did not know this. So he mailed those letters to you. And now . . .' She shrugged. 'You can make no sense of them too.'

'Have you read through these again?' said Joe.

'I never read them the first time,' said Magda. 'I still don't like reading in English.'

'Does anyone mind if I take a look at her letters?' said Julia.

Joe handed them to her.

'Hmm,' she said. 'I can see how these could be difficult to understand. Mary's thought patterns are disassociated – you can tell from how she's written all this. It probably made sense to her at the time but the order is all out of whack.'

'There's a lot there to take in,' said Joe.

'Don't forget Mary's long-term memory is strong,' said Julia. 'It's very hard for her that, since the attack, she has difficulty forming new memories. She's aware that she can't do everything she used to be able to do. I wish I could be of more help, but ultimately, only you know what you're looking for. The best I can say is to scrutinize these again and see is there anything that means anything to your investigation. To me, Mary talking about her swimming classes in Astoria Park is no big deal, but if you knew the killer swims fifty lengths a day there, then that could be important.'

'I looked at some of the drawings,' said Magda, shrugging. 'But, no. They're weird.' She pointed to the cereal box. 'On there.'

Joe flipped over the box and saw angry black mouths staring back at him, some of them big, some of them small, all of them wide open with ragged teeth. Joe passed it to Danny.

'Did she talk to you about this one?'

Magda shook her head. 'This was after a seizure. I found it on her writing desk. I can't show her that. It's too creepy.'

Danny shrugged. 'Thank you for bringing these to our attention. We'll take a look at all this, it might not mean anything, but we've got to check everything out.'

'Yes. Probably nothing,' said Magda. 'But you're here now, so maybe we could go and see if Mary can help you.'

'If you don't mind,' said Julia. 'I'll leave you to it. We're in the process of setting up a second clinic upstate and I'm under a lot of pressure.'

'That's not a problem,' said Joe.

*   *   *

Mary sat on the corner of her bed with the pages spread out in front of her. Magda sat beside her with a hand on her arm. Joe and Danny stood beside her. She had been this way for fifteen minutes. No-one spoke.

Eventually, Mary looked up. 'Something to do with mouths, hurting people's mouths. I don't think he can help it.' She pointed to her drawings and the place where the ink was so heavy and black, it had soaked through the card.

The light in the front room was on when Joe got back. Anna walked into the hall as soon as she heard the car. Her face was white.

'What is going on?' she said.

Joe walked by her into the kitchen. 'What? With the case?'

'I just got a call from Paris. The police came to the house.'

Joe didn't move. 'What?'

'To my parents' house. Three flics call to the door. My mother was frightened. She thought we'd had an accident or something. They say to her, "is everything OK?" Then they walk all around the garden. And ask can they come in the house to look too. She's seventy-five years old. She didn't know what to do. I don't think she even asked them for ID—'

Joe turned around. 'I told your parents to always ask for ID if people are calling at the door.'

'That's it?' she said. 'You told them that. What about telling them the police might call at the door! Why were they there?'

He walked over to her. 'After everything that happened last year, I asked them to look in on your parents every now and then. That's it.'

'But what have my parents got to do with anything?'

'They're part of our family. Duke Rawlins targeted my family. You had nothing to do with what went down between me and him and Riggs, but that didn't matter to him.'

'I don't understand. Did you think my parents weren't going to tell me?'

'I didn't think the cops were going to knock on the door. I thought they were just going to take a look around without raising any suspicions.'

'Do Giulio and Pam get these visits too?'

'Let me take care of them. I'm in the same country. But yes, I did put a call into Rye PD, let them know our situation.'

Anna shook her head. 'We'll never be free of this.'

'We are free,' said Joe, pulling her into his arms. 'It's over. I am not going to let someone like him ruin our lives. He is not going to come after us so soon. He's not going to risk that. We're the worst place he could be right now. New York is the worst place.'

'I don't think anything would ever stop that man getting what he wants.'

'Honey,' he said, pulling her closer. 'Listen to me. He's not coming back.'

SIXTEEN

Dr Makkar led Joe into his office. He offered him
a seat, then stood by the wall, gently swinging his
putter and guiding a fluorescent golf ball into a
green machine that fired it right back at him.

'Precision,' he said. He kneeled on an ergonomic
stool behind his desk. 'What can I do for you?'

'I have a question,' said Joe. 'What would stop
you getting your teeth fixed if they'd been injured
or broken in some way?'

He shrugged. 'Depends what you mean.'

Joe held out a brown envelope.

'Could you look at a few crime scene photos
for me? I think the perp spent some time working
on the victims' teeth or mouths for some reason
before they were murdered. These are graphic
images.'

'I'm unshockable,' said Dr Makkar, taking them
from him. He looked down, his eyes wide. 'Or at
least, I used to be. Holy crap. These are hardcore.

I liked that you said *"working"* on their teeth or mouths. *I* work on people's teeth. This guy ... wow. Wow. My breakfast is not happy.' He took a drink from a plastic cup.

'I know,' said Joe. 'So, what do you think?'

'I don't know, but your guy's got some reason for smashing these teeth in. He's not fooling around. Do you think it's a torture thing to get information out of someone? Or maybe the victims already gave away some information they shouldn't have?'

Joe shrugged. 'It could be anything.'

Makkar looked through the photos again. 'He was definitely going for a big psychological impact. It's a primal thing with teeth. That's why it freaks us all out so much when we dream they're falling out. You've had that dream, right? And it's like you're trying to imagine how your life can go on without your teeth? It's an apocalyptic thing.' He paused. 'Do you know what's so cruel about messing with people's teeth or their mouths? It's that if you don't heal one hundred per cent, there are so many reminders of your assault: every time you chew, kiss, smoke, go out in the cold, what- ever. It's there all the time. Psychologically, you could have to relive the whole thing over and over.' He looked down. 'Although, most of your victims, well, they don't have to.'

'Don't dentists have the most stressful jobs, highest rate of suicides?' said Joe.

Dr Makkar frowned. 'I see where you're going. Sure. And, man, you should see all the serial killers that've come out of dental school over the years.'

'OK, but do you think what we're looking for here is a dentist?'

'Yes, I think that's what *you're looking for*, but that doesn't mean you're right.'

Joe smiled. 'Well, what do you think?'

'I don't know.' Makkar pointed to the photo of Preston Blake that Joe had cut from the newspaper. 'But I'd say the reason someone like this guy wouldn't get their teeth fixed is that he will never ever let anyone near his mouth again. Look at those eyes, even. That is the look of a damaged man.' He turned to Joe. 'And he's not the only one.'

'You're too hard on me, Dr Mak. Anyway, look, I appreciate all this. Thanks for your help.'

'Now,' said Dr Makkar, holding on to the photos. 'I'm afraid I have some good news for you. I got a call from a doctor friend of mine who has one of the most experienced surgeons in arthroscopy visiting the Facial Pain Clinic next week and has offered me a slot for a patient. I'd like that to be you.'

Joe stared at him. 'Am I supposed to be grateful for that?'

'You're hurting my feelings here. What am I going to do with you? Your face looks so, just rigid. It's crazy. You can't look at this kind of stuff,' he pointed to the photos, 'you can't live this life without getting affected. You can't fool me. You really want to spend the rest of your life in this kind of pain?'

'No, definitely not. But I can't do surgery.'

'I'm telling you, you can.'

'What day's it on?'

'Friday – ten days from now.'

Joe sighed. 'OK. Fine, put me down. But I'd like the record to show—'

'I don't keep records for babies,' said Dr Makkar. 'Or cats, scaredy cats.'

When Joe got back to the office, everyone was gathered around Danny's desk and there was an atmosphere he couldn't quite put his finger on until Martinez opened his mouth.

'Ease yourself into the morning, that's right.'

'I was getting someone to take a look at the teeth angle,' said Joe. 'From 7 a.m. When you were in bed.'

Martinez nodded, but was looking away.

'OK,' said Rencher. 'Mary Burig is twenty-eight, single, from Boulder, Colorado, got a degree in psychology, moved to New York just over a year ago, took an apartment in the East Village, which is possibly where she was attacked.'

'What did she work at?' said Joe.

'She had a part-time job at a deli.'

'Was she dating anyone around the time of the attack?' said Bobby.

'No. Not since she got to New York,' said Joe.

'And you said she's got no memory of what happened,' said Bobby.

'No,' said Joe. 'And there's nothing we can do about that for now. She does remember a teeth thing. So I've put the word out on the teletype and updated VICAP. But whatever happens, now we know about her, it changes everything. Female vic, late twenties, happened after William Aneto and Gary Ortis, but before Preston Blake and Ethan Lowry. So Mary was the third intended victim that we know about. And she got away. And so did Preston Blake.' He raised his hands. 'How did two victims get away? What did the perp do differently? What did the vics do differently? Was it a physical thing – the vic gets a surge of adrenaline and overpowers the perp? Or a psychological thing – the vic says or does something that makes the perp stop? Or maybe he was interrupted – someone calls to the door, an alarm goes off, the police show up. We need to find out what Mary Burig did and what Preston Blake did that made them the lucky ones.'

'Yeah, real lucky,' said Danny. 'I'd give my left arm to be living in some rehab apartment or holed up like a recluse in a—'

'Huge mansion,' said Martinez.

'Yeah, well, it doesn't sound like Preston Blake's going to be too happy to talk to us again one way or the other.'

'Maybe the perp wanted them to get away,' said Danny.

'But Blake saw his face' said Joe. 'He must have been planning to kill him.'

'I guess so. And Mary was shot in the head . . . I need sleep.'

Joe laughed. 'William Aneto. Gary Ortis. Mary Burig. Preston Blake. Ethan Lowry. What is the connection? Is there a connection?'

'Back to the getting away,' said Rencher. 'There's no way from what you say about Mary Burig that she got away by overpowering the guy. He had to have been interrupted or it was something psychological.' He paused. 'Of course, he had shot her. He probably thought she was dead.'

'She's too cute to kill,' said Danny.

'Yeah, that'll stop 'em,' said Martinez.

'Maybe it was just the fact that she was a woman made some difference,' said Rencher.

'Yeah, that'll stop 'em,' said Martinez.

Joe snapped his pen in half. Everyone looked at him. He shrugged. Danny smiled.

'OK,' said Joe. 'Martinez and Rencher, can you look into another canvass at Mary Burig's old apartment building in case you're right, he was interrupted. Same goes for Blake's street, see if anyone saw or heard anything.'

'Blake will be on to Rufo again for that one,' said Danny.

'Like we give a shit,' said Joe. 'We will have

to go back and talk to him. He'll have to deal
with it.'

'Did Mary make a phone call the night she was
attacked?' said Bobby.

'Cullen is on that.'

'Maybe that's the key,' said Danny.

'Maybe the people they called are linked and
the vics are all guilty by association?' said Bobby.

'Maybe, maybe, maybe,' said Joe. 'So, let's get
the phone calls straight: Aneto calls his Mom to
say he's responsible for killing his brother. Gary
Ortis calls his former business partner just to catch
up. Mary Burig, we don't know. Preston Blake –
no phone call. Ethan Lowry – calls his ex-girlfriend
to tell her he still loves her.'

'That's two confessions we got right there,' said
Danny. 'Maybe that's what this is about.'

'Could be it's some religious nut,' said Joe. 'Listens
to their confessions. I mean, he's got to be right
there while they're making the call, otherwise they
could tip the person off and none of them did.'

'Maybe the perp's used to it. He could be a
priest . . . an ex-priest or could make out to be
one,' said Rencher.

'Yeah,' said Bobby. 'And I don't believe Ortis
was calling his business partner just for the hell
of it. He might have had something else to tell
him.'

'OK,' said Joe. 'Find out some more about him,
go back, talk to him again.'

'No problem.'

Joe took a stack of pages and spread them out in front of him. 'There are things they have in common and things they don't. Look at these.' He laid out the close-ups of each of the dead victims' faces in chronological order: Gary Ortis, William Aneto, Ethan Lowry. 'Gary Ortis's face was the most damaged. His right eye socket was completely impacted. His father had identified him by a scar on his lower back from a childhood operation. His head had been slammed against the corner of the counter top. With William Aneto, most of the facial injuries were around the mouth, but his nose was shattered. Ethan Lowry's injuries were around the mouth and his nose was untouched.

'I don't think the perp set out to create a signature, like a really identifiable MO for every crime,' said Joe. 'I think he's just doing his thing as he goes along, the best way he knows how. It's evolving. So he started bashing the guys heads off the corners of counter tops. But that's hard to do, right?'

The men nodded.

'You saw by the hand prints and drag marks all over the Aneto scene that there was some serious effort to fight back,' said Joe. 'The perp tried a similar approach again with Ortis. But then Mary Burig, a woman, survives. And Preston Blake gets away. The perp comes back again with

Ethan Lowry and we see he's finely tuned his act. He has the hammer. He seems to have done it exactly the way he wanted to. Almost tidier. More focused. Ethan Lowry is probably a good example of what he wanted to do.' He paused. 'But what's his ultimate fantasy? What is it he really wants?'

'Bashing their faces in is important,' said Danny. 'Because it's not going to kill them. So that's got to have something to do with it. And the asphyxiation . . .'

'I don't think he even realized at first that he was constricting their lungs,' said Joe. 'I think he was gone, his head was somewhere else . . .'

'Probably,' said Rencher.

'We need to talk with Mary Burig's brother, David, see if we can't find out more about her and why this might have happened,' said Joe.

It was 8 p.m. and David Burig stood in the kitchen of his Chambers Street apartment. A pot of chilli was cooking on the stove, an open carton of sour cream beside that. He was looking for a jar of jalapeños in the fridge when a call came in from the lobby.

'David? I've got a Detective Lucchesi here to see you. Shall I send him up?'

David took a deep breath. 'Uh, sure . . . Benny? Could you do me a major favor and pick me up a jar of jalapeños?'

Benny laughed. 'Yeah. I'm good with emer-
gencies.'

David went into the kitchen and took the chilli
off the stove, replacing it with the kettle. He took
down a packet of coffee.

The doorbell rang. He walked to the front door.
He could see just the top of a man's head in a
black beanie. David opened the door. He quickly
realized it wasn't a beanie, it was a mask. And the
man was drawing it down over his face. With one
step, he pushed forward, his full force slamming
against David's chest, stunning him, sending him
stumbling backwards. The door was closed. And
a gun was an inch from his face.

'I changed my mind,' said The Caller.

Danny drove the Gran Fury down Chambers
Street. Cars lined both sides.

'Give me a space, someone,' he said.

'There,' said Joe, pointing.

'Too tight,' said Danny.

'You'll make it,' said Joe. 'Come on. I'm starving.
I need to eat.'

'Before we go to Burig's place?'

Joe shrugged. 'I guess I can wait 'til after.'

Standing in his kitchen, stripped bare, David had
no control over his body as it shook, rigidly, spas-
modically and violently. The Caller watched. David
thought he could see sinews raised at his neck,

but the ridges were evenly spaced and he realized the mask the man wore was boned, finely, contoured up his neck, crafted only for him.

'What are you going to do to me?' said David. But David knew what this man did. He had never considered that a victim's first terror of knowing his death was in someone else's hands could be followed by the second terror of knowing exactly how it would unfold. David's rising fear was that fear itself would overwhelm him before he suffered the first physical wound. The more The Caller watched him, the more his body racked.

'What do you want?' said David.

'To show you why what you did was wrong. You will have the pleasure of going through exactly what the other victims did.'

'No,' said David. 'Please. I . . . no. Please don't do that.'

'Accept your responsibility.'

'I'm not responsible—'

'Tell me your big lie,' said The Caller.

'What?'

'Just tell me. Everyone has a big lie. Everyone has little lies, don't they?'

'What are you talking about? I've never lied to you. I've helped—'

'You have not helped me,' said The Caller. 'Do I look *helped* to you?'

'I don't know.'

The Caller stared at him, then shook his head.

'You have lied to me, David Burig. You have. Think about it. Ever got involved in something you knew was a violation? Of the law? Of people's trust?'

An ice cold trickle of sweat ran down David's side as he contemplated his answer. He chose silence.

The Caller stared at him. 'I want you to reveal the rotten, twisted shit scraped out from the cracks of your fractured mind.'

'There's nothing there.'

'There are a lot of dead bodies there.'

David's heart pounded, heavy and irregular.

The Caller, again, stared. This time something indefinable came to life in his eyes, a dark flame behind the whites. And he smiled.

'Come with me. Open your closet.' He gestured towards the bedroom and pressed his face close to David's. 'Show me the space under your bed. What do you hide there? What toys do you take out to play with in the dark when no-one's around?'

'Jesus Christ,' said David. 'This is what you do to people? Humiliate them. I don't know where you're going with this but—' David released a breath. 'I don't understand.'

'I don't care.'

'Please. Try me.'

'Why?'

'I could help you this time.'

'Believe me. You *are* helping me. You helped

me into your home. You helped me into your soul.'

He raised his head and stared at the ceiling. 'You helped me affirm my beliefs. You helped me, David. You can take that with you.' He wiped a hand down the black fabric of the mask. 'And you will go on helping me.'

Joe and Danny walked in through the open door of the apartment building. There was no doorman at the desk.

'Hello?' said Joe.

'These people pay all this money to feel safe in their apartments and this guy just goes out, takes a walk,' said Danny. 'Come on.'

David lay on his back on the hardwood floor, his head inches from the front door. The Caller was on top of him, pinning him down, his knees on either side of his chest.

'If you remain silent through this, trust me that I will stop at a point,' said The Caller. 'And you will survive.'

The sudden urgent siren of a fire truck made David turn his head towards the window. The glass shone with silent rain and reflected lights. Nine floors down, people walked the wet pavement. Cars drove past. And no-one knew what was happening inside his apartment.

*   *   *

Joe and Danny took the elevator to the ninth floor
and rang the doorbell. There was no answer.
Danny rang again. Still no answer.

'Do you have his number?' said Danny.

'Yeah,' said Joe, scrolling through his phone.
He dialled and waited. 'Nothing.'

'Let's go eat, come back in a little while,' said
Danny. 'He could be at the gym or something.'

The chime of the doorbell seemed a distant
memory as David Burig felt the metal of the gun
barrel pressed hard into his eye socket. It pushed
his head back against the floor, his chin high in
the air. And then it was gone. Instead, he watched
the swift descent of a hammer towards his face.
A surge of strength rushed through him, his body
still wired to fight attack in whatever small, useless
way. He closed his eyes. He lifted his head a fraction from the ground, pitching it frantically from
side to side, crazed and desperate thrashing. At
his temples, veins bulged. His jaw clamped shut.
Every muscle in his face and neck strained. His
legs bucked, the only part of him free, but not
free. His bare feet scrambled for grip on the floor,
their damp heat stopping them, sticking them to
the varnished floorboards, burning up his heels.
Laid open, bare, exposed, bucking and writhing
for his life. He waited, still rolling his head from
side to side, dizzy and sick with the movement.
For a tired second, he stopped. His breath exploded

outwards, saliva spraying into the air. Seconds followed in the quiet, eerie expectation of pain.

Nothing happened. Then he could feel it. Slowly at first. Muscular thighs on either side of his ribcage. Squeezing. The pounding in his head was dull and steady. His eyes still closed, his breathing faltered, shaken by the first sensations of constriction. He took the pressure off his neck, resting his head back on the floor, his entire focus switched to his lungs. He imagined them filled with air, maximum expansion, charging his body with oxygen, rushing it to his cells, keeping him here. He coughed, choking against the constriction.

Crushing tighter against his chest, the muscles in The Caller's legs began to tremble, then shake violently, each spasm and rise in temperature transferred to the body beneath him. He rose briefly on his knees and the air flared with ammonia and spices, a stale steam-room smell.

David could feel the moisture on his chest. A thin stream of sweat rolled down it. His head was light, tingling all over. His scalp was cold and damp. Just as his breath was leaving him, the pressure was released. His mouth shot open, followed by his eyes, faulty reflexes; the exact position The Caller wanted him to be in as the hammer crashed down on his teeth.

The blows came over and over, splitting, breaking and cracking, splintering and shattering bones, flesh, teeth. The sounds the hammer made, through the air, against his face, caught in torn flesh, were like another wound in the silence. He was secure in his achievement; David had created a vacuum where he stored up every scream that wanted to rip up his throat and take on the pain. Then it stopped. Tears streamed down his face, sobs choked in his throat, his stomach heaved. His whole body shook. He slowly opened his eyes, smearing the droplets of blood caught in his eyelashes.

The Caller reached across for his bag and took out two dental impression trays. He placed them on the floor beside him. He filled the top tray with a thick blue liquid.

'Open wide,' he said. David's mouth shook. The Caller paused. 'Stop.'

David nodded, closed his eyes and opened his mouth. The Caller slipped in the tray and pressed it hard against the bloodied roof of David's mouth, coating every surface and filling every space with the cool silicone. A chill seeped into his damaged bones, shooting pain through his head.

'Four minutes to set,' said The Caller.

David's eyes shot wide. He started to swallow uncontrollably. The Caller bent low, staring into his eyes, trying to force calm into him. He stayed that way, then grabbed the tray and pulled it free, pausing to look into it before he laid it beside him. He wiped David's mouth with a folded paper towel.

'Please,' said David, spitting blood and saliva. 'I have to look after my sister. You can't—'

The Caller pretended to consider his plea. 'OK, now the bottom teeth,' he said. 'Same again.'

David closed his eyes and tilted back his head. He wanted to hear another siren, louder than the first, one that was bringing police officers and battering rams to his door. He was restrained well, tightly bound, his wrists and hands now numb. And the blows started again, hard, fast and brutal.

David slowly opened his eyes and through the blood leaking into them, he caught flashes of The Caller and how – from somewhere closed and locked inside him, unleashed only now – he raged. As The Caller's thighs locked on, unyielding, his upper body rocked from side to side, the hammer – a relentless onslaught of strikes. Without slowing, The Caller's free hand tore at his mask, wrenching it over his head, throwing it to the ground. His face, flooded with anger, his eyes, closed and sucked into their sockets, his jaw moving, his mouth wide, his lips forming every word he wanted to roar. But no sound escaped. The message was silence.

All David could do now was take himself away. His spacious hallway became the smallest place he had ever been, but also as high and wide and deep as his greatest fear.

SEVENTEEN

'Jesus Christ,' said Rufo. He stood with his hands linked at the back of his head, staring out David Burig's window. His back was to the battered body by the door. 'What the hell is going on?'

'The guy was here, we were right outside,' said Joe. 'I can't believe it.'

'How were you to know?' said Rufo. 'How were you to know?'

'But—'

'But nothing,' said Rufo. 'We've just got to catch him. We just got to do everything we can to make sure Burig is the last.'

'It's Ethan Lowry all over again . . . without the phone,' said Joe.

'Mary Burig hadn't made a call either,' said Danny. 'Cullen just said.'

'Last call he got was from the lobby,' said Martinez, walking over. 'He asked the doorman to run to the deli for something. Burig and him got on well. Anyway, doorman figured he was safe with a "detective" in the building.'

'That'll be the last favor he'll do anyone,' said Joe.

'What do you say Henry is finally getting laid these days?' said Martinez, pointing to a small, focused crime scene tech dusting the kitchen doorknob.

'I have no idea who Henry is or what his sex life is like,' said Joe, his voice tight.

'I mean as a direct result of CSI?' said Martinez. 'Chicks dig him, they think his job is so glamorous.'

'Yeah,' said Joe. 'Meanwhile, he's here like a retard saying, "why do you need that printed?" "Why do you want a photo of that?" Because the killer might have touched it, you fucking douche-bag.'

'Yeah, I'd love to have one of those TV CSI techs at all my scenes,' said Bobby.

'Yeah and they'd go interview all the witnesses too,' said Danny.

'And they'd work through all the evidence in a nice shiny lab,' said Martinez.

'And they'd solve the case,' said Danny. 'And they would be hot.'

'Come on,' said Joe. 'It's three o'clock. We've done all we can here.'

His cell phone rang.

'Detective Lucchesi?

'Yeah.'

'Detective Scott Dolan here from Philadelphia PD. I know it's late – I was going to leave a message. We received your request for information on any dentists that had been in trouble, etc. Now, it's not dentists as such, but does the name Trahorne Refining mean anything to you?'

'No.'

'They're a company that have a lot of dealings with dental laboratories – not directly with dentists. I don't know too much about it myself. It's just that we got a visit from a Curtis Walston a few weeks back, a local kid who had been fired by Trahorne after two weeks on the job. He was fairly unhappy about the whole situation. Anyway, he had no evidence, because he said it was all burned, but he claims he found several bloodstained items of clothing that had been sent into the company for incineration.'

'I don't get it.'

'It's kind of complicated. Trahorne's business is about burning metals off of clothes and stuff that dental technicians use when they're filing down the metal parts of crowns or false teeth. Anyway, we followed up with the owner, Bob Trahorne, who basically laughed in our faces. We had no evidence and what he was saying to us was "You're taking the word of some punk over me?" There was nothing more we could do. But I just thought when I saw your report it might be of interest.

Curtis Walston is your classic disgruntled employee, but he came to us, so I don't know. You might want to come up here and talk to him yourself.'

David Burig's autopsy was six hours that could have been Ethan Lowry's autopsy until Walter Dreux showed up. Walter was a forensic odontologist, part of the OCME's Dental Identification Unit, called in for any cases that involved head injuries, decomposition, fires, bitemarks or unidentified victims.

'Walter,' said Danny. 'Dentist to the dead.'

'It's on my business cards now,' said Walter.

'How you doing?' said Joe.

'Good. You guys?'

Joe shrugged. 'So . . .'

'Don't come near me,' said Walter, walking over to the body. He flashed a smile. 'OK?'

'You need to get over that,' said Danny.

Walter had been burned on a major case because a homicide detective took notes as he was working and the attorney wouldn't allow Walter to amend what he had said when he was finished. Walter's day in court was not a happy one.

'In a half hour, I'll come out to you,' he said. 'Me and my lovely assistant here will do our thing, I will have a quiet moment and then I will give up the goods.'

He got to work and forty minutes later, came out to Danny, Joe and Dr Hyland.

'I found a gift for you. Between the upper right second bicuspid and the first molar tooth.'

'Spinach,' said Danny.

'More telling: a silicone-based dental impression material.'

'What?' said Joe.

'Someone took an impression of this victim's teeth,' said Walter.

'What? Just this victim?' said Danny.

'No, all the others too, I just didn't want to bother you with it. I was waiting 'til you were running out of leads or more bodies piled up – for dramatic effect.'

'Relax,' said Danny.

'I'll continue,' said Walter. 'Had the victim been to the dentist that day? That'd do it.'

'No to the dentist theory – and we checked that out with all the victims.'

'I can tell you the brand of material, but it won't mean a lot because they're so widely used. And no-one's going to be dumb enough to use the latest one on the market, because you could narrow that down better. What I'm giving you here is the fact that the guy took an impression of this victim's teeth.'

'Why would anyone want to take an impression of his victims' teeth?' said Danny.

'Why would anyone want to hammer the crap out of someone's face?' said Joe.

'Because he can,' said Danny.

'You think the perp could have been a dentist?'
said Joe.

'Nah,' said Walter. 'I'd say a cop.'

'Ha-ha,' said Danny.

'It's easy to do impressions of teeth,' said Walter.
'You don't *have* to be a dentist. But I have to say,
it makes sense.'

'And you dentists are known for getting stressed
out all the time,' said Joe.

'Yeah,' said Walter, 'going dental.'

'Who uses impressions once they're done?' said
Joe. 'Like in the dentist's office. Where does that
go to after?'

'A dental laboratory,' said Walter.

Joe and Danny exchanged glances. 'Holy shit,'
said Danny.

'They make all the crowns, veneers, bridges,'
said Walter. 'Some dentists use the same lab all
the time. Others spread the love around. It's whatever they want to do.'

'Is there like a society for these guys?' said Joe.

'There's formal training, college courses, you
name it. But the industry is not regulated. You
could set up in the morning.'

Curtis Walston was a gangsta rapper trapped in a
skinny white boy's body. He slouched diagonally
across a bald brown sofa, his arm up over the back.
Everything in his world was oversized – the baseball cap and shirt, the jeans, the watch, the bright

white sneakers, the widescreen TV, even the eyes
in his pale, narrow face. Joe and Danny stood by
the mantelpiece opposite him. Curtis spoke low,
with his head bowed.

'Screw Bob Trahorne, man. I took a job with
him 'cos he runs a good lab, they give good returns.
The only difference is where I worked before, we
checked through the packages, drums, whatever
that was sent in. We separated things out: the
grindings, the solids, the sweeps. I get my ass fired
'cos I's doing what I know.'

'Curtis,' said Danny. 'That's all a little technical
for my friend, Detective Lucchesi here. He's going
to need you to explain what happens at Trahorne
Refining, what goes down, how it all works.'

Curtis narrowed his eyes at Joe. 'That's cool.'
He shrugged. 'What it is, is Trahorne supplies metal
to dental technicians: gold, platinum, palladium,
silver. Dental technicians work for dentists, making
implants, bridges, crowns whatever. Dentists take
an impression of the teeth, they send that to the
dental technician who makes a model, so's he can
make the false teeth or veneers or whatever the
perfect size.'

'Tell us about the packages you get sent,' said Joe.

'When the dental technician is making the false
teeth, the base is made of metal, then the porcelain is put on top. The metal's been moulded in
an oven, but when it comes out, it ain't perfect,
there's bits of crud sticking out, some filing down

and smoothing to do. So they use this grinding
and buffing wheel that spins real fast. Little bits
of metal can get everywhere. Like what I said:
"grindings", which are sort of like shavings.
"Solids" are little chunks of metal, pieces of foil.
"Sweeps" is what the technician might wipe down
off his desk or even shake out of his hair onto a
piece of paper. The stuff gets everywhere. And this
gold and shit costs money. So what the technician will do is get a big envelope and throw it all
in: the piece of paper, the lab coat, a cloth he had
over his lap, a scrap of carpet that might have
been under his bench, a sweater he was wearing,
whatever. Or maybe, he'll throw it all in to one
of them fifty-five gallon paper drums.

'And send it to a place like Trahorne's,' said Joe.

'Yeah. Instead of throwing away the leftover
metal, he get paid for it.'

''Cos what Trahorne does is refining and
assaying.'

Danny frowned as he listened. Curtis looked
up at him.

'Assaying means they work out how much
metal is in the package and refining is about taking
it all out, separating one metal from another or
whatever. This way, there's no waste. I get the
package, take out the paperwork, then I put the
package onto a tray, it goes in the incinerator at
2400 degrees and everything gets nuked. All you
got's left is the metal. We weigh it, then send the

lab a cheque for the amount or we pay them in coins, metal – whatever they want.'

'This is a business that is run on trust,' said Danny.

'I guess so,' said Curtis. 'I mean, some dental techs weigh their package before they send it in on, like, bathroom scales, which isn't very accurate. So there's wiggle room, if you want to go that way.'

'Let me get this straight,' said Joe. 'In Trahorne Refining, when a package came in, it went directly into the incinerator without being checked through.'

'That's correct.'

'But in the lab you worked in before, you separated out these grindings, solids and sweeps.'

'Yes, sir.'

'Talk me through what happened with the package you opened.'

'OK. The package came in from Dean Valtry's lab in New York City. It's a fifty-five gallon paper drum, about thirty inches high, eighteen inches across. I weighed it. Then I opened it and put everything in a big steel tray, which goes into the incinerator. I was pulling out a lot of black clothes and I found solids like I told you about, sweepings, some sheets of paper that the sweepings had been on, a piece of carpet. I'm shaking out the clothes and I see stains.' He leaned forward. 'And I know they're bloodstains.'

'So what did you do?' said Danny.

'I left everything and went up to Mr Trahorne's

office with one of the items, a black top with a zip in it to show him. First of all I had to wait around for him – he was in a meeting. So I sat outside his office reading a magazine.' He shrugged. 'Like, a half hour later, his secretary comes out to get me. She's all, like, don't be bothering the boss for long. So I go in and Mr Trahorne asks me what I've been doing for the past half hour.' Curtis rolled his eyes. 'So I ignore that, but I tell him what happened with the package. And he listens to me and explains about how dental technicians can get blood on things if they cut their finger on the scalpels or whatever. And I'm like, I'm not a retard: this is a *lot* of blood, here. And I spread the thing out on his desk, which totally pisses him off. Then he grabs the top from me, walks me back down to "my post" he calls it and throws everything in the tray, pushes it into the incinerator. Looked me right in the eye afterwards and said, "I'm not paying you to sort. Or to take time out to bother me." I'm, like, "some dude could have got hurt." Trahorne's looking at me like I'm such a dirt-bag he can't believe I'd give a shit. That pissed me off. Then, I come in a week later and he's letting me go.' Curtis shrugged. 'I'll get other work, I know that. But, you know, I's just trying to do the right thing.'

'Mr Trahorne says you stole from the lab.'

Curtis looked up. 'OK, yeah I did. A little platinum foil. One time.'

'And he says you hold a grudge towards him because he fired you.'

'Yeah. I do.'

Danny smiled.

'I do hold a grudge,' said Curtis. 'Doesn't make me a liar.'

'OK,' said Joe.

'Also,' said Curtis, 'I ain't got no grudge against that Valtry lab. I don't know them. Why would I say this shit and imprecate them?'

'We're not accusing you of implicating them.'

He raised his head slowly and stared Danny down. 'I said "imprecate". It's a word. Look it up.'

Danny let out a breath.

Joe arrived home at 8.30 and stood in front of the mirror in the bathroom, rubbing his stubbled jaw. He slipped a blade from his razor and flicked it towards the bin. It hit the wall first, then bounced onto the floor, taking some garbage with it. He bent down to pick it up and saw a scrunched-up drugstore receipt. He glanced at the two items on it: Tara's SplashBronze tanner and something that sent his stomach into spasm: a pregnancy test. He ran his hands through the bin, looking for the box or the test. He couldn't find them. He was about to give up, when he spotted the navy plastic cap of the test and pulled it free. Tests had changed. They now had a digital read-out. No checking symbols against a leaflet. No guessing. This one just told it like it was: PREGNANT. Shaun's whole life flashed before his eyes. Joe checked the date on the receipt. It was a week old. Joe put down his razor and went to Shaun's room.

'Son, I'm going to cut to the chase here,' he said, sitting on Shaun's bed. Shaun swung his chair around from his desk.

'Yeah?'

'I hope you're . . . you know . . . with Tara . . . uh, using protection.'

'Oh my God,' said Shaun, looking away.

'I'm serious. You need to be careful.'

'This is so embarrassing. What makes you think I'm not?'

'Well, nothing. I just—'

'Did we not have this talk, like, a few years ago?'

'With everything that's happened . . . I want to make sure you're staying . . . sensible.'

'I am . . . sensible.'

'Good. Because if you're having sex . . .' He trailed off. They sat in silence.

'I'm not,' said Shaun eventually.

'What?' said Joe.

'I'm not. We're not, OK? I'm having a hard time . . . with . . . being close to someone.'

'Oh,' said Joe. 'I thought—' He stared at the floor.

Shaun stared at the floor. 'The first time with Katie, I never. I mean, you know, it didn't really

happen. And that's my last memory of . . . sex. If
I come close to that, I freeze. Like obviously, I can
get . . . you know . . . but I just don't want to go
any further . . .'

'Right. Shit. OK. Do you think . . . I mean . . .
are you really ready, Shaun?'

Shaun frowned.

'You're young, you're only just eighteen,' said
Joe, 'and if things had been different in your life,
I'd be giving you very different advice. I mean,
you can't always separate sex from emotion, whatever you might think. You have things to work
through and I'm not so sure rushing into something with another girl is the right way to go.'

'People are gonna think I'm some kind of
weirdo.' Shaun shook his head. 'I can't get Katie
out of my mind. Anything that makes me go back
to how I felt that night, I just can't do it. I have
this same dream where I meet her in the street
or in a coffee shop or whatever, she's always with
some guy and there's this feeling of hate coming
from her. I'm trying to be friendly. Then everything goes all white and when I try to reach out
to her, she slips back into this fog and I don't get
to touch her. And her face is always blank. She
doesn't smile at me. All I can think of is she died
probably hating me.'

'That's not true. She loved you. You know that.
You had an argument that night that was *because*
of how much she loved you. If she was still here,

you would have made up the next day. So she
thought it was your first time too – you wouldn't
hate someone for that. You might feel dumb, but
that's all.'

'She wouldn't have walked home alone . . .'

'Don't,' said Joe. 'You'll go over and over it
until you go crazy. Everything that happened was
out of your control. That's one of the hardest parts
about life – you don't know what's around the
corner.'

They sat in silence for a few seconds. Joe
wondered what game Tara was playing.

'Shaun, are you and Tara exclusive? I mean,
could Tara be seeing other guys?'

'Jesus Dad, bad enough you're on my case, I'm
not going to start getting into Tara's sex life with
you . . . or lack of it, thanks for your sensitivity.'

'Just, what's your relationship with her exactly?'

'OK, now you're just sounding freaky.'

Anna knocked on the door and stepped in.
'What do you think?' she said. 'New dress.'

'Cool,' said Shaun.

'You're going out tomorrow night,' said Anna,
'so I'm inviting your father to a special home
cooked meal.'

'You look beautiful,' said Joe. 'Very . . . healthy.'
She caught him staring at her chest.

'Thank you,' said Anna. 'And thank Tara,' she
said to Shaun. 'I bought some of her
SplashBronze.'

EIGHTEEN

Joe studied his reflection in the mottled mirror in the cool basement of Augie's on East 48th Street. He was wearing the same pale grey shirt and charcoal tie he wore to work that morning, but with a tuxedo that Anna had bought him in Paris two years earlier. Old Nic had discovered Augie Penrose in the seventies. He was one of New York's finest tailors. For forty years, his basement was open only to a loyal band of customers. Joe, Danny, Old Nic and Bobby, even Giulio Lucchesi, all had Augie alterations or suits.

'Beautiful tuxedo,' said Augie, 'beautiful.'

Joe nodded. 'My wife . . .'

'I saw the label was not from around here,' said Augie. 'Fancy guy. Guys give you a hard time for the European suits?'

'Jealousy,' said Joe, straightening each jacket sleeve. 'That's all it is, Augie.'

Augie laughed and walked over to him. 'Pants,'

he said, pulling at the loose waistband. 'Usually you guys come in, I'm letting the suit out,' he said.

'I'm running now,' said Joe, 'getting back in shape.'

'Yeah, I see it in guys your age all the time.'

'Really, Augie. My age is making me run?'

'For the hills. You're a handsome guy, Joe, but maybe you're looking at those grey hairs, a few lines around the eyes and wondering "Have I still got it? Do the hot chicks still check me out?"'

Joe looked down at Augie, sixty-seven years old, with his skinny, hairy white arms and his powdery pale scalp. He flashed forward twenty-five years, then looked back in the mirror to reassure himself.

'It's not over yet,' said Joe. 'Sure the hot chicks still check me out.' He smiled, but it fled quickly. Everywhere he looked that morning, women were pregnant, wheeling strollers, struggling with children and grocery bags and car seats and tantrums. Sharp surges of panic were overwhelming him. He waited for them to be replaced by something warmer. He couldn't work out whether the last year had disassociated him so much from life that he had lost all sense of what he wanted.

Augie picked some pins from a leather pouch at his hip and went to work on the waistband. 'Do you want some doughnut room?'

Joe shook his head. 'No. Give me something to aspire to.'

Nothing felt normal anymore. When Shaun was born, Joe was twenty-three, had loads of energy that was all channelled into his work. By the time the new baby was born, he would be almost forty-two and pictured himself tired and with no energy to channel anywhere. He tried to imagine himself with a stroller walking through Owl's Head Park, but the image wouldn't happen. His stomach was a knot of guilt and fear.

Augie stood up from his kneeling position at the hem of Joe's pants.

'I'm out of pins,' he said, disappearing into the back office to give the quiver in the expensive black fabric a chance to settle.

Dean Valtry sat at his desk, his manicured hands flat on the surface. In identical black glossy frames on the wall behind him was a row of photos showing eight dazzling Hollywood smiles.

'Beautiful,' said Valtry. He pointed to one celebrity icon. 'According to her dentist? She had the worst set of teeth he had ever seen. She was this breathtaking Southern belle . . . until she opened her mouth. Her teeth were rotten. She was a child model, developed an eating disorder, all she did was drink soda, eat crap. Now look at that smile. A thousand watts. That's what gets her the attention. And we did that. We gave her that career.'

Joe nodded. He was used to people like Valtry.

Cops were shit on their shoes, but they still needed to impress them.

Valtry kept talking. 'Of course, the dentists are the glory hounds. We create the perfection. They get their faces out there, in magazine ads, on TV, pat themselves on the back for my work. They just whack up the price, charge the patient five times what they're paying me – so you can imagine what they're taking in – and get their ass kissed by the rich and famous. What I do is like fine art. You know what a tooth looks like: individual, ridged, indented, curved . . . we replicate that exactly. In school, ninety per cent is a good grade. But there's only room for one hundred per cent in my line of work. When I make a crown, a dental implant, a bridge, it has to fit perfectly, like God himself put it there. Perfection doesn't do percentages.'

'It sure don't,' said Danny.

'That's how it is,' said Valtry. 'So, how may I help you?'

'Mr Valtry, do you use Trahorne Refining in Philly?' said Joe.

'Yes we do. Why?'

'We received a report,' said Joe, 'that a blood-stained lab coat was found in a package sent to them from your laboratory.'

Valtry frowned. 'Yeah, that can happen.'

Danny and Joe exchanged glances.

'Sure it can,' said Valtry. 'My technicians work

with these spinning wheels. They're mounted on lab benches and they file down metal with them. These things can break, quite explosively, actually. You could certainly get cut from flying debris.'

'That's not the quantity of blood we're talking about,' said Joe.

'Show me the coat. I'll tell you.'

'We don't have that in our possession,' said Joe.

'What?'

'It was incinerated.'

'I'm confused, gentlemen.'

'By accident,' said Danny loudly. 'It wound up in the incinerator.'

Valtry let out a snort, but slowly took in the demeanour of the two men standing in front of him. 'Just how bloodstained was this lab coat?'

Joe leaned forward. 'Enough that two homicide detectives are paying you a visit.'

Valtry paused. Joe had seen these pauses before. The person absorbs the information they're given, speeds through what he knows, weighs it all up, then decides how to play it.

Valtry threw his hands up. 'You're coming in to my office with tales of a bloodstained lab coat – no, wait – an imaginary bloodstained lab coat and *I'm* supposed to enlighten *you*?'

'Look,' said Danny. 'We've got the guy who found the coat. We have reason to believe it is linked to an investigation we are working on. We're asking for your help here.'

'This is crazy. Have you spoken with Bob Trahorne? You need to talk to Bob. He can vouch for me, my character, my reputation, whatever you need.' He gestured to the photos on his wall. 'You think someone like me, who has a successful professional relationship with New York's top Park Avenue dentists is going to be involved in a homicide? I'm going to risk my income and social . . . position in the community? Or employ someone who would be involved in a homicide? Give me a break. I'm top of my game, ask anyone. I earn a lot of money doing what I do, I don't piss people off, I make beautiful teeth. That's it. Talk to Bob. I've been dealing with him for fifteen years. I have no idea a. how that lab coat came to be there or b. if the lab coat even exists at all.'

'Yeah?' said Danny. 'You'll understand how that won't cut it with us. First off, can you tell us your whereabouts on March 13th last?'

Valtry paused, then leaned over to his computer and called up his calendar. He scrolled back six months. 'March 13th? I was at home with a very bad hangover. The night before, my ex-wife and I had dinner in Gordy's on 63rd and 8th. Gordy is my friend, with a generous hand in spirit measures. You need that while dining with a raving lunatic. You can call Gordy at—'

'But on the evening of the thirteenth you were home. Alone?'

'Alone.'

'What were you doing?'

'Watching TV. I went to bed early.'

'And on September 4th last?'

Valtry smiled broadly. 'Now that one, I've got an even better answer for. And I've got audio-visual aids.' He grabbed a remote control from his desktop and pointed it at a plasma screen on the wall. The screen lit up, showing Valtry standing at a podium in a sharp grey suit and silver and navy blue tie.

'There I am,' said Valtry, turning up the volume on the television.

Danny and Joe watched as he talked to his audience about ceramic and porcelain veneers and clicked through slides projected onto the wall of the conference room behind him.

'Where was this?' said Danny.

'The International Cosmetic Dentistry Convention, Las Vegas.' said Valtry. 'August 31st to September 5th. And that night is, as you can see from the banner, September 4th.'

'So, how many times you watched that?' said Danny.

Valtry stared at him. 'I like to learn something from everything I do, Detective.'

'It's that perfection thing again, right?' said Danny, leaning over and turning off the television.

'We're going to need to talk to all your employees, Mr Valtry,' said Joe. 'Could you please

fax a list of their names over to my colleague –
Detective Fred Rencher – at this number, please?'

'Not a problem, detectives,' he said. 'A man
who has nothing to hide, hides nothing.'

'And we'd like to come in here tomorrow
morning and speak with all of them,' said Joe.
'Would you have a room we could use?'

Valtry sighed. 'If you really feel that's necessary.'

'Everything we do we feel is necessary, Mr
Valtry. That's why we do it,' said Danny.

'Good to know,' said Valtry. 'I'll get that list
sent over. I have fifteen trusted employees, so
it shouldn't be too taxing.' He gestured to the
door.

Joe and Danny walked towards it. 'We would
appreciate your cooperation on this,' said Joe.

'Just so you know?' said Valtry, 'I *like* helping
people. It's part of what I do. My lab does pro
bono work for a facial reconstruction charity. I
want to help you. I mean you must be desperate,
right? Following up on some invisible piece of
evidence.' He shrugged. 'But one thing? If I see
or hear my laboratory's name mentioned
anywhere in a negative context because of the
investigation you are running, I will sue the New
York Police Department's ass from here to the
next century.'

Joe and Danny stopped for water in the lobby,
then walked out to the car.

'Have you ever noticed people who are pissed off never say the letters?' said Danny. 'They. Like. Saying. Every. Word. New. York. Police. Department.'

'What is going on with that lab coat?' said Joe.

'And he's got to be some kind of fruit, thinking that actress gets all her attention from her goddamn smile. It's the dual airbags that put her on the front pages. He hasn't noticed that? Christ, it took me ten minutes to find her mouth when he pointed at her. Anyway, doesn't matter one way or another, the guy's a jerk.'

'The type who could easily have a disgruntled worker,' said Joe. 'We could find out it's his own blood. Maybe he wanted to put one over on Valtry, take that smug fucking look off his face.'

'Have you been listening to me?' said Danny.

'No.'

Joe arrived home just after eleven, his whole body tensed. Anna didn't look up when he walked in. She was curled on the sofa in pyjamas too comfortable for her to be about to entertain Joe or anything he had to say.

'Hi,' said Joe. He sat beside her and pulled her legs onto his lap.

Anna glanced towards him and back at the TV. In that instant, he saw the tiniest smudges of mascara under her eyes. She wore expensive makeup. It took a trained eye to notice signs of tears. He watched her for a while, the lights from the television flickering across her face. There was an air of tired defeat about her. He knew tonight had represented all that was right in their marriage and all that was wrong.

'I'm sorry,' he said. 'We got busy.'

'You should have called.'

'I know. Did you eat?'

'No,' she said. 'Did you?'

'Yes.'

She frowned. 'And in the time you were waiting around in a diner to get served, do you think you could have called me? You knew I had planned this.'

He sighed. 'I'm tired. I'm sorry. I have so much going on.'

'I made a real effort tonight,' she said. 'For us to have a nice meal.' Tears were back in her eyes. She shook her head. 'I don't know why I'm crying.'

'I do,' he said.

She looked up at him. 'What?'

'I know.'

She read his face. 'Oh.' Her mouth hovered on a smile.

He rubbed his face hard. 'I hoped you were going to tell me I got it wrong.'

'No,' she said. 'It's true. I'm pregnant.'

'How did this happen?' he said.

'It's what happens when you don't take precautions.'

'But you're on the—'

'Not since the . . . not since Ireland.'

'And you didn't think to tell me that?'

'How did you not *know*?' Her voice was rising.

'What, did you think I knew and I was actually taking some kind of risk? That I really thought "hey, whatever happens happens and wouldn't it be wonderful to bring a child into the world"?' He surprised himself with the intensity of his anger. But not as much as he surprised Anna.

'Oh, no,' he said. 'You really wanted this, didn't you?'

Panic flickered in her eyes.

He put his head in his hands. 'That night in those little shorts and . . . you were . . .'

'I wanted to be with you.'

'You wanted to get pregnant.'

'You think I'm that calculating.'

'Funny how we have sex once last month – great stats by the way – and you manage to get pregnant.'

Tears welled in her eyes. 'Why are you being so horrible?'

'Oh, Anna. Anna, what were you thinking?'

'Looking at you now,' she said, 'I really don't know.' She tried to leave.

'Wait,' said Joe. 'Please wait. I'm sorry. I'm off balance. This is just, this is huge. It's a shock to me. I . . . I've been thinking about it all day. I don't know.'

He reached out and held her shoulders. 'I'm

worried about you,' he said quietly, 'why you
wanted this to happen. I don't know where to
start with why we shouldn't be doing this. Your
health, your age, where your head is at . . .' He
lifted her chin with his finger. 'Sweetheart?'

She cried, her eyes closed, unable to meet his.
'I'm so scared. What have I done? Being a mother
is such a . . . it's terrifying. The world is terrible. I
hate it. I never used to be like this. I mean, even
if nothing had happened to us, I'd still feel this
way: there is no peace out there. Do you know
what I mean? You can't escape to anywhere any
more. Everywhere seems to be getting touched
by . . . evil.'

'No, it's not, honey,' said Joe. 'Trust me. It's just
hard for you right now to see all the good that's
out there. And your horm—'

'Don't say it.' She half-laughed through her
tears.

Joe smiled. 'Come here, honey. Everything is
going to be OK.'

He pulled her head to his chest, then brought
it down to rest on the cushion, away from the
heart he knew was beating too hard and fast to
be any comfort to her.

NINETEEN

Magda was sitting at the edge of Mary's bed when her eyes opened.

'Hello, sleepyhead,' she said. 'How are you feeling?'

Tears streamed down Mary's face.

'Can you remember anything?' said Magda.

'David's dead, isn't he?'

'He is, honey.' Magda sat on the bed beside her and stroked her forehead. 'I'm so sorry. Can you remember anything about your seizure?'

Mary shook her head. 'No.'

'That's OK. Don't worry. You might remember again, you might not.'

'What happened?'

'You were here alone. And you had a seizure . . . I came to the door and you were lying on the floor. I called the doctor.'

Mary smiled. 'What was I doing?'

'You were just distressed, swallowing a lot . . . nothing too crazy.'

'Weird. Was I saying anything?'

'Not a word.' She paused. 'But this was on your desk when I got here.' She handed Mary a piece of plain white paper. Mary frowned. She saw her own handwriting – lecture-hall writing, the rush to absorb and preserve at the same time. In clotted black ink, the words were scattered down the page: *Shadow. Absence. Loss. Can't move. Loss. Alone. Can't move. Red. Cold.*

She stared up at Magda to ease her rising panic. 'Did you read this?'

Magda nodded.

'Freaky,' said Mary, 'what's it supposed to mean?' She read it again.

'It's just a bad dream, sweetheart. You probably wrote it just before you went under.'

'*Shadow. Can't move. Alone.* That's weird. It feels wrong.' She started gulping for air.

'It was just a bad dream,' said Magda. 'That's all that was.'

'I need to know what it all means,' said Mary. Her voice was rising.

'Nothing. Just a few scary thoughts before your seizure you must have written down. Cooties of the mind. Don't let it get to you.'

She turned as another sheet of paper caught her eye. Mary got to it first. It had three words across the centre: *All. My. Fault.* And in the bottom, David's

name exactly as she always used to write it, with
the small d curving over to meet the capital one.

She started shaking. Magda reached out her
hand for the paper.

'No,' said Mary, clinging on to it. 'No.'

Julia Embry looked around the room at the nine-
teen residents of the Colt-Embry Homes.

'Good morning, everyone. Thank you all for
coming. I wish I wasn't, but I'm afraid I'm here
with some bad news. Mary Burig has lost her
brother, David. He died on Monday. Some of you
may have seen the newspapers. He was . . .
murdered.'

Most of them seemed to have already known.
'The reason I'm telling you this is, well, some of
you know David and also, it's very important that
we're all here for Mary. She's very upset. She's
not feeling very well. She's in her room this
morning. We need to give her the space to grieve.'

She looked around at everyone. They nodded.
Some were crying.

'I know what it's like to lose someone,' said
Julia. 'Ten years ago, my son, Robin died.' She
looked down. 'I loved Robin very much. He was
only seventeen years old. I thought I could not
go on after that. But I did and I'm still here. And
you're all still here too. Some of you lost people
in the same accident that brought you here. Some
of you, sadly, have lost your fiancés, husbands and

wives or family members to . . . well, to lack of understanding. I know that's very hard for you to have to deal with. One minute your life is one way, the next it has completely changed. Maybe some man or woman who had one extra beer and got behind the wheel of their car is the reason why you're here. We can't control everything. But every one of us is here because we care. I know you've all got a lot going on, but we need to look out for Mary. Because she's in pain right now.

'It's important to remember, though, that we do not have to be defined by the things that happen to us. And certainly not the negative things. You don't want people looking at you as just people who have suffered a brain injury. I don't want people looking at me as poor Robin's mom. There is a lot more to all of us. Losing Robin was devastating, but it made me want to set up this Clinic. So some good came of it.

'Anyway, I just wanted to say please be there for Mary, you can help her through this and do nice things to make her feel better as soon as she lets you know she's up to it.'

Joe and Danny were waiting outside the door when Julia came out.

'Hi,' said Joe. 'Is it OK if we have a word with Mary?'

She paused. 'What's it about? She had a seizure this morning, she's resting.'

'It won't take long,' said Joe. 'It's just about David and some of his financial records.'

'OK,' said Julia. 'What about them exactly?'

'Why don't we go talk to her?' said Joe.

'OK. No problem,' said Julia. 'I didn't mean to pry.'

Joe's cell phone rang. 'Pardon me,' he said, falling back as they walked the hallway.

'Detective Lucchesi? It's Scott Dolan again, Philly PD. You're not going to believe this – one of Curtis Walston's buddies in Trahorne Refining has put aside a nice bloodstained black top for us from another Valtry Lab package.'

'Another one?' said Joe.

'Yeah, it came in shortly after the first.'

'You're shitting me.'

'I got it right here in an evidence bag. This guy rescued it from the furnace. He hates the boss too, thinks it was total bullshit that Walston was fired.'

'Great news,' said Joe.

'Yeah, I'm sending it your way right now.'

Mary lay curled on her bed staring at the photo of David on her bedside table. She couldn't believe he was dead. She had no-one left. No family. Then she saw the photo of herself and Julia and Magda beside it and she knew she had some people who cared about her. This was her home now. Within a week of arriving at Colt-Embry, she had felt that way. She didn't want anyone to know anything that would make it have to be any other way. She heard a knock on her door and went to open it.

'Hello, Mary,' said Joe. 'Detectives Lucchesi and Markey again.'

She nodded. 'Come in.'

'How are you holding up?' said Joe.

She shrugged.

'Well we won't stay long,' he said, 'we just have something we'd like to clear up. We were going through your brother's financial records. We know that he pays for your care here, but before your attack, he was writing cheques for some large sums of money directly to you. Can you recall why?'

Mary frowned. 'Well, he was my big brother, he always helped me out . . .'

'These cheques were for 5000 dollars a month.'

'Wow,' said Mary. 'That's a lot of money.'

'It is,' said Joe. 'Maybe you could think about that and see if anything comes to mind or if you recall how you might have spent that money.'

'Sure,' said Mary. 'But, I don't know. I really don't. I mean, I'd remember that.'

Magda Oleszak walked into the library. Stan Frayte stood in the corner staring at a large framed photo hanging on the wall. It was a blond teenage boy smiling patiently at the camera. A wooden sign that said 'gallery' was mounted high above it.

Six months earlier, Magda had cleared a space

where residents could hang framed photos of their friends and family. It was more than just about decoration, it was part of their treatment – to bring familiar faces and memories out from their dark hiding places. Everyone was encouraged to bring in photos. Mary had brought one of David.

Magda nodded to the photo in front of Stan.

'That was the first photo we hung,' she said. 'It's Robin Embry, Julia's son.'

'Really?' said Stan.

'Yes,' said Magda. 'Poor boy. Killed in a car wreck.'

'How is Mary?' said Stan.

'She's OK,' said Magda. 'It's all very hard for her. Not just the loss, but David is linked to so many of her memories of when she was well and now he's gone, I think she feels there's no-one left in the world who knew her when she was stronger, no-one who knew the real Mary.'

TWENTY

The receptionist paged Dean Valtry and offered Danny and Joe seats they declined. Valtry came out almost immediately, his smile on, his arm extended.

'Good morning, detectives. There's a conference room on the second floor,' he said. 'You can use that. It's all set up. There's water, a coffee machine. I got in some doughnuts . . . I mean, also some pastries, Danishes . . .'

'Yeah, thanks,' said Danny. 'We appreciate it.'

'How do you want to do this?' said Valtry.

'Just send them up one by one, go by the list. No need to tell them anything else.'

Valtry nodded and walked to his office.

'I hate the doughnut thing,' said Danny as they stepped into the elevator.

'What are you talking about? You love dough-nuts,' said Joe, pressing the button for the second floor.

'Exactly,' said Danny. 'Once people get the

cop/doughnut thing confirmed, they go straight to thinking all their other ideas were right. Before you know it, we're all fat, dumb, lazy and racist.'

'And sleeping around on our wives.'

'There's got to be some perks to laying my life on the line every day.'

'Yeah, I really feel my life is in imminent danger right now,' said Joe.

'Hey, anyone could walk into this conference room today and—'

'See how quickly a box of grease and sugar can disappear.'

'Well it sure as hell ain't hanging around my gut,' said Danny, patting his flat stomach.

Joe looked at him. 'Yeah, you're so hot right now . . .'

They stepped off the elevator and noticed someone was already waiting outside the conference room door – a small, bookish Asian girl in rimless glasses, with long shiny hair in a ponytail and a snug white lab coat. She wore pale panty hose and brown don't-fuck-me shoes.

'That's our guy,' said Danny under his breath.

Joe laughed. The woman jumped.

'I'm sorry,' said Joe. 'Did I frighten you? Come on in.' He opened the door.

'Yes,' she said. 'Sorry. I was a million miles away. And I hate any, uh, official stuff.'

'I don't think you have anything to worry about,' said Danny.

She sat down quietly with her hands in her lap until Joe and Danny had poured coffee.

'Let me take your name,' said Danny.

'Ushi Gahr.'

'OK, Miss Gahr—'

'Ushi.'

'Ushi, something has come to our attention and we were wondering if you could help us out.'

'I'll try,' she said.

'Have you noticed anything suspicious at work in the past few weeks?'

'Suspicious?' She thought about it. 'No.' She shook her head firmly once.

'Anything out of the ordinary?' said Joe.

'Like what?'

'Like anything you don't see every day, something that might have surprised you?'

'I can't think of anything,' she said.

'Anything that made you feel uncomfortable?'

'No.'

'Is there anyone you work with who may have been acting strangely in any way?'

She smiled. 'I wish,' she said. 'I'm afraid they're a dull bunch. Quiet, hard-working, not a lot of partying. We're nerds. I mean, I'm the wildest, I would say. Just to put it into context for you.'

Joe smiled. 'OK. Does everyone get along well?'

She nodded. 'I guess so. As long as you don't eat food from the fridge labelled with anyone else's name, there's no conflict.'

'What kind of boss is Mr Valtry?'

'Fair,' she said. 'Enthusiastic about the craft. Everyone he employs here graduated top of their class. Mr Valtry is not someone I would ever have a long conversation with or even a conversation that was in any way other than one sided, but he is not unpleasant.' She paused. 'I hope that doesn't sound too negative.'

'To me,' said Danny, 'it sounds like how most people describe their bosses.'

'I guess so.'

'So,' said Joe. 'Mr Valtry – he's very skilled at his job?'

'The work he presents to us is beautifully crafted,' she said.

'Is he strict with his standards?' said Joe.

'Yes, but that's before he hires anyone. He's not going to hire anyone in the first place who is not 100 per cent accurate. And once he has that, he doesn't need to hold anyone's hand.'

'OK,' said Joe. 'I think that's everything. Thank you very much for your time.'

Ushi walked to the door, but stopped as she was closing it behind her.

'Ask him,' she said. 'Get Mr Valtry to show you how the machines work. It's very interesting.' She gave a small smile and left.

Over three hours, fourteen more employees came through the door, none of whom had seen or heard anything unusual.

'Now,' said Danny, flicking through his note-book. 'Why the fuck would I want to see Dean Valtry make me some teeth?'

'Well, Ushi seemed like a very bright young lady,' said Joe. 'She either loves her job a lot or she's making some sort of point.'

'And if it was just about her job, she would have invited us over to *her* lab bench wouldn't she?'

'Exactly.' Joe dialled reception. 'Hi, it's Detective Lucchesi in the . . . OK . . . thank you, yes . . . nearly – could you put me through to Mr Valtry, please? Thank you. Oh yeah, they were good.' He pointed at the doughnuts. Danny took that as an invitation.

'Hello, Mr Valtry,' said Joe. 'We're all done up here. There's just one more thing – could you give us a quick tour around the laboratory before we go, just so we can get a sense of what exactly it is you do? It might throw something up we hadn't thought about.' He nodded. 'That's great. We'll be right down.'

The laboratory was small with three rows of work benches and three technicians at each one. At the back was a shared bench with most of the larger equipment.

'OK,' said Valtry. 'Listen up, everybody. You've met our two detectives already – Detectives Lucchesi and Markey. I'm going to give them a

quick run-through of what we do here at the lab,
so if you don't mind, I'll be stopping at different
benches along the way, depending on what stage
of the process you're at. Anyone doing a wax-up?'

A girl at the back of the lab raised her hand.
'OK,' said Valtry, walking down to her. Joe and
Danny followed.

Valtry turned to them. 'Here's how it works.
When you're in the dentist's chair and he takes
an impression of your teeth, he sends that to us.
We pour plaster into it and let it set so we have
an exact model of your mouth, like when you see
those joke chattering teeth.' He held up a grey
plaster model of a bottom set of teeth. 'There's a
tooth missing here and I need to make a new one,
so I start by constructing it in wax. We use a wax
pot that keeps the wax liquid and then we dip in
a spatula and build up the wax from there.

'We take the individual wax tooth and put it
in this.' He held up a small clear plastic container.
'Then we fill that with a material kind of like
plaster and let that get hard. We screw off the
base, then put it in the oven. We run the temperature up to maybe 1500 degrees Fahrenheit, the
wax is melted away and when we look inside the
plaster, there's a little hole there in the shape of
the tooth where the wax used to be.'

'I'm going to cast now,' said a guy sitting behind
Danny. 'If you want to see that.' His voice was a
painful fraction too quiet.

'Did someone say something?' said Valtry.

The guy blushed.

'This gentleman right here's ready,' said Danny, nodding at him. The guy gave a small smile.

'Ah, Kelvin,' said Valtry. 'OK. Show us what you're doing.'

'Why don't you?' said Joe.

Valtry paused. 'Pardon me?'

'Why don't you talk us through it?' said Joe.

'Kelvin is an excellent—'

'We can tell,' said Danny, 'but hey, you're the guy with all the diplomas on the wall, let's see you do your thing. After that bit of video footage I saw, I sure as hell . . .'

'Fine,' said Valtry.

He led them to a bench at the back of the lab and two small ovens with fold-down doors. Beside it was a machine he leaned into to wind a large metal centrifuge.

'What's that?' said Joe.

'A cast-off oven,' said Valtry. 'You'll see what it does in a minute. I've just wound the centrifuge there and locked it in place.'

He put on gloves and picked up some tongs, opening the oven and taking out the small plaster cylinder with the tooth-shaped hole at the centre. He placed it on the work bench.

Kelvin walked past and leaned into the cast-off oven.

'I wound that already,' said Valtry.

Kelvin frowned. 'Well, there's a screw lying down there that's popped off, so . . . did you know that, Mr Valtry? I hope you knew that,' he said, teasing the boss with the backup of two strangers.

Valtry blushed. 'I did know that. I was testing you.' He laughed badly. 'Maybe you could put that back on. And wind it again.'

Kelvin smiled as he did it.

Valtry unhooked a blowtorch from the side of the machine, pulled down the oven door and lit it from the element glowing orange inside. 'This flame here is not hot enough to melt the gold, but once I mix it with oxygen . . .' He turned a valve on a tall green cylinder beside him and a thin blue flame shot from the torch. 'I now have a flame that is extremely hot. Three thousand degrees hot. So what we're going to do is shoot the metal through the hole and when it goes in, now you get a crown made of metal, it's not made of wax any more.'

'They might need to wear the glasses,' said Kelvin.

'Yes,' said Valtry. 'Can you get our friends some glasses?'

Kelvin handed them some eye protectors. 'Look, then look away. Don't stare too long at it.'

'He's using gold today,' said Valtry, 'so we put the gold ingots into the crucible here. I take the ring—'

Kelvin pointed to the crucible. 'Uh, don't forget to preheat the . . .'

'Thank you, again, Kelvin,' said Valtry, his voice

tight and upbeat. 'I take my torch and start by *preheating* the crucible until it's a nice cherry red. *Then* I put my ingots into the crucible. With the torch here, I melt the gold until it's liquid, it takes about sixty seconds. I take the ring out, put it right here in front of the crucible. When I shut the lid, it's going to start spinning and the centrifugal action shoots the gold right through the hole and into my mould. One, two three . . .'

He shut the glass lid and a dazzling circle of white light spun with the centrifuge underneath.

'Maybe we should shut off all the gas and stuff,' said Kelvin. 'I can do that.'

'Thank you,' said Valtry.

Kelvin shut off the torch, pulled out the tube from the gas supply and turned off the oxygen.

'Right, this is done,' said Valtry. He pushed on a lever at the centre of the machine, pressed a red button, opened the lid and used tongs to take out the plaster ring.

'I'm going to leave that for an hour to let everything go back to room temperature. When I break that open, inside it is a gold tooth. After that, it's a matter of trimming and polishing. And when that's done, we start doing all the cosmetic stuff that everybody sees – adding the ceramic or porcelain or whatever. But you need that metal foundation for strength.'

'So it's the leftovers of that trimming and polishing that gets sent to the refinery,' said Joe.

'Yes,' said Valtry.

'OK,' said Joe. 'Well thanks for showing us how you work.'

'Yeah,' said Danny. 'Thanks.'

Ushi Gahr smiled at them as they walked past. Out in the hallway, Joe turned to Danny. 'Gas, blowtorches, flames, molten metal . . . very nice tools for some psycho to have to play with.'

TWENTY-ONE

Shaun Lucchesi was stretched out in front of the television with a bottle of beer in his hand and a packet of tortilla chips in his lap.

'For crying out loud,' said Joe. 'It's seven o'clock on a Monday night, Shaun. Do you really think having a beer is a good idea?'

'Uh-huh,' said Shaun, still looking at the screen. He raised the bottle to his lips.

Joe watched him until he decided he couldn't take any more.

'This is all wrong,' he said, walking over and grabbing the beer out of his hand.

Shaun sat up. 'What the hell?'

'I've had enough,' Joe shouted. 'Your attitude sucks.'

'Yeah, whatever.'

'Stop it,' said Joe. 'Just shut the fuck up.'

Shaun's mouth dropped open.

Joe sat down, rubbing his forehead. 'I apologize,' he said. He glanced over at Shaun. He looked lost. But his whole family had changed in a year. And he hadn't spent any of that time dealing with it.

Joe spoke quietly. 'Look, Shaun. I'm sorry. I'm worried about you. So's your mom.'

Shaun sighed. 'I'm fine.'

'You're not,' said Joe. 'And I know you know that deep down.'

Shaun shrugged. Joe was looking at the same bored indifference he showed his father at eighteen. He couldn't work out if it made it easier or pissed him off more.

'There really is a difference between drinking now and when I was eighteen,' said Joe.

'Yes,' said Shaun. 'You probably wore bell-bottoms while you were doing it.'

'Maybe,' said Joe. 'But seriously, it was different. We didn't drink that much, that young.'

'It's not like I've a major problem.'

'Famous last words,' said Joe. Shaun shrugged.

'Shaun, listen. You're drinking, heavily, four nights a week. It won't end well. Why are you drinking so much?'

'I'm not. No-one else is getting crap from their parents about it.'

'Maybe no-one else cares this much about their kids.'

Shaun rolled his eyes.

'Come on,' said Joe. 'I'm talking to you about
this calmly. There's no argument going on here.
But let me tell you, there will be.'

Shaun stared at the floor.

'If you're drinking to forget . . . things,' said Joe.
'That's when me and your mom get worried. We
know what you've been through more than
anyone. Your friends don't. You're just one part
of a big group. No-one there is thinking about
each individual person and whether or not it's a
good idea for them to get wasted every night. They
don't care.'

'Yes, they do,' said Shaun.

'No they don't. Has anyone had one conversation with you about what happened in Ireland?'

'I don't want to talk about it,' said Shaun. 'They
know stuff, but not from talking to me.'

'And they still think it's a good idea for you to
get wasted every night.'

'It's not down to them,' said Shaun. 'I'm my
own person. I make my own decisions.'

'Well, you're making some very bad ones. And
we're not gonna stand by and take it. So here's
the deal: you get Saturday nights to go out. Friday,
you can catch a movie with Tara or whoever, but
no drinking. Every other night of the week, you're
home here. By 10.30.'

'No way,' said Shaun. 'No way, Dad. No way.'

'Way,' said Joe. 'Way. I'm getting to you before
your mom does. She's coming in here in a minute,

but I don't want her to have to worry about anything, so I'm talking to you now, OK? You'll see more why we need your cooperation on this, why neither of us need to have to worry our son is going to end up in rehab.'

'That's so dumb,' said Shaun.

Anna walked into the room. 'Hi.' She walked over to the sofa and sat beside Shaun. He frowned. 'What's wrong?'

'Nothing's wrong,' she said. 'We just have something we'd like to tell you.'

He waited.

'We're going to have a baby,' she said.

'Who?' said Shaun. He looked at them. 'You?' His eyes shot wide, rapidly searching both their faces. 'What?' He calmed slowly. 'Oh God,' he said. 'You're not kidding.'

'Just the reaction we were hoping for,' said Joe.

'Thanks,' said Anna.

'I'm sorry, Mom,' he said, leaning across to half-hug her. 'Congratulations.' He gave Joe a small smile.

'Your mother and I . . . we're very happy,' said Joe.

'It's very early to tell you,' said Anna, 'but your father thought, just, well, I don't need a lot of stress. I hope you can help me out with that.'

Shaun stared at Joe, but looked back at Anna kindly. 'Sure, Mom. I'm sorry,' he said. 'I'm happy for you guys. I mean, it's weird, but—'

Joe flashed a glance at him.

'Come on, it's weird,' said Shaun. 'But I guess it could be cool being a big brother.' He shrugged.

Joe's mobile rang. 'I have to take this,' he said, walking over to the window. 'Yeah?'

'Joe, it's Tom Blazkow. Two things: lab results came back on that second piece of clothing from Trahorne laboratory – we got a match with Ethan Lowry's blood. And . . . we got another body.'

Dean Valtry lived and died in a soulless TriBeCa loft on Duane Street. Alive, he suited the glossy, arctic white space, its angular furniture and care-fully placed art. Dead, his blasted forehead and stiffened corpse turned it into a self-conscious installation. He lay fully dressed in a navy pin stripe suit, blue shirt with white collar and cuffs, gold tie and gold cufflinks, slumped against a long low-backed sofa. His mouth hung open.

Danny and Joe looked down.

'Death don't do percentages,' said Danny.

'Shot in the head while he was sitting on his sofa,' said Joe.

Dr Hyland looked up and nodded.

'Probably too engrossed watching himself on TV to notice the killer come in,' said Danny.

'Hey,' said Bobby, walking over.

'First precinct isn't as safe as it used to be,' said Joe.

'No shit,' said Bobby.

'What happened here?' said Joe.

'Looking like a twenty-two again, but obviously his face hasn't had the crap bashed out of it.'

Joe shook his head. 'Anyone talk to the neighbors?'

'A lot of the apartments are vacant,' said Bobby. 'Wealthy owners who come to the city couple of times a year, actors, investors, whatever. The two people who were home heard nothing. The apartments are sound-proofed and are so goddamn big, they might as well be in different buildings.'

'Let's take a walk around,' said Joe.

'At least it's not hard to see everything,' said Danny. 'Pass around some cheese and wine and we could all be at a gallery opening.'

'Yes,' said Hyland, 'and Valtry here is the work of some edgy new up-and-comer with an eye for the macabre.'

Joe nodded. 'Back in a while.'

He walked with Danny through the open plan apartment, moving around the crime scene techs.

'So,' said Joe. 'The day we find a definite link between Trahorne Refining and Valtry's lab, Valtry winds up dead.'

'Yup,' said Danny. 'You think he was part of the whole—'

'I think he *knew* who was. And I think they paid him a visit tonight.'

'It had to have been someone who worked in the lab,' said Danny.

'Maybe we need to look further – at suppliers, whoever had to come in and out of the building, whoever could have had access to those paper drums or packages going in and out.'

'But we spoke to everyone from the cleaning staff up,' said Danny.

'Well, we missed someone.'

The tour of the apartment didn't take long – a vast, clean space, all of it as tidy as the lab, as perfectly kept as Valtry's office.

'He was not lying about his attention to detail,' said Joe. 'Look – alphabetized CDs, books – who does that?'

'You do, you retard.'

'Not this much, I don't.'

Danny looked at him like he had lost his mind. 'Joe. You're the neatest freak I know.' He looked around the room. 'Makes our job easier,' said Danny. 'No searching around for anything. I'd say every piece of paper in every file in those cabinets is in the right place.'

Joe used a glove to slide open one of the drawers. The tabs were colour-coded, their titles neatly printed. Danny shrugged. 'There are not enough hours in the day for this kind of shit.'

'Yeah, well, if you organize shit in the first place, you have more hours in the day, because you don't spend them trying to find things.'

'Jesus, get a life,' said Danny.

Joe walked over to the kitchen counter and

picked up the phone. He scrolled through the numbers, writing down everything from the call log. He did the same with Valtry's cell phone.

'Last number dialled was at 6.30 p.m.,' said Joe.

'Probably when he got home from work,' said Danny.

They walked into the bedroom, which had a white brick half-wall separating it from the living space. The bed was huge, custom-made, four-poster draped in white muslin.

'He lived here alone?' said Danny.

'Yup,' said Joe.

The area was untouched, a peaceful space, far removed from the scene at the other end of the apartment.

'OK,' said Joe. 'There's something missing in this apartment.'

'Heart,' said Danny.

'Yeah, apart from that.'

'Furniture.'

Joe shook his head. 'Equipment. Machines, all that shit we saw at his lab.'

'But he works at his lab, doesn't he?'

'When he was showing us around, did you think the guy was really at home with it? Or comfortable in that environment? When he was watching himself on his television screen, I looked at his calendar and almost every evening he had a social engagement. And he's not doing technician work in the day time. He's not doing it at night. Maybe he's doing it at the weekend, but now we know he isn't. There's nothing here.'

'Yeah, but he's the big boss. He doesn't want to be fooling around with ovens and little scalpels and shit. He says to us, "what I do is fine art" means, "what my minions do is fine art".'

Joe shook his head. 'Remember the Asian girl who said we should ask Valtry to show us around? I think it's because she had her doubts about something.'

They moved into the hallway.

'So he just takes credit for his workers' talent,' said Danny. 'That's what bosses do. When we get the psycho who did this, you think it's going to be us up there on the podium?'

'Sure,' said Joe, 'but Valtry was doing more than that. He was producing physical work that made his lab rats think he was great.'

'Yeah and . . . ?'

'And I don't think it was him who was producing it,' said Joe.

They walked back to Bobby.

'Where's the doorman?' said Joe.

'Shook-up downstairs,' said Bobby. 'Guy by the name of Cliff.'

Joe turned to Danny. 'Let's go talk to him.'

They took the elevator down to the first floor. Cliff sat, pale and sweating on an orange and grey sofa in front of them. 'I didn't see anyone come in,' he said. He held his right hand over his left arm. 'I'm sorry. I got heart problems.'

'It's OK,' said Joe. 'Take it easy. You need a glass of water?'

'No thanks. I'm good.'

'You were here all evening,' said Joe.

'Yes,' said Cliff. 'I'm always here when I'm supposed to be here.'

'That's good. And no-one came to see Mr Valtry?'

'No-one came through the front door.'

'OK.'

'But we have a back entrance here. We got a lot of personalities living here, entertainment industry, models, business people and they like their privacy.'

'There's no security detail back there?' said Joe.

'No and that's the way they like it.'

'So if I had a visitor, I can tell them where that door is and they walk right in.'

'Well, they would need your private code, each apartment has one, but sure, they can come in, we're not gonna know. A car could pull right up to that back door and anyone who's been given the code can come in.'

'Do you have a code?'

'I have *a* code. Residents set and reset their own codes. Your neighbor won't know your code unless you want him to, but there's no reason you would need to give him that. If something bad happens, whoever's code was entered can be traced back to them. But that hasn't happened yet . . . until now . . . and unfortunately the guy whose code was used isn't around to tell us about it.'

'But Valtry had to have known who he was letting in.'

'Yeah, obviously not well enough. Valtry was one of the good guys, would have trusted anyone. We're all really sorry this happened.'

'So are we, Cliff.'

'So what's up?' said Danny as they walked to the car.

'What do you mean what's up?' said Joe.

'You're acting weird.'

'What's up,' said Joe, 'is that my wife is pregnant.'

Danny stopped. 'Jesus. Well, congratulations. That's . . . great news. Is it?'

Joe sighed. 'If I was a better person, yeah, maybe.'

'What's that supposed to mean?'

'I guess it's good news. Least we made Shaun think it was.'

'Chicks dig guys with babies.'

Joe laughed, then quickly put a hand to his jaw. 'Shit.'

'I'll take the kid to the park for you,' said Danny. 'I got no problem with that. I'll tell him quietly, but loud enough for the hot chicks – Mommy is with the angels.'

Joe laughed again, despite his jaw. 'You're a sick fuck.'

TWENTY-TWO

Bobby Nicotero walked into the office at Manhattan North and went straight for Joe's desk.

'Can I have a word please, Joe?'

'Sure,' said Joe. 'Go ahead.'

'Maybe out in the hallway,' said Bobby.

'You can talk to me here.'

Bobby jabbed a finger towards him, his eyes blazing. 'The hallway,' he said, turning around and walking out.

Joe got up slowly and followed him.

'Would you like to tell me,' shouted Bobby, 'what the hell is going on between you and my father?'

'What?' said Joe, closing the door behind him.

'I know you're up to something. He's doing something for you, I know he is. And—'

'What the hell are you talking about?' said Joe.

'He's acting all secretive . . .' He trailed off. 'I
guess I was wrong about him cheating on my
mom—'

'Of course you were wrong,' said Joe. 'I could
have told you that.'

'Oh, sure you could, all-fucking-seeing-all-
knowing-Joe-Lu-fucking-cchesi.'

'Are you ever going to fucking grow up?'

'Shut the fuck up.'

Joe let out a breath. 'Bobby, like it or not, I
care a lot about Old Nic. Your father's bored, he
misses the job—'

'I could care less about my father,' said Bobby.
'I'm looking out for my ma. She's worried sick
about him. She's just glad she got him to retirement in one piece. She doesn't want him involved
in your bullshit.'

'Whatever is between me and your father is
between me and your father,' said Joe.

'Yeah, just the two of you,' said Bobby. 'Nice
and tight. But he's got a wife, all right?'

'Jesus Christ, listen to yourself, you fucking
freak. I'm helping your father with his book, OK?
That's it. Cover blown. Big deal.'

'You're full of shit, Lucchesi.'

'That's what I'm doing, Bobby. Ask your father.'

'I'm not asking him shit.'

'No shit.'

'What the hell is that supposed to mean?'

'You said it yourself – you could care less about your father. He wants to do something with his time. I help—'

'What do you know about what my father wants? Nothing—'

'Bullshit, I've known him for years, we—'

'Look,' said Bobby, 'we're stuck working together on this case, that's fine with me. I can walk right back into that office and everything will be on the level. But stay the fuck away from my family.'

'What the fuck are you talking about?' said Joe. 'Get the fuck out of my face.' He walked back into the office.

Rufo was standing at his desk holding an untouched Starbucks Grande Banana Coconut Frappuccino with whipped cream. Joe looked from the drink to his boss, but said nothing.

'Everything all right?' said Rufo.

'Yeah,' said Joe, fixing his jacket, sitting down at his desk.

'So the plan is . . .' said Rufo.

'Well, we traced the last number called from Dean Valtry's house to a Marjorie Ruehling, lives in the Bronx. Danny and I'll go check it out this morning, then we got Valtry's autopsy in the afternoon.'

'Five hundred and fifty calories in this baby,' said Rufo sadly.

Danny walked over and took the drink out of

his hand. 'Want me to put this out of your misery? Or your eye line, even?'

Rufo nodded sadly.

'A moment on the lips . . .' said Danny. He sucked up a mouthful. 'Like drinking a vacation.'

Joe shook his head. 'Come on. Boss, we'll see you later.'

'Wave bye-bye to Daddy,' said Danny to the cup. Rufo had already turned away.

Marjorie Ruehling lived off Southern Boulevard in the Bronx in the only apartment block on the street that wasn't newly renovated, for sale or about to be torn down. Joe rang the bell for 6E. An elderly voice crackled through the intercom.

'Yes?'

'Marjorie Ruehling?' said Joe.

'Yes,' she said. 'Who is this?'

'My name is Detective Joe Lucchesi with my partner, Detective Danny Markey from the NYPD. We'd just like to come in and talk to you about something.'

'What?'

Joe shook his head at Danny. 'Are you acquainted with a Mr Dean Valtry?'

'I'm going to come down now,' she said. 'And you can show me your nice badges.'

'OK, ma'am.'

Five minutes later, a skinny woman in her sixties

with a huge caramel-coloured bouffant and a peach velour tracksuit opened the door and studied the two badges. She opened the door wider and led Joe and Danny into a small, square, grey lobby lined with mailboxes, most of them overflowing.

'That man you mentioned – Valtry,' she said. 'He called here last night.'

'So you know him?'

'Not really. He was a friend of my daughter, Sonja, from way back. You'll need to talk to her. She'll know more. He was calling to speak with her.'

'Did you pass on the message to her?'

'There was no point,' said Mrs Ruehling. 'I knew she was out with her husband. And Valtry didn't want to leave a number.'

'Could we get a cell phone and address for Sonja?'

'Better than that. You can come in for coffee. She's on her way over.'

Marjorie Ruehling's apartment was a bland colour chart of creams, beiges and browns flowing between carpets and sofas and cushions.

'How did Mr Valtry seem to you on the phone last night?' said Joe.

Mrs Ruehling shrugged. 'Like I said, I don't know the man, but . . . I guess he seemed . . . he was talking quickly. That was the main thing I noticed. The phone call was over quickly after he told me to get her to call.'

'Was he speaking clearly?' said Joe.

'Yes,' she said. 'He seemed impatient, that's all.'

'OK,' said Joe.

They all stopped when they heard keys in the front door.

'Oma?' Sonja called from the hallway.

'German for grandmother,' said Marjorie. 'We're in the living room,' she shouted to her daughter.

Sonja Ruehling walked in. 'Hello . . . what's going on?'

Her mother smiled. 'It's OK,' she said. 'These are detectives. No big deal. Just about last night.'

Sonja frowned.

'Someone called your mother's home looking for you last night,' said Joe. 'Dean Valtry?'

'Dean Valtry?' She turned to her mother. 'What did he want?'

'He didn't say,' said Mrs Ruehling. 'Just you were to call him.'

'Did he leave a number?' said Sonja.

'No,' said Mrs Ruehling. 'It's all very funny. Why don't *you* ask him?' she said to Joe.

'How do you know him?' said Joe to Sonja.

'We . . . look, why don't we go into the kitchen?' said Sonja. 'Oma, you don't mind, do you? There's no point in you getting into all this.'

'As long as you fill me in later, I'm fine right here.' She took an apple from the table beside her and started peeling it with a knife.

Joe, Danny and Sonja moved into the kitchen.

'OK,' said Sonja. 'This is all strange. I know Dean Valtry because I dated his friend. But years ago, when I was twenty-one, twenty-two.'

'I'm sorry to have to inform you that Mr Valtry was the victim of a homicide last night,' said Joe.

'Oh my God.'

'Yes. And he tried calling your mother's house several times yesterday. He was looking for you. She didn't want to give out your number. We just want to know why he would be calling you.'

'I have no idea.' She lowered her voice again. 'We weren't even particularly close. I mean, to be honest, we didn't really get on, God rest him.'

'Tell us some more about how you met,' said Joe.

'I worked at Feelers, this bar in the East Village. One of the guys I worked with, his name was Alan Moder and we got together and Dean Valtry was his friend. That's how I knew him.'

'When was the last time you saw Dean?'

'Years ago. What has he been doing?'

'He was boss of one of the top dental laboratories in New York.'

Sonja leaned back in her seat and smiled.

'You look surprised,' said Joe.

'I am. He was ambitious, so from that point of view, I get it. But from what I gathered, he wasn't that good.'

'Where did you get that idea?'

'Alan. They were in college together. It was

funny, Alan dropped out and he was the one with the talent.'

'But Valtry opened the lab.'

'Yes, but Alan did a lot of what got Dean's company noticed. Alan worked for Dean.'

'Does Alan have his own lab?'

'I have no idea where Alan Moder is or what he does.'

'It ended badly,' said Danny.

'Very. Let's put it this way – last time I saw Alan Moder, he was screaming obscenities at me in front of my work colleagues in a beautiful French bistro on 29th Street, seven years after I dumped him in the most shitty way possible, so he would never come near me again.' Her laugh was bitter.

'Yikes,' said Danny.

'I should be over it, I mean, I am over it, obviously,' she said, 'but you know when you just think – what a shit. I was twenty-two years old, madly in love. I thought he was too until I caught him with a woman over twice his age, some fat, wealthy woman who even I knew he didn't give a damn about. So that's my Alan Moder story. I'm going into way too much detail. It's just I've never got it off my chest. I'm married now. Alan showed up that time in the restaurant, trying to get me back after that witch he went off with died. So there you have it.'

'Back to Valtry,' said Danny. 'Can you think of

any reason he would have wanted to get in contact with you?'

She shrugged. 'No. The three of us hung out together all the time, but it was more that he was Alan's, like, only friend and so I was lumbered with him. He was – we just weren't close. I'm still shocked he's dead.' She shook her head. 'It's so weird he tried to call me. That's going to bug me. Let me know when you find out.'

'Sure,' said Joe. 'What was Valtry like?'

'He was fine,' said Sonja. 'Boring, if anything. Bookish, but dumb. Terrible combination,' she laughed. 'The type who tries to seem more intelligent, better than everyone at everything . . .'

'Was he ever violent?'

'Dean?' She laughed. 'No. Why do you ask?'

'Just covering as much ground as we can, now that we have you here,' said Danny.

'Seeing that Alan Moder is the only link you can think of to Valtry,' said Joe, 'do you know how we could get a hold of him if we needed to?'

'I wouldn't be surprised if he still worked for Dean.'

'No,' said Danny. 'We've been through employee records. He's not there.'

'I don't know then. Let me think. He was from Maplewood, New Jersey, but I'd say he's never been back there. He had a major falling out with his family. It was all very dysfunctional. But you

could try them. His father's name was Tony.' She
shrugged.

'OK,' said Joe. 'Thanks a lot for your help.'

Shaun Lucchesi walked into the kitchen past his
mother and grabbed a carton of juice from the
fridge. He drank from it, then put it back in.

'You will be pleased to hear it's over between
me and Tara.'

'What?' said Anna. 'Why would I be pleased to
hear that?'

Shaun stared at her. 'Are you for real?'

'What? I . . . she was cute,' said Anna.

'Sure,' said Shaun. 'You now think cute is, like,
emaciated.'

'She had a pretty face.'

'Under all that makeup.'

Anna turned to him. He smiled and shrugged.

'Want to hear something funny?' he said.

She nodded.

'I bought her a special edition of *Romeo and
Juliet* because she told me how much she loved it
and when I gave it to her she said, "Oh my God.
It was the *movie* I liked. Leonardo di Caprio is so
hot."'

Anna laughed. 'Oh la la.'

'I know.'

Bobby Nicotero sat at his desk in the twentieth
precinct. He worked well there. His shift had

finished three hours earlier, but he didn't want to go home. He read through copied pages of statements, making notes, highlighting, cross-checking. Nothing new was showing up. He sat back in his chair and started thinking about his two boys. He had a day off the next day – his first for weeks. They were going to the Sea, Air and Space Museum. He smiled. Then he turned back to his notes, drawn to a section of text, highlighted roughly in blue. Something finally clicked into place. He just needed to check one more thing.

Anna was lying on the sofa watching television and flicking through an oversized book of fabric samples. Joe arrived home and went straight upstairs to the bedroom. She followed him up.

'Hi,' she said.

'Hi.'

'How are you?'

'Fine. How are you?'

'Fine.'

He pulled off his suit jacket, then his shirt and tie.

'Shaun broke up with Tara,' said Anna.

'Really?'

Anna nodded. 'Yes.'

'Yeah, I never ended up with the girls my ma didn't like.'

'You didn't like her either.'

'That's not the point. It's all about Mom. I think

maybe it's like a dog whistle. You send out some repel signal that's only picked up by girls who look like tramps. Which is exactly what teenage boys are looking for.'

Anna slapped Joe's shoulder.

'What?' he said, smiling. 'It's OK. I'm past that phase.'

'We could have another boy and have to go through it all over again. Or worse – a girl to keep control of.'

Joe said nothing.

'What?' said Anna. 'What's wrong?'

'Nothing,' said Joe.

'There is something. We have barely had a conversation this week—'

'I'm pretty busy, Anna.'

'Me too.'

'I'm sorry,' he said, yanking his belt from his trousers, 'if I sometimes can't connect your level of busy with mine, OK?'

'That's not fair.'

'Life's not fair. Who says life's fair? The shit I see . . . I could care less if stripy wallpaper is making a fucking comeback. Can you see how that might not matter to me?'

Anna stared at him. 'No-one can ever win with you, can they? You arrogant—'

'Whoa, I'm not *arrogant*,' said Joe. 'I'm just not living up in the clouds . . .'

'Up in the clouds?' she shouted.

It spurred him on.

'Yeah, making up these fake little worlds where everything is perfect and everyone is happy and the sun is shining and all the people are sitting on the sofas or dancing around their fucking kitchens and bedrooms in their cute underwear with their perfect bodies, with big smiles on their faces and—'

'Are you OK?' Anna said, her voice softer.

'No! No I'm not.'

'You've changed so much.'

Joe rolled his eyes. 'Why do women say that shit?'

'What?'

'Look – it's not a bad thing if I have changed, Anna. People change. At forty, you want to be married to some immature asshole with no clue about responsibility or no major ambition who likes to get drunk every weekend with the guys? You can't start idealizing this guy you married.'

'That's the thing, it's not idealizing you. I didn't need to. You were—'

'Don't give me that crap. I used to drive you nuts, same as always.'

'We never fought like this.'

Joe looked down. 'No. We didn't.'

'What is *wrong* with you?' said Anna.

'OK. You want to know? You really want to know? I'm furious! You know, I've tried to be cool, but I'm not. We have one more year before

Shaun goes to college and I thought great, just the two of us, you know? I cannot believe that right when I think my life is going to go one way, someone hits rewind and I'm right back where I was eighteen years ago. I feel like I've worked my ass off for nothing, Anna.'

'That's not how it is.'

'Yes, it is! I feel paralysed here! This baby feels like an excuse for something.'

'What do you mean by that?'

'Like an excuse for you not to have to face what has happened to us. An excuse for you not to have to go out there—' He pointed to the window.

'Out where?' said Anna.

'Anywhere,' Joe shouted. 'Anywhere! Look at how you've been living. You've hardly gone outside the door, you fall apart when you do, you're here all day, in the evenings—'

'I'm depressed!' she shouted.

'Exactly,' shouted Joe. 'Which is why we should not be having this baby. Who wants to bring a kid into this home?' It hung there in the silence.

'We have a wonderful home,' said Anna. She started to cry.

Joe sat down on the bed. 'Doesn't feel that way,' he said. 'Or maybe I've forgotten. I don't know any more. I don't think about it. I never think about us any more.'

'I know,' said Anna, pressing her sleeve against her eyes.

He looked up at her. 'I . . . love you so much, you and Shaun. You're everything to me. But we're not the same. I mean, things have changed.'

'Maybe the baby will . . .'

Joe shook his head sadly. 'That's one hell of a scary job for a newborn.'

TWENTY-THREE

The sun beamed down through a slice in the grey sky over Denison, Texas. Wanda Rawlins held her hand up to the television set, the bones in her fingers rigid and spread.

'I have been clean and sober for—' The telegenic preacher, his grey hair smooth and waxy, paused for his audience to fill in their 'time spent walking with Jesus'.

'Sixteen years, three days and seven hours,' said Wanda.

'Before I walked with Jesus I—'

'Danced with the devil.' Wanda's voice was as fiery as the man with the headset microphone striding the stage in the crowded white marquee.

'My salvation was—'

'Vincent Farraday.' Wanda shouted. She was talking about her husband, the singer who plucked her off a strippers' stage in Stinger's Creek, cleaned her up and welcomed her into this loving home

in Denison, forty miles south. The studio audience had already answered 'The Lord'.

'Oh yeah, the Lord,' said Wanda. 'Duh. My
salvation was The Lord and Vincent Farraday.'

The preacher stood with his arms outspread,
his hips thrust forward. 'My power is in—'

'My sobriety,' said Wanda.

'My love,' said Wanda.

'My destiny,' said Wanda.

'My denial. My detachment. My ice cold soul.'
Duke Rawlins stood in the doorway, gripping the
frame above his head, his long, lean body rocking
gently back and forth. The audience cheered.

'Dukey,' said Wanda, struggling to get up from
the floor.

Duke looked at the television. 'You won't recall
this, Mama,' he said, 'but it was soap operas you
used to watch. All day sometimes. I would run all
over the house, all over the yard. I would come
in to you, lying there and I would have scratches
and bruises and dirt on me, just, you know, to
see . . .' He shrugged. 'And you would lean your
head around me, use all your weakness to push
me aside and you would say, "Mama's got some
other people's lives to watch."' He smiled. 'Well I
see now that Mama's got her some Jesus to watch.'
His face twisted into an expression of the hate
down deep and rising.

Wanda's eyes were love and fear and sixteen
years, three days and seven hours of veneer.

'You've done some very bad things, Dukey. A lot of people want to talk to you. That detective in New York . . .' Duke's expression stopped her. She raised calming hands. 'But I understand why now,' she said, 'why you did those things.'

Duke tilted his head.

Wanda nodded. 'I understand. The devil entered my body with the sin of my ways. I opened my lifeblood to him and he flowed right in. He rested alongside you in the womb. And he grew alongside you. And when you came out of inside me, he was gone. And the only place he could . . .'

Duke had a new laugh for this, one he had never used before, high and staccato and minutes long. 'You crazy motherfucking bitch,' he said at the end. 'Damn, you're crazy. Maybe the crazy fairy fucked you up the ass. He went in one way, the devil went in another. Maybe they met in the middle, had themselves a little party. Hell, maybe I joined in.' He laughed again and started walking towards her.

'I want to help you, Dukey. I want to redeem—'

'Yourself, Mama. As per usual. You want to redeem yourself.'

'No, no!' said Wanda. 'I'll do whatever you want. You need money? I got money.' She pointed at her pocket book. 'I won't tell anyone you were here. You can even stay here! I won't tell a soul.'

Duke let her panic run its course.

'I'll . . . what do you need, Duke? I'll do it. I'll . . . whatever it is.' She saw how he was looking at her. She stumbled back, grabbing for the cell phone on the arm of the pretty pink sofa. She held it in her trembling hand. Duke's right leg shot out and kicked it away.

Wanda screamed. 'You broke something.'

'So did you,' said Duke.

Wanda sat with her back to her son's chest. He sat behind her, taking the full weight of her body, his legs wrapped around her, pinning hers to the ground. With skills honed throughout his child-hood, he quickly wrapped the tourniquet around her left arm, pulled out a syringe and shot the purest heroin to ever course through Wanda Rawlins' veins. Her stricken face was quickly replaced by one he knew better: the slack one; the face that danced on shiny poles, the face that stood outside the school gate, the face that baked burned cookies, the face that opened his bedroom door to johns whose needs no woman could ever meet.

One hour later, Vincent Farraday arrived back from the grocery store and walked in on the wife he thought he'd saved – her body limp, her eyes dark and glassy. She gave a half smile and turned back to the TV.

Vincent turned to the twin teenage girls standing beside him.

'Your mama is not feeling well,' he said. 'I'm thinking, let's go on that vacation a day early. Go pack your bags.'

Vincent Farraday took off his hat and rubbed his head over and over. He pulled out a handkerchief and pressed it to the corner of his eyes.

The preacher's voice rose from the television through the quiet. 'And if a house be divided against itself, that house cannot stand.'

The audience cheered.

'And whoever rewards evil for good, evil will not depart from their house.'

TWENTY-FOUR

Joe sat at his laptop with the VICS file opened. The last time he used it, he had added the photo of David Burig. Now he added Dean Valtry. The faces of five murdered men looked out at him from the screen. And underneath was a photo of Mary Burig. He shifted the boxes around and made two sections that he separated with a thick red line. To the left were Gary Ortis, William Aneto, Preston Blake, Ethan Lowry. To the right were Mary Burig, David Burig and Dean Valtry. Joe drew a black border around Preston Blake and Mary Burig – the ones who got away. Then he focused on the three names to the right of the red line – the line that marked the point when the motive changed. He had no doubt that the killer knew Mary Burig, David Burig and Dean Valtry. Joe just had to figure out how. And who else could be next on that list.

*   *   *

The steps to Preston Blake's house were edged with crisp brown leaves, blown by a wind that had whipped up out of nowhere in the warm afternoon. Danny and Joe stood waiting on the front step after ringing the doorbell.

'I can just feel my retina being scanned,' said Danny. 'Or maybe my ass. He's taking some kind of outline of my ass to make sure it fits with the groove I left on the sofa from the last visit.'

Joe leaned close to Danny's ear. 'Shut the fuck up, he can probably hear you.'

'Yeah. Well. He. Can. Probably. Read. Our. Lips. Any. Way,' said Danny.

They rang the doorbell and knocked again.

Joe pulled out his phone and dialled Blake's number. It went straight to voicemail.

'Mr Blake, it's Detective Joe Lucchesi, here. We're right outside. We'd like to talk to you about a few things. We don't want to hold you up too long.'

One minute later, the door opened and Preston Blake stood in front of them, his face passive. He leaned out, glanced past them, onto the street, left and right, then looked at their badges.

'Come in,' he said. He brought them to the same room they had been in before, guided them to the same sofa.

'We appreciate this,' said Joe.

Preston Blake shrugged.

'How have you been doing?' said Danny.

'Great,' said Blake, his voice flat. 'How's your investigation?' He smiled.

'That's why we're here,' said Joe, 'we've a few more questions for you.'

'Go ahead. For what it's worth.'

'Have you ever come across a David Burig?'

'Why do you ask?'

'Just connecting a few dots.'

'No. I don't know a David Burig.'

'What about a Dean Valtry?'

'No. Are these guys suspects?'

'Like I said, their names have come up, we're just cross checking things. We were looking to see if maybe you knew them or if there's anything else you might have remembered.'

'Look, about remembering stuff, no, OK? I told you that. This is something I've gone over in my mind constantly. I'm not going to start randomly remembering extra details later on. It just doesn't happen that way.'

'For some people, it does,' said Danny.

'Not me.'

'Have you been reading the papers?'

Blake stared at them. 'No thanks,' he said. 'Not any more. My reluctance probably started around the time my house was under siege.'

'We didn't leak your name,' said Joe. 'We gave you a promise. And it's just not in the interest of the investigation.'

Blake frowned. 'So it wouldn't have helped to

have me out there – just in case the killer wanted
to finish me off.'

'He would have known where to find you if he
wanted to do that. Look, there's no point in going
over old ground . . .'

'Maybe I believe you, Detective,' said Blake.
'And you,' he said to Danny. 'But what about the
rest of your men? Do you trust them? All of them?'

Joe's phone rang. 'Excuse me,' he said, standing
up and walking a few feet away.

'Joe, it's Denis Cullen. I'm running a check on
that Alan Noder guy and—'

'Moder,' said Joe. 'M-O-D-E-R.'

'Oh, shit, sorry. That's why it wasn't adding up,'
said Denis. 'Someone wrote it down here—'

'Danny's scrawl. Not a problem.'

Joe sat back down. 'My apologies. Back to the
article – if it helps, I will call the journalist right
now and try again to get his source. You know
how they are about that, though, right? It's not
going to be easy. But if I do it, if he gives me that
information, it will be dealt with.'

'There's no need to call him,' said Blake. 'I'm
over it. It's done now. I guess I'll be forever linked
in every article, website, whatever. I don't think
anyone gets how hard that is.'

'I get it,' said Joe.

'That's why I thought maybe it wasn't you
personally.'

'Look, we need your help. I'm sure you can

understand why. We've had years talking to people, just talking and you'd be amazed at what can come back to people when they have to tell a story more than once—'

'A story,' said Blake. 'That's how you see it. That's how the press see it. A nice little story. An angle.'

'Come on,' said Joe. 'You know what I mean. I'm not—'

Blake stood up suddenly. 'I'm sorry. Would you excuse me, please? I just remembered. I've got a client coming to pick up a piece. Let me just bring it up.'

He left them sitting there.

'He isn't as pissed as I thought he'd be,' said Danny.

Joe let out a long breath. 'He's hard fucking work.'

'You have to watch what you say the whole time,' said Danny.

'He looks like shit,' said Joe.

'Why not get his teeth fixed?'

'Dr Mak says he's too scared.'

'That's what he says about everyone . . .'

'Well because you've brought it up, you can be the first to know: I am scheduled for surgery.'

'You what?' said Danny.

'Yes,' said Joe. 'Decision is made.'

'Like major surgery?'

Joe smiled. 'Like probably the most minor surgery you can get.'

Danny laughed. 'Then what's the point?'

'It's supposed to really work and it doesn't screw you up for ages, no major recovery time. I can go in, get it done, come out again, go right back to work. I'm doing it for you . . .'

Danny shook his head. 'I'm in shock here.'

'Yeah, well, I've had enough with the pain.'

'When you going in?'

'The end of the week – a slot came up . . .'

'Does Rufo know?'

Joe nodded. 'He's always happy when people address their problems.'

Danny smiled. They sat in silence for a while.

'You know something?' said Joe. 'He said "up".'

'What?' said Danny. 'Who?'

'Blake. He said, "Let me just bring it up". Last time we were here, he told us his workshop was upstairs. If that was the case, he'd be bringing the jewelry down.'

'So?' said Danny. 'So he brought the thing upstairs, now he's bringing it down.'

'Why has he been gone ten minutes?' said Joe, standing up.

'Jesus, relax,' said Danny. But Joe was already drawing his gun.

Danny sat up, then stood up. 'What are you doing?'

'I'm going to find him.'

'Put the gun away – the guy's probably gone to take a crap and he's going to freak out if he comes back and that's in his face. We're here to mend a few bridges, not fucking burn them down.'

'I don't think he's coming back,' said Joe, walking into the hall, through the hanging bookshelves. He looked carefully at the ones that were moving, very slightly, coming to rest after being knocked against.

'Mr Blake?' Joe called out. 'Mr Blake?' He heard nothing. He looked at Danny. He was also drawing his gun. Joe pointed to the basement door. Danny pointed to the stairs that led to the second floor. Joe shook his head and walked towards the basement door and slowly turned the knob.

The basement was still, airless. Joe shone his flashlight up to the ceiling, the light tracking across a wide wooden beam stretching overhead with a notch at its centre. He continued slowly down the stairs, the flashlight sweeping across glossy industrial grey steps and walls. Danny followed slowly behind.

'Mr Blake?' said Joe. 'Mr Blake?'

Silence. They reached the bottom of the steps. Joe moved the flashlight over a thick work bench with a small shelf above it that held clear plastic boxes of wires, metals and clasps. Mood boards on the wall behind it were inspirations for the jewelry that was pinned to bronze velvet backing in front of them. Spools of soft black leather hung from the shelf onto the bench top. Tools were lined up along the surface: a mandrel, burrs, pliers, filing discs.

'Told you he worked downstairs,' said Joe. He slid open one of the six small drawers down the right-hand side of the desk. It was empty.

'Look,' said Danny. He walked over to a machine standing four foot tall in the left-hand corner. The upper part was a small oven, mounted on a blue base with retro red and black start/stop buttons and clunky dials.

'The Oakville Gas Appliance Co.' Joe shone the light on the wide-tracked blocky caps embossed on the steel door, its enamel finish worn away by years of high temperatures.

'Motherfucker,' said Joe. 'That's like an old-style version of the oven Valtry used to burn off the wax.' He pointed to the dials, the top one marked AIR, with a dial that from numbers one to eight could increase or decrease the flow. Underneath, was a dial marked GAS, that could be turned from OPEN to CLOSED on a scale of one to five. To the right was a temperature gauge, set at 1500 Fahrenheit, below that, another dial with a red and green light.

'Blake makes jewelry,' said Danny. 'He burns metal.'

'Blake's the fucking perp,' said Joe. 'He's been fucking with us. He's the fucking perp.'

Danny stared at him. 'Holy fuck.'

'It's the same deal – make a mould in wax, burn it off, shoot the stuff through . . . you get a ring or you get a crown.'

'Holy fuck,' said Danny. He glanced down at the oven, panic in his eyes. 'That's off, right?'

'Yeah. The dials are at neutral, no lights on. Anyway, we'd smell gas or feel the heat.'

'Fuck me,' said Danny, staring at Joe, shaking his head. 'Son of a fucking bitch.'

'Let's take a better look around.' He reached over and hit a light switch on the wall behind the bench. No light came on. He turned to Joe and their eyes locked.

Rufo sat at his desk in front of two massive piles of papers, trying to decide which would get his attention first.

Denis Cullen knocked and walked in. 'I think we might have a problem,' he said. 'I've been trying Joe for the last half hour and I'm getting his voicemail. His cell is always on and—'

'No-one's cell is always on,' said Rufo. 'Come on.'

'You know what I mean,' said Denis. 'And he was waiting for information. He was out in Preston Blake's house with Danny, right? And I checked the address – 1890 Willow Street. That's exactly the address I got for this other guy I was doing a background check on. Alan Moder.'

'Who the hell is Moder?'

'A friend of Dean Valtry from college. I ran his records, I got last known address this house on Willow Street.'

'Any other residents in the home?'

'At that same time –1994 – I've got a Mrs Joan Blake.'

'Any Mr? Any children?'

'This is weird. I've come up with Mr Preston Blake. But I did a search and this Preston Blake died in '94. And he was, like, sixty-seven at the time.'

'And the last known address for Alan Moder was there?'

'Yup. So he went off the radar around the same time as this Preston Blake died.'

'Looks that way.'

'Well that's too good to be true, isn't it? Let me try Lucchesi again.' He dialled Joe's number, then Danny's – both went straight to voicemail.

Joe and Danny froze as the dull roar from above fused with a rumbling vibration that penetrated the walls, the floors, everything solid that surrounded them. Joe looked up and saw how quickly the notched beam snapped as the weight from the ceilings above crashed down. He caught a glint of silver as something plunged down towards him. Danny grabbed for his arm and pulled his focus, mouthing something he couldn't hear, pointing desperately towards the work bench. Joe watched as Danny's face, then his body, were swallowed up, quickly disappearing into a thick cloud of acrid dust.

TWENTY-FIVE

Anna Lucchesi knocked lightly on Shaun's bedroom door. He didn't answer.

'Honey? I know you're in there.'

Silence.

'I have something for you,' said Anna.

'Come in,' he said, his voice quiet.

Anna pushed open the door. Shaun was lying on the bed, in black sweatpants and a blue T-shirt. His eyes were red and swollen. She sat down beside him and put a hand gently on the side of his face.

'I know this is a difficult day for you,' she said. 'How are you holding up?'

He shook his head. 'Not. I just want to be on my own.'

'That's not always the right thing,' said Anna. She paused. 'I miss Katie too, you know.'

'I can't believe it's been so long.' He started to cry.

'I know.' She rubbed his hair. 'I got you this,' she said, putting a new scented candle on the bedside locker. 'I know it's Katie's candle you like, but just, if you like the smell, I thought . . .'

He put his hand on top of Anna's. 'Thanks, Mom. At least you remembered.'

'Your father has a lot on his mind,' said Anna. 'You know that.'

'I just know it's not us,' said Shaun.

'That's not true,' said Anna. 'Let me tell you something about your father you might not realize. He's old-fashioned, Shaun. He might look cool—'

Shaun laughed.

Anna laughed back. 'What? He does. Kids are so mean . . .'

'OK,' Shaun said. 'He doesn't look too nerdy.'

'OK,' said Anna. 'But what I'm saying is, he's old-fashioned. He believes in protecting us from all the horrible things he has to deal with. And you know what? He feels he didn't do that last year. And he's decided not to face that. I'm not getting all heavy with you, you don't need to hear all this stuff. But you just need to remember your father is a human being. And he cares a lot about us.'

The darkness in the basement was absolute. The deafening roar had died away, leaving behind isolated sounds of objects shifting slowly from where they'd originally fallen – loads being taken, then given up. A chunk of plaster had plunged from the ceiling above, trapping Joe and Danny under the work bench, pressed shoulder to shoulder, their bodies cramped and strained from choking and coughing.

'What the fuck?' said Danny.

He got no response. 'Joe?' He pushed against him with his elbow.

'My throat,' Joe managed. He coughed again, dry and hoarse.

'You hurt?' said Danny.

'I don't think so. You?'

'My neck.' His chin was forced against his chest. 'Can you see anything?'

'No. But . . .'

Danny managed to turn his head slightly to one side. 'Shit, Joe. The gas.'

'What gas?'

'The cylinder. There. For the oven. It's just lying right there.'

A small chunk of plaster crashed down from the ceiling sending up more dust and debris.

'Jesus Christ,' said Danny.

'It's OK,' said Joe. 'Anything that was going to fall down has fallen and the gas is only a problem if there's a fire.' He started coughing uncontrollably. 'My throat. I . . .' He tried desperately to suck in a breath, but nothing seemed to be working.

*   *   *

Blaring sirens shattered the quiet streets of Brooklyn Heights. The first fire truck arrived within five minutes of a call from one of the neighbors. The door to the basement was under the front stoop. The Forcible Entry team rushed to it – one with a Halligan tool to break through, the other, the can man, ready with a small fire extinguisher, a quick fix before the hose lines were ready.

The officer beside them shouted out. 'Hello? Hello? This is the fire department. My name is Johnson. Is there anybody in there?'

'Yes,' shouted Danny. 'Two of us. We're police officers.'

'Well, hang in there, we're going to get you out of there.'

'Hurry,' shouted Danny. 'My partner is not breathing . . .' He paused. Joe stared at him. Danny continued. '. . . very well. My partner is not breathing very well.'

'OK,' said Johnson. He turned away and shouted. 'Let the Chief know we got two police officers in here.' He turned back. 'What are your names?'

'Danny Markey, Joe Lucchesi, Manhattan North Homicide,' said Danny.

'Anyone else in the building?'

'I don't know,' said Joe, his voice weakened by his aching throat. 'I don't think so.' He coughed.

'The blast was deliberate,' shouted Danny.

'OK,' said Johnson. 'You think there's a possibility of a secondary explosion?'

'Nah, he's done, he's done,' said Joe.

'But the owner uses gas for his work,' shouted Danny.

There was silence from outside. Joe and Danny waited. They heard the crackle of Handie Talkies and voices outside, hushed this time.

'OK,' shouted Johnson. 'Guys, we got a small fire at the door we need to take care of, OK? Nothing to be alarmed by.'

Danny looked at Joe. 'Oh shit. Oh shit. This is not the way I'm going. No way.' He tried to lean forward and push at the chunk of ceiling that wedged them in.

'Danny, Danny, calm down,' said Joe. 'We're not going to be able to move that. The fire is not near us. Can you feel any heat? Can you smell anything?'

'No. But anything could be in this fucking place – more gas, flammable shit. I don't know. He could have planted more stuff. It's an old building—'

'Calm down,' said Joe. 'They know what they're doing.'

'This is my worst fucking nightmare,' said Danny. 'My worst nightmare.'

He clawed again at the plaster, then pushed with his palms. He struggled desperately to move his feet against it, to press his back to the wall and gain leverage. But his body stayed as trapped as it was when he crouched under the bench. Before long, he lost all feeling in his hands as he slammed them uselessly over and over against the plaster. Then he hammered with his fists, splitting the skin across his knuckles, oblivious to the pain and the sweat pouring down his face and soaking into his shirt and trousers.

Outside, houses were evacuated along the block, residents gathered at the far end of the street behind the barricades, camera and videophones ready to capture the next disaster. Three fire engines and two more fire trucks arrived. A F.A.S.T. truck struggled to find space on the narrow street. Rescue 2 and Squad 1 followed – elite teams of experts with specialist equipment. Over twenty-five firefighters gathered in front of the building.

Joe could see more than Danny. There was a jagged gap wide enough for him to look through. In the darkness, a small glow had struck up in the corner by the door. Through the haze of dust, it looked warm and unthreatening. When his eyes adjusted, he could see the fire, every flame like a flickering warning signal, powerful and unpredictable. He tried to see what lay around the fire to feed it, but it was just a series of jumbled shapes, each object indistinguishable from the next. Through the confusion of the FE team trying to break the door down, metal on metal, heavy boots on concrete, urgent voices, was a sound like gushing wind. Joe watched as the flames shot high, then low again, then spread out across the floor towards them. They had caught what looked like paper drums. The same ones Blake used to send off the bloodied clothes.

Danny had his eyes closed, but he couldn't miss the light flaring behind them.

'No,' he said, simply. 'No way. Tell me that's not—'

'They're at the door,' said Joe. 'They'll be inside any minute.'

Outside the Handie Talkie struck up and they both heard Johnson telling his men to back away from the door.

'Aw Jesus,' said Danny.

Tiny wisps of smoke drifted across the basement. The fire started to crackle. And very slowly, Joe started to feel heat at his shoulder. He felt Danny jerk beside him. He could see the whites of his eyes in the darkness. He was tearing up.

'Listen to me,' said Joe. 'The fire department is here, OK? They are right outside that door and we're their priority. They like to get people out alive. They're going to put that fire out. They need to make sure they're not putting themselves in danger first. Worst case scenario? The fire hits the gas tanks and then? We'll be blown to shit. But we won't feel a thing. What I'm saying is there is no chance of us burning alive in here. Trust me.'

'Man . . .' said Danny, 'I don't know.' Then he took a huge breath and roared: 'Johnson? Johnson? What the fuck is going on out there?'

But his voice was drowned out by the door crashing in. The FE team charged through, blasting the fire with extinguishers. The air was thick with smoke and dust, the floor littered with beams and exercise equipment and chunks of heavy ornamental plaster from the parlor floor above. They rushed to the work bench where Danny and Joe were trapped.

'We're going to clear this debris and get you out of there,' said Johnson. 'How you doing in there?'

'Good,' said Joe. 'We're doing good.'

Danny was slumped in the corner with relief, his hand over his face, the other hand still gripping Joe's arm.

Johnson spoke into his Handie Talkie. 'Chief, we got a partial collapse in the rear of the building. We just put out a small fire to the front of the first floor. Officers at the scene say there was an explosion while they were looking for a possible suspect. He could still be in the building.'

Joe shook his head. 'Probably not.'

The three firefighters were joined by more, forming a line to pass out the broken plaster, timber and rubble that blocked in the work bench. As soon as the space was large enough, Danny and Joe crawled out and stood up slowly, their faces covered with pale grey dust, their eyes rimmed red.

'Thank you,' said Joe.

'Not a problem,' said Johnson.

'Yeah – thanks,' said Danny. 'Let's get the hell out of here.'

Joe paused to look up through the shattered ceiling. He shook his head slowly.

They made their way through the basement door into the heat of Willow Street and crowds of firefighters, police and EMS crews, standing around between fire trucks, squad cars and ambulances. They were led to the back of an ambulance where they were checked over by an EMT.

'You should really go to the hospital,' she said.

'No thank you,' said Joe.

The fire marshal walked over to them. 'Taye Harris. How you doing?'

'Not doing too bad,' said Danny, shaking dust out of his hair.

More firefighters gathered around them.

'What happened?' said Harris.

Joe shrugged. 'We were inside, questioning a victim . . . he disappears, we go looking for him down in the basement.'

'I flicked a light switch,' said Danny, 'then, bam.'

'Looks like it was a BLEVE,' said Harris.

'Blevy?'

'Boiling Liquid Expanding Vapour Explosion,' said the marshal. 'Something was rigged in there,

we'll know more later. See – the third floor there
– the one window above the front door.'

Danny frowned. 'What?'

Harris pointed. 'We call the basement the first
floor. Next floor up is the second floor or parlor
floor where the front door is and see, above that
is the third floor.'

'Right, I see,' said Danny.

'Well, the roofman says he thinks the explosion came from the equivalent room to the rear
of the building. You were lucky the fire was so
contained,' said Harris. 'If that had gotten into the
cockloft, it would have run to the front and taken
off. I think what happened was something shorted
in the basement.'

Danny breathed out.

'You know what we call that room?' said Harris.
'With the bay window? It's small, there's usually
only one way out and in a fire where there's no
access to the interior stairs, you're trapped. We
call it the dead man's room.'

Rufo jogged over to them, his small hands
clenched. 'What are you doing, Lucchesi, bullshit-
ting here – get to the hospital, the both of you.'

'We're not going to the hospital,' said Joe. 'We're
fine. A few cuts and bruises, that's it. I'll fill out
a Line of Duty injury report—'

'Yeah, when you get back from the hospital.
I'm not giving you the option,' said Rufo. 'Look
at you, you're covered in crap. You don't know

what's under there. You can't see shit.'

'I think I'd know if I'd been hit by something,' said Joe.

'Me too,' said Rufo. 'Cos it would have knocked some sense into you. Now, go. To the hospital. Now.'

Joe and Danny looked at each other. 'Fine. OK. I'll drive,' said Joe.

'Thanks, guys,' he said to the firefighters.

'I'll be in touch when I know more,' said Harris.

'Here's my card,' said Joe.

Danny and Joe went to the ER at Long Island College Hospital and were given the all-clear by a doctor within ten minutes. They washed their faces in the men's room and were in Cody's on Court Street within an hour and a half of being dragged out from under Preston Blake's work bench.

Joe knocked back a shot of vodka. 'What the fuck was that about back there?' he said. '*My partner is not breathing.*'

'What if it was true?' said Danny. 'What if that fucking ceiling fell down on your head and killed you and you left a young son and a pregnant wife behind you?' He stared at Joe. 'Ain't you happy to be alive?'

Joe stared back.

'Weren't you a few seconds away from being a dead man?' said Danny. 'How did it feel not to breathe?'

'Jesus, Danny.'

Joe watched his partner. He was paler than he'd ever seen him, his face a sheen of sweat. His eyes were running all over the room.

'Yeah, well . . .' said Danny. He drank from his beer, his fingers almost straight, to take the pressure off his bloody knuckles. 'This is all the medical treatment I need today.' He ordered another beer.

'I was thinking about him. Or her. When I was in there . . .' said Joe.

'Who?'

'The baby.'

'Good,' said Danny. He raised his bottle and hit it off Joe's second glass of vodka. 'Cheers.'

'Cheers.'

'So,' said Danny. 'You still going along to the benefit tomorrow tonight?'

'I'm tired,' said Joe. 'But, yeah. For a few hours. Cullen's a good guy. And, you know, I got my tux altered.'

'Split the seams again . . .'

'An inward alteration, actually.'

'Inward.' Danny shook his head. His hand trembled as he raised his beer to his mouth. 'You want to know what I was thinking about when I was in there?'

'What?' said Joe.

'The rule of nines.'

Joe frowned. 'What? The burns thing?'

'Yeah, that diagram of the body to work out

the – what is it? – TSA? Total Surface Area of
burns. With all the different sections marked out
with percentages? I couldn't get it out of my head
when I was in there, when I smelled the flames.
The head and the arms are nine per cent each.
The front of the torso and the back are eighteen
per cent each. The legs are eighteen per cent
each . . .'

'Yeah?' said Joe slowly.

'Know what that adds up to?' said Danny.
'Ninety-nine per cent.'

Joe nodded. 'And?'

'Do you know what's the remaining one per
cent?'

Joe started to smile.

'Yeah,' said Danny. 'Your . . . genitalia. I'm lying
there in the dark and I'm thinking my nuts could
go up in flames at any minute. And I'd be marked
off in the hospital as having one per cent burns
and, you know, my prognosis mightn't be too bad.'

Danny's face was so serious, Joe was afraid to
laugh.

'But that's not what was freaking me out,' said
Danny. 'I was thinking – one per cent for such a
huge part of my life. The centre of my fucking
universe. The source of my marital problems. And,
obviously, some of my marital happiness. But I'm,
like, it could all be over, just like that. And I was
thinking of Gina and all the grief from this one
per cent and—'

'Excuse me for just one second,' said Joe, holding up a hand. He walked across the floor to the men's room, opened the door of the stall, pushed it closed and laughed silently until tears streamed down his face.

He walked back out and Danny was sitting in the same position, frowning. 'One Line. One per cent. One year on, still no answers. One life. It's a small word – one. And it can mean so fucking much.'

'One deep and meaningful detective,' said Joe. 'Right. I need to call Anna.' He dialled Anna's cell. He got voicemail. 'Honey, it's me. Me and Danny got caught in a building collapse earlier. I'm just calling to say I'm OK, I got checked out at the hospital. I'm fine. Sorry I'm leaving this on your voicemail. See you later. Love you.'

He turned to Danny. 'OK – has your life finished flashing before your eyes? Are you fit to work?'

Danny nodded and knocked back the last of his beer. They lasted an hour back at the office before they both went home.

TWENTY-SIX

Joe arrived at the house and went straight into the living room. He pulled off his jacket, threw it on the back of the sofa, sat down, turned on the television and put his feet up. He channel-hopped until the screen became a blur. Anna walked in.

'What happened?' she said, kneeling in front of him, putting her hand to his face.

He struggled up. 'Sorry, I was drifting off,' he said. 'I'm OK. We went to check this house out, the guy had rigged it up—'

'Rigged up? Like a bomb?'

'Nah. It was nothing, something small. It just shook us up more than anything.'

'I was so worried,' she said. She wrapped her arms around him.

'You never need to worry about me, honey, OK? You just take care of yourself. Of the two of you. And that big guy upstairs. That's all that matters.'

She kissed him.

'Honey?' he said. 'I'm sorry. About every-thing . . . how could I have been such an asshole?'

'It's OK,' said Anna.

'It's not,' said Joe. 'I was a total jerk. I hope you can forgive me. I haven't been there for you.'

She squeezed his hand. 'Me neither.'

'Let's start again,' he said. 'From right now. You, me, Shaun and . . . little Giulio.'

They looked at each other and laughed.

Danny arrived home to a quiet house. The kids' toys were all tidied away in boxes in the living room. Everywhere was neat. He went into the kitchen. He pressed play on the answer machine. It was his own voice, choked up and broken: *Honey, if you get this, it's me. I've been in an accident . . . it was terrible . . . a fire . . .* ' His breath caught. '*Please, sweetheart. Change your mind. I . . . the kids need me . . . us.*' He didn't care about how desperate he sounded. He just cared that she had heard this message and she had still gone. He listened to the last of it. '*I need you. I love you . . . we're a team.*'

He reached down and opened the drinks cabinet. He pulled out a bottle of whiskey.

'You total asshole,' said Gina, rushing over to him from the door. She whacked him across the shoulder. 'You asshole. You scared the shit out of me.' She hit him again. Then she hugged him tight. Tears spilled down her cheeks. 'You asshole.' She kissed him on the lips. He kissed her back.

'Where are the kids?' he said, looking behind her.

'With my ma.'

'You're not going to leave me, are you?' said Danny.

'No,' she said. 'Now, get me a glass . . . you asshole.'

The following morning, Joe and Danny were back in the office at eight. Joe took out his notebook and found Sonja Ruehling's number.

'Mrs Ruehling, it's Detective Joe Lucchesi. We were wondering if we could speak with you again as soon as possible.'

He nodded to Danny.

'We just have some questions to clear up, that's all,' said Joe. 'Yeah, OK. Sure. We'll see you there.'

They drove to a coffee shop near Sonja Ruehling's office on 43rd Street. She was waiting for them in a corner with three large coffees in front of her.

'Thanks,' said Joe. 'OK, we need to know a little more about Alan Moder. We're having problems tracking him down.'

'Alan? OK. You mean what he looks like and stuff?'

'Whatever you got,' said Danny.

'OK. Dark brown hair, brown eyes, long face . . .

long body too, actually. A cyclist's build, he cycles
or, at least, he did. He was from Maplewood, New
Jersey. He's, well, he would be . . . I guess, thirty-
three years old now.'

'Actually,' said Joe, glancing down at his notes,
'he's thirty-five.'

'Ugh,' she slapped the table. 'The guy is, like,
unbelievable.'

'What do you mean?' said Joe.

'He's such a liar,' she said. 'He's thirty-five. I
mean, that's not what's bothering me, but it's like,
even now, he is getting to me with his bullshit.'

'He was a bullshitter,' said Danny.

'He was a pathological liar,' said Sonja. 'I know
it's one of those terms that's thrown about out
there, but he really was. He could not help himself.'

'What do you mean exactly? What did he lie
about?'

'Everything,' she said. 'What time he got up in
the morning, what he had for breakfast . . . like,
you would come down in the morning and there
would be a pan with bits of scrambled egg at the
bottom and he would say, "I just grabbed a bagel."
Or I'd say, "where'd you get the shirt?" and he'd
say one store, then I'd see the label and it would
be from somewhere totally different.'

'Men,' said Danny.

'It's not that. It sounds like none of this was a
big deal, but it was. I didn't know where I stood
with him. And I'd make excuses. If little things in

his stories didn't add up, I'd put it down to bad memory. A lot of guys have bad memories, right?'

'I do,' said Danny. 'Drives my wife crazy.'

Sonja smiled. 'And can you imagine how good a liar you can get by practising with all the little lies? How much easier it would be, then, to lie about the big things?' She shook her head. 'It makes me so mad. He would be there all the time defending himself. It would wear you out. And in the end, you start to feel like you're the freak. That was the worst part.'

'You said the other day that it ended badly,' said Joe.

'When I caught him cheating, I left. I had suspected, but I thought I was being paranoid, of course.'

'Did you confront him there and then?'

'No. That's not my style. I turned and walked out. I left him a note. And I was gone.'

'Did he try contacting you afterwards?'

'For a few weeks after, once or twice, nothing too heavy. In the meantime—'

'Was he ever violent?'

'What?' she said. 'No.' She looked at both of them. 'You don't think . . . ohmygod . . . you don't think he had something to do with Dean do you?'

'We're just talking here,' said Joe. 'Sorting through some information.'

'Well he was never violent. I mean, that time in the restaurant when he went nuts, but there was never anything physical . . .' She slowed down as she realized she was probably saying something they had heard over and over from innocent people found sucked into homicide investigations.

'Sorry, I interrupted you,' said Joe. 'What were you about to tell us?'

'Just that for a while after we broke up, I was obsessed with finding out why Alan was like that, more to convince myself that I wasn't crazy for going out with him, do you know what I mean?'

'Makes sense,' said Danny.

She nodded. 'It turned out most of what he told me was bullshit. He said his father was a multi-millionaire, they owned homes around the world, his mother worked in the United Nations as a translator. The detail he gave me was unbelievable—'

'We see that all the time,' said Joe. 'Liars give way more detail than people who are just telling the truth.'

'I mean, some parts of it were true,' said Sonja. 'His family did live in a huge house in a nice part of Maplewood, but they hadn't a lot of money. His father had built the house – he had a construction company. Then it went bust, so they had the house but no money, even though they looked like they did and their parents seemed to encourage them not to say or act otherwise. So I think from very early on in Alan's life, he was trained to lie. And I think it went from there. He had, like, six brothers and sisters, but was only close to this one sister. But she died. He wasn't responsible, but he felt he was, because he covered for her the night she was going out. She and a group of friends were going to hang out by this quarry which, if her father had known, he would have forbidden her to go to, because it was unsafe, there had been major rain that week. Anyway, Alan covered for her and she fell while she was at the quarry, the ground gave way, whatever. And she died shortly afterwards.'

'How do you know that was true?' said Joe.

'Well, that was the final straw for his parents. They cut him off completely. I knew it had to have been something big for them to do that. Dean Valtry confirmed the story, he knew people involved. Also, I spoke with Alan's mother, so I had it all squared away. I felt terrible for him because of it all. But wouldn't you think that would *stop* him lying? That's how obsessed he was.'

'Do you think he could be any different now? Any more likely to tell some of the truth?' said Danny.

She smiled. 'I'd say it's even more difficult now to work out if he's lying. I'm not a stupid person. And he fooled me. That was years ago. He's a seasoned pro now.' She shrugged. 'Also, there's more than one way to lie: sometimes, he'll tell you the whole truth, sometimes a doctored truth and then there's the all-out fantasy stuff.' She looked at the two detectives. 'For Alan, there is no distinction between telling the truth and telling a lie, so when he's sitting right there in front of you, you will not see a flicker of a change across his face, nothing that you would be familiar with in a regular person. You won't see a tic, he won't touch his face a certain way, he won't blush, he won't sweat, he will calmly sit in front of you and lie through his teeth.'

Back at the office, Joe's phone rang.

He picked up. 'Yeah?'

'Detective Lucchesi? It's Taye Harris, fire marshal.'

'Hi, good to hear from you.'

'Just to fill you in, we found three propane cylinders in the rubble and some scraps of tape. So I'd say your guy left the cylinders in a taped-up room, releasing gas. So you wouldn't have got any odor even if you'd have been up there. That rear room was the source point. It was used as a gym. You were lucky you weren't hit with any of that equipment falling down. '

'How did it all happen?' said Joe.

'The switch your partner flicked. It's real easy to create an explosion. Looks like your guy used a light bulb. You soak a bit of twine in gasoline, wrap it around a light bulb base, just above the screw. You light it, let it burn a little, then dip it in water. That creates a crack. The bulb is intact, but basically, once you switch it on, you've got a naked flame in the room. He just set up the switch in the basement, made it look like it was going to light down there . . .'

'Jesus,' said Joe.

'Guys do it in prison,' said Harris. 'Nice way to take someone out. They crack the bulb and fill it with glue they've robbed from the shoe department or the woodwork room, wherever. When the cell doors are unlocked at meal times or exercise times, a guy will hang back, slip into the other guy's cell and swap the regular bulb for the one with the glue. The guy comes back to his cell, turns the light on, there's an explosion, he's covered with flaming glue he can't get off and basically, he's burned alive. Sometimes they won't bother with the light bulb, they'll just throw some glue over the guy, then throw a match after it. I don't care how many tattoos you have, everyone's terrified of being burned alive.'

Joe glanced over at Danny.

Heavy rain pounded the green awning of the Bay Ridge Manor. Denis Cullen stood underneath, smiling as he saw Joe and Danny running in, holding their jackets over their heads.

'Thanks for coming, fellas,' he said. 'I didn't expect to see you here after yesterday—'

'Don't worry about us,' said Joe, putting on his jacket. 'It's a pleasure.'

'This is my daughter, Maddy,' said Cullen. She stood with her arm around him, leaning lightly against him, pale and thin, with bright blue eyes.

'You look beautiful, sweetheart,' said Danny. 'It's very nice to meet you.'

She gave him a huge smile. 'Thank you,' she said. 'You too. What happened yesterday?'

'Someone gave Detective Lucchesi here a pretty big fright,' said Danny. 'He was crying, you should have seen him. Like a baby.'

She laughed.

'Your daddy's done some pretty cool things in this investigation we're working on,' said Joe.

Maddy smiled again and hugged Cullen's arm.

'My wife gave me this for you,' said Joe, reaching into the pocket of his tuxedo. He handed her a bracelet of pink beads.

'That's so sweet, thank you,' said Maddy. 'How did she guess I was wearing pink?'

'The wives are the real detectives,' said Cullen. 'We know that from Mom, don't we, sweetie?' He squeezed her shoulder gently. She laughed.

'Go ahead in,' said Denis. 'Get a few drinks into you.'

TWENTY-SEVEN

Magda Oleszak looked out from under the hood of a black waterproof jacket as she pulled the zip closed under her chin.

'Are we crazy going out in this?' She turned to the support staff standing next to her in the lobby of the Colt-Embry Homes.

'No,' shouted the residents.

Magda smiled. 'OK then. Let's get soaked.'

Mary made a move for the door. Magda grabbed her arm gently. 'Are you sure you won't join us for dinner?'

'Yes,' said Mary.

'Or I can come with you?' said Magda. 'And we can meet the others before the movie?'

'I'll be OK.' Mary held up her phone and switched between a screen with written directions to the church and one with a map from there to the movie theater. 'I just want to be alone. But thanks, Magda. I'll see you all at eight.'

She gave a small wave, pulled up her hood and dashed out into the rain.

St Martin's Church was empty but for the last of the congregation from evening mass. They were spread out across the pews that bordered the centre aisle or standing by the altar, putting money in slots to light candles. The smell of incense and wet umbrellas hung in the air. Mary kneeled in one of the pews near the back, setting her bag on the seat behind her. She prayed to each of the statues mounted high on plinths along the walls. She lost herself in the words, shutting out the sounds around her. She felt close to David, close to her parents, far away from all the bad things that had happened. She knew the intensity of her faith was a side-effect of her injury, but at least it was a positive one. She was at ease reciting childhood prayers that had been locked away safely in her long-term memory. She loved discovering new prayers, reading them from little cards, comforted by how right it was to find positivity in the darkest times.

After half an hour she picked up her bag and walked to the door, reaching into the front pocket to take out her phone. It wasn't there. She patted the other pocket. Nothing. Her heart immediately started to speed. She glanced around to see if anyone was watching her but then, she didn't care. She shook the contents of her bag all over the damp tiles: makeup, notebooks, loose pages, a hairbrush, Band-Aid, headache pills . . . things rolled away from her, paper blew into the air, but all Mary could see was that her phone wasn't there. Her phone was her memory. And now it was gone.

'No,' she said out loud. 'This is not happening to me.'

She pulled the lining of her bag out, checking it for holes. She started to cry. Her panic rose, pounding through her body. Her fingers trembled as she tried to drag everything back into the bag. She managed to stagger down the steps of the church, out the gate and make her way onto the street, where she grabbed the first person she saw.

'I'm looking for the Colt-Embry Clinic,' she said.

The person shrugged and walked on. The fourth person Mary asked pointed ahead, directing her left and then giving more instructions that Mary knew she wouldn't remember. She pulled her notebook out and wrote it all down, ignoring the woman's reaction. She walked quickly, then jogged, her eyes moving back and forth between the notebook and the pavement in case she had dropped the phone on the way to the church. She arrived at the apartment building to the warmth of the light at the empty reception desk. Everyone had left. She steadied her key with both hands as she unlocked the main door and ran in. She made her way quickly to the elevators, pressing the button for her floor, desperately trying to talk herself calm. Her phone would be on her bed, she left it there, or it would be on the floor, or it was by the sink in the bathroom, or it was on the kitchen counter top or it was gone. Maybe it was gone. It was definitely gone. But didn't she have it in the lobby? She couldn't recall. All her fears gripped her internally, there was no outward show. If anyone saw her, all they would think was that she was determined, not that her lifeline was gone and she could fall apart at any moment. She imagined being found again by Stan or Magda or Julia curled into a ball on the floor like a crazy woman.

She made it to the second floor, rushed past the library. She got to her apartment door and was pushing on it before she even had the key turned. She burst in and ransacked the place, pulling out drawers, turning over cushions, sweeping things onto the floor, falling to her knees to look under every space a phone would or would not fit. She stopped suddenly. She could hear a noise coming from further down the corridor. But she didn't care. She just needed to find her lists, her names, her whole life, lost in one tiny silver product.

She didn't hear him come in behind her. He was so quick, he held her in his arms and had his

hand clamped around her mouth before she had
time to scream.

For the second time in his life, Preston Blake sat
in a small room with Mary Burig. His skin was
covered in a film of greasy sweat that bled into
his scalp, leaving his hair limp and flat against his
forehead. He pulled a handkerchief from his pocket
and rubbed furiously at his face, throwing it, damp
and grey, to the ground when he had finished. He
studied Mary, searching for signs of recognition.

Mary could feel the tightness of dried tears on
her skin. They had streamed down her cheeks as
he carried her away, brought her to one of the
vacant apartments, sat her on the chair. The walls
had been painted that day. The carpet was covered
in sheets. Most of the furniture was gone or
protected with plastic covers. There was a ladder
and paint pots in the corner, some machine she
didn't recognize, brushes, newspapers, mugs, a
radio. An overpowering smell of onion filled her
nostrils. She looked around the room and saw one
halved on a plate in the corner to absorb the paint
fumes. It was dried out and useless. She couldn't
stop shaking. She still had her coat on and pulled
it around her to keep her warm, even though she
knew that the cold wasn't the problem.

The memories Mary had of the man sitting
opposite her were fragmented, the same broken
narrative she tried to put back together before her

seizures. A plug-in light, glowing on a baseboard, a tall figure standing in her office doorway, his voice strangled, his breathing shallow, "*I need your help I need your help I need your help, sit down. Don't do anything else. Just fucking listen to me, OK? Just listen to me. I'm looking for a little help here, OK? OK? I think I'm losing my mind. I just need you to listen to me. OK? Listen. That's all. That's your job, right? To listen and to help.*" Recoiling from him, he must have been only six or seven years older than her, but looked so much older, worn down . . . beyond her knowledge, "*Are you listening to me? Help me. I don't want to be who I am. Please help me. Stop me. His teeth. Liar. He was a fucking liar. I can rebuild some of the damage. But he's gone, he won't come back. I'm going to do it again. I'm going to kill again.*" Then David arriving, angry, protecting . . .

Mary shook her head. 'No,' she said. 'I don't remember.'

Blake tilted his head, saw the confusion in her face.

'What are you going to do to me?' said Mary.

'I don't know.'

'Did you kill my brother?'

'Yes.'

'Why?' Her voice was pleading and desperate.

'I made a mistake.'

'What do you mean?'

'I mean, I thought I could be prepared. For prison. For anything. But I made a mistake. I was wrong. I tried. It didn't work. And all I wanted then was to stay free. And I would have stopped killing . . . after you.'

'Please don't—'

He stared at her. 'I didn't start out this way. I just . . . something snapped. I wanted confirmation. That's all. I tried to make friends with people . . .'

'You must have some people who care about you.'

'Not everyone has friends. Not someone like me. Maybe beforehand . . . but not now.'

'Maybe you left it too late.'

'What?'

'For help.'

'That would suit you to think that way.'

Mary said nothing.

'You're nearly normal, aren't you?' said Blake.

Mary nodded.

'That's got to be hard.'

She stared at him.

'We're tied together by lies,' he said.

'You and me?' said Mary.

He nodded.

'No,' said Mary. 'We're not. Lies were just – something to you.'

'They *are* me. But . . . they're everyone.'

'That's not true.'

He laughed sadly. 'That's my point. It *is* true. You called me a freak, remember? You kept

screaming at me to get out and calling me a freak.
I lost it. I know I did. But I'm not a freak. It turns
out really I'm not. Everyone lies like me. No-one
wants to admit it. I'm just proving it. Push people
far enough and they'll tell you the truth. But why
do you have to push so far?'

Lies had been a huge part of Mary Burig's life and
what had led her to this point, what had brought
Preston Blake into her world. It was the evening
before her final exam. She sat in one of four quiet
corners at Tewkes, the deadest bar in Boulder. Her
Biopsychology textbook was spread out on the
small round table in front of her with notes written
in the margin. She knew how her mind worked.
Intense bursts of studying right before an exam
paid off. She kept up with most subjects all year,
but for the ones she didn't, she could concentrate
all her energies in a twelve-hour session and still
come out on top. She waited an hour, focused on
reading, wired on coffee.

Then Jonny Tewkes walked in, the son of the
owner, followed by most of his class on the trail
of free beer. Mary kept her head down. But Jonny
had seen her and walked over, pulling out the
stool opposite her and closing the textbook shut.

'Mary Burig. Now is not the time.' He smiled.
She smiled back. 'No. It's way past the time.'
'When's the exam?'
'Tomorrow morning.'

'Then you're done. You need to relax for the evening. In preparation.'

Mary rolled her eyes.

'You do psychology, right? So isn't it proven that sex releases endorphins and they make you relaxed and happy?'

'So we've just skipped straight to that then?'

'Not at all. I'm obviously going to get you drunk first.'

'You really are such a loser.'

'A sincere one. I can not stop thinking about last week.'

She smiled. 'Me too.'

'So, what's your problem?'

She opened her book. 'This.'

He shook his head.

'Look,' said Mary. 'Let's hook up tomorrow night, OK?'

'I can't keep this up for twenty-four hours.'

She smiled. 'From what I saw . . .'

A waiter came over with a beer and a glass of white wine.

'Cheers,' said Jonny.

'One mouthful,' said Mary, reaching for her wine.

Mary didn't make it to her final exam. She didn't graduate. And after months of partying with Jonny Tewkes, she moved in with him to the apartment above the bar and took a job as a waitress. But alcohol-fuelled sex and constant conversations about having it, could sustain her only so long. And Jonny didn't have much more to offer.

Mary left. She moved to New York. She opened a small office in SoHo that David paid for. The plaque on the wall had read Mary Burig, Psychologist. It sounded right to her. Her friend reproduced a University of Boulder Certificate and created a Masters certificate to go alongside it. He knew she was bright. She'd helped him get off drugs in his sophomore year. He knew she could help other people. David didn't agree with what his sister was doing, but he covered for her then and right through their first meeting with Julia Embry.

Mary stared at Blake. One word flashed into her mind: CORRUPT, a mnemonic from college for the symptoms of Antisocial Personality Disorder: Cannot follow law. Obligations ignored. Remorseless. Recklessness. Underhandedness. Planning Deficit. Temper. Mary realized she also ticked some of those boxes.

Blake raised his voice. 'Did you hear me?'

'I'm sorry,' said Mary. 'I was thinking.'

'I wonder how your brain works now,' said Blake.

'So do I,' she said. She looked away. 'Did it make a difference?'

'What?'

'Killing those people. Did it prove to you what you wanted it to prove? That you're normal, that everyone else is just like you, that you're not . . . a freak?'

'Everyone is just like me,' he said. 'Everyone lies. Everyone who told me I was a freak was wrong.'

'Why am I here?' said Mary.

'Because I wanted to see you. Because I want to get away with my crimes now. Because I think it might be too late.'

'You can't blame me for what you've done,' said Mary.

'I want to give you something,' he said.

Mary started to shake. She was watching the gun in his right hand.

'And what I will give you is time,' said Blake, standing up. With his left hand, he started to pull something from his pocket. She could see a flash of silver in the moonlight through the window. He was handing her back her phone. Giving her a lifeline. Letting her go. She reached out and took it from him.

Suddenly, the door behind him flew open and he jerked around. Mary shut her eyes tight, aware of an explosion of light and gunshot. The window behind her shattered. She flung herself flat on the floor and clawed her way towards the door. Screams, more gunshot, footsteps, a terrible smell. She could feel something warm on her face, something trickle down her cheek. She wiped it away before it could reach her mouth. As soon as she got into the hallway, she ran. She could hear the random workings of the building that went on all day and all night, sounds she would never notice, only that now she was alone and it was dark and she was afraid. She cried quiet, desperate tears.

She made it to the elevator bank. A sign told her it should not be used in the case of a fire. She thought about how quickly it would get her down to the first floor, to the lobby, to the outside. Then she imagined being trapped in there. Anyone could push a button on any floor and step into that tiny space with her. She turned her head and knew the only way to go was back towards the emergency stairs, back through the half-finished renovation. She ran, under the eerie black void of missing ceiling tiles, exposed wires, conscious that all around her were doors to empty apartments.

She burst through onto the landing and decided to go up a floor instead of down. She gripped hard to the banister, dragging herself up. She could hear her name being called urgently, over and over, echoing up the stairwell. She pressed her hands against her ears. *Shut up. Shut up. Shut up.* Everything was closing in on her. She didn't know what she'd seen. She could add it to all the other jumbled up thoughts and images her mind could no longer process. She hated it. She hated it so much.

On the third floor she found a vacant apartment and closed the door gently behind her. She was confused by its orientation; as she made her way to the window, she didn't know what view she would see. But what was there made her heart want to burst – the room overlooked the flowerbed she had planted with David. She never knew what memory could take root, why one memory could stay and another would not. Tears streamed down her face. She wiped them away and in the dark, couldn't see that they were mixed with blood. She stayed at the window, thinking of her brother, his kindness, his smiling eyes, his—

A shadow crossed the wet grass and Mary slammed herself back against the wall. Her chest was tight with panic. She slid down the wall, then gripped the window sill and slowly pulled herself up to take another look out.

She slumped back down and stayed that way for over an hour before she decided she had to do something.

TWENTY-EIGHT

The banquet hall was a sea of pink balloons, floating out of the centre of round tables with bright white cloths. The tables were starting to fill with women and young children. The older teenagers and men gathered at the bar.

Rufo stood alone near the buffet table, dressed in a three-button tuxedo, drinking a vodka.

'Boss,' said Danny, slapping his back, 'now's the time to get that "after" picture taken for the slimming magazine.'

Rufo cupped a hand around his ear. 'Is that a compliment I'm hearing?'

Joe walked over, 'Jesus, Sarge. Nice threads. New hair cut.'

'See?' said Rufo turning to Danny. 'That's the way to do it.'

'Brown-nose one-oh-one,' said Danny.

'You got to admit that's a great tux,' said Joe.

'Get a room, you guys,' said Danny.

'This,' said Rufo, 'is Armani. Two thousand dollars, I swear to God. This guy I was doing security work for? When he saw me drop all the weight, gave it to me as a gift.'

'Sure,' said Danny. 'No strings attached. Rrrrring rrrring, rrrrrring rrrring.' He put an imaginary phone to his ear. 'Hello? Sergeant Rufo? Hi, yeah, listen I got a few parking violations, first degree murder charges I could use your help with . . .'

'No-one can just do a nice thing for someone in your world,' said Rufo.

'I'm going to the bar,' said Danny. 'Drink? That's a nice thing.'

Joe nodded.

'I got one on the way,' said Rufo.

'Maddy's a sweet little kid,' said Joe. 'I hope she'll make it.'

'Doesn't bear thinking about otherwise,' said Rufo.

Danny was surrounded on all sides by oversized college kids gripping their ID, their golden ticket to getting wasted. He was grateful only when they hid him from someone he really did not want to see. He grabbed his drinks and rushed back from the bar with his head bowed.

'I just saw one of my exes,' he said, handing Joe his beer.

'Yeah?' said Rufo.

'It happens all the time,' said Joe.

'Someone from when Gina and I were on a break,' said Danny. 'This girl was nuts. Every night out with her, she would end up, a drink in each hand, dancing on a table. You could be at a wake, she'd find a table to dance on. I carried her home more times than I can remember. In the end, I couldn't take any more and it broke her heart. I had to say to her, 'Ba—'

'Barbara,' said Rufo, smiling to a woman in an emerald green gown, taking her hand and guiding her past Danny towards him. He kissed her on the cheek. 'This is my . . . partner, Barbara Stenson. This is Danny Markey. And you've already met Joe.'

Danny opened and closed his mouth twice before he spoke. 'Uh, nice to meet you, Barbara.'

'You too, Danny,' she said, squeezing his hand too tight.

'Can I get you anything to drink?' said Joe.

'This is my third soda and lime,' said Barbara, 'and there's only so many you can drink. I quit drinking a few years back and I still wonder how I could physically put away so much liquid in one night.' She laughed.

'There was Barbara spending years knocking back vodkas while I was busy eating all the pies,' said Rufo. 'I wonder would we have liked each other if we met back then.'

'Sad thing is we wouldn't, because back then when my nights were all a blur, I wound up with the biggest losers.'

Joe laughed louder than anyone.

Barbara squeezed Rufo's arm. 'I needed to wait a few years to catch myself a good guy.'

'Joe, why don't we leave these two lovebirds alone?' said Danny.

Joe was still laughing as they walked away. 'So you think you broke her heart?'

'Can you fucking believe she's with Rufo?'

'As a matter of fact, I can,' said Joe.

'There's too much love in the room tonight,' said Danny. 'I can not handle it.'

'Let's see what food's on offer here,' said Joe, wandering to the top of the buffet table.

'I'm in the mood for a little roast beef,' said Danny. 'Lots of it.'

'I'm thinking turkey,' said Joe.

Joe and Danny sat at a table with two beers and two plates piled with food. Danny was eyeing Barbara Stenson smiling and laughing with Rufo.

'What does she find so funny?' said Danny.

Joe glanced over. 'Probably the fact that you keep staring at her. That you treated her like shit and now she can come back to haunt you. That you might actually be at her wedding to your boss . . . there's lots of things she could be laughing at right now. The idea that—'

'Shut the fuck up.'

'Think about it,' said Joe, 'she marries Rufo, he's at home bitching about work, she's never going to take your side—'

'I've got to tell him—'

'Are you out of your mind?'

'Is that your phone?' said Danny.

Joe stared at him.

'I'm serious,' said Danny, 'it's vibrating against my chair.'

Joe reached back to his jacket hanging on the back of his chair. He pulled out his phone and answered.

'Hello? Hello? Hello . . .' He shook his head at Danny. He was about to hang up. 'Mary? I can't hear . . . you're where?' He listened. 'OK. Your door's locked, right? Stay right where you are. Don't move, OK? And when you hang up what I need you to do right away is call 911. Can you do that? They'll keep you on the line—' He paused. 'No, no. They'll send some patrol officers over. And we'll be right behind them. You hang in there, OK? You'll be fine.' Joe turned to Danny. 'Jesus Christ, that was Mary Burig. She said something about the perp being in her building. And she's on her own. But . . . you know, it's Mary . . .' Joe shrugged. 'Come on. We better go check it out.'

Mary's thumbs hovered over the buttons 9 and 1. Outside in the hallway, someone was calling her name. Her heart pounded. She put the phone down.

Joe and Danny pulled into the empty parking lot outside the Colt-Embry Homes. There were no patrol cars. The building was in darkness.

'What the fuck?' said Joe.

'Maybe they pulled up around the back,' said Danny.

'Why would they?' said Joe. He turned to Danny. 'Shit. She never fucking called them.'

He grabbed the radio. 'Manhattan North Homicide portable to Central K. Be advised we're at Colt-Embry Homes on 21st Street in Astoria. We have a possible murder suspect at the location. We need backup.'

They ran to the side of the building. The front door was ajar. The lobby was empty, the lights off. Joe pointed behind the desk to where the ceiling of the short corridor was exposed, its floor tiles hanging by thick cables along both sides of the wall. Behind it was the fire door and stairs that would take them to Mary's apartment on the second floor.

Joe walked up the stairs first, trying to limit the noise from his new dress shoes. Danny followed him.

'We're going direct to her place?' Danny whispered.

'Yeah,' said Joe.

They reached the second floor landing. Joe stopped to retie the laces of his left shoe.

'Fuck these shoes.'

They walked down the hallway. Twice, his right foot lost its grip, but he managed to keep his balance. He forgot to give his shoes to Anna before he came out. She would have scored the bottom of them with a pen-knife or roughed up the surface with an emery board. He brought his mind back to focus. The only thing he could hear were Danny's footsteps beside him and the buzz of the fluorescent light above.

Mary heard footsteps approaching from the end of the hallway and the jangle of Stan's keys. She pushed open the door slowly and placed one bare foot onto a tile she was expecting to be cold. It was warm and wet. Her foot slid from under her. As her head hit the cold hard floor, the last thing she saw was Stan's utility belt . . . covered in blood.

Joe and Danny opened all the vacant rooms along the second floor hallway and found no-one. Mary's apartment door was wide open and her belongings strewn everywhere. Drawers were opened, cushions were turned over, bags were emptied.

'This does not look good,' said Joe.

'Mary?' said Danny. 'Mary?'

It didn't take long to search the small apartment. They found nothing. They ran upstairs to the floors above, throwing open the unlocked doors. They moved down the stairs, pushing through the back door into the lobby.

'Whoa,' said Joe, pointing at a streak of blood on the tiled floor.

'That was not here when we got here.'

'No way,' said Joe.

They ran towards the door.

'Where is she?' said Danny.

Joe glanced out into the dark. 'And where the hell's our backup?'

'Look at that,' said Danny.

Two uniforms were taking their time walking up the path. Danny gestured them forward. They ran towards him.

'The woman who called this in is not here,' said Danny. 'But we haven't searched the entire building. Perp goes by Preston Blake or Alan Moder, he's six foot tall, mid thirties, medium build, dark hair, heavily scarred chin, may be accompanied by a female, Mary Burig, late twenties, five four, slim build, long dark hair, very pale blue eyes. Unknown method of escape.'

Magda Oleszak ran through the parking lot of the Colt-Embry Homes, past the patrol cars that had just arrived and straight into a uniform standing at the door.

'What's happened?' she said.

'Who are you?' said the officer.

'I work here. My name is Magda Oleszak. I'm looking for my friend. We were going to the movies, over two hours ago. I thought she was in the group. Someone said she was. I should have checked. Is she OK? Is she in there? Why are you here? Her name is Mary.'

'We were responding to a possible break-in. Please, ma'am, I'm going to have to ask you to step back. If you could go talk to one of my colleagues.' He pointed to a second patrol car that was pulling into the lot. 'They'll take care of you. It's not safe for you to be in the building right now.'

Joe dialled Rufo's number from his cell phone.

'Boss? It's Joe. We're at Colt-Embry. Looks like Blake was here. No sign of Mary Burig. We got some blood on the floor. That's it.'

'You think the perp's still in the building?'

'We don't know. We're waiting on more backup from the One-One-Four.'

'Let me round up the guys from the bar. Be right over.'

Julia Embry pulled up to the scene in her car and jumped out. Magda got out of the patrol car and ran towards her.

'Is it Mary?' said Julia. Her eyes were sunken in her pale face.

'I don't know,' said Magda, crying. 'I don't know what's happening.'

'Oh God, I hope Mary's OK,' said Julia. She started to run towards the building.

Magda held her back. 'They're not going to let you in.'

'Why not? I need to get in there. I need to see what's going on.'

'Everyone's at the movie. Mary had left but was to follow on from the church. I left one of the girls to wait for her in the foyer. She said Mary was there. I mean, it was the cinema, it was dark, I should have checked.'

'It's not your fault,' said Julia.

'I should go to the church—'

'Don't go anywhere,' said Julia. 'The police will tell us what we need to do.'

'I've been trying Mary's phone, but she's not answering,' said Magda.

'This is so terrible,' said Julia. She watched the detectives moving around inside the lobby. 'There's nothing we can do. Someone has to tell us something.'

Joe ran through the lobby and hammered on the glass door for the uniform to stand out of the way. He jogged down the path to Julia and Magda.

'Detective Lucchesi,' said Julia. 'What's going on? Where's Mary?'

'We're trying to find her,' said Joe. 'She called us. Someone broke in—'

'Oh my God,' said Julia.

'Mrs Embry, are there keys to all the apartments?'

'Yes. They're in my office.'

'I can't let you go in there right now, but if you could let me know where they are . . .'

'Bottom left-hand drawer of my bureau, inside a makeup bag.'

'OK. That's great. Are your security cameras operational?'

'No,' said Julia. 'Sorry. They're temporarily down because of the rewiring.'

'OK,' said Joe. 'What I'm going to need you to do is one of the uniformed officers is going to take you and Miss Oleszak to the hundred and four-teenth precinct. If you could wait for me there, I'll come by and speak with you in a couple hours, OK? I know that's hard at this time, but I'm afraid that's what we're going to have to do.'

Julia nodded. 'That's OK. We can do that.'

Rufo stood in the lobby with the rest of the task force. Most of them were straight from the benefit.

'I'm feeling a little overdressed for this particular party,' said Rufo. 'March of the fucking Penguins. And someone, open the door, get the fumes out. Jesus.'

Joe walked over.

'What happened?' said Rufo.

'We got here – no Mary,' said Danny. 'And she hadn't called 911.'

'We called it in to the Oné-One-Four twenty minutes later when we got here,' said Joe. 'We're waiting for more of them to show.'

Rufo looked down. 'One streak of blood, that's it.'

'Crime Scene's on the way,' said Joe.

'So talk me through this again,' said Rufo. 'She

called, said there was someone in the building, said specifically it was Blake?'

'Yeah,' said Joe.

'I have to ask the question. This Mary is . . . challenged. So can we believe what she's telling us? I mean could this be all in her head?'

'No way. I heard her voice,' said Joe. 'She was terrified. I don't think she's going to be that freaked out by something she's imagined.'

'If I find out I could have stayed at the bar . . .' said Rencher.

'How many apartments are there?' said Rufo.

'Twenty – some of them are empty, they're being renovated,' said Joe. 'Then there's a communal room on every floor opposite the elevators – a library, a dining room, a TV room.'

'Right,' said Rufo. 'They haven't all been searched. Let's go.'

'Where's Bobby and Martinez?' said Joe.

'Martinez is not exactly in great shape. I told him to stay where he was,' said Rufo. 'I left him hanging out with some old lady.'

'Bobby didn't show,' said Pace. 'I think he's doing security at a runway show in Bryant Park.'

Joe shook his head.

Mary lay in the darkness, deprived of most of her senses; her body was cold and numb, her eyes useless, her ears ringing with the endless drone of an engine. 'Just a short trip, everything will be fine, nothing to worry about,' he had said. Twice. But he was shaking and he knew she'd made the phone call and he couldn't look at her. When he reached over her, a droplet of sweat had trickled down his face and landed, stinging, into her eye. He didn't notice.

She could not stop crying. 'Where are you taking me? Where?'

'Please be quiet, please, please.' He kept saying it over and over.

'I can't,' she screamed. 'I can't.'

He stayed silent, just glancing back at her every now and then to make sure she hadn't twisted her way out of the restraints. She was curled on her side, her legs tied together at the ankles, her hands bound tight at the wrist.

'I am all alone in this world now,' she roared. 'I have no-one! I have no-one! Why are you doing this to me? Why? Why? Why?' She started retching.

'Try not to throw up. You'll have to stay that way. I can't stop.' He hadn't gagged her because she looked so fragile. He knew she was the type to be sick.

She pitched forward and retched again. Her mind couldn't handle any more. Her body was taking up the fight. She had felt so close to being taken away from danger. And now she was in total blackness with rain hammering loudly on the roof and on the windows, drilling into her head, making her struggle harder and harder to be heard. Words didn't work. He didn't want to hear them. She knew she could stop speaking. But she had no control over the rest. Her sobs cut right through him, agonizing wails that trailed off into whimpers, like a sick child without the voice to express her pain. But Mary did have a voice, she just lost the will to use it.

Hope was a white light to Mary. It was a guide. It was visitation and resurrection and redemption and ascendance. It was all good things. Here in the dark, she searched for it inside. There was no other way. Prayers ran quickly through her mind; to St Joseph, St Pio, St Anthony, St Jude. She moved on to the rosary, ten decades, fluent words her memory had never let go of. She finished with the Confitior; 'I confess to Almighty God and to you my brothers and sisters / That I have sinned through my own fault / In my thoughts and in my words / In what I have done / And in what I have failed to do . . .'

She thought about what she had done and what she had failed to do.

It was 5 a.m. when Joe and Danny got back to the office. Rencher, Blazkow, Martinez and Pace were all still at their desks. Joe rubbed his eyes.

'Anyone got anything?' said Joe.

'Nada,' said Rencher.

'A hangover,' said Martinez. 'Already.'

'Yeah, and some grandma's phone number,' said Rencher.

'Anyone get a hold of Stanley Frayte?' said Joe.

'No.'

'All the other squads have been told what to look out for,' said Danny.

'So,' said Joe, 'we've got no Stanley Frayte. No Mary Burig. No Preston Blake. Fucking great. Blazkow – can you do a victimology on Stanley Frayte?'

'Sure. But I can sleep now, right?'

'We all need to get some sleep,' said Joe.

His cell phone rang.

'Joe? It's Taye Harris, fire marshal.'

'How you doing?' said Joe. 'Sorry I didn't get back to you earlier. Things have been crazy.'

'I heard. That's why I'm calling so late, early, whatever. Joe, I don't think your perp made it out of the building alive. I think we got your perp.'

'What?' said Joe. 'Can't be . . .'

'Well, we got a body . . .'

'But the scene was clear. I thought there was no-one—'

'I know. I know. I've talked with the officers involved and because it was a crime scene and the search was expedited, the primary and secondary search reports were given as negative. They didn't have a lot of time. The body was in the curve of the bay window at the front of the house. Behind a large sofa. When my men went in to ventilate the place, they had to pull down some heavy curtains covering the window to get the air circulating. No-one saw him. He was concealed there for several hours.'

Joe paused. 'The bay window. He was in—'

'Yeah,' said Harris. 'The dead man's room.'

TWENTY-NINE

Joe and Danny drove to the Office of the Chief Medical Examiner.

'We have been up twenty-four hours,' said Danny as they walked in.

Joe yawned. 'I know.'

Dr Hyland came down and led them into the room where a body was laid out under a white sheet.

'Just to warn you, he's in pretty bad shape,' said Hyland. He lifted the sheet. The first thing Danny and Joe saw was a badly burned arm and hand. Something gold glinted on the finger. They both leaned closer. It was their high school ring. They locked eyes.

'Jesus Christ,' said Danny.

'It's Bobby.'

At the twentieth precinct, Pace checked Bobby's desk where his notes were still laid out. He had come to the same conclusion as Cullen about Blake's address.

'He must have just decided to call into Blake on his way home from work,' said Joe. 'Blake freaked, knew we were on to him.'

'I should have been with him,' said Pace.

'If he didn't say anything to you . . .' said Joe, shrugging. 'Jesus Christ. He's got two little boys.'

Danny shook his head.

'I better take care of notifying Old Nic,' said Joe.

Most people knew that Bobby Nicotero and his father weren't close. But everyone knew that didn't matter today and it would never matter again.

Victor Nicotero knew when he saw Joe at the door at 8 a.m. His hand was shaking as he let him in.

'Nothing about this is right. It's all wrong,' he said, struggling. 'I'm at the wrong end of a notification here. Jesus Christ. What happened?'

Joe tried to clean up the details. Old Nic didn't buy it, but pretended he did. He sat in silence, staring.

'Patti's up there, sleeping away her last night before her whole world is turned upside down. I don't ever want to wake her up, Joe.' His voice cracked. 'When he was a kid, Bobby worried about me all the time,' said Nic. 'Used to drive me nuts. He'd cling on to me, wouldn't let me go.' Tears welled in his eyes. 'I know how he feels.' He let out a desperate, mourning sob. 'I don't want to let him go.' He searched his pocket for the handkerchief. 'We were getting somewhere,' he said. 'I think we were getting somewhere.' He looked up, his eyes red and watery. 'What was his problem with me, Joe? Where did I go wrong? I don't mean with him, he's a good kid, but . . .'

'Families,' said Joe, handing him a Kleenex. 'We don't ever know, do we? But I know when a son loves his father, Nic. I do. And Bobby did. He looked out for you. In his . . . his own way.'

Nic smiled. 'Angry way.'

'I'm not saying that,' said Joe. 'But yeah, he wasn't straightforward about it. But he gave a shit. You know, he went crazy with me last week.'

'He did?'

Joe nodded. 'Yup. Made me take it outside.'

Nic smiled. 'That's my boy.'

'He wouldn't do that if he didn't give a damn,' said Joe.

The office was quiet. No-one knew what to say. Pace had gone home. Cullen had arrived in.

'I can't believe they just didn't find him,' he said.

'It was chaos,' said Joe. 'We didn't want them tramping all over any evidence. We didn't know what could be in there.'

'Yeah, Blake's whole life was run from that home. The dental work for Valtry, the—'

'Whoa,' said Joe. 'Did you see any dental stuff down there?'

'Yeah,' said Danny. 'Remember? The pliers, the burrs—'

'Yeah, but there were no teeth, no models, no porcelain – none of the shit we saw in the lab.' He looked at Danny. 'We need to get back to the house . . . I think he's got Mary in there.'

Danny and Joe parked the car on Remsen Street and walked to Willow Street. They stopped a short distance from Preston Blake's house.

'Our only way in is through the basement door under the stoop,' said Joe, pointing. 'The collapse has blocked everything off from the back entrance.' They walked up to the door – it was padlocked and had a Gravoply tag slapped on it from the fire department and a number to call if you wanted to gain access.

'I'll call ESU,' said Danny.

Fifteen minutes later, two Emergency Services guys showed up and broke through the door into the damp basement, the smell of smoke still strong in the air.

'There it is,' said Joe, 'the trapdoor down to the basement he doesn't fucking have.'

An overpowering stench hit them as soon as they lifted it. They jerked their heads away. Danny clamped a hand over his mouth.

'Jesus Christ,' said Joe. 'That is fucking—'

Danny took his hand down, wiping the tears that streamed from his eyes. 'Unbelievable. That is . . .' He breathed out. 'Christ.' He stared down at the vertical ladder.

'I'll go first,' said Joe. 'Shine that flashlight down there.'

He held the beam steady as Joe climbed down. He handed him the flashlight and followed him into the small cramped space.

'What the fuck is this?' said Danny. Joe swept the flashlight left to right, its beam broken up by the bars of a prison cell. A TV was mounted on the wall in front of it. Joe reached out for the light switch beside it.

'No!' shouted Danny. 'No switches.'

'Jesus Christ,' said Joe, snapping his hand back. 'You scared the shit out of me.'

Danny walked over to the cell, his throat constricting as he closed in on the source of the smell. In the corner beside the bed lay a bucket of human waste, the liquid almost evaporated, the solids breaking down, covered with breeding maggots. Adult flies swarmed around it, landing along the rim, travelling back and forth to a plate of spoiled food on a tray by the door. Joe shone the light on the pale china and could see the tiny olive-green specks of excrement they left behind. Danny rushed out towards the ladder, but managed to ride out the nausea without throwing up.

'Why would anyone live like this?' said Danny, holding his handkerchief loosely over his face.

'He's a broken man,' said Joe. 'Probably came

down here only after the first victim. The guy hates himself, probably thinks this is all he deserves.'

'What he deserves is his head shoved into that bucket,' said Danny. He choked back another wave of nausea.

'You're making yourself sick.'

'I have got to get out of here.'

'Look,' said Joe. He pointed to the dull plaster models of teeth scattered from a box on the bed. He shone the flashlight across two shelves mounted above it with neat rows of tiny animal skulls, jewels glistening in the cavities.

Pinned to the wall above a small desk was a single cracked and yellowed handwritten note, the top of it ripped from a lined spiral notebook. Joe leaned in to read it:

The wicked are estranged from the womb: they go astray as soon as they be born, speaking lies.

Their poison is like the poison of a serpent: they are like the deaf adder that stoppeth her ear;

Which will not hearken to the voice of charmers, charming never so wisely.

Break their teeth, O God, in their mouth: break out the great teeth of the young lions, O LORD.

The rest of the industrial grey walls had been covered with photocopies of the same script, side by side, edges overlapping, layer upon layer.

'I bet that's the note,' said Joe. 'From Sonja Ruehling. That was his kiss-off.'

Danny shook his head. 'It is so fucked up . . . Jesus Christ.'

Joe crouched down and looked under the bed. 'Wallets,' he said. He pulled some of them out, looking through them at the faces of the unchosen victims. 'If they only fucking knew.'

'And upstairs, you had this beautiful shiny home? Jesus Christ,' said Danny.

'You never know, do you?' said Joe. 'What shit people hide beneath the surface.'

'Where are you, you fucking freak?' shouted Danny.

Rufo sat at his office with his head in his hands. Joe and Danny knocked and went in.

'I'm in shock here,' said Rufo. 'I can't believe Bobby.'

'I know,' said Joe. He looked down. 'He probably went there because I was giving him a hard time, wanted to check it out before he came to me with the information . . .'

'Don't be an idiot,' said Rufo gently. 'Where we at now?'

'We've found Blake's fucking dungeon, but no-one in it,' said Joe. 'Stanley Frayte's home has been searched and nothing's come up so far. No sightings of Mary.'

'All we can hope is that Blake does something to draw attention to himself,' said Rufo. 'Our first contact with him was because he reached out to us.'

'Yeah,' said Joe. 'But I think that was his way of putting himself forward as the exact opposite of what he was, this pathological lying thing. He knew he was good at it. He could get close to us, get off on the whole victim role and maybe find some shit out at the same time.'

Rufo let out a breath.

'You know Blake was the one who got in touch with Artie Blackwell about that article,' said Joe.

'Artie told you that?' said Danny.

Joe nodded. 'Yeah. Maybe our near-death experience brought something out in him . . .'

Cullen rushed into the room. 'Guys. I've found something. I don't really know what to make of it. But you might want to take a look.'

'What's this about?' said Julia Embry, struggling to pull out the seat opposite Joe in a canteen reeking of disinfectant and vegetables.

Joe helped her with the seat. 'It's about your son, Robin.'

She held a hand to her chest. 'Robin?'

'I know you never got any answers from that night and the driver was never caught . . .'

'Oh my God,' she said, raising her hand to her mouth. 'Did you find out who—'

Joe nodded. 'Yes, I did. And if you want, I can let you know.'

'Yes,' she said, 'of course I want to know. Why wouldn't I—'

'You could trust me that I know who it is, that this person is not an evil person, that they're not a danger or—'

'I'm sorry, detective, I do trust you, you seem like a good person. But you know I've never got closure and I need closure and if it's right here staring me in the face, I'm going to take it. Why wouldn't I?'

'Because it's going to come as a shock—'

'Who?' she said. 'Who did this to Robin? Just tell me.'

'Stanley Frayte.'

Her eyes registered shock, but her whole face seemed to collapse with sadness and disappointment. Joe could barely look at her. He pulled a clean handkerchief from his pocket. He was going to hand it to her, but her head was slumped onto her folded arms on the table and she was sobbing so hard, he could barely move. He tapped her arm lightly and put the handkerchief in front of her.

'I'm so sorry to have had to tell you,' he said. 'But I know you never got closure. I know how hard that is. He may have taken the opportunity to leave because of the police attention. He probably felt we'd figure it out sooner or later.'

Julia shook her head and managed to draw breath long enough to tell Joe it wasn't his fault.

She reached out and dragged the handkerchief towards her, covering her entire face with it, then wiping her eyes and blowing her nose before she looked up at him. She broke down again and it was several minutes before she could speak. Joe sat quietly, looking out the window, listening to the sounds in the parking lot outside.

'The Christmas lights in the house,' she said. 'Were . . .' she sobbed, '. . . Robin and I always put them up. Then when Robin died – my husband. But when he left me . . . it was Stan who helped. He could do that with me and not . . . how could he do that? Why am I even thinking of Christmas lights right now? That's the first thing I thought of . . .'

'Stanley must have made the decision never to come forward for whatever reason. And then he realized he couldn't live with that guilt. It takes a split second to decide to keep on driving. And there's no going back. The next best thing for him was to reach out to you in some other way. I guess that eased his mind. I'm just guessing.'

'You see all kinds of things in your job. Do you think what he – did not coming forward – was wrong?'

Joe shrugged. 'Stan made a huge mistake. He had worked hard to get where he was at that time. He was thinking of his own family. He wasn't thinking—'

'Of mine. Of me. But he is such a . . .' she choked on the words, '. . . kind man.'

'I don't doubt that.'

'How did you know it was him?'

'When we picked him up for mailing the letters for Mary, I thought we'd got our guy. He looked guilty. And when he was in the interview room, it was like he was relieved. But when we told him why we'd taken him in, he seemed surprised. We knew he wasn't the killer, but after, I thought maybe there was something else going on with him. I thought it might have been some scam he was working . . . We checked him out . . . We reached out to the detectives on the case and they had the last few letters of the truck company's name that a witness had seen leaving the crime. She'd got one of them wrong . . .' He shrugged. 'We put it together.'

'Stan was here from the start of the building project – the Clinic,' said Julia. 'He offered us rates that I know were below his usual. He was never late. He was polite. He was loyal. He didn't drink, didn't do drugs. He had such a good heart.' She shook her head. 'How am I supposed to feel about this? What am I supposed to do?'

'I don't know,' said Joe.

'How did I not see it from him? Nothing. I never got any sense . . .'

'I'm no shrink,' said Joe. 'I've never been to one in my life, but I'd say if you go back and start to think about every incident and every word that passed between you and Stanley Frayte, you might never make it through.'

Julia stared ahead. She nodded. 'And maybe that would diminish all his *good* work,' she said. 'I've already gone over and over my last conversation with Robin and it's enough to drive anyone crazy. It's the old cliché – it was a fight. Our last exchange of words was angry. And I can never go back and change that. You're so used to getting the chance to make up after an argument, that you expect the chance will always be there. The person storms off and you say "fine – go", knowing you can apologize a little while later.' She shrugged.

'I'm sure he felt the same way,' said Joe. 'I'm sure he thought he'd be coming back in that door to sort it all out.'

Julia gave a small smile and turned her head to stare out the window.

It was late evening when they got back to the office. The atmosphere was grim. The only thing worse than a stalled investigation was riding a rollercoaster of promising leads to nowhere.

'Do you know what it is tomorrow?' said Joe.

'No,' said Danny.

'My surgery.'

Danny laughed. 'You looking for a way out? You looking for me to say – you can't go now, you're too tired or the case will fall apart without you?'

'That'd be great,' said Joe.

'Yeah, well I'm not,' said Danny. 'You need this.

You want to know it's an expert who's drilling into your face, right? Not some student doctor. This is your one chance.'

Joe bowed his head. 'Drilling into my face . . .'

'Yeah, well that's what it is.'

Joe sighed. 'So do I go or not?'

'Go,' said Danny. 'You're off work a day. We'll survive without you. You can have a rest.'

'Who the fuck rests in a hospital, I'd like to know.'

'Well, whatever.'

Joe stood up. 'OK. OK. I'll go home, catch a few hours sleep, then I guess I'm going in.'

Danny stood up and reached out his hand. 'Don't worry. We got things under control.'

'OK. Let me know.'

'Man, I want to wish you the very best of luck with the operation.'

Joe paused. 'Thank you.'

'Any last words?' said Danny.

'Very and fucking and funny.'

'I'll store them up for you,' said Danny.

'Right,' said Joe.

'Right,' said Danny. 'I'll see you . . .'

'The day after tomorrow.'

'Are you *really*—'

'Yes I am. Shut the fuck up.'

'I'll call Anna for the update.'

'OK.'

'You're DNR, right?'

THIRTY

'Detective Lucchesi?' A tall thin man walked into the ward. 'I'm Dr Branfield, I'll be carrying out your procedure this morning.'

'How you doing, Doctor?' said Joe.

Branfield smiled. 'Well, *I'm* fine. Just to reassure you, what's going to happen is a minor procedure, I've performed more than any other surgeon in the U.S., so it's like a walk in the park for me. And it will be the same for you . . . if you usually walk lying down and sedated.'

Joe made the effort to smile.

'You have nothing to worry about,' said Branfield, 'it will all be over and done with in about thirty minutes. And before you know it, you'll be going out of your way to eat steak.' He walked away. 'See you in theater.'

Four words Joe thought he would never have to hear in his lifetime. His stomach was empty, but it felt like it weighed a ton. He lay back on the pillow with his arm above his head. *What am I doing?* His phone beeped. It was a text from Anna: 'Good luck. We're all thinking of you! XX'

'Ready to rock?' said a bright voice from the doorway.

'Sure,' said Joe, against every single impulse in his body and mind.

He found himself on a gurney, staring up at the ceiling, watching the lights fly overhead as he was being wheeled in for his anaesthetic. The male nurse guiding him along was talking at high speed about his cell phone coverage and how bad it was in his new apartment. Joe felt like punching him. His hands were already in fists, tight and rigid by his side. He tried to relax, but something had happened to his breathing, stalling it like a car out of gear. The nurse glanced at him.

'You'll be fine,' he said. 'Take some deep breaths. Honestly, it will make all the difference. In. Out. In. Out.'

Joe locked eyes with the nurse and realized he was now the only person who could stop him from getting up and running out on the street in a gown. He synched his breathing with him and turned away.

'Now,' said the nurse, his voice cheery. 'It's all good.'

'Thanks,' said Joe.

'Pardon me?'

'Uh, thanks.'

'Oh, not a problem. OK, here we are.'

Joe's head jerked towards the door. 'Quick. Great,' he said.

'In we go.'

He delivered Joe into the waiting surgical team and said goodbye. Joe didn't want him to leave. In a corner of the room, a doctor was turning away from the group of theater nurses, laughing. A nurse moved over to Joe and introduced him.

'This is Dr Graff, your anaesthetist.'

'Hello,' said Dr Graff. 'OK. This is the first step towards you feeling a whole lot better.' He smiled. 'But if you've made it this far, I guess I'm telling you something you already know.' He smiled again. 'OK. I'm going to give you a little something and before you finish counting down from ten to zero, you'll feel yourself go under . . .'

But Joe wasn't thinking about going under. He was thinking about telling somebody something they already knew. Lying on his back, naked and vulnerable, everything started to slot into place. He struggled up from the gurney.

'It's OK,' said the nurse. 'You'll be—'

'I'm sorry,' said Joe. 'I gotta go.'

Martinez brought two cups of coffee to Danny's desk and handed him one.

'Milk, two sugars,' he said.

'God bless your memory,' said Danny. He

glanced at his watch. 'I'd say Joe is going under round about – now.'

Martinez sat at the edge of the desk.

'How long's he gonna be gone?'

'Just a day or two,' said Danny.

'I'd hate to have anything done to my face,' said Martinez, stroking his jaw. 'Anyone fucking with you like that. I don't even get the whole laser eye surgery thing. Totally freaks me out.'

'Yeah, well I guess Joe's desperate.'

Danny's cell phone rang. 'Yeah?'

'Get the hell over to the hospital.'

'Joe?' said Danny. 'Holy shit! Aren't you in surgery? Where are you right now?'

'Not dressed enough to be standing in a hospital hallway on a payphone,' said Joe.

'Have you been administered any medication?'

'Just hurry the fuck up.'

'You got clothes there?'

'No. I'm going to do this one naked. Course I've got clothes. I just need to find my room.'

'I'm on my way. What about your surgery?' But he didn't wait for an answer.

The drive through Westchester was familiar to Joe – he had stayed in his father's house in Rye with Shaun when they came back from Ireland. Today, they were seven miles further from the city in a quiet stretch of countryside, a perfect setting for the second Colt-Embry Clinic. They followed the blacktop road that curved through the half-finished gardens and led to the main building. They walked past the empty reception desk and stopped at a stack of signs, edged in protective cardboard, leaning against the walls. They had yet to be mounted, but showed with a neat black arrow the way to Julia Embry's office. They knocked, but opened the door without waiting. Julia jumped and half-staggered up from her chair.

'Where is Mary?' Joe was shouting.

Julia was pale. She nodded. 'She's here. She's safe.'

'Do you know how many people are out looking for her?' said Joe. 'Are you out of your mind?'

Danny put a steadying hand on Joe's arm. Joe pulled away from it.

'No,' he said. 'What the fuck is going on here?'

Julia started to cry.

'No fucking tears,' said Joe. 'Quit it with the fucking tears.'

'Joe, come on,' said Danny. 'Calm down.' He turned to Julia. 'Mrs Embry, we're glad Mary is safe.'

'Thank you.'

'Where is she?'

'In the new apartments. I moved her out here early. I couldn't watch her go through any more. I know she was the one who got in contact with you. And I know you've been kind to her. But her life has been turned upside down and I didn't

want her to go through any more. I couldn't face
it.'

'Is Stan here too?'

'Yes.'

'Jesus Christ,' said Joe.

Julia sat back down in her chair. 'You have a
close family, Detective, I read about you,' she said.
'And it's a different dynamic than when you don't.
Stan, Mary . . . they can disappear without people
paying too much attention. They have no family
to panic when they're gone. How many missing
person reports are filed—'

'Let me stop you right there,' said Joe. 'I'm
genuinely concerned. Have I come across as
someone who thinks human beings are disposable?'

Julia's face burned. She avoided his stare. 'I'm
sorry. No, no you haven't.'

'Thank you,' said Joe. 'Because you need to
know there are a lot of people in my line of work
who care – me, my partner, the entire task force.
We care about the people we meet. You think I
come in contact with someone like Mary Burig,
she disappears and we're all going to forget about
her? Yeah, you might be able to sleep at night
knowing she's safe. But maybe I can't. Maybe I'll
wake up wondering what I did wrong. What if it
was you? How would you feel?'

'I'm sorry.'

He shook his head. 'Look, I can't argue with
what you want to do with the clinic,' said Joe.

'And what you *have* done, how many people you've helped. There should be a million of these clinics all over the country.'

'Thank you,' said Julia. 'That means a lot.' Tears welled up in her eyes. 'I don't know how I got into this mess – I'm sorry.' She looked up at him. 'How did you know?'

'I see people cry a lot,' said Joe. 'I see real tears and fake ones. When I told you about Stan and Robin, I saw real tears. But I knew you were crying for another reason. I got the impression I was telling you something you already knew. Does that make sense? You know sometimes you see people cry at a funeral – and you just get from them that something else is going on. That's what it's like.'

She smiled sadly. 'You're right. I was crying for something else.'

'For what?'

'Because it reminded me yet again that I had a son who wanted to die.'

'What?'

'Robin drove straight into Stan's path.'

'And you believe that?' said Joe.

'Yes. Life was unbearable at home. I knew he wasn't . . . well. It was all too much for him. He had attempted suicide before. Stan confirmed what I had suspected.'

'How did you know about Stan?' said Joe.

'He broke down and told me. It was as simple

as that. After he had been working for me for
years. He said he just couldn't take the guilt. He
said me being nice to him made it worse. He
couldn't just leave, because he knew how important he was to me, but he couldn't stay because
every day, he felt like a fraud.'

'How did you react when he told you?'

'Well, I was devastated.'

'But you recovered . . .' said Joe.

Julia looked up at him.

'You recovered when you realized you had
someone for the rest of your life that would do
anything to make up for taking away your child.'

'I'm not that cynical,' said Julia.

'Come on,' said Joe. 'You knew what you were
doing.'

'It's not like that,' said Julia. 'Stan had become
a really dear friend. I lost my son, I lost my
husband. I could not lose someone else. I just
couldn't. No-one could bring Robin back. Stan
wasn't a bad person. There was nothing to be
gained by shutting him out.'

'It sounds to me like a little circle of people—'

'Of friends,' said Julia. 'Families have blood ties.
We had . . . different loyalties. But we were all
friends.'

'OK. What happened that night at the clinic?'

'The killer came back for Mary. No-one was
in the building except me. I heard noises in one
of the apartments, so I walked in. He swung

around and his gun went off. It was a reflex. He wasn't aiming. He missed me. I was screaming, Mary was screaming. Stan came rushing in and . . . Stan shot him. It was self-defence. It all happened so fast.'

Joe's face was impassive. Inside, he was raging. 'What happened to Mary?'

'It was all so confusing, the noise, the gunshots . . . she crawled past us and ran down the hallway. We were all in shock. She hid in one of the rooms. I ran after her.'

'Where was Stan?'

'He . . . wrapped the body in the sheets that were in the room, then in plastic and . . . buried him.'

Joe shook his head. 'So that's when Mary called us?'

Julia nodded. 'I guess so. I told Stan to find her and take her away to the new clinic. She'd made it down to the supply room in the lobby. You probably ran past it on your way in . . .'

Danny let out a breath.

'It was terrible,' said Julia. 'It nearly broke Stan's heart having to take her away the way he did. He had to restrain her. Someone he cares about so much—'

'You and Stan are going to have to come with us,' said Joe. 'And we need to see Mary.'

'She's just outside. Please, though, let me call Magda Oleszak and tell her. Maybe you can bring

Mary to her. I don't want her having to come to
the police station.'

'OK,' said Danny.

Mary was kneeling in front of the flower-beds,
slamming her hands on top of them, weeping and
crying out her brother's name. Joe walked across
the grass towards her and watched her destroy
the freshly planted flowers, leaving orange and
yellow petals strewn across the soil.

Joe hunkered down beside her. 'Mary?'

She looked up at him, tears shining in her pale
eyes.

'Mary. Did you see something?'

Tears spilled down her cheeks. Joe laid a gentle
hand on her shoulder.

'You're not in any trouble, Mary.'

She shook her head. 'I have to be.'

'No,' said Joe. 'You don't.'

She bowed her head and cried harder and
harder.

Julia turned to Joe. 'This clinic is my life. I just
didn't want it associated with any negative
publicity. We're just about to open this one. There's
a lot at stake. A lot of people's lives depend on us.
I am so terribly sorry for how this has ended. But
it was for the best intentions.' She paused. 'Do you
know what it's like to want something at all costs?'

EPILOGUE

The sulphurous smell of death filled the crime scene tent that stood in the quietest corner of the grounds behind the Colt-Embry Homes. The flower-bed ran through the centre, its bright blooms in contrast to everything around it: the steady rainfall on the roof, the set faces of the detectives, the body under the surface.

A tall blond crime scene tech stood in front of Danny and Joe, squeezing the contents of a clear plastic bag to blend the powder and water inside it.

'Dental stone,' said Joe, shaking his head.

'Makes sense,' said Danny.

The technician crouched down by a boot print and released the liquid so it poured slowly around the ridges without disturbing the soil. He let it spill out over the top, then stepped back and sealed the bag. Three more technicians used small shovels and sifters to gradually expose the body, buried just two feet under the surface.

One of them looked up. 'So someone finished him off for you.'

Joe looked through him.

'Least you got him,' said the tech.

Joe shrugged. 'You know what? I have a funeral to go to Saturday. The guy you're digging up there killed one of my men. We did not *get* him . . . not the way we wanted.'

'I was ready for a perp walk,' said Danny. His tone was flat.

Joe stared at the leather cuff on Blake's stone-white wrist, his hand half-pushing through the soil as if he was trying to reach out.

'The beetle,' said Joe. 'I was right. He had all that leather in his house . . .'

'Nice work, detective,' said Danny.

'Come on,' said Joe. 'Let's go get some air.'

Shaun was sitting alone at the dinner table when Joe got back.

'Where's your mom?'

'I don't know.'

'I heard about Tara . . .'

Shaun nodded.

'How are you doing?'

Shaun smiled at him. 'Dad, it's OK. You don't have to talk to me about stupid stuff when, like, Old Nic's son has died and you nearly got—'

'How you are doing is what I'd like to know,' said Joe, shrugging. He grabbed a plate and helped himself to spaghetti.

'I'm OK,' said Shaun.

'Good,' said Joe.

'My heart will go on.' He was smiling.

Joe laughed. 'Look . . . about college . . .'

Shaun's smile faded. 'Yeah?'

'Well . . .'

'Look, I'm going to college, Dad, OK? I have another few months before my applications have to be in. I need to think about it.'

'But you *are* going? That is what you want?'

Shaun rolled his eyes. 'Of course it's what I want. It's just it was all too much trying to think about it. I mean, it's deciding where I want to live for the next few years, what I want to do with my life. That's big stuff.'

Joe breathed out. 'Well, I'm glad.'

'How are you?' said Shaun.

Joe raised his eyebrows. 'Me? I'm great.'

Shaun didn't question him.

Joe's cell phone rang – private number. He stood up and walked into the darkened living room.

Duke Rawlins' voice was quiet menace: 'The grave was a beautiful touch.'

'Yeah? I thought you'd like it,' said Joe.

'You got your old friend to take a little trip here, didn't you? I guess he did as you told him. Paid some teenage dirtbag to dig right alongside Donnie. There's not a whole hell of a lot of space there. Probably fit a small woman. Or a child.'

Joe said nothing.

'He can't be much of a friend if you sent him my way,' said Duke.

Joe's heart pounded as he thought of Patti Nicotero, already bereaved.

Rawlins' voice was quieter when he spoke again. 'I guess you knew it was the one place I'd come back to. You couldn't stand not knowing where I was for all those months, what I was doing, who I was doing it with . . .'

Anna walked into the living room. Her eyes sparkled. Her hair was newly cut. It fell to her shoulders, dark and shiny, split at one side. He smiled at her. She held out her arms. Her white top rode up and he could see her tiny belly. He was hit with love, regret, fear, guilt, shame. She opened her mouth to speak. Joe held a finger to his lips, but kept smiling. And listening.

It's a powerful thing to be up close, sucked into the dead space of a killer, having to touch him, observe him, get answers from him, invest in him. Most people saw Duke Rawlins only in a photograph in a newspaper, from a safe remove – where they couldn't sense what was rotting from inside him. In the flesh, it seeped out every way it could – through the soulless eyes, through unbrushed teeth and unwashed skin. Joe had forced Anna to cross that boundary unprepared. She was torn from the comfortable world Joe had helped create and plunged into Duke Rawlins' twisted little universe. It felt like an illusion now, that Joe had sold her some bullshit dream he could never follow through on.

Joe looked at Anna and a shiver ran up his spine. Duke Rawlins had stalked her, held her, breathed on her, carried her, struck her, drawn a knife across her perfect skin . . .

Anna turned to leave and looked back at Joe over her shoulder, her eyes lighting up, her smile going right to his heart.

He hung up the phone.

One thing Rawlins hadn't done: he hadn't broken her.

ACKNOWLEDGEMENTS

Thank you to my agent, Darley Anderson and everyone at The Darley Anderson Literary Agency – an amazing and talented team.

Thanks to Editorial Director and legend, Wayne Brookes.

Thanks to Amanda Ridout, Lynne Drew and everyone at HarperCollins.

To Tony Purdue and Moira Reilly – thank you for your hard work and fabulous company.

I am so grateful to all the experts who helped with my research. Special thanks to Stephen A. Di Schiavi, retired NYPD Homicide Detective. Thanks also to George Farinacci, Lieutenant FDNY and Dominick Albergo, retired NYPD Detective; Reggie Britt, former First Grade Homicide Detective, NYC; David G. Aggleton and associates; Paul J. Cascone, Senior Vice-President of Technology, The Argen

Corporation; Professor Marie Cassidy; Andrew Dalsimer MD; Dr Alice Flaherty; Paul Keogh; Professor Nicholas Manos; Elliott Moorhead; Dr Paul Siu; Elton Strauss MD; Joanne P. Tangney; Dr Erin Grindley Watson.

Thanks to Kelly O'Hara for being so generous with her time and knowledge.

For everything they give to those lucky enough to come their way, thanks to Sue Booth-Forbes; Maureen and Donal O'Sullivan and family; Anna Phillips; Mary Maddison; Maggie Deas and Matthew Higgins.

To my wonderful and supportive family and friends – you make it all worthwhile.

Special thanks, always, to Brian and Dee.

If you enjoyed *The Caller*, read Alex Barclay's debut novel *Darkhouse*.

PROLOGUE

New York City

Edgy hands slid across the narrow belt, securing it in place on the tiny eight-year-old waist. Donald Riggs pointed to the small box attached.

'This is like a pager, honey, so the police can find you,' came his lazy drawl.

'Because you're going home now. If your mommy is a good girl. Is your mommy a good girl, Hayley?'

Hayley's mouth moved, but she couldn't speak. She bit down on her lip and looked up at him, beaming innocence. She gave three short nods. He smiled and slowly stroked her dark hair.

The fourth day without her daughter was the final day Elise Gray would have to endure a pain she could barely express. She breathed deeply through anger and rage, guilty that it was caused more by her husband than the stranger who took away her child. Gordon Gray's company had just gone public, making him a very wealthy man and an instant target for kidnap and ransom. The family was insured – but that was all about the money, and she didn't care about the money. Her family was her life and Hayley, her shining light.

Now here she was, parked outside her own apartment at the wheel of her husband's BMW, waiting for this creep to call her on the cell phone he left with the ransom note. Yet it was Gordon who dominated her thoughts. The insurance company had told the couple to vary their routine but, good God, what would Gordon know about varying his routine? This was a man who brewed coffee, made toast, then lined up an apple, a banana and a peach yoghurt – in that order – every morning for breakfast. Every morning. *You stupid man*, thought Elise. *You stupid man and your stupid, stupid, rituals. No wonder someone was waiting outside the apartment for you. Of course you were going to show up, because you show up every day at the same time bringing Hayley home from school. No detours, no stops for candy, just right on time, every time.*

She banged her head on the steering wheel as the cell phone on the seat beside her lit up. As she fumbled to answer it, she realised it was playing *Sesame Street*. He'd actually set the tone to *Sesame Street*, the sick bastard.

'Drive, bitch,' each word slow and deliberate.

'Where am I going?' she asked.

'To get your daughter back, if you've been behavin' yourself.' He hung up.

Elise started the engine, put her foot on the gas and swung gently into the traffic. Her heart was thumping. The wire chafed her back. By calling the police in that first hour, she had set in motion a whole new ending to this ordeal. She just wasn't sure if it was the right ending.

Detective Joe Lucchesi sat in the driver's seat, watching everything, his head barely moving. His dark hair was cut tight, with short slashes of grey at the sides. He questioned again whether Elise Gray was strong enough to wear a wire. He didn't know where the kidnapper would lead her or how she would react if she had to get any closer to him than the other end of a phone. He had barely raised his hand to his face when Danny Markey – his close friend of twenty-five years and partner for five – started talking.

'See, you got the kinda jaw a man can stroke. If I did that, I'd look like an idiot.'

Joe stared at him. Danny was missing a jawline. His small head blended without contour into his skinny neck. Everything about him was pale – his skin, his freckles, his blue eyes. He squinted at Joe.

'What?' he said.

Joe's gaze shifted back to Elise Gray's car. It started to move. Danny gripped the dashboard. Joe knew it was because he expected him to pull right out. Danny had a theory; one of his 'black and whites', as he called them. 'There are people in life who check for toilet paper before taking a crap. And there's the ones who shit straightaway and find themselves fucked.' Joe was often singled out. 'You're a checker, Lucchesi. I'm a shitter,' he would say. So they waited.

'You know Old Nic is getting out next month,' said Danny. Victor Nicotero was a lifer, a traffic cop one month shy of retiring. 'You goin' to the party?'

Joe shook his head, then sucked in a sharp breath against the pain that pulsed at his temples. He could see Danny hanging for an answer. He didn't give him one. He reached into the driver's door and pulled out a bottle of Advil and a blister pack of decongestants. He popped two of each, swallowing them with a mouthful from a blue energy drink hot from the sun.

'Oh, I forgot,' said Danny, 'your in-laws are in from Paris that night, right?' He laughed. 'A six-hour dinner with people you can't understand.' He laughed again.

Joe pulled out after Elise Gray. Three cars behind him, a navy blue Crown Vic with FBI Agents Maller and Holmes followed his lead.

*   *   *

Elise Gray drove aimlessly, searching the sidewalks for Hayley as though she would show up on a corner and jump in. The tinny ringtone broke the silence. She grabbed the phone to her ear.

'Where are you now, Mommy?' His calm voice chilled her.

'2nd Avenue at 63rd Street.'

'Head south and make a left onto the bridge at 59th Street.'

'Left onto the bridge at 59th Street.' Click.

The three cars made their way across the bridge to Northern Boulevard East, everyone's fate in the hands of Donald Riggs. He made his final call.

'Take a left onto Francis Lewis Boulevard, then left onto 29th Avenue. I'll be seein' you. On your own. At the corner of 157th and 29th.'

Elise repeated what he said. Joe and Danny looked at each other.

'Bowne Park,' said Joe.

He dialled the head of the task force, Lieutenant Crane then handed the phone to Danny and nodded for him to talk.

'Looks like the drop-off's Bowne Park. Can you call in some of the guys from the 109?' Danny put the phone on the dash.

Donald Riggs drove smoothly, his eyes moving across the road, the streets, the people. His left hand moved over the rough tangle of scars on his cheek, faded now into skin that was a pale stain on his tanned face. He checked himself in the rear-view mirror, opening his dark eyes wide. He raised a hand to run his fingers through his hair, until he remembered the gel and hairspray that held it rigid and marked by the tracks of a wide-toothed comb. At the back, it stopped dead at his collar, the right side folding over the left. He had a special lady to impress. He had splashed on aftershave from a dark blue bottle and gargled cinnamon mouthwash.

He turned around to check on the girl, lying on the floor in the back of the car and covered by a stinking blanket.

It was four-thirty p.m. and five detectives were sitting in the twentieth Precinct office of Lieutenant Terry Crane as Old Nic shuffled by, patting down his silver hair. *Maybe they're talking about my retirement present*, he thought, narrowing his grey eyes, leaning towards the muffled voices. *If it's a carriage clock, I'll kill them.* A watch he could cope with. Even better, his boy Lucchesi had picked up on his hints and spread the word – Old Nic was planning to write his memoirs and what he needed for that was something he'd never had before: a classy pen, something silver, something he could take out with his good notebook and tell a story with. He put a bony shoulder to the door and his cap slipped on his narrow head. He heard Crane briefing the detectives.

'We've just found out the perp is heading for

Bowne Park in Queens. We still don't have an ID. We got nothing from canvassing the neighborhood, we got nothing from the scene – the guy jumped out, picked up the girl and drove off at speed, leaving nothing behind. We don't even know what he was driving. This is just from the father who heard the screech from the lobby. We also got nothing from the package the perp dropped back the following day, just a few common fibres from the tape, nothing workable, no prints.'

Old Nic opened the door and stuck his head in. 'Where'd this kidnapping happen?'

'Hey, Nic,' said Crane, '72nd and Central Park West.' With no clues to his retirement present apparent in the office, Old Nic moved on, until a thought came to him and he doubled back.

'This guy is headed for Bowne Park, you gotta figure the area's familiar to him. Maybe he was going that way the day of the kidnapping, so he could have headed east across 42nd Street to the FDR. I used to work at the 17th and if your guy ran a red light, there's a camera at 42nd and 2nd might have given him a Kodak moment. You could check with the D.O.T.'

'Scratch that carriage clock,' Crane said to the group, winking. 'Nice one, Nic. We're on it.' Old Nic raised a hand as he left. 'You just want to hug the guy,' said Crane as he put a call in to the Department of Transportation. Thirty minutes later, he had five hits, three with criminal records. But only one had a prior for attempted kidnapping.

Joe could feel the drugs kick in. A warm cloud of relief moved up his jaw. He opened and closed his mouth. His ears crackled. He breathed through his nose and out slowly through his mouth. Six years ago, everything from his neck up started to go wrong – he got headaches, earaches, pain in his jaw so excruciating that some days it was unbearable to eat or even talk. Strangers didn't react well to a dumb cop.

Hayley Gray was thinking about *Beauty and the Beast*. Everyone thought the Beast was mean and scary, but he was really a nice guy and he gave Belle soup and he played in the snow with her. Maybe the man wasn't all bad. Maybe he'd turn out to be nice too. The car stopped suddenly and she felt cold. She heard her mommy shouting.

'Hayley! Hayley!' Then, 'Where's my daughter? You've got your money. Give me back my daughter, you bastard!'

Her mommy sounded really scared. She'd never heard her shout like that before or say bad words. She was banging on the window. Then the car was moving again, faster this time, and she couldn't hear her mommy any more. Donald Riggs threw open the knapsack, his right hand pulling at the tightly-packed wads.

Danny reached for his radio to run the plates of the brown Chevy Impala that was driving away from Elise Gray: 'North Homicide to Central.' He waited for Central to acknowledge, then gave the number. 'Adam David Larry 4856, A.D.L. 4856.'

Joe was on Citywide One, a two-way channel that linked him to Maller and Holmes and the 109 guys in the park. He spoke quickly and clearly.

'OK, he's got the money, but he hasn't said anything about dropping off the girl. We need to take it easy here. We don't know where he has her. Everyone stand by.'

Danny turned to him and gave his usual line. 'And his voice was restored and there was much rejoicing.'

Halfway down 29th Avenue, Donald Riggs stopped the car, reached back and lifted the blanket.

'Get up and get out of my car.'

Hayley pulled herself onto the seat. 'Thank you,' she said. 'I knew you'd be nice.'

She opened the door, got out and looked around until she could see her mother. Then she ran as fast as her little legs could carry her.

Joe and Danny were behind Riggs now, Agents Maller and Holmes behind them. Danny was holding for the information on the car. Joe was distracted. He had a feeling this was bad; the kind of bad that happens when everything is too easy, when the maniac is so fucked up, it gets scary calm. He looked at Danny.

'Why would the guy give this woman her child back without a scratch?' He shook his head. 'It's too easy.'

He slammed on the brakes and, arm out the window, waved the Crown Vic ahead of him. Agent Maller gave a quick nod and took the right, eyes locked on the car ahead.

Joe turned around and saw the swaying shape of a mother and daughter reunited. Too easy. He got out of the car, grabbing his vibrating cell phone from the dash. He flipped it open. It was Crane.

'We got your perp.'

'Brown Chevy Impala,' said Joe.

'Yup. '85. Riggs, Donald, white male, thirty-four, born in shitsville, Texas, locked up for petty larceny, scams, bad cheques, collared at the scene of a previous kidnapping.' He hesitated.

'And be advised, Lucchesi, he was done for C4 in Nevada in '97. We got ourselves a boom-boom banjo-player.' Joe dropped the phone, his heart pounding.

'I got ESU and hostage negotiation on stand-by,' Crane said to no-one.

Joe began to run. He willed his heart to carry the new pace his legs had taken up.

*　*　*

Donald Riggs had reached the corner of 154th and 29th. He rocked back and forth in his seat, skinny fingers clenching the wheel, eyes darting around, taking in everything, registering nothing. But something caught his eye. Behind him, a black Ford Taurus pulled into the kerb and a dark blue Crown Vic overtook it. A rare heightened awareness flared inside him. He kept driving, his breath shallow as he slowed to a stop at the next corner. Then a sudden burst of activity drew him in. Two men stepped out of a Con Ed van by the entrance to the park. They walked quickly to the back and pulled open the doors. Two others stepped out. In the rear-view mirror, the dark blue car loomed back into sight, driving alarmingly on the wrong side of the road. Donald Riggs lurched across the passenger side, grabbed the knapsack, pushed open the door and tore out of the car towards the park. By the time Maller and Holmes screeched to a stop seconds later, the four FBI agents in Con Ed uniforms were surrounding an empty car. 'Go, go, go,' roared Maller and all six men ran for the park.

'You used my pager!' says Hayley, amazed, pointing down at the belt around her waist and the black box with its flashing yellow light. Her mother stands up, confused, searching out anyone who can understand what this is, but knowing in her heart the answer. Her pleading eyes stop at Joe.

* * *

'You stupid bitch, you stupid bitch, you stupid bitch . . .' Donald Riggs is running wildly across the park, clutching at his knapsack, concentrating on a small dark object in his hand. He stops, rooted. His eyes widen and deaden as his mind and body shut down. Then a twitching, afterthought of a movement connects the thumb of his right hand to the black button of a detonator.

Elise Gray knows her fate. She makes a final grab for her child, hugging her desperately to her chest. 'I love you, sweetheart, I love you, sweetheart, I love you.' Then a frightening, shockingly loud blast tears through them, the bright light stinging Joe's eyes as he watches, now motionless. Then red and pink and white, splattering grotesquely, as a confetti shower of leaves and splintered bark falls around the place where a mother and daughter, seconds earlier, didn't even make it to goodbye.

Joe was absolutely still, paralysed. He couldn't breathe. He felt a new throbbing pressure in his jaw. His eyes streamed. He slowly sensed warm concrete against his face. He pulled himself up from the pavement. Too many emotions flooded his body. The radio on his belt crackled to life. It was Maller.

'We lost him. He's in the park, heading your way, along by the playground.'

Now one emotion overrode all others: rage.

* * *

'I don't think your mommy was a good girl, Hayley, I don't think your mommy was a good girl,' Riggs was howling, ranting, rocking wildly, bent over, his face contorted. He clawed desperately at the inside pocket of his coat. Joe burst through the trees, suddenly faced with this deranged display, but ready, his Glock 9mm drawn.

'Put your hands where I can see them.'

He couldn't remember his name. Riggs looked up; his arm jerked free, swinging wildly to his right and back again, as Joe pumped six bullets into his chest. Riggs fell backwards, landing to stare sightless at the sky, arms outstretched, palms open. Joe walked over, looking for a weapon he knew did not exist.

But something did lie in Riggs' upturned palm – a maroon and gold pin: a hawk, wings aloft, beak pointing earthwards. He had been gripping it so tightly, it had pierced his palm.

Ely State Prison, Nevada, two days later

'Shut up, you fuckin' freak. Shut your fuckin' ass.
I got National Geographic in my fuckin' ears
twenty-four/seven, you sick son of a bitch. Who
gives a shit about your fuckin' birds, Pukey Dukey?
Who gives a fuckin' shit?'

Duke Rawlins lay face down on the bottom
bunk of his eight by ten cell. Every muscle in his
long, wiry body tensed.

'Don't call me that.' His face was set into a frown,
his lips pale and full. He rubbed his head, disturbing
the dirty blond hair that grew long at the back, but
was cut short above his chill blue eyes.

'Call you what?' said Kane. 'Pukey Dukey?'

Duke hated group. They made him say shit that
was nobody's business. He couldn't believe this
asshole, Kane, knew what the kids used to call
him in school.

'This hawk has that wing span, this hawk ripped a jack rabbit a new asshole, this hawk is alpha, this hawk is beta, and this little hawk goes wee, wee, wee, all the way home to you, you sick son of a bitch.'

Duke leapt from his bunk, sliding his arm from under the pillow, pulling out a pared-down, sharpened spike of Plexiglas. He jabbed it towards Kane, who jerked his head back hard against the wall. He jabbed again and again, slicing the air close enough to Kane's face to let him know he meant it.

The warden's voice stopped him.

'Lookin' to book yourself a one-way ticket to Carson City, Rawlins?' Carson City was where Ely's death row inmates took their last breath.

Duke spun around as he unlocked the door and pushed into the cell. The warden smoothed on a surgical glove and calmly took the weapon from a man he knew was too smart to screw up this close to his release.

'Thought you might like to read this, Rawlins,' he said, holding up a printout from the *New York Times* website.

Duke walked slowly towards the warden and stopped. The pockmarked face of Donald Riggs jumped right at him. KIDNAP ENDS IN FATAL EXPLOSION. Mother and daughter dead. Kidnapper fatally wounded. Duke went white. He reached out for the paper, pulling it from the warden's hand as his legs slid from under him and he slumped on to the floor. 'Not Donnie, not Donnie, not Donnie,' he screamed over and over in his head. Before he passed out, his body suddenly heaved and he threw up all over the floor, spraying the warden's shoes and pants.

Kane jumped down from his bed, kicking Duke in the gut because he could. His laugh was deep and satisfied. 'Pukey fuckin' Dukey. Man, this is quality viewing.'

'Get back to your business, Kane,' said the warden as he turned his back on the stinking cell.